Early Praise for *You Will Be Peter*

"My friend Jerry Lathan has long been focused on Peter. This novel is a product of his study and determination to advance a deeper understanding of the humanity of the man, Peter, as well as the enormity of his impact. This novel provides new insights into this incredibly consequential life."

—The Honorable Jeff Sessions, former United States Attorney General and US Senator (Alabama)

"There can be no doubt that Jerry Lathan and Steven Manchester are gifted and talented writers ... and *You Will Be Peter* is a perfect example."

—Joan van Ark, actress, *Knots Landing*

"I have spent my entire life as a Christian, yet I never had the insight into what it must have been like to be a disciple of Jesus Christ. The novel *You Will Be Peter* opened my eyes into the men and women who ultimately shaped my faith. Thoroughly researched and biblically accurate, *You Will Be Peter* is an exciting, emotional roller coaster into the life of the man who became the 'rock' upon which the Christian faith would be established. Unlike traditional scholarly works, this book gives us a glimpse into the true man known as Simon Peter...a man familiar with hard work, who shared emotions like all of us, ranging from compassion to anger ... love to despair. This is a fascinating read that will inspire anyone who is interested in learning more about Peter and those disciples who would lead a movement that changed the world. Reading it has made me a better man, husband, and father. The authors of *You Will Be Peter* have done a tremendous service to anyone desiring a better understanding of the origins of Christianity…for that I am grateful!"

—Robert F. Barrow,
Lieutenant Colonel, US Army, ret.

"Although I am a pastor, I am not a Biblical Scholar or Theologian. I found the overall telling of *You Will Be Peter* to be very accurate, while also learning a great deal—lots that I can use in my sermons. With the story being told from Peter's direct point of view, I was able to internalize the chief apostle's passions and feelings. I loved the brotherly relationships—especially the four-man fellowship—formed amongst the Apostles; how they shared many hardships that brought them even closer. They are real characters in this story. *You Will Be Peter* also humanizes Jesus with many smiles and even laughter, offering a fresh perspective on the Bible. I was happy to find that I didn't get stuck in the words. Instead, it was more about getting lost in the emotions. I read the manuscript twice, learning new things the second time. I intend to read it again."

—Pastor Dylan Mello,
Christ and Holy Trinity Episcopal
Church, Westport, CT

"What a thought-provoking way these authors have made Peter come alive by asking the same questions I ask myself every day: *What did Jesus ever see in me?* and *He must have seen something I either lost or can no longer see in myself.* Even today, we as Christians must all ask ourselves these same two questions. Great job! I look forward to your writings on all the disciples."

—Jerry Carl,
US Congressman, Alabama's first district

"Step into the captivating world of Simon Peter, the Everyman who defied all odds to become the Founding Father of Christianity. In *You Will Be Peter*, Jerry Lathan and Steven Manchester expertly weave history, faith, and redemption into an emotionally charged biography. With meticulous research and storytelling artistry, this unique perspective reveals the real person behind the legend—a journey of transformation that will resonate with readers for generations to come."

—Orsayor L. Simmons,
book blogger, *Book Referees*

"In *You Will Be Peter*, Jerry Lathan and Steven Manchester have done something exceptional. They take readers beyond the devotional and the doctrinal into the story of the greatest disciple. In Peter's sorrows and triumphs, we enter the sacred the same way we enter our own lives—as a story. Lathan and Manchester's unique talents in bringing alive daily experiences invite us to transcend what we think we know for a real encounter with Peter and with Christ. Their work takes us beyond scholars and saints to a world where we journey into the greatest story ever told and make it our own story."

—Rev. Andrew Stinson, MA, MDiv,
**Senior minister, First Congregational
Church of Fall River**

"In *You Will Be Peter*, Jerry Lathan and Steven Manchester tell the story of Jesus's final years as seen through the eyes of his disciple Simon. Regardless of your belief system, you will relate to Simon, an Everyman who contends with questions, doubts, and awe as he joins the band of brothers surrounding and supporting Jesus. Lathan and Manchester humanize Simon, allowing readers to experience what he and his fellow apostles experienced—while bringing history to vivid life. An absorbing read!"

—**Judith Arnold,**
***USA Today* bestselling author**

"In *You Will Be Peter*, Jerry Lathan and Steven Manchester bring to life Jesus's first apostle, Peter. In this thoroughly researched and fully imagined volume, Peter becomes much more than simply the character of often-told Bible verses. We meet him as a real person, with both his virtues and flaws fully exposed. Written with all the immediacy of a novel, we meet the man as he changes into the man Jesus needed him to be. It isn't often such a monumental historical figure is depicted so well as a living, breathing human being. This book does that and more."

– **Donna Foley Mabry,**
Wall Street Journal* bestselling author of *Maude

"*You Will Be Peter* is pure inspiration! Lathan and Manchester expertly articulate this biblical history, immersing the reader in the past. Walking alongside Jesus, chronicling the first years of his ministry through Peter's (Simon's) point of view captures an entirely different perspective of this humble yet majestic story. A truly moving testament, it is a compelling narrative, inspiring the reader to live a

Christlike, more meaningful life. I couldn't put it down and when I had to, I couldn't wait to get back to it. I was moved to tears many times, and I already knew how the story ends. *You Will Be Peter* is a story of belief, faith, love, and, most importantly, the ultimate sacrifice."

—Shannon L. Gonzalez,
book blogger, *Literarily Illumined*

"I sometimes struggle when I read the Bible. Without an understanding of what the culture was like, it is difficult for me to relate and understand. This wonderful story about Peter, Jesus's rock and cornerstone of the church, was eye-opening. It helped me to understand Peter and relate to his actions and reactions. It brought him to life. He was not a perfect man; he struggled like we all do.

You Will Be Peter follows Simon Peter from the time that he is called to follow Jesus until his death. It shows his uncertainties, how he struggled to understand Jesus's teachings and his jealousies over his fellow disciples. It humanizes his fears and denial of Jesus. It gives insight into the era that he lived and how these times helped mold him. I loved this story. It gave me a look behind the scenes of life during Jesus's time on earth. It helped me to understand Peter, the man. He was just like me with all the same human struggles and questions. It made me realize that God has a plan for all of us."

—Diane Moyle,
Book Bug **Blog**

"Jerry Lathan and Steven Manchester have written a wonderful book. *You Will Be Peter* is the story of young Jesus and his rag-tag group of apostles in the early days of his quest to change the world.

The reader walks with Peter as he leaves his wife, his home, and his life's work as a fisherman in the Sea of Galilee. Peter becomes a true believer and Jesus's right-hand man. He follows Jesus, who is attracting ever-growing crowds, performing miracles, and choosing the band of men who will become his apostles.

Lathan and Manchester have found a way to make *You Will Be Peter* contemporary, relatable, and just plain wonderful. It's a great story and an amazing book."

—John Lansing,
bestselling author of *The Devil's Necktie*

"*You Will Be Peter* is a dynamic way of reading through all four gospels. As we follow the involvement of Peter's interactions with the Savior, we receive the gift of learning the historical background of where these events fit into the whole story. The words of Jesus are untampered with, which means you are not engaged in a critical reading, but rather with the joy of discovery. There are plenty of 'aha' moments on every page."

—Pastor David H. Stewart

"Following the path of Saint Peter when he was a mere lowly fisherman to his role as founder and head of the Christian church has been an incredible literary journey. Jerry Lathan and Steven Manchester have brought to life the epic story of not only Saint Peter and the beginning of the Christian faith, but also the trials that Jesus, his disciples, and the faithful followers had to endure. This relatable novel is so beautifully written; I didn't want it to end. I can't wait to see *You Will Be Peter* on the bestseller lists."

—Beth Worsdell,
author, host of *The Witty Writers Show*

"I am familiar with the stories of Jesus and his disciples, but reading *You Will Be Peter* made me feel like I was walking alongside them. Although Simon Peter had his doubts, for every doubt came proof that Jesus's word is the way of the Lord."

—*Charlotte Lynn's Reviews*

"*You Will Be Peter* transports the reader back in time to experience the thoughts, lessons, and dangers faced by the apostles who followed Jesus. Although their journey is not without pain, we learn exactly what it took to bring Christianity into being. After experiencing *You Will Be Peter*, our prayers take on a much deeper meaning and new appreciation of all that was sacrificed for us. Above all, faith is the key. Read this amazing book!"

—Deb Guyette - *Single Titles*

"*You Will Be Peter* takes us into one of the most well-known and relatable characters in the Bible. We get to see not just his zeal and humanity, we're able to better understand ourselves as well. This is the kind of book where the characters come to life, and we're all better off because of it."

—Cyrus Webb,
publisher of *Conversations Magazine*,
Top Amazon Reviewer

"In *You Will Be Peter*, the reader is transported right into the heart of the story, becoming Simon's friend, even part of his family. The reader watches Simon struggle with his beliefs, as the fisherman witnesses the world change before him. Following each step of Jesus's ministry, I was captivated by just how heart-wrenching Simon's life must have been, from his humble beginnings to his triumphant restoration in Jesus. Simon Peter's life is forever changed, as is every reader who picks up this novel. I can easily give *You Will Be Peter* five out of five stars."

—**Kathleen Smith,**
Reviews from the Heart

"Jerry Lathan and Steven Manchester have written a profound and thought-provoking montage, bringing in the history of Simon Peter's life in a fresh perspective with depth and heart. We can each be a rock, too!"

—**Lauri Schoenfeld,**
host of *The Enlightenment Show*

"*You Will Be Peter* by Jerry Lathan and Steven Manchester is a beautiful, well-written account of an ancient story written for modern times, and it is done perfectly.

The authors took me back in time flawlessly with descriptive scenes, brilliant dialogue, and emotions that touched my heart and at times had me wiping away a few tears. Pulled in by the writers' words, I was standing right there next to Simon Peter when he first met Jesus on the banks of the River Jordan, a young man in his twenties—and I never left throughout the three-year journey the story takes us.

You Will Be Peter is a masterpiece of self-discovery, redemption, courage, and sacrifice. It's must-read for all generations that will stay with you long after you have read it. You will come to adore and know Simon Peter just as I did."

—Tina Hogan Grant,
award-winning author of The Tammy
Mellows trilogy, host of *Read More Books*

"Lathan and Manchester's epic telling of Peter's story chronicles his inner monologue and his outward devotion with painstaking detail—faithful to the Scriptures. Pick up these pages and journey in the shoes of the fisherman, from the shores of the Sea of Galilee to the Jordan Valley; from the home of tax collectors to the Garden of Gethsemane; from fishing nets to fireside; and ultimately from the upper room to the upside-down cross. With expert craftsmanship, the authors carve out a tale of hope, encouragement, devotion, and love from the Rock of the apostles."

—Reverend Don Bliss,
East Freetown Congregational-
Christian Church

You *Will* Be Peter

You *Will* Be Peter

A Novel

JERRY LATHAN

WITH STEVEN MANCHESTER

Forefront
BOOKS

To my parents, Delvin and Eveleen Lathan,
who brought me up with a foundation of faith in God

and

For Nancy Ann Manchester,
who taught me to "keep the faith"

CONTENTS

Acknowledgments.. 19
Author's Introduction 21

PART 1:
MEETING JESUS, YEAR 1:
SIMON'S LIFE TAKES A NEW DIRECTION

Chapter 1: Four Brothers..29
Chapter 2: "We Have Found the Messiah!" 37
Chapter 3: You Are Simon...45
Chapter 4: Six Stone Jars 61
Chapter 5: Passover in Jerusalem.....................................73
Chapter 6: Quenching a Thirst in Samaria 89
Chapter 7: Fishers of Men 103
Chapter 8: The Big Man of Capernaum 117
Chapter 9: Matthew, the Tax Collector 129

PART 2:
THE MINISTRY OF JESUS, YEAR 2:
PETER RECEIVES HIS COMMISSION

Chapter 10: Too Many People to Count.............................145
Chapter 11: Loaves and Fishes 163
Chapter 12: Who Do Men Say I Am?...............................183
Chapter 13: Never Alone..199
Chapter 14: Open Your Eyes 211
Chapter 15: His Time, Not Ours 225
Chapter 16: Raising Lazarus..239

PART 3:
FAILURE AND REDEMPTION, YEAR 3:
SIMON FALLS, PETER RISES

Chapter 17: Palm Leaves and the Children 257

Chapter 18: Setting the Table............................. 269

Chapter 19: Wolves and Sheep........................... 281

Chapter 20: They Know Not What They Do..................... 293

Chapter 21: No Greater Love............................. 307

Chapter 22: Where Were You?........................... 319

Chapter 23: Go and Tell Peter 333

Chapter 24: Sweet Redemption 347

Chapter 25: I Am with You Always 361

Chapter 26: No More Fear 371

Epilogue: I Am Peter.......................... 377

Afterword 391

Selected Bibliography........................ 393

Meet the Authors 395

ACKNOWLEDGMENTS

For my faithful wife and partner, Terry, whose personal faith, endless support, and encouragement made it possible for me to pursue the dream of writing this account of the life of my hero, Simon Peter. And for my children, Brittany, Adam, and Rachel, the pride of my life.

A special thank-you to Father Eamon Kelly in Magdala, Israel. Dr. Achia Kohn-Tavor, archeologist and guide in Jerusalem and Galilee. Efrat Sharoni, guide in Israel. Dr. David Trimble for sharing his knowledge of Koine Greek and his understanding of the earliest written form of the Gospels. Special acknowledgment goes to William Thomas Walsh for his book *Peter the Apostle* (New York: Macmillan, 1948). Walsh's thorough and impeccable research contributed greatly to scriptural validity and the time line of this story.

—Jerry Lathan

Paula, my beautiful wife; my children—Evan, Jacob, Isabella, and Carissa—and my beloved family, for whom I have been incredibly blessed. You are my foundation.

—Steven Manchester

Our BETA TEAM: Dan and Sue Aguiar, Les Barnett, Frank Barrow, Peter Blackwell, Bob and Keigh Butler, Hunter Finch, Brian Fox, Tom Gastall, Terry Lathan, Dylan Mello, Sue Nedar, Mary Lou Nicholson, Tim O'Connell, Todd Parent, Sue Maxwell

ACKNOWLEDGMENTS

Rasmussen, Claude Tetreault, Mike Thompson, Mark Tremblay, and Hen Zannini.

AUTHOR'S INTRODUCTION

Although Simon, the son of Jonah, is one of the most important figures in the history of mankind, nothing in his birthplace, family, or early existence could ever point to the enormous impact his life would have. In their first ever meeting Jesus said to him, "You are Simon," then Jesus added this odd statement, "You will be called Peter." Hence the title of this biographic novel.

Every good biography ever written contains two essential elements: a subject whose life is interesting, based on their accomplishments or experiences, and the story that is well-told. Jesus started their relationship by choosing Simon to be the founder of a religious faith and a church that did not yet exist; a faith that remains the largest organized religion on earth, counting its numbers in the billions. It is hard to imagine a more important or interesting accomplishment than to be the Founding Father of the most influential and enduring institution in the history of humanity.

From a rough and brazen fisherman to Jesus Christ's first chosen apostle, Simon Peter—the Everyman—became the founder of the early Christian church. Unfortunately, this Founding Father of Christianity is often reduced to a caricature, usually depicted in modern culture as an old, white-bearded man standing at the gates of heaven, holding the keys. This historical biography has been written so that readers will get to know Simon Peter for the real person he was.

You Will Be Peter is written to be real and relatable, capturing the three-year ministry of Jesus Christ through the eyes of

Simon Peter. It is an emotionally charged story told by living, breathing characters who lived at one of the most pivotal times in history.

In *You Will Be Peter*, the research has been conducted. The timeline is accurate, depicting the actual steps taken by Jesus and his early followers. As the story is fleshed out, historical and political context becomes clear. Just imagine what the men and women who followed Jesus Christ were thinking. Imagine the dialogue shared between them, as they followed Jesus into history.

Living in Capernaum in Galilee, Simon Peter's life was filled with competing interests. He struggled—as we all do—to make the right decisions. In search of the Messiah, he met Jesus on the banks of the Jordan River, naively believing the Messiah would be a military or political figure sent to stand against the injustices of their Roman-dominated world.

In this unique perspective of the earliest days of the Christian church, readers will meet a strong, healthy young man in his late twenties—and get to know him. Although Simon Peter was not very well-educated, he was a natural leader. He did not travel in the circles of power. He was not a member of the elite. He was not wealthy or well connected, nor was he a gifted man with some great talent or born into a legacy that offered him anything more than a common life.

Simon bar Jonah was impetuous, decisive, and passionate about his beliefs and pursuits. He was loyal, faithful, and trustworthy. Although he could have a foul mouth, he was the kind of friend anyone would be lucky to have—until he was not. Toward the end of Jesus's life on earth, Simon played the role of treacherous liar and coward—betraying Jesus.

Simon was many things that we can all relate to. Whether known to others or not, each of us knows our own failures. We can all relate to the times when we have disappointed ourselves

22

and even those we love, the times when we were Simon—even when we wanted to be Peter.

You Will Be Peter is a vivid and heartfelt tale of faith and surrender, of betrayal and redemption; it is a unique perspective of the beginning of the most enduring and important institution in all of history—the Christian church.

You Will Be Peter paints with words an age-old story told from a new set of eyes, enhanced by the sights, sounds, and smells of that time, bringing the reader directly into each scene. This story is told so you may picture in your own mind the events from two thousand years ago that still impact our lives today.

Perhaps you have noticed that he is called Simon, Peter, and Simon Peter. This is exactly what Jesus did—calling him the name that fits the moment. The title of this book comes from the first words Jesus said to Simon:

You are Simon.

You will be Peter.

The Gospels call him Simon or Peter over sixty times and in almost equal numbers, more than all the other apostles combined. Half the time he is Simon. Half the time he is Peter. Peter steps out of the boat and walks on water. When he doubts and starts to sink, Jesus says with disappointment, "Simon, why did you doubt?"

I hope and trust that you will enjoy *You Will Be Peter* as you contemplate your similar journey, living with the understanding that we are all Simon, working toward the day when we will be Peter.

If Simon Peter, the Everyman, could start a movement that has lasted two thousand years, what can his story tell the modem reader? *Just imagine ...*

Jerry Lathan
Mobile, Alabama
2024

Without Jesus, I am nothing.

—*Simon Peter bar Jonas*

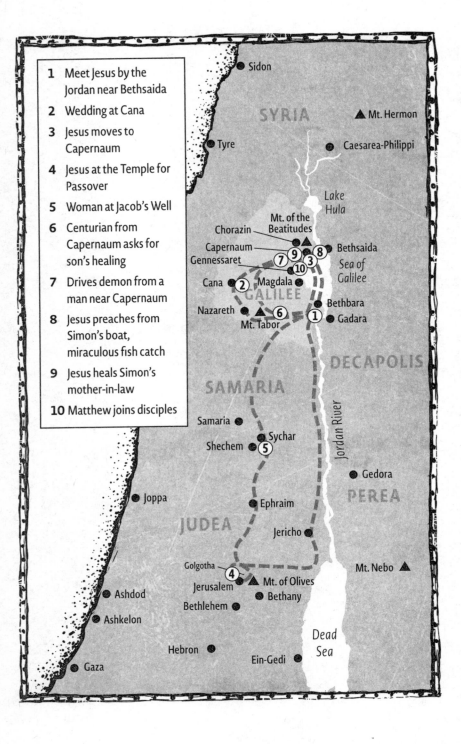

1 Meet Jesus by the Jordan near Bethsaida

2 Wedding at Cana

3 Jesus moves to Capernaum

4 Jesus at the Temple for Passover

5 Woman at Jacob's Well

6 Centurian from Capernaum asks for son's healing

7 Drives demon from a man near Capernaum

8 Jesus preaches from Simon's boat, miraculous fish catch

9 Jesus heals Simon's mother-in-law

10 Matthew joins disciples

Sidon

SYRIA

Mt. Hermon

Tyre

Caesarea-Philippi

Lake Hula

Chorazin

Mt. of the Beatitudes

Capernaum

Bethsaida

Gennessaret

7 9 8

Sea of Galilee

3

10

Cana 2 Magdala

GALILEE

Bethbara

Nazareth 6

1 Gadara

Mt. Tabor

DECAPOLIS

SAMARIA

Samaria

Sychar

Shechem 5

Jordan River

PEREA

Gedora

Joppa

Ephraim

JUDEA

Jericho

Golgotha

Mt. Nebo

4

Jerusalem Mt. of Olives

Bethany

Bethlehem

Ashdod

Ashkelon

Dead Sea

Hebron

Ein-Gedi

Gaza

PART 1

MEETING JESUS

YEAR 1:
SIMON'S LIFE TAKES
A NEW DIRECTION

CHAPTER 1

FOUR BROTHERS

Capernaum, Galilee

Simon slowly opened his eyes. With a heavy sigh, he finally surrendered to a second night of relentless insomnia. Taking care to be as quiet as humanly possible, he swung his feet onto the cool, earthen floor and rose from his warm bed. Standing upright, he turned to ensure that he had not awakened his wife. *She'll be up soon enough, tending to a full day of chores,* he thought, smiling at her beloved silhouette. Stretching out his stiff muscles, he stifled a yawn before stealing one last look at her and slipping out of the room.

Simon found his worn sandals, robe, and light coin purse, and headed out the front door.

As he passed through the threshold, he tapped the mezuzah—a small case affixed to the doorframe containing a tiny scroll of parchment inscribed with a prayer—and then kissed the fingers that touched it.

Stepping onto the desolate street, he released the yawn that had been clawing to be freed. *I need to get some sleep soon,* he thought, shaking off the last remnants of the yawn. *I don't know what's keeping me up, but I can't remember the last time I've felt this tired.*

In the predawn hour, the spring air felt unusually cool on his olive-toned skin—*especially for this late in the season,* he thought.

In no particular rush, Simon made his way from his mother-in-law's humble home, heading southeast toward the docks at the Sea of Galilee.

During the four-minute walk to the docks, a sliver of waning moon was settling in the east over the Golan Heights, reflecting in the gentle ripples of the sea, providing just enough light for him to make his way safely. It didn't matter. Although he'd experienced very little of the larger world, he'd spent his entire life in this place—all twenty-eight years, from his birth to this drowsy moment—and could have walked each step blindfolded.

At the top of the last rise in the road, he slowed his gait before stopping to gaze at the magnificent sea below him. Peering hard for a solid minute, he realized it was still too dark to make out the docks or his forty-foot boat tethered to them. Instead, he closed his eyes and surrendered to the other senses that he trusted just as well. While the cool air caressed his neck and arms, his nose and ears took over, painting a fairly detailed picture of this challenging life on the sea.

The soothing rhythm of the lapping surf gave way to the echo of wood banging against wood. *One of the boats has too much slack in the tie line,* he surmised. He wasn't completely done shaking his head when the faint smell of decomposing fish filled his nose. *I wonder if James caught anything last night?* He opened his eyes in search of his boat—the largest of the fleet—but the dark, ghostly forms in the distance were still only recognizable in his imagination.

Moving a few steps to his left, Simon claimed a seat on the largest rock he could find, situated just on the west side of the road. He was sure this perch would offer the best view of the sea below when the sun decided to make its grand entrance in the east before him. Not three seconds passed before he adjusted his position, sliding free from a jagged fist that protruded from the center of the massive granite stone. Finally comfortable, he closed his eyes again and smiled—his mind flashing back to so many wonderful memories.

Simon could see himself and his older brother, Andrew, learning to swim, their fear and panic giving way to a lifelong love of the water. His mind drifted back to the childhood home nestled in the small village of Bethsaida, where the Jordan River flows into the Sea of Galilee. He saw his strict father, Jonas, working the boat's unfurled sails—teaching his boys to fish while reciting passages from the Torah as he went about his tasks. In time, Simon and Andrew buried the hardworking man, but not before he'd passed on all the knowledge needed to earn an honest living on the Sea of Galilee.

Simon could picture every detail of the warm afternoon he'd married his wife beneath their simple chuppah. He then recalled moving into his mother-in-law's house, where Andrew, his brother and business partner, had come to live with them.

There's no better place on earth than Capernaum, Simon thought, without acknowledging his lack of travel. His village sat on the northern shore of the Sea of Galilee, nearly two miles from where the Jordan River flowed into it. Amid the warm, sweet air, amazing views of the sapphire waters sparkled for nearly thirteen miles to the south, while the snowcapped summit of Mount Hermon jutted out in the north. Capernaum was a small cosmopolitan of Palestinian life situated on the main roadway through Galilee. As the eastern outpost, both Roman and temple taxes were collected there.

Tax collectors and Romans, Simon repeated in his head, the thought causing a plume of bile to rise from his stomach and settle at the back of his throat.

Opening his eyes, Simon was happy to discover that the first rays of sunlight had struck the body of water, making it shimmer like a billion morning stars. After all these years, all the grueling hours of fishing, the sight still stole his breath. *It's not the easiest life,* he confirmed, *but it's a good one.*

Having recalled his father's many lessons, Simon took pause to spend a few minutes in grateful prayer—as well as to seek wisdom and perhaps settle the deep worry that was stealing away his sleep. *Yahweh,* he prayed, *watch over Andrew and John on their travels to find the answers they seek. Please shroud them in Your angels and keep them safe from harm.*

Andrew had been obsessed over the coming of the Messiah, vigilant for any sign of the Holy One while learning everything he could.

If only, Simon thought, grinning slightly. *The Romans would finally get exactly what's coming to them!*

The first rays of morning light were suddenly trampled by a full sunrise, as a stiff sea breeze moved up the hill and became trapped in Simon's sinuses. *We've had a recent storm on the water,* he recognized, knowing that this was anything but a good sign toward the previous night's catch.

Starting down the hill, he could now make out the distinct form of his boat bobbing alongside the dock, occasionally banging against it. *You should know better, James,* he thought, shaking his head. *How long have we been doing this?*

Arriving at the dock, he called out for James, hearing his friend's muffled reply from below deck. Simon hopped aboard, taking notice of the empty nets clustered on both sides of the top deck. *Not a single fish,* he confirmed.

Cursing under his breath, he kicked at the wet nets piled before him. Frustrated, he stomped toward the bow of the boat and screamed out at the sky—when he suddenly caught himself and went silent. Turning back, he spotted James standing there, looking defeated.

James was the brother of Simon's best friend, John. They looked so much alike that neither one of them could deny the other. At just over six feet tall, James was wiry but strong. His lean, sinewy muscles had been trained by years of hard labor, working the nets. His real strength, however, remained concealed to the eye. *Although James isn't all that assertive and usually as quiet as a field mouse, he's as solid as they come.* Simon smiled. *There's no one more dependable.*

James broke the awkward silence, offering his version of the night's fruitless efforts. "Sorry, Simon," he muttered. "We did what we could, dragging the nets for hours...but with the storm..." He shook his head. "Nothing."

Simon looked the younger man in the eye. "I'm the one who should be sorry," he said, apologizing to his loyal friend for the outburst. "I know you did your best," he added, trying to offer a few words of comfort. "With both of our brothers away, and you with only one deckhand, I shouldn't have expected much." *James was like his little brother,* and he chastised himself for the flare-up.

James nodded his gratitude, then added, "The storm in the south did not help."

With Andrew and John away... Simon repeated in his head. *Is that why I haven't been able to sleep?*

James did all he could to fight off the grin. With Simon's thick neck, wide shoulders, and bulging biceps, nothing seemed funnier to James than when the brute attempted an apology, no matter how genuine. *Simon's a bull,* James thought, stifling a laugh, *but he's our bull.* He studied the shorter figure standing before him. *The man's been there for me my whole life, like a second brother, sticking up for all of us...even when he's been wrong.* James continued to fight back the laugh. *Which is most of the time.*

The examples of Simon's impetuous behavior were endless, but James only needed to think back a few weeks to recall a good one.

It had been a long day of fishing. After taking their catch to market, they decided to share a drink at the local tavern. "We'll meet you there," Simon had told Andrew, who was concluding their business with one of the least corrupt money changers.

They weren't two steps into the dark tavern when James watched Simon's face burn red, his nostrils beginning to flare. Without a word of warning, the small group's impulsive leader made a beeline to one of the tables, his large hands balling up into punishing fists as he went.

"You stole some of my gear!" Simon roared at Yussif, a fellow fisherman who had allegedly wronged him. "I know you did!"

Yussif adamantly denied the accusation. "I did no such thing, Simon," he swore, his eyes filled with shock and confusion. "Your brother..."

Simon lunged forward, cutting him off—and striking fear into the tavern's other patrons.

Without further investigation, Simon hissed, "Don't you worry, Yussif. I won't turn you into the Romans." He swung once, his massive stone fist smashing into Yussif's cheek, knocking him clean off the rickety wooden chair.

As Simon pounced on the man, Andrew stepped into the tavern. "Simon, stop!" he screamed. "I loaned out the fishing gear to Yussif two days ago. Stop!"

James returned from the memory and chuckled. Poor Simon begged Yussif's forgiveness for two weeks before the man finally grew tired of the groveling and relented.

But that's Simon, James thought, shrugging, *a head full of rocks and a heart made of gold.* He slapped his bulky friend's back. *But there's no one in the world I'd rather have by my side when the dark clouds roll in and life gets rough.*

Simon, James, and the deckhand began the task of scraping and scrubbing the nets for transfer to the drying racks. After several minutes of welcome silence, James posed a question—as if he were reading Simon's mind. "So, what do you think John and Andrew have found on their trip?"

One of Simon's eyebrows rose, inspiring his square head to do the same. He pondered his childhood friend's question. *Andrew and John left three days ago to walk down the west side of the Sea of Galilee, past the outflow of the Jordan, so they could visit John the Baptizer again.* Simon recalled when he'd also visited the eccentric man. At the time, he remained suspicious of the gossip, skeptical that a wild man dressed in camel skins could actually be preparing the way for the Lord. *But he's definitely anti-authority,* Simon thought, *and there have been more and more rumors of miracles and signs that the Messiah is drawing near.* Simon felt a bolt of hope strike his heart, turning his weathered forearms to gooseflesh. *Please, Lord, let it be so.*

Simon turned to James. "Whatever Andrew and John have found, they need to get home and let us in on it." Wearing his famous grin, he snickered. "Besides, they've ducked out on work for long enough."

They all laughed, even the deckhand.

What have they found? Simon wondered.

CHAPTER 2

"WE HAVE FOUND THE MESSIAH!"

Capernaum, Galilee

The morning was growing old, with Simon struggling to decide when to head out to fish. He peered out onto the horizon to see a line of boats belonging to the local fishing fleet. "As long as they stay away from our spots," he complained out loud.

James nodded in agreement, his head remaining on his work.

The Sea of Galilee was a clear freshwater lake, stretching for thirteen miles in length between green banks, with ten cities thriving along its shores. Crossing from one side to the other took just over three hours of sailing time. Fishing was normally abundant, and as drift-net fishermen, Simon and his crew were able to provide well for their families.

As of late, Kinneret sardines had become the primary catch. These small, salt-brine pickled fish were a staple of Israel's diet, especially for those who lived in the Galilean area. Although full baskets and casks were taken to market in Magdala on a regular basis, a strong demand remained.

Still, the life of a fisherman was not for the weak of spine, creating gruff and rugged men—the opposite of social elites. Besides as a fisherman having to read the wind and the stars,

Simon learned time and again that his environment was as uncontrollable as his own emotions. The Sea of Galilee was moody and subject to swift, dangerous changes in the weather, resulting in stretches of stingy catches and volatile storms. Situated over seven hundred feet below sea level, the strong winds of the hills on both sides of the sea made for a climate unlike most. For Simon and his Galilean friends, this was the only thing they knew.

Making final preparations for their next sail, Simon spotted Andrew and John approaching over the hill in the distance. *They're finally back!* he thought, exhaling heavily; it felt like he'd been holding his breath for days. He could feel a weight lift from his shoulders. Looking toward the sky, he whispered, "Thank You, Yahweh." Simon wasn't sure if this great relief was due to his brother and best friend being safe or because he'd longed to hear about their discoveries. *They look excited!* he thought, the truth of it raising his long-held hopes to an all-time high.

As the men jogged closer, both Simon and James jumped from the bow of the boat onto the sand, preparing to greet their brothers. As Andrew and John approached, both beaming from ear to ear, Simon studied his lanky brother. Andrew was a slightly shorter—and thinner—version of himself, the man's eyes normally revealing more details than his tongue. Although Andrew was older by three years, the brothers shared a mutual respect, with Andrew usually allowing Simon to play the dominant role. *Andrew's more thoughtful and considerate,* Simon admitted to himself, *but in most cases, he's happy to let me run things.* He chuckled. *But not when it comes to issues of faith.* Andrew was passionate about his beliefs, bordering on overly zealous. And being so cerebral, Simon was surprised to see such excitement in his normally reserved brother.

"Well?" Simon screamed out.

The men quickened their pace, shortening the distance.

"We have found the Messiah!" Andrew yelled back, his tone filled with equal amounts of pride and joy. "We will be delivered!"

For a second, Simon lost his breath. *Can it be true?*

By now, Andrew was upon him, nearly jumping into his thick arms. "It's true, brother," he said, answering the question that was never asked aloud. "We saw him with our own eyes." Tears swelled. "We saw the Lamb of God, who takes away the sins of the world," he added, his voice cracking from emotion.

Simon looked at John, who was wearing a smile that threatened to break his face in half.

Overwhelming emotion had clearly stolen his words. He merely nodded.

Squeezing both of Simon's shoulders, Andrew gazed into his eyes, revealing that his words were true. "Simon, we've found the man we've been praying for our entire lives."

If that's true, then anything is possible now, Simon thought, *even the downfall of the Romans!*

Andrew was bursting at the seams to share the good news but had to remind himself to slow his speech so that each one of his words would be understood.

"Simon, we walked for days before we reached John the Baptizer in Bethabara on the banks of the Jordan. And you can't imagine how long the line was. It stretched from the edge of the river to the acacia groves. John's ministry has spread far and wide, brother. There were so many believers waiting to be baptized!" Coming up for air, he looked to John for an affirming nod, which he swiftly received.

Both of Simon's eyebrows snapped to attention.

"Then, John the Baptizer pointed to a man his own age and stopped speaking for several seconds. That's when he said, 'Behold, the Lamb of God, who takes away the sins of the world!'

"The whole crowd turned to look and saw a young rabbi about our age, dressed in long robes."

"Our age?" Simon repeated.

Andrew nodded, his mind speeding faster than his tongue. "Then this young teacher asked John to baptize him. 'But I need to be baptized by you,' the Baptizer told the teacher, 'and yet you come to me?' And the rabbi said, 'Permit it now.'" Andrew became emotional. "So, the Baptizer immersed him right there in the Jordan for all to see. And that's when a dove appeared."

"Yes, the dove," John repeated, his face happier than Simon had ever seen.

Andrew nodded. "The air changed—"

"A cool mass of air descended upon us," John interrupted, excitedly, "clearing the heat and humidity."

"As the clouds rolled back," Andrew said, reclaiming the floor, "rays of sunlight illuminated the scene."

"Then there was a voice that came from nowhere . . ." John added.

The men paused, clearly caught up in whatever had come next in the scene that was still so vivid to them.

A voice? Simon wondered. What voice?

"The voice of God," Andrew explained, his tone lowering in reverence. "Yahweh said, 'This is my beloved Son, with whom I am well pleased.'"

Simon stared quietly at Andrew, then at his best friend as he tried to comprehend the scene his brother described. "This voice you heard," he asked, "truly, it was the voice of God?"

Although John's emotions froze his tongue, his face and eyes confirmed Andrew's account.

"Who is this young rabbi?" Simon asked, excited but still skeptical.

"His name is Jesus. He's a carpenter from Nazareth." Andrew took a deep breath, trying to slow his ramble. "The Baptizer pointed at Jesus again and repeated those same words, 'Behold, the Lamb of God. Behold him, who takes away the sins of the world!'"

Simon's eyes went distant in thought. Then he held up his hand to stop the storytelling while he considered this remarkable tale. After gazing across the waters of Galilee to the distant hills of the south, where this event had occurred, Simon returned his attention to his brother.

Andrew couldn't help but feel excited for them both—for all the people of Israel. *We have waited so long*, he thought. His brother's piercing eyes misted over from the years of suffering and fading hope.

"So, John and I followed Jesus," Andrew explained, "and we stayed with him, listening to him until four o'clock in the afternoon. Jesus announced he would be leaving to pray and fast in the wilderness. He then told John the Baptizer that he was going to prepare himself for his ministry, and that he would take forty days and nights to fulfill the prophecies."

"Forty days and nights?" repeated Simon.

"Yes," replied John and Andrew in unison. "Forty days and nights."

"That's when we started for home to share the news," John added with a nod. "It took only a day and a half."

Simon considered the distance before whistling. *A day and a half?* he thought. *They were moving.*

Andrew shook his brother's shoulders. "I have no doubt that Jesus is the Christ," he added excitedly. "We have found the Messiah, brother. We have found Christ!"

Simon's eyes continued to well up.

"Don't forget about the vipers, Andrew," John chimed in. Although he'd allowed his friend to break the good news, he wasn't about to let some of the important details go unrecorded.

"Oh yes … yes!" Andrew was overcome with another surge of adrenaline that rushed through his bloodstream like sweet wine through a new wineskin. "John the Baptizer called the Pharisees vipers, saying they were worthless!"

"He what?"

Andrew nodded, knowing his brother would enjoy the fact. "The Baptizer disapproves of the Pharisee-snakes as much as we do, Simon. He loathes the wealthy hypocrites, who live better than all of us … and in the name of God."

"Really?" Simon smiled wide.

"At one point, he asked that the Romans and tax collectors not extort money or take more than what they're supposed to," Andrew added.

"And he told the common people to share food and clothing with those who don't have any," John reported, clearly tired of sitting quietly on the sidelines.

Andrew nodded. "He rejects tradition and authority."

"Good for him," Simon whispered.

John nodded, excitedly.

"Good for him," Simon repeated, his eyes darting from his elder brother to his best friend, John.

John laughed out loud. From the time they could walk, he and Simon had been inseparable. They learned to fish together with their fathers, Jonas and Zebedee. They attended Hebrew school together, learning the Torah, the first five books of the Bible written by Moses. They even celebrated Passover side by side each year.

Even though he was thinner and a few inches taller than Simon, they were equals in every way that counted. However, as John was more contemplative and polished than Simon, he was slower to action and more thoughtful. He studied Simon's strong face and smiled. *I've always loved the thickheaded mule like a brother,* he thought.

"Every word Andrew has said is true," John told his best friend. "We've found the Messiah, Simon."

Without further detail, John turned to his brother, James, and winked. "And I plan to write down everything I can remember."

∝ • ⊃

I hope it is true. It must be, Simon thought, feeling excited. *The two best men I know have sworn to it, so it must be.* In a moment's time—a flash—his mind filled with fantasies of all that might be.

For years, Simon had been tormented over the injustices of his world. *How could Yahweh's people suffer so badly and for so long?* he wondered. *Enslaved for generations only to be liberated from the Egyptians when Moses parted the Red Sea. Then we were left to wander aimlessly around the desert, lost for forty brutal years.* He snickered. *And if that's not bad enough, once we returned to our own lands, we were oppressed by the savage Romans.* It made no sense to him. It never had.

Now it was his generation's turn to suffer. From the Roman dictators to the High Pharisees, Simon and his people were treated like pariahs. The injustice of it twisted his stomach into slipknots. Worse yet, the Jewish people's passive response to all of it went against his nature. *Fire should be fought with fire,* he'd always believed, *and muscle with muscle.*

Since he could remember, he lived his life feeling torn, his heart and mind engaged in steady combat. Like one of the storms that wreaked havoc on the Sea of Galilee, his thoughts and feelings were tossed about like a small boat on the massive, churning waters.

The Messiah is exactly what we've been waiting for, he thought, grinning. *These Roman dogs have no idea what's coming. The Messiah will be a great leader!*

Simon bar Jonas loved engaging in wishful thinking, even when it was not foretold in the Scriptures. For the next few minutes, he allowed himself to daydream about war and glory and a conquered people finally being liberated.

Sweet deliverance!

When Simon emerged from his fantasies, he looked at his brother and smiled. "Do you think we should go back?"

"Back?" Andrew asked, clearly hoping they were thinking the same thing.

Simon drew in a long breath and exhaled. "Well, we have time to prepare, so let's make a plan," he announced. "When we learn this Jesus has returned, we can have James sail us down to the south of the sea. James can leave us and then head back to fish, while you, John, and I will travel the rest of the way together to meet Jesus in Bethabara. What do you think about—"

Andrew leaped into his arms, where the brothers shared a hug. This was not a common practice on the docks, but neither man cared.

If only I could get a few winks of sleep, Simon thought. *But what are the chances now? The Messiah is here!*

CHAPTER 3

YOU ARE SIMON ...

Capernaum, Galilee

The next few weeks passed quickly. Fishing was good and the emerging glories of spring in Galilee made daily life a pleasure. Travelers from all sides of the Sea of Galilee were sharing stories of the baptism of Jesus. The hopeful tales and descriptions of Jesus made their way among the communities that surrounded the region of Galilee. Again and again, Simon and the others heard of the miracle: the voice of Yahweh, the baptism, and the dove. Although they continued in their daily lives, the topic was never far from their minds.

Simon had, of course, shared all the stories with his wife, making plans in his mind to go and see for himself.

After just a few weeks had passed, word arrived in Capernaum by a boat that had just sailed from the south, that Jesus had returned to the area.

The morning light had not yet entered their bed chamber when Simon and his wife discussed his upcoming trip.

"How long will you be gone?" she asked.

"I'm not sure," he admitted, stifling a yawn.

"Not sure?" she repeated, a hint of disapproval in her voice. "So it's that easy for you to leave me and Eema?"

He rolled sideways, throwing his thick arm around her torso. "It's never easy leaving you, my love," he vowed. "Not even for a day." He paused. "But Andrew says he's found the Messiah...and I need to go see for myself."

She sighed heavily, surrendering to the fact that her stubborn husband had already made up his mind.

"I won't be long," he promised. "And I'll send James back to take care of the fishing and to look after you."

She sighed again; her breath was lighter this time, less emotional.

She's starting to warm up to the idea, he decided.

"Why don't you just send James?" she asked; it was her final attempt at keeping him home.

"Because James might never return," he teased, "and I will." Although she tried to conceal her smile in the darkness, Simon caught it. "I'll always come back," he whispered, kissing her cheek. "Always."

"I know," she said. "Just don't be too long, OK?"

"I won't," he whispered, kissing her again.

At first light, once Simon had offered his wife a proper goodbye, he, Andrew, John, and James set out for Bethabara, sailing down the length of the Sea of Galilee until they reached the beginning of the Lower Jordan River, where the river leaves the sea and continues its path south to the Dead Sea. From the docks, James sailed back north to home, while Simon, Andrew, and John followed the paths on foot along the river and its surrounding floodplains.

On land, the Galilean crops were as plentiful as the abundance of fish in the sea. Spring flowers were in bloom. Shimmering fields of grain, silvery groves of olives, the towering date palm orchards, and emerald vineyards blanketed the lush countryside. Simon surveyed the fertile landscape, noting the stark difference from the rocky hillsides on his northern end of the sea. Here, in the south, the land was flatter along the river and the crops reflected a diverse abundance.

"God is good," Andrew commented, surveying their surroundings. Simon gawked at his brother, prompting him to explain further. "He's given us all we need."

Although Simon grinned, he said nothing.

"What?" Andrew asked. "You don't agree, brother?"

Simon's grin broke into a smile. "We're about to find out, aren't we?"

Punching Simon's arm, Andrew joined in the laughter. "I already have," he said, "but if you need to see it with your own eyes, then—"

"I do," he interrupted, returning the punch. "That's if you don't mind." Andrew stopped laughing, rubbing the sting out of his arm.

As the men walked on, they talked about the possibilities for the future.

"So you must believe me and John, or you would never have traveled all this way," Andrew prodded.

Simon snickered. "Of course, I do. I never doubted either of you." He stopped to look into his brother's eyes. "It's because I do believe that we're making this trip." His eyes widened. "Why wouldn't I want to see the Messiah for myself?" He half-shrugged. "I'm not stupid."

"I agree," Andrew quickly countered, adding a grin.

Simon chuckled. "Although I haven't been as single-minded as you in finding Messiah, Andrew, I've always shared your deepest wishes." He nodded. *I'm not sure anyone wants the Messiah to come into power more than me ...*, he thought before releasing a war cry. "And return the twelve tribes of Israel back to their former glory!"

∝•∞

As the brothers walked, each was content to be alone with his own thoughts. They finally arrived at the very place that Andrew had described. The quiet setting surprised Simon. *For whatever reason, I was expecting a crowd,* he thought.

Scanning the area, his eyes searched hard for the Chosen One. As if it were a dream, he watched as Jesus Christ, the great prophet promised by Moses, quietly approached them.

Time stood still.

Searching for his next breath, Simon was rocked with a sensation he'd never experienced before. This was not physical nor even emotional; it went much deeper. It felt like his soul was trying to scream out.

Wearing the most loving smile, Jesus locked eyes with Simon and closed the distance between them.

Laboring to breathe, Simon heard the distant echo of his own voice: *Could it be you, Lord?*

The entire world felt like it had stopped spinning as a quiet but overwhelming sense of complete bliss enveloped Simon. Although he felt like he was experiencing the moment outside of his body, Simon was sure of one thing: he revered this man—this stranger—as he had never revered or loved another before.

Jesus of Nazareth was a tall man, with a lean, muscular build, the clear result of his occupation, as well as the many miles he'd traveled. At thirty years of age, his tanned, gentle face looked gaunt, as though he'd fasted for weeks. His brown hair matched his beard, and his chestnut-colored eyes were magnets, drawing everyone into his almost hypnotic gaze.

Simon was drawn right in, completely awestruck.

Standing face-to-face, Jesus cleared his throat, breaking Simon's trance. Humbled, Simon waited.

"You are Simon, son of Jonas," Jesus told him. "You will be called Peter [Cephas]."

Although he nodded—or thought he did—Simon thought, *What?* He was immediately unsure whether he had missed something he should not have. But the weight of the moment continued to sweep him away in a tsunami of emotions that he could neither recognize nor define.

As Simon stood in shock, Jesus turned away.

What did he just call me? Simon asked himself. *A rock?* His mind raced to recount the exact words that were just spoken to him. *You will be Cephas, or Peter,* he repeated in his head. *The rock?* His vision blurred, as he struggled to understand. *Did he really just call me a rock?* He inhaled deeply a few times. *What does that mean?*

Simon looked to his left to find his brother smiling at him. "Told you," Andrew said, his face radiating pure joy. "I told you, brother."

"I know, but..."

"But?"

"He said I will be called Peter," Simon whispered.

Andrew matched the shrug. "Then that's what you will be called."

What? Simon thought, feeling as lost as a child.

The following day, accepting his invitation, Simon, John, and Andrew followed Jesus into Galilee, where the rabbi found a man named Philip.

"Follow me," he told the new disciple.

Philip agreed without reluctance. Being from Bethsaida, he knew Simon and the others very well. Philip then sought out Nathanael—also known as Bartholomew—and told his friend, "We have found him, whom Moses and the prophets wrote: Jesus of Nazareth, the son of Joseph."

"Can any good thing come out of Nazareth?" teased Nathanael, smirking.

"Come and see."

Once John joined them—surprised to see that others had already been added to the group—the five men began following Jesus wherever he went.

John turned to Simon, gesturing toward Nathanael and Philip. "New recruits?" he whispered.

"The more, the merrier ... I guess?" Simon said.

John shrugged. "I guess," he repeated. "And I don't think we've seen the last of them."

∝•✕

"I've been invited to a wedding in Cana with my mother," Jesus shared with the small group, "and I'd like you all to join me."

Each of the men quickly accepted.

"I love weddings," Simon said, picturing his wife's beautiful face.

"I remember," John teased him. "You could barely stand at your own after all that wine."

"Barely stand?" Andrew repeated. "If it wasn't for fear of his new wife's wrath, he would have fallen asleep halfway through the celebration."

They all laughed.

As they started their journey west toward Cana, walking on faith, Simon used the time to consider the benefits as well as the risks. *We're stepping into the great unknown,* he realized, *but I've always wanted this.* He'd longed for such an opportunity. *I just hope I've made the right decision.* He looked at his friend and brother. *I hope we all have.*

Fear began wrestling hope and was starting to win. *My father entrusted me with his trade,* he thought. *Can I just give up fishing and walk away? I mean, James will only be able to handle the strain of working alone for so long.* He shook his head. *And what about my wife, home alone . . . wondering and worrying?*

He stopped—literally—taking a moment to calm his breathing and break the negative cycle of thoughts that was making him feel dizzy.

John stopped alongside him and waited, without a word spoken.

Proceeding up the long, dusty road that leads from the Jordan Valley into the steep Galilean hills, Simon tried to process everything, struggling to make sense of it all. *Sure, I've always been impulsive,* he thought, *but I've never left my family, my work . . . to follow a man I barely know.* He shrugged to himself. *Maybe that's what faith is.*

He stared at the back of the rabbi, his new master, and was filled with as much fear as excitement. *You will be Peter [Cephas], the rock,* he repeated in his head. *Who says that? And what on earth does it mean?* He tried to shake it off but couldn't. *What was Jesus saying to me?*

While Simon wrestled with all the jumbled thoughts, he watched as Jesus turned around and looked directly at him. The man's mischievous smile made Simon think that Jesus could read his every thought and doubt.

Simon nodded, affirming that he was with him on every step— *even if I have no idea where this road might lead.*

Jesus returned the nod, marching on.

Simon and John walked side by side, as they had their entire lives, both feeling a mixture of excitement and uneasiness. It was their first trip with the Messiah, with no idea of what to expect.

"Nervous?" John asked, masking his own anxiety.

"Not at all," Simon fibbed. "Although I don't want to disappoint Jesus," he said, shrugging. "I'm still not sure why he picked me."

"Either of us," John admitted.

"Where do you think we're going?" Simon asked.

"To a wedding, right?" John quipped.

"You know what I mean. Do you think we'll be stopping anywhere along the way?" He looked back at Nathanael and Philip. "Maybe to pick up more recruits?"

"Your guess is as good as mine, Simon." They walked in silence, but only for a minute.

"Is it a friend's wedding, or a cousin's?" Simon asked.

"I'm not sure."

"Do you know anything?" Simon asked, fighting off his own grin.

John slapped his bulky arm. "As much as you do."

A few minutes passed. Simon tried to embrace the silence, but it was a futile attempt. "Are we stopping in Nazareth to meet the rabbi's family?"

"I don't think so." John stopped to peer into Simon's eyes. "You're like a young boy in Hebrew school. If you have so many questions, why don't you just ask the rabbi yourself?"

Simon considered this, before shaking off the idea. "No, Jesus looks like he has much bigger things on his mind." He grinned. "I'll save my questions for when I really need to ask them."

"Well, that'll be a first."

This time, Simon slapped John's arm, making his best friend cringe.

"Go easy, you clumsy ox," John muttered.

Simon laughed aloud, drawing looks from the others. "You're a fisherman, John," Simon replied. "You should be a bit hardier."

The friends laughed, making Jesus smile, as though he'd heard the entire childlike exchange.

It was dusk when Jesus finally halted the troop. "We'll camp here for the night."

Jesus had stopped at the crest of the hill where the entire Jordan Valley was visible below. Simon looked across the Sea of Galilee at the sun setting over the Syrian hills to the west. He wondered when he would see this familiar landscape again. Returning to the practical chores of the moment, Simon, Andrew, and John went off to find long branches to trim down and fashion into tent poles, while Philip and Nathanael hurried off to locate kindling and firewood.

Upon returning to camp, Simon watched as Jesus started the night's fire. Using a wooden spindle, he spun it back and forth on a separate piece of dried wood. The friction eventually created a few sparks that were quickly transferred to dried grass and moss.

He's not afraid to pitch in, Simon thought.

Using the ropes and tarps they had carried, the enthusiastic crew made quick work of erecting three improvised shelters, tents that would protect them from the elements.

By nightfall, the six weary men huddled around the crackling fire, which they used to cook the food they'd packed in cheesecloth for the trip. They also warmed themselves as well as the water they used to bathe.

Exhausted, Simon was happy for the chance to rest his aching bones. They'd traveled many hours and just as many miles, climbing up through rough and rocky terrain.

As Simon rested on one elbow, the fire dancing on his friends' faces, he became entranced by Jesus's words.

"Truly I tell you, unless you change and become like little children, you will never enter the kingdom of heaven," he warned. "So, whoever takes the lowly position of a child is the greatest in the kingdom of heaven. And whoever welcomes one such child in my name welcomes me."

Even though Simon could not truly understand the rabbi's puzzling lessons, he watched as John wrote much of it down. *Maybe I should have paid closer attention in school?* Simon thought, feeling envious that his friend was so proficient at turning blank papyrus into the written word. But for Simon, reading and writing remained a skill better left to others. *I can make out enough to get by, but I never really took the time necessary*, he thought, chastising himself.

Deciding to turn in, Simon bid his good nights and headed for the tent. After prayers— pleading for God to watch over his loved ones—he lay down, his head stuck just outside the shelter. There was something serene about being able to sleep beneath God's great firmament, a beautiful blanket of stars provided above to keep him warm.

He hadn't finished counting a half-dozen cricket chirps before the world turned to a single pinpoint of light and disappeared. Sleep finally claimed him.

Simon awoke from the first good night's sleep he'd enjoyed in days. *Maybe even weeks?* After a breakfast of sweet dates and bread, he brushed his teeth with a dried bone and rag and offered his prayers.

As dawn broke, it took little time to break down the camp. By morning's early light, the men were back on the road, marveling at all the sights to behold in lower Galilee. It was a flourishing countryside, known for its warm climate and rolling lands. Acres of wildflowers and blossoming trees were intermingled amid large swaths of deep green. The fertile land was home to abundant vineyards and thriving fruit orchards.

As they walked, Jesus insisted that they enjoy the gifts God had provided them.

Breakfast on the go, Simon thought as he cracked open a large, succulent pomegranate.

"God will provide," Andrew commented, peeling his own piece of sweet, juicy fruit.

"Indeed," John managed, his mouth stuffed with figs.

John loved to travel, and the excitement he felt over this new adventure was making his hair stand on end. He and the boys were usually stuck out on the water, so this was a welcome jaunt.

YOU WILL BE PETER

The road to Cana had leveled off, and the walk was easier. With a new skip in his step, John was taking in their wondrous surroundings. Strolling along like a tourist, he glanced back and spotted his friend Simon skulking behind the group. He slowed his stride, waiting for the stout man to catch up.

"You look troubled. What's on your mind?" John asked.

Simon glanced sideways, his eyes swimming in uncertainty. "Oh, I don't know, John," he quipped, "I thought I'd just take a walk and…"

John laughed. "I get it. Trust me."

"This is crazy," Simon said, lowering his voice to a whisper. "On one hand, I've never felt so excited and proud. I think we were chosen by the Messiah!" He shrugged. "Though I still can't understand why."

"I know," John said as he let out a chuckle. "It's going to take a while for that to sink in with me too."

Simon went silent.

"But on the other hand?" John asked.

It took a dozen more steps before Simon could form his thoughts into words. "Did you hear what the rabbi said to me? 'You will be Peter.' Who says that?" He shrugged. "And what does that mean?"

For a while, John couldn't find the words either. With a half-shrug, he grinned. "I think you'll find out when the time is right."

Simon shook his head, trying to erase any doubts or worries that left him unsettled.

"Well, whatever happens, at least we're in it together."

John threw his arm over his friend's shoulder. "Always," he vowed.

Simon looked over at Andrew and nodded. With a smile, Andrew returned the bonding gesture.

"Except for your brother," Simon joked, "who's back on the water, fishing for all of us."

John grinned. "Yeah, James has always been lazy like that."

They both laughed.

Walking through rolling fields of swaying wheat, Jesus continued on. With the five disciples at his heels, he answered questions, allowing them the time they needed to ponder his answers. To Simon, they all sounded like children, learning from their abba. But I like it, he decided. Something in him enjoyed the feeling of nostalgia.

For the rest of that day, they followed the road that skirted the southern slope of Mount Tabor. When they reached the major road from Magdala, they discovered they were not alone. More traffic than Simon had ever witnessed flowed along on both sides of the road. From ox-drawn carts to Roman chariots pulled by raven-black horses, a nearly constant plume of dust encircled them, causing them to shield their mouths and noses. Merchant caravans of camel trains transported exotic wares from the farthest reaches of the world.

The world is so much bigger than Capernaum, he thought, excited to discover more of it.

On the third day, Simon looked to the north to see many villages tucked among the hills. Beyond them, the snowy peaks of Mount Hermon stood guard. To the west, a faint yellow line of beach bordered the great sea, making him think of home as the group forged on.

Nestled in the midst of the green hills sat a little town of white-washed houses with flat red roofs. Tall, plumy palm trees provided a canopy of shade. *We've reached the outskirts of Nazareth,* Simon realized. Vibrant bursts of colors betrayed each home's magnificent flower garden.

Wow!

But Jesus kept on walking.

"We're not stopping at your home, Rabbi?" Simon asked for them all.

Jesus shook his head. "My eema has also been invited to the wedding. You will meet her at the feast this evening."

"Do they know we're coming?" Simon asked.

Jesus smiled patiently. "You will be welcome, Simon. Trust me."

The full midday sun accompanied them as Simon tromped along, continuing to work out the reasons for the impromptu trip.

Jesus seems to be what the prophets have foretold so far, he thought, as he went back and forth between faith and doubt.

Simon then recalled his wife's beautiful face, the sudden glimpse making him smile. He recalled how awkward he'd felt trying to explain it all to her. *I've never gone to a wedding without her,* he thought. *But she was more than understanding when I announced the trip.*

"I know who you are and what you want, Simon," she'd told him. *"And I know how hard you've searched for this. I won't stand in your way, husband."* She was beyond supportive; she was unconditionally loving. *I miss her already,* he thought.

"What an adventure!" John exclaimed, yanking Simon from his thoughts.

"Yes," he said, incapable of concealing anything from his child-hood friend.

"You're still struggling with it, huh?" John said. "Talk to me."

Simon half-shrugged. "We've been asked to join the Messiah. I can't imagine a greater blessing..."

"We've already agreed on that."

"But..." Simon muttered.

"But?"

Simon slowed his gait. "I worry about the business we've built. If we don't catch fish, then we can't pay our bills."

John threw his arm over Simon's shoulder. "It's why we left James behind: to tend to our duties." He smiled. "And we've spent our entire lives teaching him." He nodded, confidently. "James is solid. He can be counted on."

"I know that, John. I would never question James's loyalty," Simon said, turning quiet again. "But I also have a wife who—"

"Who will be looked after by James as well," John interrupted. "You've been blessed with a woman of great faith, my friend."

"Yes," Simon agreed. "She's the blessing of my life."

"She'll be fine." John searched his friend's eyes. "Have some faith yourself."

Simon's worry was slowly replaced by peace. "You're right."

"Of course, I am," John teased, gesturing toward Jesus with his head. "Besides, I have a sense that he'll provide whatever is needed."

Simon gazed at their leader, who walked with purpose at the front of the small throng. "I have that same feeling."

The friends trudged along in a comfortable silence as Cana appeared just over the rise. Although Simon was excited for the wedding celebration, he longed for his wife. *I do miss her. She would enjoy this celebration.* Even in the company of all these men, he felt oddly alone.

He turned his face to the sky. *Thank You, Yahweh, for looking after my family while I'm away from them,* he offered in silent prayer. *And for James, for seeing that my work gets done. Please let me do Your will and become the servant I'm meant to be.*

CHAPTER 4

SIX STONE JARS

Cana, Galilee

All six travelers arrived in the village of Cana late that Wednesday afternoon. As they traversed the final hill, the valley revealed more orchards and crop fields. *Galilee really is beautiful*, Simon confirmed. *Hopefully, its vineyards produce wines that are just as fine.* He was still smiling as they grew closer to the houses huddled together on the hillside.

As they approached the village, the sounds of children's laughter and joyful conversations were intermixed with the loveliest music. Even a braying donkey sounded happy.

Simon was marveling at the masonry workmanship of the larger buildings, carved from limestone and granite, when Jesus announced, "It appears that we've arrived in time." The rabbi's smile revealed that he wasn't surprised.

The traditional wedding procession from the bride's father's home to the bridegroom's was underway. While the minstrel troop played at the front of the convoy, a squad of servants handed out dates to children along the road and wine to those of a more seasoned age.

A young girl about fifteen years old, her dark, curly hair protruding from behind a white bridal veil, walked alone. Some of her relatives carried sprays of flowers, while others bore lit torches.

Wonderful, Simon thought. He loved his Jewish customs and celebrations.

Dusk was starting to creep in as the parade's onlookers clapped and praised the bride's semi-concealed beauty. Jesus, Simon, and the others applauded before joining the back of the line, proceeding on to the bridegroom's home, where the young man would carry his betrothed over the threshold of their new marital home.

Upon arrival, Jesus gestured for his disciples to remove their sandals at the outer door before proceeding onto the courtyard, which was being used as the reception hall.

From the first step in, Simon was impressed by the stone courtyard, which had been decorated for the great celebration. Adorned in ornamental rugs and cushioned couches, low tables were arranged for the guests to dine; each person would be expected to lay on one elbow with their feet positioned away from the table.

While servants scurried to and fro, carrying food and drink, Simon and his brethren washed their hands and feet, complying with the precepts of the ancient law. Upon drying their extremities, each was officially welcomed with a cup of water drawn from one of the large stone jars.

The sweet notes of a talented musical duo permeated the warm air, the harp and flute creating a simple but elegant symphony.

Quenching his thirst, Simon looked around. *Flowers,* he noted, *there are flowers everywhere.* He nodded his appreciation. *They've turned this courtyard into a garden.*

Beyond a table overlaid with bowls of fruits and nuts—even a stack of sweet date cakes—Simon spotted the intricately decorated chuppah. Ivy, flowers, and greens were wrapped around four legs that had been fashioned from cedar timbers, approximately eight feet in height. It was just wide enough to host the bride, bridegroom, and officiating rabbi. The entire wooden frame was covered in a canopy of flowers—yellow, white, pink, and red—which had been strung together to create breathtaking strands of garland.

The sight of it instantly brought Simon's thoughts back to his wife. No, he scolded himself, quickly pushing the melancholy out of his head. *I'm here now, and I need to be here ... and she understands.*

Catching the first whiff of roasting lamb, Simon turned to see Jesus and an older woman locked in a lengthy embrace. The disciple needed no introduction to understand the scene. *She's his mother.*

Mary was beauty in its purest form. She was not tall, but above medium height. Her oval face was slightly bronzed by the sun. Beneath black, slightly arched brows sat a pair of gentle, olive-colored eyes. Her hair was light and her nose slender, much like her hands. *But there's something more,* Simon thought, considering it. *She has an unmistakable aura,* he finally decided, *a striking beauty that can only come from within.* He studied the embracing pair further, while they swayed in each other's arms. *And she must be the most beautiful woman, having given birth to the Messiah.*

Breaking from the hug, Jesus and Mary held hands, exchanging a long, blissful look that revealed more about their sacred bond than any words ever could.

Jesus then turned to face his disciples. "Mother," he said, "I would like you to meet my students."

Without thinking, Simon was the first to step forward. Jesus smiled. "Mother, this is Simon Peter."

Rock? Simon swallowed hard, as he considered the peculiar title.

"Simon," Jesus said, "this is my mother, Mary."

It was the second time in the simple fisherman's life that he could feel the air leave his lungs, only to remain lost while he fumbled for the right words. *Silence.*

Mary was gracious, even angelic. "I hope my son is taking good care of you?" she jumped in.

Simon smiled. "He is," he managed.

As though offering her blessing, she nodded once.

John was the next to step forward, while Simon's mind spun in circles. *What must it be like to be the mother of the Messiah?* he wondered, seeking out one of the servants for another cup of water. *And what will it take for the rest of us to truly follow him?*

Mary had arrived a few days early to help with the wedding preparations. The bridegroom's family were dear friends. From assisting with the seating arrangements to helping decorate the chuppah, she did what she could. The family was not wealthy, but they had splurged on this feast. In fact, they had provided several large jars of wine.

Now, seeing her son, it felt like the celebration had finally begun. *But Jesus is too skinny,* she worried. *He needs to eat more to keep up his strength.* She shook her head. *It will be harder for him to take care of others unless he starts taking better care of himself.* She stared at him, her heart gushing with love and pride. *I can only pray that the world treats him with kindness.* Her eyes misted over. *His ministry will bring so many risks.* She looked skyward. *Please, Yahweh, watch over our Son.*

Simon was trying not to stare at Mary, or at least not get caught, when the wedding ceremony commenced. The bride, bridegroom, and rabbi took their respective places beneath the processional, the canopied altar of eternal love and commitment.

Standing side by side, the young couple entered their ever-lasting bond before family and friends. With a blessing, the rabbi commenced the services, where the smiling bridegroom took his wife according to the Law of Moses of Israel.

By the time Simon paid attention to the words, the ceremony was complete. The bridegroom lifted his new wife's veil, kissing her publicly for the first time. The applause was deafening, loud enough to keep any sorrow or worry at bay for the entire night.

At least I paid attention at my own wedding, Simon thought.

The young groom signed the contract, vowing to honor and keep his new bride. Good wishes and prayers were then heaped upon the married couple.

Simon looked at Andrew and John, and grinned. They were beaming as well, ready to celebrate the happy nuptials. *Let's go enjoy the party!*

Servants began drawing water from the huge stone jars, holding some twenty gallons each, and transferring the liquid into basins for the guests. Hands and feet were washed again as everyone prepared to eat.

The master of the feast kicked off the festivities with the blessing of the wine. With a raised cup, he called out, "Blessed are You, Lord, our God, the King of the universe who brings forth the fruit of the vine. Amen."

"Amen," Simon repeated. As he lifted the cup to his lips, he turned to see Jesus looking at him. The two men exchanged a smile before raising their cups even higher to each other. When they claimed their seats, Jesus was positioned at a place of honor.

As a rabbi from Nazareth, Jesus was expected to be seated with the other most honored guests, near the bridegroom and the bride.

Olives, cheeses, loaves of bread, and cucumbers were already set out on the long tables. Candied dates and sweet dessert cakes were abundant. Famished from their long journey, Simon wasted no time indulging. *Delicious!*

As the guests reclined on the couch cushions, the servants lit candles and lamps before serving platter upon platter of food. Simon focused on the lamb and vegetables, mopping up his plate with several chunks of unleavened bread. At one point, he noticed Mary directing the servants to continue filling Jesus's plate. He chuckled. *A mother's love is a mother's love,* he thought, *Messiah or not.*

Soft music played, the harp and flute floating just above the well-lit courtyard. The wondrous buzz of joyful conversation and laughter filled every inch of the space. Knowing only one another, Simon, Andrew, John, and Philip huddled together and broke bread, spending the meal getting better acquainted. The wine didn't hurt as each was willing to share.

Nathanael was from nearby and helped introduce the group from Bethsaida and Capernaum.

"We're fishermen by trade," Simon told Nathanael, gesturing toward Andrew and John.

"And my brother James is back home running the business for us," said John, nodding. "He's also a follower of Jesus."

Simon raised his cup. "To James," he said. "Someone has to work." They all laughed.

"How difficult was it to leave the fishing behind?" Philip asked.

Simon cleared his throat, preparing to answer for them all. "It's all we've ever known," he admitted. "It isn't difficult. It's impossible."

Every man nodded that he understood.

"We don't yet understand why, but we're all compelled to follow," John commented as he looked at Jesus, who was playing a silly table game with the children.

"Where do you think we'll stay tonight?" Nathanael asked.

"Stop worrying about these things," Andrew said, as though he'd known this man his entire life. "Jesus will provide." He paused. "I think our only job right now is to trust and to learn."

"To watch," John, the scribe, added.

Simon nodded in agreement but thought about Jesus and real signs of power. *He needs to claim his throne publicly.*

As the disciples continued to fill their bellies, loosen their tongues, and bond, Simon looked around and smiled. *No Romans. No tax collectors.* His smile widened. *What a perfect evening.*

"I'm told that Jesus was a gifted craftsman, a carpenter," Nathanael commented.

"But he no longer practices his craft," Philip countered.

"Sure, he does," John said. "He's building a kingdom."

Each man raised his cup to honor the declaration.

As the hours passed, Simon noticed that the bridegroom's parents had welcomed several uninvited guests. *Very hospitable,* he thought, watching as the crowd grew larger. *I just hope the wine holds out.* He took another sip, draining his cup.

The sounds of joy echoed throughout the courtyard. Friends and strangers alike sang and danced; they held hands and spun in circles like overgrown children. More toasts were followed by the clinking of red-clay cups. As the adults celebrated, drinking heartily, their giggling youngsters ran about. The little ones were drawn to Jesus, where he sat reveling in their contagious laughter.

The servants refilled cup after cup, the wine flowing as freely as everyone's dancing. And the food never stopped either. Bread, olives, and cheese. More meats. More lamb. Simon grabbed his midsection. *I feel like I'm going to explode.*

After the dance of Miriam, another round of wine was served.

As the night grew older, the moon rose above them. Wall torches licked at the darkness, while the candles turned to stubs. Whispered gossip began to travel throughout the reception hall. *The wine has run out.*

Simon and the others shook off the ridiculous rumor.

"Run out of wine?" John said. "It's only the first day."

"Maybe they'll dilute what's left?" Philip suggested.

Nathanael shrugged. "From what the servants are saying, there's nothing left to dilute."

Can't be, Simon thought, glancing over at the adjoining room where the ladies were gathered around a separate table. He saw Mary, her beautiful face looking troubled. Concerned, he quickly got to unsure feet, taking a moment to steady himself.

Mary stood in the doorway looking at Jesus, trying to get his attention. Jesus stood and walked toward her. With perked ears, Simon became focused on their exchange.

"The wedding hosts have no more wine to serve their guests," Mary reported to her son, panicked for her friends. "They're sure to be humiliated."

They exchanged a long look.

"What has that to do with me?" Jesus asked, gently. "Mother, my time has not yet come."

Mary reached for Jesus's hand and stared into his eyes. Her tongue said nothing, but her long gaze at her son settled the matter. She finally smiled before turning to the servants.

"Do whatever he tells you to," she commanded.

Besides Simon, many others were now watching the peculiar scene unfold.

Six huge purification jars, holding some twenty gallons each, were propped against the outer wall. These were the same water pots that had been drawn from when each guest arrived. The jars were made of stone, a material considered pure as it was unlikely to break or stain, making its contents unclean.

Without fanfare, Jesus confidently told the servants, "Fill the jars to the brim with water."

They did as they were told, filling each to the very top.

"Now draw it off," commanded Jesus, "and bring it to the master of the feast." His calm voice offered no hint of the true power in his words.

As the servants began to pour the liquid from the crocks into smaller vessels, they saw that it ran red. It had the smell, color, and taste of wine.

There was a collective gasp.

After tasting the wine, the master of the feast called for everyone's attention. "People, please listen."

The crowd quieted.

"At every wedding I've ever officiated, the hosts have always served the best wine first." He half-shrugged. "Then later, when everyone has drunk their fill and their senses are dulled..."

A few people laughed, Simon the loudest.

"The hosts serve the poorer wine," the feast master added. "I mean, who would ever notice?"

This time, everyone laughed.

"But not at this wedding," the man said, both his voice and cup being raised higher. "They have reserved the best wine until now." He took another sip. "And it is the best I've ever tasted."

As a new round of applause erupted, one word screamed in Simon's buzzing head: *How?*

He looked to his master. *Jesus turned the water into wine. Wh—what?*

The servants hurried to refill everyone's cup.

The feast master raised his glass to offer a new toast. "May this marriage be as pure and fruitful as this delightful wine."

Simon caught Mary nod her gratitude toward Jesus, who merely smiled, returning the nod.

Jesus obviously couldn't deny his mother, Simon thought, *the woman who gave him life.* Simon took a sip of the new wine. *Whoa, this is amazing!* He looked at John to see if his friend shared his opinion. But John was already seated back at the table, his hand flying across a new sheet of papyrus. *Word of this will spread quickly,* Simon predicted.

Not everyone was aware of the miracle that had transpired, but Simon and the rest of the disciples were.

Andrew hurried over, but before the man could speak, Simon blurted, "Did you see that?"

Andrew nodded. "I did."

"What just happened here?" Simon asked.

His brother laughed. "I believe Jesus has given us a taste of his amazing power."

Simon shook his head. "Unreal."

"For some, probably. But we've just seen it with our own eyes, brother."

"We have." In shock, Simon took a sip. "Have you tried the wine yet?"

Andrew nodded. "I've never had anything like it."

Simon agreed. "A taste of heaven," he commented, taking another sip.

"Indeed," Andrew said.

By now, the wedding reception was back in full swing, with guests conversing and laughing as they enjoyed the plentiful wine.

Standing off in the shadows, Simon still questioned his own eyes. *How could it be? Turning water into wine?* He looked at the six stone jars. *And Jesus gave more than was needed.* The extraordinary feat was so difficult to grasp that it generated more questions than answers. *How do I make sense of the impossible?*

New candles replaced the old, and the party lasted late into the night, and even the next day. Singing, laughing, dancing, arms draped over shoulders; it was a time of great joy.

But Simon had retreated deeper into his own mind. *Turning water into wine?* he kept repeating in his head; it had become a mantra.

Confusion eventually gave way to enthusiasm. Simon hoped, *By Jesus turning water into wine for all to see, it's only the beginning.* His newfound leader had begun to exhibit his power, confirming Simon's greatest hopes.

He looked at Jesus, thinking, *I will follow you anywhere.*

At that very moment, Jesus turned and peered directly into his eyes. With a smile, he nodded that he understood.

Anywhere, Simon repeated.

CHAPTER 5

PASSOVER IN JERUSALEM

Capernaum, Galilee

Much to Simon's delight, Jesus came from Nazareth to Capernaum to live with him and his family. Sandwiched between farms on the east and forests on the west, the Messiah settled into one of the many humble limestone homes. The town of Capernaum was large enough for royal officials, as well as a contingent of Roman soldiers, to call home. Its white-walled synagogue sat atop a black basalt foundation, its gleaming, red-tiled roof revealing its significance within the community. The docks at the fishing port of Capernaum were only a healthy walk away.

Jesus informed his followers, "I am going to Jerusalem for the Passover, and I would like you all to join me."

"Yes!" Simon called out, never bashful about sharing his thoughts and feelings.

Jesus laughed.

Passover was the annual Jewish holiday that took place in the spring, attracting droves of pilgrims to the Holy City of Jerusalem. All twelve tribes of Israel celebrated the time when God had used Moses to free the Israelites from slavery. The Lord had smitten the land of Egypt on the eve of the exodus, sparing the firstborn of the Israelites.

Simon was excited. He loved visiting Jerusalem—the Mount of Zion, the capital of Judaism. Three times a year, they offered sacrifices of goats or doves. As Simon recalled, his only pilgrimage took place when he was twelve years old, taking the lengthy trek with his dad and Andrew. It was a rite of passage into manhood. *That first visit was an unforgettable experience.*

As the group prepared to leave for their journey, they bid their goodbyes to family and friends. Filled with mixed emotions, Simon kissed his wife. It felt much like the first time they had kissed, innocent and sweet. "We won't be gone long," he whispered into her ear.

She pushed him away enough to peer into his eyes. "You'll be gone for as long as you need," she replied, blessing his pilgrimage with another kiss.

With bulging packs slung across their chests and shoulders, the men took up their walking sticks and started down the dusty trail.

Although the land east of the Sea of Galilee had less vegetation, the rainy season had brought their entire world into full color. While Jesus led the band along the familiar road by the river, Simon took it all in, breathing as deeply and peacefully as he could ever recall.

Moving south beyond the Sea of Galilee and Mount Hermon, Simon and his brethren asked questions. Jesus answered each one.

I wonder if I'm the rabbi's favorite, Simon thought, a few hours into the trip.

John and James, however, were relentless in their pursuit of the master's attention. "Rabbi, do we have to wait for the harvest before burning away the chaff?" James asked.

"What do you mean?" Jesus asked.

"The nonbelievers," John said, jumping in to help his brother. "Should they not be stricken down until they submit?"

"As the Romans do?" Jesus asked with a wry smile.

Although Simon smiled over the lively exchange, he was clever enough to keep his mouth shut. For once, he was happy to keep his sandal out of his mouth. Even he realized, *Jesus did not come to gather slaves or force people to believe. If so, many would have already been drowned in the Jordan. Freewill was the key. Faith is a choice,* he decided.

Both James and John shrugged, the younger brother running his index finger across his throat in a mock display of execution.

Jesus laughed, surprising Simon. "Ah, the Sons of Thunder," Jesus said, nicknaming the zealous, outspoken brothers.

Sons of Thunder? Simon pondered this, unsure if it was a term of endearment. It didn't take long to come to his final decision. *It doesn't matter,* he thought, taking his rightful place beside the Messiah. *I'm definitely his favorite.*

En route later that day, Simon continued to contemplate the miracle at Cana. *It happened,* he thought. *Jesus turned water into wine. But how?* He then pictured the deep bond shared between Mary and her son. *The things love will make us do,* he thought, grinning to himself.

Just then, Jesus turned to him and smiled.

Simon tried to wipe away the thoughts. It was impossible. They walked on, each man lost in his own daydreams.

Although Simon understood that the Messiah had power— *I've witnessed it with my own eyes*—he was concerned that there weren't more signs. And each one should be a public display, he thought, imagining greater things. *We need everyone to know! It doesn't make any sense to keep it secret. If Jesus performs miracles but seeks no credit, how will the word spread? How will the Romans know?*

Jesus turned to him again. This time, he was not smiling. "Not yet, Simon," he said. "The time has not come."

Nodding that he understood, Simon felt unsettled but not surprised that the man could read his thoughts. *So, you'll reveal your plan when the time is right, then?*

Jesus's loving smile returned.

As if seeing the spring bloom for the first time, Simon breathed in the beauty of the nature that surrounded them. The warm air was sweet and heavy. Golden-colored blossoms of wild mustard led to larger patches of ruby-red poppy fields. A stunning row of oleander shrubs lined the water's edge, while pink-flowered peach trees claimed the higher ground. It was a scene from a dream.

Buffalo, gazelle, even the occasional ibex could be seen going about their business. Simon looked skyward to see a pair of tiny birds at play. *They've been following us for a while,* he thought, before realizing, *They've been following the Messiah, just like us.* Smiling, he kept his head on a swivel. He didn't want to miss a single detail. *Everything feels like the first time now.*

The Jordan Valley was in full bloom, its rich soil proving fruitful for all sorts of trees. From walnuts, which normally enjoyed a cooler environment, to palm trees, which grew best in hot air, they were all able to thrive side by side.

Beyond the acacias and willows were wine vineyards, palm orchards, and fig groves completing the stunning portrait.

On the road, the raggedy band of pilgrims passed merchant caravans heading north to Galilee, their wagons being pulled by donkeys, oxen, or camels. Simon imagined all the exotic wares—jewelry, spices, rugs—he could never afford to buy his wife. He grinned. *Thankfully, she doesn't care about such things.*

"OK, that's good for today," Jesus announced, suddenly stopping. "Let's camp here." They'd reached the dark cliffs of Mount Quarantania, just outside of the ancient city of Jericho.

Plopping down, Simon couldn't have been happier. His feet were aching terribly, and he was tired of spitting out dirt. Evidently, the heavy labor of pulling nets had not prepared him for this type of travel.

Andrew looked at his brother and chuckled.

"I have blisters growing on my blisters," Simon said, removing his sweaty sandals.

"It'll get easier," Andrew said, shrugging it off. "It's just a matter of training the body."

Simon agreed, thinking, *And the mind.*

Later that evening, after eating a portion of bread as well as some fish, figs, and dates they had brought along, they settled in for the night.

No sooner had his makeshift shelter been erected when Simon completed his prayers.

Thank You for the blessing of this journey, Yahweh, and for protecting those I love.

To the low drone of several whispered conversations, which he was all too happy to avoid, Simon passed out from exhaustion. Insomnia had become nothing more than a bad memory.

In the morning, the group skirted past the flowery city of Jericho. In stride, Simon craned his neck to catch a glimpse of its skyline. *The merchants and their wares. The architecture.* Such details were left to Simon's old memories and his childlike imagination.

"How are you holding up?" John asked, walking beside him.

"Never been better," Simon said. "I have a feeling we're about to witness some amazing things soon."

Smiling, John nodded. "I think you're right. Although I have no idea what they might be." He half-shrugged. "And I'm done trying to predict."

Simon was still laughing when a bolt of pride ripped through his body. They had already made their ascent through the hill country of Judea and were turning onto the road that led to the Mount of Olives. "Jerusalem's getting close," he said, his voice sounding odd even to him.

John laughed. "You'll always be that twelve-year old boy," he teased.

Maybe, Simon thought.

Walking uphill, they headed toward Jerusalem, leaving the view of ancient Jericho and the Dead Sea behind them. They moved on to Bethany, a small village on the southeastern slopes of the Mount of Olives, just outside of Jerusalem. Strolling through the small marketplace, Simon spotted one of the vendors hawking seafood.

"From the waters of Galilee, boys!" he called out. "Fish from our own nets!" John, Andrew, and James nodded proudly.

Jesus chuckled.

Walking through his homeland toward Jerusalem, the seat of pride for his people, Simon's chest swelled with pride as he remembered everything he'd witnessed along their journey, all the beauty of the landscapes, along with the craftsmanship and hardworking ingenuity of the Jewish people. *How could anyone not be proud to be a Jew?* he wondered. Although it often meant suffering, he was a member of God's chosen people, carrying the weight of the Father's promise to Abraham. *Yahweh will keep His promise.* Eternal hope was his birthright.

The first sight of Jerusalem in the distance stole Simon's breath. His bulging forearms were covered in goose bumps, while the hairs on the back of his neck stood on end. He looked toward his teacher at the head of the column. *Will he perform such an undeniable miracle here that even the most ignorant nonbelievers will have no choice but to crown him king?*

Simon looked up. The temple of God—constructed of the purest marble, the roof covered with gold—stood high above Jerusalem. *Remarkable,* he thought.

The light was fading fast; the sun was diving below the horizon but not before shooting off a few final bursts of breathtaking color. Then, like a healing bruise, the sky turned from blue to purple to black.

Jesus halted the troop. "It is late," he said. "We will camp here for the night and enter the Holy City in the morning with a fresh set of eyes." He grinned. "And feet."

No one complained.

Preparing to sleep, Simon unfurled his bedroll. The clear night sky from atop the Mount of Olives was spectacular. With a half-empty belly and throbbing feet, he slowly drifted off to the most vivid fantasies.

Jesus will take over the world, with me by his side, Simon thought, painting one mental detail after the next into his long-believed masterpiece. *He'll deliver a great speech, leaving the mob in awe. The Pharisees, even the Sanhedrin, will be stunned into silence. The Roman monsters will step up to quell the gifted speaker, the radical, and will be crushed into oblivion.* He smiled. *At last, the sandal will be placed on the other foot!*

Simon could feel a triumphant roar launch from his diaphragm and try to leap from his mouth. He held it back. No matter how excited he felt, he held back. *Soon,* he thought, closing his eyes. *Soon.*

Unlike the night before, sleep did not come easy.

Jerusalem, Judea

The world was still covered in a film of morning dew when Jesus and his disciples made their way down the steep path past the Kidron Valley and entered the Holy City through the Beautiful Gate—also known as the Gate of Nikanor. Simon stood shoulder to shoulder with the Messiah, surveying the chaotic scene. They watched as the crowds of devout pilgrims hurried through the Court of the Gentiles to make their sacrifices in the temple.

In awe, Simon scanned the magnificent building. The massive structure had been ornately carved from stone; its flat-topped red roof reached toward heaven. *The Holy of Holies,* he thought. He pictured the temple altar in all its extravagance, with priests scurrying about.

Jesus was suddenly startled, drawing Simon's attention. His master was focused on the vendors that were lined up just inside the temple, selling live animals—doves, goats, sheep, lambs—to be sacrificed in worship.

"Every year, the prices go up," one of the disgruntled buyers complained. "You're a crook!"

"If you don't like it," the vendor yelled back, "then you can approach the altar empty-handed! I don't care either way."

Supply and demand had been created by a system of price-fixing, established under the Jewish theocracy. It clearly wasn't working.

Cursing under his breath, the buyer threw his denarii onto the table. "Thief!" he repeated, snatching up the small, bleating goat.

Simon watched as Jesus's face turned angry; this was not a cruel look but one worn by a man in authority who was convicted to right a wrong.

Here we go, Simon thought. *This is exactly what I've been waiting for!*

Picking up some cords, Jesus wound them into a whip as he marched toward the money-changer tables. With a single grunt, Jesus overturned the first table. "Take these things and leave now," he barked at the pigeon vendors. "Do not turn my Father's house into a den of thieves!"

My Father's house? Simon thought.

The hard-edged money changers were paralyzed in fear. As Jesus flipped over one table after another, the sound of coins bouncing off stone echoed past the scurrying pilgrims. He then whipped the animals to drive them out. Many people fled amid the chaos.

Although Simon felt provoked—this type of violent response being familiar territory—his master's behavior still struck him as unexpected. He remembered the scripture, *Zeal for thy house shall consume me.* He nodded. *Who else could say "my Father's house" in such an honest tone?*

Drawn by the raucous crowd, some of the chief priests led the Pharisees to the scene, who immediately questioned Jesus. "On whose authority do you act?"

Jesus peered at them. "Destroy this temple, and in three days I will raise it up," he vowed.

"It took Herod the Great forty-six years to build this temple," retorted one of the hissing Pharisees, "and you will build it up in three days?"

Jesus did not clarify the remark.

Three days? Peter repeated; he was as confused as the hypocrites who questioned Jesus. *But it doesn't matter whether I understand the comment,* he decided, feeling compelled to protect his master. Stepping forward, he took up a defensive position between the men he hated and the man he loved.

Jesus held their stare and never blinked.

On the second day in Jerusalem, while Simon and the others followed Jesus, they were able to do some people watching.

Jerusalem is so different from Capernaum, Simon thought. Amid the labyrinth of streets, the melting pot of cultures and ethnicities created a symphony of different tongues, a beautiful song. *Not everyone is poor here,* he recognized. Instead, a real socioeconomic class system had been established. Wages were higher, but so were the prices. Competing smells of roasted lamb and ox dung filled the air. *As I remember,* Simon thought, *the food and drink aren't any better here.* He nodded. *I prefer the fresh fish from home any day of the week.*

The marketplace was many times larger than the one in Capernaum, or even those in Tiberius and Sepphoris. Brass lanterns, fine silks, and gold jewelry were available to all. Even large draft animals, such as oxen, cattle, and rams, were tethered to stakes, each for sale. Caged birds, covered in cloth to keep them calm, were stacked against the clear blue sky. And among it all, Romans were watching from the shadows, prepared to pounce and impose their will.

Maybe this place isn't so different after all, Simon thought, peering at the ever-present oppressors.

As they traveled the city, rumor had it that the Messiah was being discussed among members of the Sanhedrin, the council of seventy elders.

Simon was ecstatic. *Now we're talking! Surely the more people hear about Jesus, the more they'll be persuaded to join him. Many hands will make light work of overthrowing the Romans!*

Word also reached the group that Nicodemus, one of the High Pharisees, was requesting a private meeting with Jesus.

"No," Simon blurted, as though answering for his master.

Jesus looked at him. "Yes," he countered.

"But, Rabbi, how do we know if this man can be trusted? He's in league with the Romans!"

"I will meet with Nicodemus," Jesus confirmed, without further discussion.

It was decided that the clandestine introduction would take place under the cover of darkness at the upper chamber of a friend's home.

"Rabbi," Simon pled, worried sick over the risk. "At least let me escort you, in case–"

"Do not worry," Jesus said, cutting him off. "John will accompany me."

"But—"

Jesus placed his hand on Simon's arm. "I'll be fine."

From a distance, Simon watched as Jesus, his identity disguised by a hooded cloak, was escorted by John to a torchlit rooftop, where they disappeared.

Ugh, Simon thought, checking the home's perimeter. *All clear.*

He lingered in the shadows, ensuring that no more Pharisees or Romans arrived. No one did. *John will give me the details when we get back*, he decided.

By reputation, Nicodemus was a timid old man. *But I still don't trust him*, Simon thought. He couldn't remember feeling this anxious. *It's my job to protect the Messiah, not John's.*

Hours later, the moon was at its zenith when Jesus and John returned safely, with Simon discreetly shadowing their every move. They weren't back for more than a few minutes when Simon grabbed John, physically dragging him out of everyone's earshot. "So, what happened?" he asked.

John's face looked radiant, inspiring a pang of jealousy in Simon. "I stayed just outside the door the entire time, taking notes," he replied, referring to his tablet.

"Well?"

"Nicodemus had many questions," John reported. "They talked about a new kingdom that is coming, though I'm not sure Jesus was talking politics."

Of course he was, Simon thought.

John went on. "Jesus told the priest, 'I didn't come to deliver the people from Rome, but from sin and from death.' And he said that 'to enter the kingdom of God, a man must be reborn.'"

Reborn? Simon repeated in his mind, already lost.

"Jesus told Nicodemus that God did not send His Son into the world to condemn it. He sent His Son to save the world through Him. Then the master said, 'Whoever believes in me will not be condemned, but whoever does not believe stands condemned already.'"

Simon nodded.

"Simon," John's eyes began to fill from emotion, "Jesus then said, 'For God so loved the world that he gave his only begotten

Son, that whosoever believes in him should not perish, but have everlasting life.'"

While his best friend continued with the meeting's recap, Simon's mind drifted off. He couldn't help it. He was more focused on what had transpired in the temple the day before. He could only see the manifestation of what he wanted in the Messiah.

"For God so loved the world..." John began to repeat.

"That's great, John," Simon said, cutting him off, "but did you see what Jesus did with those money changers' tables yesterday?" He slapped his friend's arm. "The Romans have no idea what's coming!"

John lowered his tablet. "Yeah, Simon. I saw it."

Jesus and his disciples left the Paschal Feast, following one of the good stone Roman roads westward to the hilly countryside of Judea. Each step tested their sandals' wooden soles.

They weren't far from the city when Simon noticed several travelers dressed in Pharisee tunics. He turned to Andrew. "We're being spied on," he whispered, gesturing with a flick of his head.

Andrew appraised the scene before nodding in agreement. "Vipers," he whispered, echoing John the Baptizer's insightful assessment.

Later they stopped to camp in the open countryside in the hills of Judea. From there, they would need to veer east to the Jordan River. It was there they learned that John the Baptizer had been arrested by King Herod's men. It was hardly surprising to Simon, his anger flaring at the news. *The wild man has converted many believers, which makes him a threat to the crown.* He thought about it. *But I doubt they'll kill him. John's considered a prophet by many and much too popular with the people. The last thing Herod wants on his bloodied hands is a martyr.*

The news shook Jesus. In an instant state of sorrow, he announced, "We'll be returning at once to Galilee."

No one in the group was sorry to leave Judea.

"Not by way of the Jordan," Jesus added, "but through Samaria."

Worried looks were exchanged among the group. This was a dangerous and treacherous trek, and each one of them preferred the longer route.

"Are you joking?" Simon blurted. *Why?* he wondered. *It's just not worth the trouble. We'll be denied food and lodging. And the road is a dangerous one, infested with violent thieves and even the chance of a mountain lion attack.*

"It will take us half the time," Jesus said.

"It's safer to go around Samaria by way of the Jordan Valley," Simon pointed out.

Jesus shook his head. "We are going through Samaria," he repeated.

Simon looked to his friends. Everyone was thinking the same thing, yet no one questioned it further.

Jesus had spoken. They were prepared to follow.

A day's walk north of Jerusalem, they came upon a highland village known as Karioth. As Jesus preached there, he singled out a man, Judas Iscariot, who stood alone in the crowd.

Jesus told him, "Follow me."

Wait ... what? Simon wondered, quickly sizing up the stranger. *Why him?*

With dark eyes, Judas had a pale face with pencil-thin lips along with a slight build. As a Galilean, Simon naturally disliked the Judean right from the start.

"Yes," Judas answered, seemingly happy for the offer.

The man appeared likable at first. Upon being recruited, he hurried off to gather food, water, and other supplies for the group.

Andrew approached his brother. "Judas is obviously resourceful," he whispered. "He was able to obtain some things we need."

Simon shrugged. "He'll be useful, I guess," he said, unsure about how he felt. The band of disciples was growing. *I'm not so sure that's a good thing.*

CHAPTER 6

QUENCHING A THIRST
IN SAMARIA

On the road, Samaria

Jews and Samaritans had always disliked one another, maybe even hated one another. The house of Israel had been divided into two kingdoms: Samaria to the north, containing ten tribes, and Judea to the south, which was dominated by Jerusalem and the two southern tribes. This division took place after the death of Solomon and during the reign of his son, Rehoboam, as the people revolted against heavy taxes.

In these days, many did not even understand the reasons for the division. They only knew that Judea and Samaria were life-long enemies, despising each other to the very bone.

Most Jews avoided travel through Samaria at all costs, preferring to take the longer route—Jerusalem down to the Dead Sea, rounding by Jericho, then traveling up the Jordan Valley—in order to sidestep any contact with the heretics.

"At the very least, we'll be facing insults," Simon whispered to John, James, and Andrew.

"If not beatings," Andrew added.

"We'll see about that," Simon snapped back defiantly. He had already steeled himself, preparing for combat.

James grinned. "There's also a chance we'll get robbed along the way." They all laughed nervously, drawing looks.

Simon looked to Judas. Jesus had already appointed the new disciple the group's treasurer. A leather bag of coins was girded to his reedy waist, producing very little jingle. It was all they had to purchase the absolute essentials. "What are they going to rob?" Simon asked.

"Maybe Judas himself," Andrew whispered. This time, they stifled the laugh.

The group picked up the pace to make camp in Bethel by nightfall. Each man took his turn, pulling a small wooden cart on wheels. James volunteered more time than most. Unless someone asked to take his turn, James quietly forged on.

It was the middle of April and warm, each rise and descent in the road staining their tunics in sweat. Mild hunger had become an accepted way of life, but now they needed to drink often to fight off their thirst.

They set up camp that night just inside of a single tree line. Wood was plentiful for tent poles, as well as for firewood, used for cooking and bathing. Dinner conversation, however, was limited. Everyone was exhausted from the three-day trek.

At one point, Jesus stood and announced, "I need to pray ... alone." He took a few steps and disappeared from the fire's light.

Simon felt uneasy when his master was away from his sight.

"Relax," John said, shuffling closer to him. "You don't think Jesus has more protection than we can provide?"

Simon nodded in agreement. "I know, I know," he said, but he still didn't like it.

"Just because we can't see ...," Andrew began.

Simon's eyes flew up to find Andrew's. "I said I know," he barked, returning the circle of friends back to silence.

Later, when Jesus returned from his prayers, most of the others were asleep—but not Simon. He stayed vigilant to ensure his teacher's safety.

As Jesus headed for his shelter, he looked at Simon and smiled. "Good night," he said.

"Good night, Rabbi," Simon answered from the campfire's dying light, watching Jesus disappear into the homemade tent. *I wish I could hear his prayers*, he thought.

Sychar, Samaria

The following day, they traveled through high barren hills until reaching swaying fields of grain.

At a hilltop above the plain of Samaria, Jesus stopped. "This is it," he announced. "The city of Sychar."

At last! Simon thought, overjoyed for his raw feet.

He looked at his master. Jesus was clearly worn out; the rabbi was weary, giving the first signs of human weakness.

The scent of roses lingered in the air. While drops of sweat flowed down his back, Simon surveyed the place. *That's strange*, he thought, *not a rosebush to be found*.

From this elevated area, he looked out onto the plane of Samaria. One of Herod's ruined palaces stuck out in the distance. An arcade of massive monuments, marble pillars dominated the view. *Shrines made by men*, he thought, snickering. *The Samaritans with their false temple*. A rivalry had always existed between the Samaritan temple and the true one in Jerusalem. *Their teachers have corrupted the wisdom of Israel. They even fought against us in the Maccabean wars*. He shook his head. *It's no wonder we hate them!*

But this was still hallowed ground. They were standing beside the deep cistern that Jacob and his twelve sons had dug by hand to store rainwater. *Jacob's Well*, Simon thought, still struggling to understand why Jesus had chosen this place as their destination.

He looked back. Jesus was still resting. Simon approached. "Rabbi..."

"Simon," Jesus said, "I'm told that we've run out of food, so you and the others will need to go into Sychar to resupply."

Simon's instincts kicked in, launching him straight into defense mode. "You shouldn't be here alone, Master."

"John will stay back."

"John?" Simon asked; it sounded like a gasp. *Again? He couldn't believe it. I'm being dismissed again!*

"I'll be fine," Jesus told him, adding a smile. "I need you to look after your brothers for now."

This order was something Simon could follow. *Jesus obviously knows something I don't.*

He still didn't like it, but he accepted it.

"John," Jesus called out, "Simon and the others are going into town to get food. I need you to stay back with me."

Simon searched his friend's face to ensure that he wasn't feeling smug about it. Neither John's eyes nor lips ever flinched.

"Let's go," Simon told the rest of them. As they walked down the hill, he thought, *Not much can happen in this desolate spot. Besides, John will fill me in again when we get back.*

For a brief moment, he met John's eyes. It was long enough to shoot his best friend a dirty look.

They both grinned over the childlike exchange.

En route to the market, Simon spotted a woman dressed in dirty rags walking toward them, carrying a jar and rope to draw water from the well. *A woman traveling to the well alone this late in the morning?* he wondered, looking up. The sun was high in the sky. *She's obviously been shunned by her own people, or she would have drawn her water with the other women hours ago.* He shook his head.

Dishonorable, filthy people, he thought, feeling the acid swirl in his belly. *They have the gall to treat us like we're the parasites.*

As they passed each other on the hill, Simon tried to meet her gaze. But she kept her eyes on the ground, avoiding all eye contact.

Just as the guilty or shameful would do, Simon decided, allowing himself to pass the harshest judgment on her.

The Samaritan marketplace was one big blur for Simon. The narrow streets were bustling with people he never wanted to meet. Vendors were lined on both sides, selling food, clothing, animals. *Much like Capernaum,* Simon thought, catching himself. *Well, not really.*

He looked to James and Andrew. "Go with Judas and purchase whatever we need."

"You mean whatever we can afford," Judas commented.

Simon took a deep breath, exhaling slowly. "Buy whatever you can."

"That will only leave us with ..." Judas began.

"Whatever you can," Simon repeated. "We'll worry about tomorrow, tomorrow." He shrugged. "Jesus will provide."

Andrew smiled. "Amen," he whispered.

While the three men hurried off to complete their task, Simon wandered the market stalls, his jealous thoughts consumed with being elsewhere. *Why John? Why not me? That's my role.*

During his walk, Simon offered as many foul looks as he received. Twice, he wanted to fight men who refused to drop their gaze. *But the master will not approve,* he decided, struggling to restrain himself.

The walk back was more like a jog, with Simon anxious to get back to Jesus and John. This time, they didn't pass anyone on the hill. Instead, they returned to find Jesus sitting alone with that same Samaritan woman at Jacob's Well.

"What?!"

Everyone was shocked. *It's unheard of for a rabbi to speak with the opposite sex in public,* Simon thought.

John was seated off to the side, a sheet of papyrus in his lap.

Simon was not happy. *How could my master converse with such an offensive creature?*

And what is John doing, just sitting there without protest?

"There must be a good reason ..." Andrew began.

"Does Jesus not know who he's speaking with?" Simon barked, disgustedly. "What a disgrace!"

In shock, they watched as Jesus, wearing a broad smile, stood. Overjoyed, the woman ran from the well, singing Jesus's praises, leaving her water jar and rope behind. "I have met the Messiah! I will tell everyone," she yelled. "Everyone!"

Her mood only added to Simon's confusion. *She was completely miserable when we passed her earlier on the hill. And now ...*

He watched as she ran and skipped down the grassy knoll, yelling her praises as she went.

As a man of strong curiosity, Simon could hardly wait to draw John aside. But he knew better than to make it obvious in front of their master.

"We have food, Rabbi. Eat," he said to Jesus, gesturing toward the sack of bread and other provisions that James carried.

Jesus shook his head. "I have food of which you know nothing," he said. "My food is to do the will of Him who sent me and to accomplish His work. Do you not say there are four months yet, and then comes the harvest? I tell you, raise your eyes to the fields, for they are already white for harvesting." Jesus was not looking at the wheat field but to the Samaritan city beyond it.

Although Simon didn't understand, he didn't question it.

When it was safe, Simon pulled John aside and questioned his friend. "Please tell me why Jesus was speaking with that filthy woman," he said, his tone a mix between a hiss and a whisper.

John looked at him, his eyes looking as impatient as their master's. "I'm writing it all down," John said. "Do not interrupt me."

Annoyed, Simon nodded.

Finishing his journal entry, John turned back to Simon and recounted the entire exchange between Jesus and the Samaritan woman.

"Give me a drink," Jesus said to her.

"How can a Jew ask for a drink from me, a Samaritan woman?" she asked, holding up her bucket.

"If you had known the gift of God, and he who is saying to you, 'Give me a drink,' you would've asked him, and he would've given you living water."

"Sir, you have nothing to draw with, and the well is deep. Where then have you got the living water? Are you greater than our father, Jacob, who gave us the well and drank from it himself?"

"Everyone who drinks this water shall thirst again, but whoever drinks of the water that I shall give him shall not thirst anymore. But the water that I shall give him shall become in him a fountain of water, leaping up into everlasting life."

"Sir, give me that water, so I may not be thirsty, and I do not have to come all the way here to draw."

"Go, call your husband, and return with him."

"I have no husband," she admitted.

"You have answered well," Jesus said. "You have no husband, for you have had five husbands, and the one you now have is not your husband. What you have said is true."

"I am rejected by others," she said, lowering her head in shame.

"I know, but not by the Messiah."

"I see, sir, that you are a prophet. Our forefathers worshiped on this mountain, while your people see the place where one wants to worship is in Jerusalem."

"Believe me, woman, the time is coming when you shall worship the Father neither on this mountain nor in Jerusalem. You worship what you do not know. We worship what we know, for salvation comes from the Jews. But the hour is coming. Yes, he's here now, when the true worshipers shall worship the Father in spirit and in truth. Indeed, the Father wishes for such to be His worshipers. God is a spirit, and His worshipers must worship in spirit and in truth."

She wept softly. "I know that Messiah, he who is called Christ," she said, composing herself, "is coming. He will tell us everything."

Jesus nodded. "I am He."

As tears rolled down her cheeks, she fell to the ground overwhelmed with joy. "I am going to tell everyone."

John looked up from his tablet.

"Is that all of it?" Simon asked.

John nodded. "Is it not enough?"

Simon sighed heavily. *It's absolutely unacceptable!* Given his lifetime of prejudice, John's report did not curtail the disappointment he felt in his master. "The Samaritans are unworthy people," he whispered. "They don't deserve the Messiah."

"And who are you to decide that?" John snapped back, rebuking him for his ignorance.

"I was chosen by Jesus," he argued.

John shook his head. "And so was she," John explained. "Jesus told her so."

Although Simon was listening, he struggled to hear. Even in his state of disgust, he somehow knew that his dislike of the woman spoke so much more about himself than her. Once again, he questioned his choices. *I've walked away from fishing and my family to wander around in the world... only to end up here?* He thought about it. *And for a ministry I barely understand.*

Jesus looked at him and nodded.

Simon returned the nod before focusing on his competing thoughts. *I know that Jesus has his reasons,* he thought, *but I still don't care for it... or understand.*

Just as John finished his story for Simon, the Samaritan woman returned with a crowd at her heels. "Come and see the man who told me all I ever did," she yelled. "Can this be the Christ?"

Due to one woman's passionate testimony, the people of this despised nation sat at Jesus's feet, listening to his every word. He explained who he was and what he wanted from all people.

Simon's head whirred. *But the Samaritans are heretics,* he thought, *the lost sheep of Israel.*

"We have heard him ourselves," the Samaritan crowd exclaimed, "and we know that this is truly the Savior of the world!"

Simon looked to the other disciples for confirmation that this was actually happening. They were also in shock.

The crowd of new converts begged Jesus, "Please stay with us."

He agreed to stay for two days, quenching their great thirst.

While Simon's skin crawled, he scratched his thick head. *Two whole days in Sychar!* It felt impossible to view these people on equal ground. Somewhere deep inside his conflicted mind, he knew there were reasons for all of this—reasons he did not understand. *I just need to keep the faith,* he decided, trusting that something good would come.

Two days later, they left Samaria and headed back out onto the road. The group settled into silence, each man trying to reconcile what had just occurred. Jesus gave them the freedom to do so.

Reaching the Galilean hills, they left the hot, dry Samaritan desert behind them.

Green, Simon thought, trying to refocus his attention by taking in his surroundings, *I've never seen so much green in my life.* He thought to himself, *Blue is my color, though.* He watched as Jesus forged ahead at a healthy pace.

A mile later, the tall group leader guided them onto one of the main roads.

That's odd, Simon thought. *Jesus usually likes to stay off the main roads.*

Cana, Galilee

That afternoon as they walked near Cana, a Roman centurion seated upon his magnificent steed rode up on the rocky road and halted the group, his silver breastplate glittering in the sun.

Now what? Simon thought, hurrying to Jesus's side.

The man was clean-shaven with close-cropped hair. He wore a crimson, sleeveless tunic made of wool beneath leather armor. His blue cape, bordered in yellow, was tied in the front by an ornate bronze brooch. Besides the impressive breastplate, his armor consisted of shoulder pieces, forearm and shin guards, and a helmet to match. His feet were protected by heavy-soled, horseshoe-nailed sandals.

Simon knew this man. He recognized him from Capernaum.

As a centurion, he was the captain of more than one hundred foot soldiers. Simon knew that the man's skill and courage in battle was exactly what defined his rank. *I wonder how many Jews this man has killed?*

Then another thought entered Simon's mind. *Jesus's fame is spreading faster than I realized. This is proof.*

"You are Jesus of Nazareth?" the imperial soldier asked, settling his warhorse.

"I am."

As if it even mattered, Simon took a step forward. Jesus silently extended his arm, causing Simon to step back.

"I have heard of your many miracles," the centurion said, looking down from his horse, "such as the wine at Cana."

Jesus nodded.

"I implore you, sir, to heal my son," the Roman said. "He is paralyzed, suffering terribly back in Capernaum." He shook his head. "Even now, he may be dead."

Without hesitation, Jesus explained, "I will come and heal him."

The centurion shook his head. "Lord, I do not deserve to have you come under my roof. But just say the word. I, myself, am a man of authority, with soldiers under me. I tell this one, 'Go,' and he goes. I tell that one, 'Come,' and he comes. I say to my servant, 'Do this,' and he does it."

When Jesus heard this, his face filled with amazement. Smiling, he turned to his followers. "Truly I tell you," he announced, "I have not found anyone in Israel with such great faith. I say to you that many will come from the east and the west and will take their places at the feast with Abraham, Isaac, and Jacob in the kingdom of heaven." He paused, his smile disappearing. "But the subjects of the kingdom will be thrown outside, into the darkness, where there will be weeping and gnashing of teeth."

Swallowing hard, Simon froze in amazement at Jesus's words and his demeanor.

Jesus turned back to the centurion. "Go, and let it be done just as you believed it would." Studying Jesus's eyes, the Roman opened his mouth to speak but paused.

Jesus offered a confident nod, his eyes sparkling with truth. The man smiled wide.

Jesus has healed the man's son, Peter thought, aghast. *He's granted the Roman's wish!*

Nodding his gratitude, the officer kicked his horse's hindquarters, speeding off.

First, Samaritans. Now Romans. Is there none of our enemies that Jesus won't help? Simon wondered, his mind flashing back to his childhood teachings.

Decades before, the Romans had conquered Jerusalem, declaring Herod the Great as "King of the Jews." From there, the Jews were assimilated into their culture of strict laws and government. Although the Romans prided themselves on their fine engineering—building cities and roads—they were best known for their well-trained army, ruling the vast empire by force.

And now, the Messiah was helping one of these oppressors.

Jesus and the group marched on, with Simon shaking his head.

"You will see, Simon Peter," Jesus called out, without ever turning his head. "You will see."

CHAPTER 7

FISHERS OF MEN

Capernaum, Galilee

A day later, as they passed Magdala on the road back to Capernaum, Jesus and his disciples were met by a pack of chattering children. This was becoming commonplace. Wherever they went, Jesus was a magnet for the excited younger people. This time, however, it was their message that was different.

"The soldier's son is healed," they sang to the group. "It's a miracle!"

Simon looked at the others, exchanging smiles. *Everyone in Capernaum and around Galilee knows now,* he realized.

Other children ran toward them as well as several adults. "Jesus has performed a miracle!"

As Simon's chest swelled with pride, his tired gait turned to a strut; he felt like a bona fide hero returning home from war.

Several people swarmed Jesus. Simon quickly intervened but was rebuked by Jesus. "It's OK, Simon," the rabbi said.

His anxieties aside, Simon loved the scene. He was returning home to his own people as the head of Jesus's entourage. *I knew I made the right decision,* he told himself, thinking of his wife's approval. His pride gushed over.

Besides the centurion's son, pilgrims traveling from Jerusalem had brought back word of Jesus's miracles. This only made the crowds swell in size.

The next day, Jesus preached to the huge crowd in Capernaum and healed several people, with Simon standing nearby as his confidant and defender. As he watched and listened, one thing became immediately clear: *The crowd is looking for healing more than for sermons.*

Still, whenever Jesus spoke, a reverent silence washed over the crowd; they were quickly enchanted by the rabbi's words.

After a two-day celebration of food and drink at Simon's house, the Sabbath arrived.

They all walked the few short blocks to the packed synagogue, with Jesus seated alongside his disciples, as well as the common parishioners. The priest, or ruler of the synagogue, read from the Torah. Simon could have recited many of the Sabbath rituals in his sleep. Only now, he knew to pay closer attention to every word.

He looked at Jesus, who was worshipping beside him, thinking, *As the priest speaks, the prophecies are being realized.*

At the conclusion of the service, Simon's serene thoughts were shattered by a man possessed by evil. "Jesus of Nazareth, have you come to destroy us?" the demoniac man cried out. "I know who you are, the holy one of God."

Some onlookers scurried away in fear.

Even before Simon's instinct to protect Jesus moved him to action, Jesus rebuked the evil spirit. "Be silent," Jesus said, "and come out of him."

As the man convulsed, the demon cried out before leaving the trembling body. The man was healed.

What? Simon thought. *Jesus commanded the foul spirit with authority, and it obeyed him?*

The crowd was shocked, but no more than Simon and the other disciples. It was the first exorcism they had ever witnessed.

This is going to spread like wildfire, Simon thought, as he, Jesus, and the other disciples headed back to his house. Simon shook his thick head from side to side. The powers of Jesus were boundless.

Still, with all the signs and wonders Simon and his brothers had witnessed, it was wonderful to be home. Before getting back to the fishing nets, Simon decided to accompany his wife to the marketplace. *I hate shopping,* he thought, *but I love her.*

Strolling through the community's social center, Simon absorbed each detail. From unsavory types to Pharisees, there were all walks of life milling about. Two Roman guards, huddled in some dark corner, looked at Simon. They both sneered at him as he passed.

So much for goodwill, Simon thought. *Their captain's son has just been saved by my rabbi, and they'd still rather slit my throat than look at me.*

"Stop," his wife whispered, as though hearing his thoughts. She slapped his arm.

He nodded, trying desperately to peel his gaze away from them before it became trouble.

Naturally proud and defiant, he wrestled against the surge of rage.

While the sun beat down, creating a terrible thirst, he finally refocused on the world that unfolded before him—leisurely strolling through the world he cherished, among people he'd known and loved his entire life.

Wares were transported in wooden carts, pulled by mules—*if the cart's owner is lucky.*

Their products included everything from fruits—dates, grapes, pomegranates, papayas, and figs—to nuts. *The walnuts and pistachios are my favorite,* he thought.

Without being asked, his wife bagged up both, making him smile. She also purchased a small cask of olives, a basket of vegetables, and a skin filled with oil to refill their night lamps. "Do we need wine?" she asked, stepping up to a stack of stained wooden casks.

Simon maintained his grin. "We could always use more wine."

She added two swollen wineskins to their cart. Spices—whatever she couldn't gather and dry herself—also made it into the cart, as did incense.

Two stalls over, they passed a rack of animal pelts and skins. These were hanging right beside a pen of live animals, imprisoned by barred sticks of wood, latched by heavy twine. "That seems insensitive," Simon pointed out, drawing another playful slap.

The manure-laden hay produced a deep stench. Simon inhaled deeply. Even though the marketplace's smells were a mix of fragrant and foul, he somehow liked them all. *It's home.*

The next hour was much of the same: they filled woven baskets and red-clay vases. Whenever possible, they ducked beneath the wooden pergolas, draped in colored fabrics that shaded the narrow alleys from the sun.

In one corner, a disabled beggar held out his dirty palm. "Some help, sir?" Although the vagabond's eyes appeared to see, they were completely devoid of life.

"God bless you," Simon told him, dropping a denarius into his outstretched hand. Simon couldn't tell who was more surprised by this act, the vagabond or himself. It was the first time he'd ever given to a beggar, and he enjoyed it.

His wife grinned, clearly impressed by his recent growth.

Simon continued to take it all in—the sounds of the bustling marketplace, the hum of people laughing and talking. Above it all, a yelling match was underway between the tax collector—Rome's favorite Jewish pet—and another unhappy customer at the head of the charlatan's long line.

Protected by a Roman guard, the taxman collected tributes of silver from paupers who could barely afford to put bread on their tables. Either that, or they were jailed—while their debts compounded. *I'm not sure which man I dislike more,* Simon thought, *the Roman guard or the tax collector.* He snickered. *But why choose when I can hate them both?*

While Simon's wife pawed through some fine linens they could never afford, Simon spotted one of the High Pharisees, a religious elitist dressed in his sharp robes, pass them by. The bearded man's entire face was framed in judgment as he stared down his nose at Simon—*and everyone else beneath his office.*

Moving on, the happy couple stopped briefly to watch two women crush grapes by foot to be fermented into wine.

Simon thought of Cana. *I wonder if I'll ever taste wine like that again?* He grinned.

"What is it?" his wife asked.

"Nothing," he said.

She stared at him but let it go.

Everything, he thought.

Passing the local tavern, an onslaught of laughter hit him in the face when the front door opened and someone stepped in. Instinctively, Simon took a step in the same direction.

"Not today," his wife said, grabbing his arm. "You've been away for a while. Today, you're all mine."

He grabbed her hand, intertwining his fingers with hers. Wiping his sweaty brow, he looked back at the tavern. *A drink would be nice right about now, though,* he thought. He could picture himself betting on one of the usual fistfights or playing a few games of knucklebones—anything that men wagered on to keep the boredom at bay.

"You're right," he told her. "I'm all yours."

A short while later, it was dusk when Simon and his better half walked home. The streets were nothing more than dirt and rock, with some straw strewn about. Simple stone-archway buildings were made of wood and stone, their flat roofs a poor comparison to those in Jerusalem. Stone walls marked territories, with latched gates creating a false sense of security. Palm trees and flowerbeds were transformed into silhouettes, as torches affixed on either side of wooden doors were being lit. The smoke of burning fires wafted on the warm breeze, making Simon inhale deeply.

Capernaum is nothing extravagant, he thought, *but it's home.* He threw his arm around his wife's waist. *It's everything I'll ever need.*

That night, their shadowed silhouettes, illuminated by candle-light, danced on their small bedroom's wall.

Simon awoke before first light and stared at his sleeping wife. *I do love this woman,* he thought before tiptoeing out of the house and heading down to the docks. *I can't wait to smell the air,* he thought, *and taste the sea on my tongue.* He had been looking forward to fishing again. *I never could have imagined how much I'd miss this grueling trade.*

As he descended the final rise, he could hear the faint sound of the waves, the rhythm of its ebb and flow lapping at the shore. He picked up the pace until he was standing right at the water's frothy edge. Looking out, he saw that the waning moonlight had carved out a swath of light, like a shimmering road sign, pointing toward the horizon, toward the hope of better days.

He then looked to his left. *The boat's exactly where we left it,* he thought, expecting nothing else.

Unlike the merchants and their small fleets, Simon and Andrew piloted an independent fishing vessel. *Even Zebedee has four ships, crewed by John, James, and ten other men,* he thought. *But it's just me and Andrew on our rig.* He smiled proudly. Their boat was seventeen feet in the beam, with seven-foot depth of hold. Lug rigged with a sturdy main, the mast was located center-rear. *She can fit six men comfortably.* He chuckled. *She's a hulk of a water sled.*

He was excited to unfurl her sail to the wind, imagining that he and his brother would go to market with a full day's catch, the larger fish strung on loops of twine, with the smaller sardines taken in baskets or casks.

He inhaled deeply a few times before closing his eyes. "Thank You, Yahweh," he said aloud, "for the blessing of this life. Help me to do Your will always."

As the sun made its full appearance, Simon and Andrew were already on the water—smiling and laughing. After lugging their gear on board, the simple rigging was prepared to sail.

Blue skies, hosting a few slow-moving clouds, promised a good day ahead. *But the air is still,* Simon realized. *Hopefully, we can catch a breeze at some point today.*

"What time are John and James going to start fishing?" Andrew asked.

Simon shrugged. "Whenever Zebedee tells them to." Casting away the lines from the dock, he pushed off with an oar. The sweet sound of splashing water made him smile.

The Sea of Galilee was two hundred feet deep in some places, and it took nearly a half hour to reach one of Simon's favorite fishing holes. For the next few hours, he and his brother threw nets overboard, drift fishing as they went. But each time they pulled the nets back on board, the lack of weight made Simon cringe. *Empty again!*

This went on for several more hours—empty net after empty net.

Frustrated, Simon blurted, "This isn't good! We've been gallivanting with Jesus for weeks and haven't made a penny!"

"Gallivanting?" Andrew repeated.

"Bills are due, Andrew," Simon added, "and they're starting to add up." Looking out across the water, he shook his head. "If we don't catch fish soon, and lots of them, then we're in real trouble."

Andrew opened his mouth to speak but thought better of it. "We will," he finally muttered; it was nearly a whisper.

With hands as tough as leather, arms and shoulders as hard as steel, Simon hurled the large net back into the water with a grunt. *Please, Yahweh,* he silently prayed, peering into the cobalt sky. *Please fill these nets. And the heavier, the better.*

He waited until he couldn't take it any longer. From the first tug on the net, he could tell there wasn't a single sardine caught up in it. "No!" he roared. "We can't catch a break!"

"Or a breeze," Andrew added.

Fishing was backbreaking work; but when the effort produced zero results, it was infuriating. There was nothing worse than smelling like old fish and new sweat when the boat's hold was empty. *There must be a better life,* Simon thought, enraged. *Something more than this!*

"We'll be fine," Andrew said. "We just need to keep the faith."

Simon's eyes closed to slits. "No, brother," he hissed, "we need more than faith. We need fish … or we'll never be able to keep the tax collector at bay."

They sailed back to the dock in silence.

Staring at the empty nets and bare cargo hold, Simon felt completely disheartened. *We've been on the water all day,* he thought, *and not a single fish.* He shook his head. *We're in serious trouble.*

As they continued to sail north back to the dock, Simon heard an unusual sound coming from the shore. It was an approaching crowd, people shouting with excitement. He leaned in, looking harder.

About a mile east of their docks in Capernaum, the crowd covered the hills sloping down to the beach. Jesus was preparing to teach, and a huge crowd was gathering to see him. With a glance at Andrew, who was manning the tiller, Simon tacked their empty boat toward the scene unfolding on the beach.

Surrounded by the mob, the rabbi stopped at the water's edge. As Jesus commenced his latest sermon, the crowd pressed in even closer to him.

Peter and Andrew reached the shore, beaching the boat.

"Simon," Jesus called out, "may I use your boat as a pulpit? The crowd has grown, and the people may hear me better if my voice carries on the water."

"Of course, Rabbi," Simon said, noticing that two new disciples—Thaddeus and James the Lesser—had joined Jesus's side.

Upon boarding, Jesus stood at the bow and offered his sermon. "The net gathers fish of all kinds." He looked back at Simon.

The fisherman snickered; Andrew abandoned his work of cleaning nets and sorting the gear to listen in. Most of the crowd was seated, hanging onto their rabbi's every word, enthralled.

"The same is true for the kingdom of heaven," Jesus explained. "After the net is full, the fisherman proceeds to the shore, sits down, and sorts the fish. The good are placed in barrels. The bad are thrown away." He nodded. "It will be the same at the end of the age, separating the evil from the righteous." He looked directly at Simon and Andrew. "Bring forth and gather."

Although Simon nodded, the entire sermon felt like sea salt being poured into an open wound.

When he finished, Jesus disembarked. He turned to Simon, telling him, "Put out into the water a bit farther and let down your nets for a catch."

Simon's head snapped up. "Master, we have toiled all day and caught nothing." They exchanged a long look before Jesus repeated his same words.

Sighing heavily, Simon relented. "All right, Master," he said in surrender, "at your word."

He and Andrew shoved off a short distance from the shore and cast their nets. Simon waited impatiently.

Jesus smiled at him; it was the kind of smile that indicated he knew something that Simon didn't.

The boat rocked once and then twice before nearly capsizing from a great weight pulling it down. Simon and Andrew pulled hard at the first net, which was teeming with jumping fish. Overflowing with blue and redbelly tilapia, sardines, biny, and carp, the net threatened to break open.

Seeing this, Zebedee and his sons quickly rowed over to assist. Simon's boat began to take on water as Zebedee and his sons helped muscle the second catch onto their own boat.

Andrew was giddy. "I told you, Simon. I told you!"

Simon's chest ached from emotion. *How could I have ever questioned him?* he thought. *How could I have doubted?*

Jesus watched, smiling.

The second net was so overloaded by a shoal of fish that it broke open, spilling a mountain of fish onto Zebedee's deck. Filled to the gunwales, both boats nearly sank.

Jumping out of the boat, Simon sloshed through a few feet of water before he reached the sandy shore. At Jesus's sandaled feet, he dropped to his knees. "Depart from me, Lord. I am a sinful man," Simon pleaded. "I am not worthy. What do you want from me? Anything you ask, I will do."

"Follow me," Jesus answered, looking at Simon, Andrew, John, and James. "I will make you fishers of men."

Through tearful eyes, Simon looked up at his master. "I will."

Jesus reassured him. "Fear not, Simon. From here on, you shall be catching men."

What? Simon thought. *Catching men?*

"You will gather as many as possible, all kinds." Smiling, Jesus nodded. "I will sort them out later."

Slowly, Simon realized this was a full-time job offer. *The trial run has come to an end,* he thought. *It's time to fully commit.* Several weeks and just as many miles had already passed, with he and the other disciples following Jesus and witnessing his powers. They'd now arrived at their final decision.

"I will," Simon repeated, louder.

The fishermen beached the boats, leaving the lucrative catch of fish to be sold by Zebedee's men. They followed the Lord along the shore back to Capernaum. Simon, Andrew, James, and John exchanged knowing looks—each man knowing he was giving up the sea for a new life.

Although Simon's heart burst with joy, one worry continued to nag. *What about my wife?*

Just then, a family friend sprinted onto the beach with urgent news. "Simon, your mother-in-law is very ill with fever!"

Jesus and his disciples departed the shore, hurrying back to Simon's home.

This woman, who was ill with fever, not only meant something to Simon but to Jesus as well. She'd taken good care of him since their arrival in Capernaum.

Upon entering the house in their corner of Capernaum, Simon could hear an awful coughing fit from the back bedroom.

They quickly stepped into the room to see that the poor soul was moaning in bed, a wet cloth draped across her forehead, the covers pulled up to her chin. *She's not well at all*, Simon thought, listening to her uneven and labored breathing. He looked to his wife. Her face was awash in paralyzing worry.

"Eema's fever has spiked," his wife reported, her voice cracking from panic. "She's burning up." As she tried to make her mother comfortable, the elderly woman began mumbling something unintelligible.

This is bad, Simon thought, swallowing hard.

Without a word, Jesus approached the sick woman's bed. Placing his hand upon her hand, he closed his eyes in prayer. With a gentle squeeze, the coughing immediately ceased. He then lifted her up, as if she were a child. "Leave her," Jesus commanded.

Opening her eyes, she sat straight up and gasped like it was her first breath of life.

She looks normal, Simon thought. *She is completely healed.* Like his sobbing wife, he was suddenly overcome with emotion.

The old woman bounded out of bed to compose herself. Then, as if nothing was ever wrong, she announced that she was going to prepare food and tend to her guests.

Overjoyed, everyone laughed—unsure of how else to react.

Jesus embraced Simon's wife, the long hug healing her of any further worry.

Even Simon could see that in that hug, more than words were exchanged. *A knowing. A peace offered.*

After the holy embrace, she pulled Simon to the side to speak. "Did you see how Jesus just healed my eema?" Clearly, she had now seen all she needed to see.

Simon nodded. "I did."

"He is the Messiah, husband," she said; her tone was urgent, pleading. "You must go and do what he tells you." She grabbed his weathered face. "You haven't only been called, Simon, you have been chosen. Your true path is before you. Although I may not be with you physically, I am always with you." She was obviously excited, proud—even feeling blessed to make any sacrifices she could for the man who performed these miracles.

Simon gazed into her moist eyes. *Until now, she's allowed me to travel with Jesus,* he thought. *Now, she's demanding that I go.* He kissed her.

As they broke bread, celebrating Eema's new life, Simon considered his new place in the world. *After all that's happened, of course I need to follow him.* He grinned. *No matter where it takes me.*

While Andrew filled mugs with water, Simon looked to his wife. "Oh, and there's something else," he said.

"And what's that?"

He smiled. "Do I have a fish tale to share with you!"

Everyone laughed—even Jesus.

CHAPTER 8

THE BIG MAN OF CAPERNAUM

Capernaum, Galilee

It was a great honor that Jesus was living in Simon's home. The fisherman was thrilled that his own community had accepted the Messiah. *And in my opinion, Jesus's radical teaching is badly needed.* Between Roman dominance and high taxes, not to mention a lack of control over their homeland, Jewish life felt like it had been deteriorating year after year.

One morning, the Lord arose and went quietly out into the darkness. Hearing this, Simon sprang from his bed and summoned Andrew. As they searched, they found the rabbi alone, praying. "Let us go elsewhere to the neighboring villages and towns, so I may preach there," he told them. "I will also heal and cast out demons. I have come for these reasons."

As the rising sun wiped away the morning dew, the group shared a hearty meal of goat stew, bread, and sips of wine. As they broke fast, preparations were made for the journey—with Simon, Andrew, and John making the proper arrangements.

"How long do you think we'll be gone this time?" Simon asked.

"As long as it takes," Andrew said, adding a wink.

Shaking his head, Simon looked to John.

"Your guess is as good as mine," John said, shrugging.

Simon nodded that he understood. "Then let's pack enough bread and water for a very long walk," he said.

All three men smiled.

"We'll figure out the rest of it on the road."

After a quick round of goodbyes, they headed out onto the road again.

Jesus led them through the hills, where they traveled from town to town. Simon noticed the crowds had become so large that Jesus could no longer enter the towns. Instead, he needed to preach outside of them in vast, open areas.

As commanded, the Lord preached, healed, and cast out demons wherever they went.

Believers were gathered in droves.

At the end of the first week, on the Sabbath, the disciples had run out of food and were hungry. "We need to stop and eat," James called out to no one in particular.

Jesus stopped before sweeping his arm across the cornfield and orchards. "There is plenty of food," he told them.

"But it is Sabbath, Rabbi," Andrew reminded him.

Jesus nodded. "If you are hungry, eat."

Simon and the rest immediately gathered armfuls of grains and fruits, roasting the bounty over a new campfire.

As they greedily ate, they enjoyed one another's company and conversation.

"I could eat two loaves of bread and three dozen figs," Simon said, his mouth half-full.

"Haven't you already?" one of them called out.

Even Jesus was laughing when several Pharisees, who happened to be in the area, approached the dinner party. "Why have your followers plucked grains and fruit, and then cooked and eaten from the fields on the Sabbath?" they asked Jesus.

He stood. "Have you never read what David did when he was hungry and entered the house of God when Abiathar was high priest?"

Simon jumped to his feet, taking his place beside Jesus.

"Of course, we know this story," one of the Pharisees said. "David ate the showbread."

"Right," Jesus said, "which is not lawful for anyone to eat, except for the priests." He nodded. "And David also shared it with those who were with him."

They looked at each other, but neither one could concoct a proper response.

"The Sabbath was made for man, not man for the Sabbath," Jesus reminded them, "and the Son of Man is Lord, even of the Sabbath."

Their arrogance immediately changed to anger, and they stomped away.

When Jesus finally found Simon's eyes, the fisherman repeated, "Even of the Sabbath."

Smiling, Jesus nodded before returning to the cooking fire and the rest of their meal.

A few days later, the roving band encountered a pilgrim, who was limping and stumbling toward them. His face distressed and his eyes filled with dread, he was holding one of his arms.

Simon recognized the symptoms. "Leper!" he called out, halting their group. "Do not come any closer," he warned the contagious man before covering his own mouth. If necessary, he was prepared to physically defend his master.

The marked man suffered lesions and open wounds on his neck and arms. Other patches of skin looked faded. His eyebrows were nonexistent, while swollen ulcers covered his pitiful face.

His body will eat itself until there's nothing left and he's dead, Simon thought, ensuring that his band retained a safe distance of four cubits between them and the diseased drifter.

Jesus took a step forward, causing a pang of fear to jump-start Simon's heart.

"Master, don't..." the disciple blurted.

Jesus raised his hand. "It's OK, Simon. Be still," he said, moving closer to the suffering man.

The other disciples also called out for the Messiah to stop.

But Jesus ignored their pleas, his face set with a compassionate conviction that Simon had never witnessed before.

He has no concern for his own safety, Simon thought, his heart racing out of his chest.

"Please," the leper sobbed. "Please..."

Jesus was now less than a foot away from the man.

"Lord, if you are willing, you can cleanse me," the anguished soul claimed, sobbing.

Taking a final step forward, Jesus's eyes moistened.

Jesus's heart has been moved, Simon realized.

"I am willing," Jesus said, placing his hand on the man's rotting arm. "Be cleansed."

As the man wept, Simon watched the leper's ulcerous face resume a healthy color and texture. It was instant. *He is healed!*

Even now, after witnessing multiple miracles, the group stood paralyzed in disbelief.

The leper checked his body, his sobs turning to giddy laughter. "It's a miracle!" he squealed. "I knew it. I knew it!"

This man is whole again, Simon realized, his mind wandering in search of the meaning.

Jesus nodded. "Do not say anything to anyone," he told the man. "Please do this one thing for me."

Jesus does not seek his own honor, Simon thought. *How does that help his ministry?*

"But what do I tell people?" the healed leper asked.

"Go and show yourself to the priest," the Messiah advised. "Let him inspect you to see that you were cleansed. Then make the proper offering in the temple, as Moses commanded, and go on your way."

To the continued disbelief of the others, the two men embraced—until the man ran away to share his miraculous news with his priest.

My bet is that he'll tell everyone he knows, Simon predicted. *How could he not?*

Although the disciples were shaken over the frightening exchange, Simon looked at Jesus and couldn't help but wonder, *Why hide your power? What's the point?* He finally resigned himself to the thought, *Jesus knows what he's teaching and the reasons he's performing these miracles.*

After several more weeks of travel, Jesus announced they would return to Capernaum. The word of the healed leper had spread throughout the land, as the group returned home to their village by the sea.

The people could hardly wait for the Sabbath sun to go down. Once the final sliver of light ducked beneath the horizon, they flocked to Simon's house, presenting Jesus with their own infirmities or sick friends.

"The ill have come out en masse to be healed," Simon said.

"Do you blame them?" Andrew asked.

John nodded. "If someone I loved was ill, I'd do anything to get them to Jesus."

Simon thought of his mother-in-law and nodded. "Me too," he muttered.

One after another, they entered Simon's courtyard, where Jesus lay his gentle hands upon them. Each arose strong and well.

Simon's home had become a type of a community clinic, and he was surprisingly pleased with it. In truth, he loved all the attention, reveling in his high position beside the miracle-working preacher and his revolutionary movement.

I have always had my family's love and support, Simon thought, *and now I have my community's respect and recognition.* He couldn't help but bask in the honor and glory of his new political status.

As word spread across Galilee, a mob gathered in and around Simon's home. Although Simon was determined to protect Jesus, he told John, "There's no way I can stave off this growing crowd."

"Not unless you can grow a couple dozen more arms," John replied, grinning. James and Andrew both smiled.

Ignoring them, Simon thought, *There's nothing that will stop them from hearing Jesus speak.* He nodded. *I can understand their determination.*

"Jesus is a gifted orator," James commented.

"And not because of his fiery tone or from beating on his chest," John added.

"Unlike others who can draw large crowds, Jesus is different," Andrew chimed in. "His words are filled with true wisdom and conviction."

Simon thought about it. "He's real," he added. They all looked at him.

"Exactly," John said.

At the start, the crowd wished to discuss the story of the nets, as well as the incredible miracle at the wedding at Cana. After Jesus had satisfied their hunger for the legendary tales, he offered his sermon.

"Be dressed and ready for service. Keep your lamps burning, like men waiting for their master to return from a wedding banquet. So when the Son of Man comes and knocks, they can immediately open the door for him. It will be good for those servants whose master finds them watching when he comes." He looked toward his disciples. "But understand this: if the owner of the house had known what time the thief was coming, he would not have allowed his house to be broken into. You must also be ready, because the Son of Man will come at an hour when you do not expect him."

Although Simon did not really understand, he knowingly nodded—unwilling to reveal his confusion. Even when Jesus spoke in riddles, he knew each of his master's words were inspired. "Is this parable intended for us," he whispered to John, seeking help from his trusted friend, "or for everyone?"

Overhearing the question, Jesus, not John, answered. "Only a faithful leader will be put in charge of his master's servants to provide for their needs. If he does his job well, when the master returns, he will put him in charge of all his possessions."

Simon stood straighter.

Jesus's knowing eyes lingered awhile longer before he gazed back upon the crowd.

Returning to his lesson, he said, "But suppose the servant says to himself, *My master is taking a long time returning*, and he starts to beat the other servants and get drunk? Returning on a day and time that is least expected, the master will cut him to pieces and assign him a place with the unbelievers." He took a deep breath, pausing. "The servant who knows his master's will and does not get ready or does not do what his master wants will be punished."

Jesus looked back at his disciples. "For those who have been given much, much will be demanded in return," he said, raising an eyebrow. "And for those who have been entrusted with much, much more will be asked."

Simon matched his master's nod, for himself as well as his brethren. *So, with great responsibility, like we've been given, comes real accountability.* He smiled to himself. *I think I'm starting to get some of this,* he thought. *I'm ready.*

Later, the crowd grew uncontrollably larger, even a few Pharisees now peppered among them. The good word was spreading. As the Messiah's self-proclaimed bodyguard, Simon felt more concern rise within him. His recent feelings of glory and honor had clearly come with a price.

While Jesus preached, the mob's mood was becoming nearly hysterical. The Pharisees were anything but pleased with this. People pushed closer toward the doors and windows, trapping those who were inside the house.

Simon's pride was now entirely replaced by the fear he felt for his master's safety and his home.

"God does not see some as worse than others," Jesus told the people. "We must all repent for our sins or perish."

Simon nodded. *All must repent or perish,* he repeated for himself.

"What about prayer?" one of the villagers yelled out. "How are we to pray?"

"It's better to go into your room, shut the door, and do it in private," Jesus answered. "Pray to your Father who sees you in secret. The same is true for giving to the needy. Don't let your left hand know what your right hand is doing. Give generously without thinking about it. Do not do it for show or to impress others. Don't even congratulate yourself in private. Always give in humility."

"By whose authority do you teach?" one of the angry Pharisees howled above the crowd.

Listening hard, Simon realized that he had heard this question several times.

Jesus ignored the man and his deceptive question.

"Answer me!" the self-righteous leader roared. Jesus still ignored him.

The moment passed, when a different voice called out from the roof, causing everyone to look up.

The awful sounds of wood and roof tiles being ripped off made Simon cringe. *My poor house,* he thought, picturing his wife's stores being pillaged or destroyed. *Raisins, prunes, dates, nuts, pistachios, walnuts. Even some of the herbs that she dries up top—dill, mint, sage, rosemary, and coriander. They're all as good as gone.*

But as these strangers hooked a paralyzed man to the roof hoist—normally used to lower baskets of vegetables and dry goods—Simon realized that these people were anything but thieves. *They're just desperate to get near the Messiah ... but my house!*

Opening the roof by the power of faith, they tore off more roof tiles and wood by hand, creating a hole wide enough to lower a full-grown man by rope.

Enraged by this, Simon looked at Jesus.

Jesus simply raised his hand.

But my house? Simon repeated in his head. *My roof?*

Jesus nodded at him, offering a sense of calm.

By now, the people were lowering a paralytic man into Simon's home for Jesus to heal. "He has been paralyzed since childhood," one called out. "He has no hope but you, Rabbi."

Simon watched in disbelief, seeing that the man's skinny legs were terribly misshapen.

"If you are willing, Rabbi," the cripple told Jesus. "You know you can."

Jesus looked at the paralytic man, now seated awkwardly on Simon's floor. "Son, be of good heart, your sins are forgiven."

The man began to weep softly.

"Only God can forgive sins," an enraged Pharisee yelled out, "and a man who claims to do so by his own authority must either be God or else a blasphemer." The Pharisees were beside themselves. "Why does this man talk this way?" they implored the crowd. "He's blaspheming!"

The room went silent, the crowd waiting for Jesus to react.

How can Jesus stay so calm? Peter wondered, marveling at his teacher's serenity.

Jesus turned to them. "Who is this who speaks blasphemies? Who can forgive sins but God alone? But I ask you, which is easier to say: your sins are forgiven, or rise up and walk?" He nodded. "It's easy to say, but better to show you … so that you may know that the Son of Man has the authority on earth to forgive sins." Taking two steps closer to the Pharisees to emphasize his authority, Jesus stared them down.

By now, the religious elitists' faces were painted with fury, their unblinking eyes locked on Jesus.

Jesus returned his attention to the paralytic. "I say to you, my son, rise. Take up your bed and go home."

While the crowd held its collective breath, the sobbing man rolled onto his knees before managing to get to his feet, standing for the first time in memory. He swayed once and then twice before steadying himself in front of Jesus's smiling face.

Stunned by the miracle, the crowd erupted in cheers.

Although it was a relatively peaceful gathering, the Romans now caught wind of it and arrived to restore order.

"Thank you," the man cried, taking another step.

"Now go on," Jesus told him.

Withdrawing, the Pharisees huddled together like hungry vultures, conspiring in whispers. They were afraid of Jesus, even jealous of him.

"Jesus will be sought out for his comments about forgiving sins," John suggested.

"And for blasphemy," Andrew added.

Simon surveyed the group. Each man was also concerned for his own safety.

As the men joined in group prayer, Simon could hardly contain his anger at the Pharisees. *These religious intellects, educated men who interpret the Scriptures, love to tell others how to worship and live their lives,* he thought. *No different from the Romans; they also enjoy wielding power over us.* The role of the Pharisees was to enforce Jewish law and uphold ancient customs and traditions, but they had no qualms about overstepping those sacred boundaries.

For Simon, their vile reaction to Jesus only added more confusion to an already bewildering journey. *Jesus just performed the most incredible miracle, and they still want him punished.* He shook his head. *How can they accuse him of blasphemy when he proved his own words right before their eyes?* This rocked Simon to his core. *I just hope they don't decide to make a martyr of him.*

With the crowds now dispersing, Simon's mind spun wildly. *Jesus healed a leper and now a paralytic man,* he thought. *I guess that's part of the deal for a leader who will crush the Romans?* In all he'd experienced, he remained single-minded about the Jewish people reclaiming their power. Unfortunately, Simon bar Jonas only ever saw what he wanted to see.

By the time they reached a trusted friend's home, Simon was drunk on confusion. He could not believe it, but he actually felt ready to get back on the road and resume the nomadic life. *I'm not sure where it's more dangerous,* he pondered, *staying at home or heading back out into the unknown.*

CHAPTER 9

MATTHEW, THE TAX COLLECTOR

Capernaum, Galilee

Days later, the loud buzz continued through Capernaum and all of northern Galilee.

Simon was following Jesus through the marketplace when he spotted a dark silhouette standing in the shadows. He peered hard, trying to identify the man. It's *Matthew, the publican,* he realized, his chest tightening. *The worst among us.*

Simon could picture Matthew's dark hair and matching almond-shaped eyes. The Roman loyalist also had a slight build—though with all his money, he was clearly well fed. *Even Matthew's smile looks devious,* Simon thought, unable to tell whether the taxman could see him staring. He didn't care.

Shaking his head, Simon thought, *Matthew was born a Jew, raised a Jew, and yet he chose to align with the Romans and collect their taxes from his own people.* Simon considered all the suffering the man had caused. *All the years of trouble, being broke and unable to pay on time. All the penalties that accumulated.* Continuing to gawk at Matthew, he could feel his stomach threaten to reject his breakfast. *All those times Andrew and I found ourselves in a bind, each one taking extra hours and heavy labor on the sea to dig ourselves out.* He tried to calm his breathing. *And I've known many others who've had it worst at the hands of this cold-blooded traitor.*

Simon tried picturing his friend Shmuel's pitiful face, which had been hidden within a Roman cell for months. *A long drought and a bad crop were all it took. Unable to pay, Matthew turned the poor man over to the Romans to be jailed for his debts.*

He spit on the ground in Matthew's direction. *Traitor!*

Ignoring the insult, Matthew stood in the shadows of Capernaum's bustling marketplace. All walks of life strolled past him—some Pharisees, even a Roman centurion sitting on horseback, patrolling the community center, alive with activity.

Matthew looked up. The sun felt strong today, causing him to stain another neck scarf.

The sounds of the market hardly changed from day to day; there was a hum of people laughing and talking, with the occasional yelling match taking place over a one-sided deal.

"You're a thief," a prospective customer wailed.

"And you want everything for nothing," the vendor countered. Matthew enjoyed watching these spirited barters the most.

Long wooden tables, shaded by large sails of faded cloth, were staked down by wooden poles. Scales, occasionally tipped to benefit the money changers, were normally the cause of the screaming matches. *Today's no different,* he thought, coming out of the shadows to peruse some of the wares.

The finer products included copper and bronze works, Egyptian pottery, Greek urns, rugs and tapestries, jewelry, perfumes, and herbs from the East. *These luxuries reach far beyond most people's budgets,* Matthew thought, *but not mine.*

Keeping his eyes down, Matthew moved on. Fired clay pots and casks contained all the essentials, while wine jars, narrow at the bottom, rested upright on slotted wooden shelves.

Hanging from the pergolas, recently dyed fabrics were strung up, baking in the sun. Besides these pergolas and staked tarps, some trees created a canopy of relief from the sun.

Thank Yahweh, the tax collector thought, wiping the sweat from his brow.

Smoked and pickled fish hung on racks, creating a distinct aroma that dominated the square. Matthew reviled the pungent smell. Most smells in the marketplace were a mix of fragrant and foul; he somehow detested them all. *And this place is as close to home as I'll ever know,* he told himself, snickering.

On the market's perimeter, livestock—including goats, sheep, and chickens—cackled and complained from their barred pens, as though they were pleading to avoid the axe. Matthew sidestepped the animals as he did most humans.

A few cubits away, he happened upon a disabled beggar, who extended his dirty, trembling hand. "Please, sir, some..." the homeless soul began to say, before noticing whom he was addressing. He quickly retracted his hand, as well as his half-finished request.

As always, Matthew ignored the pathetic creature.

Dressed in their fine robes and linens, two Pharisees looked down on Matthew with sneering superiority as they passed by. *No different from any of the other locals,* he decided. *Everyone looks down on me.* He watched as these self-righteous men, who not only taught Jewish law but enforced it, interacted with the commoners. It was intriguing how people were repelled by their very presence. *They're most definitely hated,* he thought, *but maybe not as much as me.* Being shunned was something he and the religious elite shared in common. *But at least I have the comfort of money.* He thought more on it. *I could never relate to* the *Pharisees*. As odd as it seemed—even to him—he thought, *They're too dishonest.*

Matthew passed the pawnbroker's stall. For some, it was their last stop before squaring up their Roman debts with the tax collector.

One of the men standing in line spat at Matthew's feet. "Thief," he hissed as Matthew passed.

"Rat," his friend murmured.

Ignoring their usual insults, Matthew, the tax collector, scurried along until arriving at his counting house.

As Matthew unlocked his small fortified booth, his assigned guard, Claudius, took his post to the right of the iron-barred window. Although the Roman legionary thought less of the tax collector than the other Jews, Matthew thought, *He's probably the closest thing I have to a friend.* The very idea made him wonder briefly about his own life—but only briefly.

A man of few words, Claudius was all business. Reporting directly to the Roman prefect, Pontius Pilate, he was charged with protecting the district's taxes while also imposing the Roman way of life on the Jewish rabble he was forced to associate with.

Matthew surmised that the soldier didn't care for his assigned post. *But taxes are collected to help fund the empire,* Matthew thought, *so it's an important job.*

Dressed in a blood-red scarf, Claudius wore a crimson tunic beneath leather armor, embossed with the gold eagle that represented the greatest empire on earth. His long sword was girded to his lean waist, and his heavy leather sandals were tied up his calves. His helmet was forged from metal, with a leather chin strap that covered his ears and cheeks.

Matthew nodded his usual morning greeting. And, as was the norm, Claudius ignored the friendly gesture. *That's my best friend right there*, Matthew thought ruefully.

Protected by an iron-barred window, Matthew locked the door behind him. Although he felt physically protected, the rest of him remained terribly vulnerable. He looked around. *This is my life*, he thought. Being good with numbers, he'd taken the job knowing that his skill set was a perfect match. But the price he had to pay was far higher than he could have imagined. *Insulted, spat on, shoved—and that's a normal day.*

As Matthew inventoried his surroundings, the irony was hardly lost on him. *I'm languishing in a dreadful cage I created for myself.*

Shaking it off, Matthew lit the oil lamp to warm and liquify his wax pot. He arranged a ream of papyrus, his wax seal at the ready. His thick ledger, filled with the district's accountings, was opened to a fresh page.

Taking a deep breath, he looked out toward the line of unhappy faces that was forming beyond his window, each person waiting to be victimized by the Roman Empire once again. Most would be asked to surrender money they needed for the basic essentials. Instead, they were paying Rome to keep its cruel and heavy yoke hung around their necks, choking the life out of them. Even Matthew understood. *To suffer is one thing, but to be asked to fund the pain was something else entirely.*

It was an injustice that reached beyond criminal. It was sinful.

A dark silhouette appeared above the Capernaum synagogue, the chief rabbi lifting the shofar horn to his lips and giving it three long blasts.

It had been a quick day for Matthew, with retail hours shortened. *Tough luck on the commoners*, he thought, *Shabbat has begun.* Hardly inconvenienced, Matthew was happy to close his booth. There was no work from sundown on Friday until an hour after the sun set on Saturday. *At least the Romans haven't taken that from us,* he thought. *Not yet anyway.*

As they parted ways, Matthew nodded toward Claudius. The stern legionary peered at the tax collector like he was looking through him. Matthew received nothing in return.

Leaving the marketplace, citizens greeted one another with, "Shabbat shalom." But not for Matthew. He was greeted with nothing but scornful silence from faces that stopped smiling and looked away.

After arriving home and lighting the Shabbat candles, Matthew offered the meal's blessing.

"In love and favor, God made the holy Shabbat, our heritage, as a reminder of the work of creation. It is first among our sacred days and a remembrance of the exodus from Egypt. O God, You have chosen us and set us apart from all the peoples, and in love and favor have given us the Sabbath day as a sacred inheritance. Amen."

Seated alone at his table, Matthew tried to enjoy the Shabbat meal. As he honored the old Jewish traditions each week, he remembered what it was like before his family had exiled him. The bittersweet memories filled him with such sorrow that he quickly turned them off. Instead, he focused on the here and now.

Although I wear the finest clothes, he thought, *I have nothing. Although I eat the richest foods,* he realized, *I have nothing. Although I drink the best wine, I have nothing.*

On face value, Matthew's life appeared better than most of his people. In reality, there was nothing further from the truth. He had riches and wealth, but he was empty. He had no one to share his success with. *Although I'm accomplished, it means nothing,* he thought. *Although I am known by many, my acclaim is not envied by anyone.* He had betrayed his people by deciding to work with the Romans.

He scanned his empty table. *I'm not just lonely,* he realized. *It goes well beyond that.* His eyes filled. *I'm alone.*

As he did at each Shabbat meal, he struggled to find a possible path out of his own predicament. *What else could I do?* he wondered. *Become a fisherman or a stonemason?* He shook his head. *It's probably too late for me now. I've traveled so far down this road that there's no turning back.* He felt a deep sense of dread. *I've made my choices, and I am condemned for them. It will take nothing less than a miracle.*

A tear broke free and traveled down his cheek as he again recalled the days when he celebrated Sabbath with his family and friends. *But my greedy choices ended all of that.* He shook his head. *So many bad choices…*

In silence, he finished his meal—alone.

Simon and his fellow disciples were following Jesus through the marketplace when the Messiah stopped in front of the barred window at Caesar's customhouse. Jesus and Matthew, the despised publican, gazed quietly at each other.

What's this? Simon wondered, getting nervous. He'd seen the same exchange when Judas had joined their group.

"Please don't tell me…" Andrew whispered to Simon.

Simon shook his head. "Can't be," he said. "The Romans were born Romans, but Matthew chose to betray his own people."

After a long silence—with Jesus and Matthew staring at each other—Jesus told the despised man, "Follow me." He said nothing more.

What? No!!! Simon blurted in his head. *He can't be serious!*

Shocked looks were exchanged among the group.

"Rabbi," Simon blurted, immediately protesting on everyone's behalf. "I know this...this tax collector. Do you have any idea who Matthew is? What he's done?"

Jesus nodded. "I do."

Turning away, Simon threw up his hands in frustration. "Why this guy?"

Jesus took pause, waiting quietly until Simon turned back. "I came to call the sinners," he finally answered, his eyes emitting patience.

Simon looked at the counting booth to see that Matthew had already abandoned his job, falling in behind Jesus and their little group with nothing more than his tablet.

Simon was not happy. He had heard Jesus, but he didn't like it. Matthew took his place beside Simon.

How could anyone not be proud to be a Jew? Simon wondered again, recalling their trip to Jerusalem. This time, the question meant something quite different.

Matthew, for his part, could not believe it. Peering through his eyes and into his soul, Jesus smiled. "Follow me," he said.

Without the slightest hesitation, Matthew began locking up his booth, happy to bid farewell to Claudius and all the grief this miserable life had caused him. Matthew was amazed at himself and at Jesus. *This is the answer I've been waiting for,* he decided.

The wardrobes of perfumed clothes, the finest sandals with heavy wooden soles, even the jewelry he wore that was coveted by those who had none—he was happy to let it all go. *It was all earned from blood money, anyway, doing Rome's bidding by bleeding my own people dry. No more!* he thought. *Maybe there will even come a time when it's safe for me to walk the streets alone.* Finally given the opportunity to make a righteous choice, he wasn't about to squander it.

As a logical man with a keen sense of observation, numbers made sense to Matthew— much more than intangible concepts such as faith. Yet, he could not deny his eyes and ears. He had heard of the many miracles Jesus had performed and of the crowds that flocked to hear the rabbi preach. Nor could Matthew deny his gut. Every fiber in his being screamed that he should do exactly as this man asked. *Follow!*

Taking the first few steps, he couldn't believe how easy it was to walk away from his work, his entire world. *This is the miracle I've been praying for,* he confirmed in his mind, not yet understanding the enormity of the blessing. For as long as he could remember, no one else had looked out for him, so he had no choice but to look out for himself.

But that's behind me now, he thought, smiling. *Give up everything to gain everything. I was lost, and now I'm found.*

He wanted to jump for joy. No more living a life in quicksand with no way out. He had heard enough about Jesus that he was more than willing to take this giant leap of faith, forfeiting it all and stepping into the great unknown.

Matthew looked back once. *Claudius is going to miss me,* he thought, the ridiculousness of it making him grin. With each step farther away from the prison he'd created, his breathing became lighter.

As they walked, Jesus dropped back behind the group to think in silence. Ordinarily, Simon would adjust his position as well. He didn't. He kept marching forward, all the while glaring at the newest recruit. *I heard what Jesus said*, he thought, *but I just don't get this one. Why?*

Matthew was clearly sharp with numbers and words. *He's more of a thinker, like John*, Simon surmised, *but it's the depth of the man's heart that I question.*

As if on cue, John stepped up beside him. "This will be interesting," he said, pushing his friend's button, his tone low.

Simon shook his head. "The worst thing that anyone could ever call me is a coward, and in my opinion, this man is beneath that," he said, less concerned about his volume. "Cowardice would be a compliment for Matthew."

A few of the others looked in their direction.

As they continued to walk, John drifted behind Simon. He was too smart to be ensnared by his best friend's emotional tirades.

This gave Simon the time and space to define why he hated the tax collector so much. *He forgot his own people, betraying us in the most unimaginable way. And for what?* Simon wondered. *A bigger home? Better food and clothing? Social status?* He shook his head. *It can't be that. He's the lowest of the low.* He continued to gawk at the newest disciple. *I wonder if the tax man took delight in his work. It seemed like he did.* He snickered. *I'll have to ask him.*

Matthew looked in Simon's direction but quickly looked away.

Simon felt like his throbbing head might explode right off his shoulders. *Matthew has been our enemy's puppet for years, and he did his job very well.* He looked back at Jesus and then over at Matthew. *I'm sorry, but I can't… I cannot stand the man!* Sucking in a deep breath, he put his head down and pushed on.

Jesus called for a dinner party in the north district, the hillside with the best views of the sea below. It was where the wealthy and immoral lived—Matthew's crowd. At the rabbi's request, Matthew was tasked to host the event for Jesus, his disciples, and a various mix of sinners. People were invited regardless of their social or moral status. It was Jesus's will.

In a torchlit courtyard, long tables were lined with fruits, nuts, meats, cheese, wine, and flowers. Both savory and sweet, everything was there for the taking. *Such an overabundance of food and drink,* Simon thought. *It's more indulgent than what the boys and I enjoyed at the Cana wedding.* Still stinging from this new recruitment, he felt incredibly uncomfortable. *This is not my world,* Simon told himself, looking around, *and these are not my people.*

He was sampling some goat cheese, bread, and olive oil when he asked John, "Is there going to be a wedding tonight?"

John chuckled, unable to restrain his amusement at his friend's sarcasm. Andrew glared at his brother to lower his tone.

"Sorry," Simon said, "but I don't see a chuppah." His brother shook his head and moved away.

A few Pharisees arrived, peering into the courtyard to steal a peek at who was in attendance.

Simon turned to find Jesus looking at them, his eyes set in stern authority. *I've seen that same look before,* Simon thought, proudly realizing that he'd identified a pattern.

Glancing at the Pharisees, then at Jesus, then back again, Simon thought, *Here we go again!*

The Pharisees appeared shocked, watching as Jesus broke bread with unholy people, the dregs of society. Furious, they spotted Simon and drew him aside. "How is it that your master eats and drinks with the publicans and sinners?"

I wonder that myself, Simon thought.

"The healthy have no need of a physician," Jesus blurted out across the courtyard while taking three steps toward them so he would be heard, "but the sick do. I did not come to call righteous people, but sinners."

Simon pondered this.

Although the religious snobs were invited to join the festivities, they quickly declined. "Their presence defiles us. They've never offered guilt sacrifices at the temple."

"I desire mercy more than sacrifice," Jesus replied, reciting the scripture.

Even Simon knew, *The Pharisees wouldn't be caught dead with tax collectors and prostitutes.*

The Pharisees warned Jesus, "There are righteous men on the lookout for you, and they are weighing every word you say."

Simon stepped up to defend his master.

Jesus stopped him with a raised hand, allowing the Pharisees to have their full say.

When given an order, Simon did not always understand, agree with, or like it, but he still followed the order—always. *All this trouble for what?* he wondered, shaking his head. *Jesus must know something the rest of us don't.*

Returning to the table, Simon couldn't look away from their host. *Matthew's own parents disowned him. So why pick him?* He looked around the table. *As if Judas wasn't enough?*

"What shall my job be?" Matthew asked the master, breaking Simon's train of thought.

"Write what you see and hear," Jesus told him.

Like John, he gladly accepted the new role of scribe. It was clear instruction, something he could obviously understand and embrace. "I'll record all I witness," he humbly vowed.

Seeing this, Simon remained quiet, troubled. *No more living in luxury*, he thought, continuing to study the new disciple. *No more fleecing your own people.*

But there was something about Matthew that seemed different, as though experiencing Jesus's grace had already made him a new man.

Simon sat for a long while in silence. *Jesus picked him for a reason*, he finally decided, looking to the Messiah. *He chose us all to play a role. I only wish I knew what mine was.*

At that moment, Jesus looked his way, raising a knowing eyebrow, and smiled.

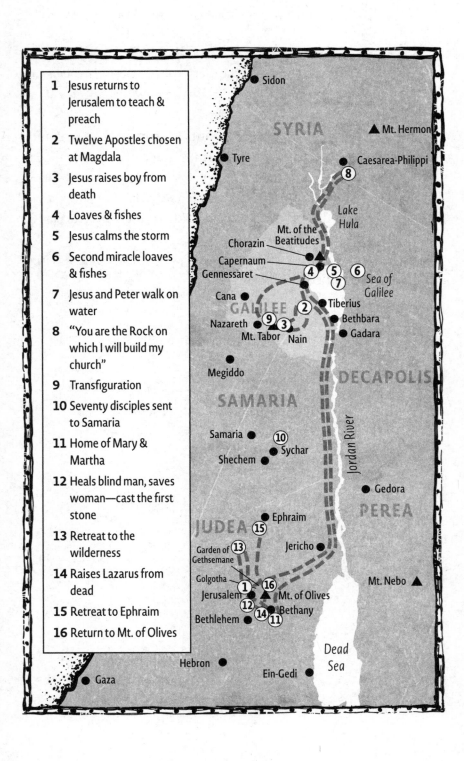

1 Jesus returns to Jerusalem to teach & preach
2 Twelve Apostles chosen at Magdala
3 Jesus raises boy from death
4 Loaves & fishes
5 Jesus calms the storm
6 Second miracle loaves & fishes
7 Jesus and Peter walk on water
8 "You are the Rock on which I will build my church"
9 Transfiguration
10 Seventy disciples sent to Samaria
11 Home of Mary & Martha
12 Heals blind man, saves woman—cast the first stone
13 Retreat to the wilderness
14 Raises Lazarus from dead
15 Retreat to Ephraim
16 Return to Mt. of Olives

Sidon
SYRIA
▲ Mt. Hermon
Tyre
Caesarea-Philippi
8
Lake Hula
Mt. of the Beatitudes
Chorazin
Capernaum
Gennessaret
4 5 6 Sea of Galilee
7
Cana
GALILEE
2 Tiberius
Nazareth
9 3 Bethbara
Mt. Tabor Nain Gadara
Megiddo
DECAPOLIS
SAMARIA
Samaria
10 Sychar
Shechem
Jordan River
Gedora
PEREA
Ephraim
15
JUDEA
Garden of 13
Gethsemane
Jericho
Golgotha
Mt. Nebo ▲
1 16
Jerusalem ▲ Mt. of Olives
12
14 Bethany
Bethlehem 11
Hebron
Ein-Gedi
Dead Sea
Gaza

PART 2

THE MINISTRY OF JESUS

———————

YEAR 2: PETER RECEIVES HIS COMMISSION

CHAPTER 10

TOO MANY PEOPLE
TO COUNT

Jerusalem, Judea

Following some debate, Simon and the others accompanied Jesus to the Holy City of Jerusalem for their second time together—one year into Jesus's ministry. Simon was pleased to be making the trip again. He loved visiting the bustling city.

After the weeklong hike down the Jordan Valley, past Jericho and up the steep hills, they arrived at the outskirts of Jerusalem.

Breaking camp among the ancient groves near the Mount of Olives, the newly awakened group crossed the bubbling spring at Kidron, where they filled their jugs and skins with fresh water. A few yawns later, they were crossing the Kidron Valley.

Although Simon could see the great city before him, it was the eclectic sounds that made the fisherman's bulging forearms turn to gooseflesh. The growing buzz was clearly a mix of people and animals, a cacophony of hawking vendors and bleating animals.

Simon exchanged looks with Andrew, John, and James. Each man was smiling from the anticipation of this newest adventure.

Every step closer to the city's ancient walls only added to Simon's excitement. Picking up the pace, Jesus and his disciples entered the Holy City through the Gates of Damascus and joined the horde of pilgrims.

After several days of preaching to whomever would listen, the Sabbath arrived. The sun had just reached its zenith when, on the streets outside of the temple, Jesus healed a paralytic man suffering from a withered hand. By now, this was not an unusual occurrence for Simon or the other disciples to witness.

This merciful act infuriated the Pharisees, as Jesus's work had been performed on the Sabbath—prohibited by law. The high priests were quick to remind him of the fact.

Their outrage is becoming a pattern, Simon thought, maintaining a calm pulse. *Jesus doesn't need my help to handle these squawking vultures.*

"My Father is working till now," Jesus told the religious elite, "and I also work."

This angered the Pharisees even more, making Simon smile. *Squawking vultures blinded by their own self-righteousness,* he decided.

Even Simon knew that the rabbi's answer was referring to the prophecies foretelling that the Messiah was coming. *And he is right here with us,* Simon thought, his smile widening, *right now.* Considering this, a feeling of inexplicable bliss overtook him. *My teacher and friend.*

Jesus further explained who he was. "He who does not honor the Son does not honor the Father who sent him," he said. "Indeed, indeed, I say to you, he who listens to my word and believes him who sent me possesses eternal life."

The high priests now appeared to be gnawing on their tongues. Pure blasphemy!

Jesus is not crazy and he's obviously not an imposter, Simon thought, *so why do the leaders of Israel continue to brush aside all the evidence of this, refusing to recognize him as the true Messiah?*

In the hours and days that followed, Simon pondered his master's enemies until he began to see that these venomous men were a real and viable threat to Jesus and his ministry.

The temple was ruled by two exclusive groups, the Pharisees and the Sadducees.

Influenced by the Maccabean War and now empowered by their Roman occupiers, their job was to enforce Jewish law, ensuring that all mandates were strictly observed by the people.

Although Simon lacked their education, he understood that these finely dressed men were more concerned with keeping customs than keeping the faith. *They love wealth and power, and have been corrupted by both,* he surmised, shaking his head. *They're more concerned with ceremonial washings and fasting than with their people's well-being.*

Making their way through the temple market, Simon turned to his best friend. "And to think that I once looked up to these snobs," he whispered, gesturing toward a group of Pharisees huddled together in gossip.

Maintaining his leisurely pace, John nodded. "They've forgotten their place and why they wear those expensive robes." His face turned stoic. "Instead of preparing our people for Jesus's coming, they've neglected their duties. They'd rather hoard the glory for themselves." He stopped for a moment. "As Jesus would say, 'They have failed to feed their sheep.'"

Simon grinned. "He sure would." But the smile quickly left him. Just the sight of these conspiring men made his skin crawl. *Their spies are always watching—in the synagogue and the streets—hoping to inform against Jesus. Whether it's because we plucked a few ears of corn on the Sabbath, or because Jesus healed some poor soul at the wrong hour, they've made it their mission to bring whatever charges they can against him.* He stopped long enough to stare holes into the back of their smug heads. *They're probably conspiring against Jesus right now, trying to figure out how they can finally destroy him.*

John grabbed his arm, pulling him forward. "Relax, Simon. They'll get what's coming to them. Don't you worry about that." He grinned. "After seeing everything we've seen, I can't imagine that Yahweh is all that pleased with a single one of them."

Picking up the pace, Simon looked skyward. "I definitely like our chances better."

Near Magdala, Galilee

"It is time for us to leave Jerusalem," Jesus announced, looking skyward as if he were confirming the decision. "For now."

Simon saw his master's face turn serious, wondering what it might mean. *For now?*

Leaving the Judean hills, Jesus led his troop back up the Jordan, north to the inland sea. It did not take long for the news to spread of their location. The rabbi instructed them to board a boat and put out into the deep, leaving the massive crowd complaining on the shore.

Before Simon and the other fishermen could relax on the water they missed, they arrived on the banks near Magdala, beneath a small hill—the Horns of Hittin.

As was becoming customary, Jesus sauntered off to engage in solitary prayer. Simon hated this part of the routine—*Jesus going off alone, unprotected.* But he kept the distress to himself. *The others will only remind me that he has much stronger protection than me.*

To quell his angst, Simon got busy, helping to set up their newest camp and working the only way he knew how—hard. Singing his usual hymns, even James the Lesser's angelic choir voice couldn't soothe him.

Jesus returned that night in the darkness. "I have decided to choose twelve apostles," he announced, taking a seat at their campfire, "one for each of the sons and tribes of Israel."

Although Simon had no reason to believe he would not be one of the named twelve, his mind and heart were instantly engaged in battle. His mind told him that he was guaranteed a position. *How could I not be?* he asked himself. *He calls me "the rock."* His heart, however, fluttered with uncertainty. As Simon waited to hear more, he felt as if someone had reached into his chest and given his heart a firm squeeze.

Concealing his own worries, he looked across the fire at Andrew, John, and James, offering each man a supportive nod. They were all sitting up straight now, equal amounts of hope and fear swimming in their dark eyes.

Simon then looked sideways to Jesus. *He's obviously prayed a lot on this,* he thought, *and he knows each one of us—who we are and where we come from.* Simon scanned the uneasy circle. *Such different personalities and points of view,* he realized. *A doctor, a salesman, a publican, as well as men who have either worked the land or else made a living on the sea.*

Jesus leaned toward the fire so that everyone could see his face. "Simon Peter," he announced as the first of the apostles.

Simon didn't realize he'd been holding his breath. Exhaling, he felt a heavy yoke lift from his shoulders, freeing him.

Mercifully, Jesus quickly listed the others. "Andrew. John and his brother, James. Philip. Thomas. Thaddeus. Bartholomew. James the Lesser. Matthew. Simon the Zealot. And Judas."

Besides the disciples who had not been chosen, everyone was breathing easier now. Simon couldn't help but glance over at Matthew and Judas. *Jesus must have his reasons,* he thought, still unable to reconcile these men.

"Each of you will have the power to heal the sick and cast out devils," Jesus told them. This news caused even more surprised looks across the dancing flames.

Simon's mind whirled with the possibilities for the future, the incredible opportunities set before him. *At thirty years old, I'm one of the founders of the Messiah's new kingdom!* The sudden sense of unbridled glory made him feel lightheaded. Simon felt the soft gaze of Jesus fall upon him. He turned to see Jesus smiling at him.

In the weeks that followed, Simon noticed that Jesus was spending a great deal of time with Matthew—alone. As they conversed at a distance, Matthew recorded their exchange. Simon was tempted to inquire about this with Jesus but decided against it. *It's no secret that Matthew isn't my favorite,* he thought, *and I'm sure Jesus would remind me of that.*

Instead, he spoke to John, the group's other scribe. "What do you think Jesus and Matthew are talking about all the time?"

John half-shrugged. "I'm not sure, Simon. I haven't been invited into their conversations."

"And that doesn't bother you?"

"Should it?"

Simon smirked. "You're also Jesus's scribe, aren't you?"

John shook his head. "Jesus tells me what he wants to tell me, and I record his words. If he needs me, he calls for me. I don't worry about anything else." He returned the smirk. "I trust him, Simon."

"I trust him too," Simon snapped back, quick to defend his position.

"Then don't concern yourself with what Jesus and Matthew are doing. I'm sure it will be revealed to us in good time."

Sighing heavily with his typical impatience, Simon nodded. "I know," he said. "I know."

But when?

Although the fire had died, a full moon lit the night sky with soft light, allowing only the brightest stars to flicker and shine. Simon gazed for a while, wondering whether his wife was looking at the same moon. I *hope she is,* he thought, *and that she's thinking of me too.*

Tabgha, near Capernaum, Galilee

Jesus and his newly appointed apostles traveled on, reaching a hillside near Tabgha. It didn't take long for the crowd to find them. Word had spread that Jesus would be teaching. Several hundred began swarming the incline, crying out for Jesus, begging him to teach them and heal their infirmities.

After many months of Jesus's preaching, his prominence was extraordinary. *His fame has spread,* Simon realized, *and his name has power, inspiring strong emotion.* Simon felt torn. On the upside, these were wonderful things. But on the downside, it attracted droves of strangers who could turn unruly and dangerous at any time—*and without warning.*

The crowd kept amassing, swelling like the Sea of Galilee before a storm. Hundreds were multiplying into thousands before their eyes. The people were happy, yearning to learn.

Unfortunately, there were more worshippers than Simon had ever seen. *This isn't good,* he thought, his level of vigilance elevated to an all-time high. Unable to contain his fear, he looked to John. "Will you look at all these people?"

Together, they scanned the hillside, watching as the crowd swayed like a wheat field in a breeze.

John rested his hand on Simon's shoulder. "The crowd is why we're here," he said, nodding. "For the people to hear Jesus and to bear witness to his truths." His eyes narrowed. "Haven't you figured that out by now?"

Simon shrugged.

"Jesus knows what he's doing," John added. "We'll be fine." He smiled. "He'll be fine."

Simon continued to scan the massive gathering. *Like the stars above the Sea of Galilee*, he thought. *Too many people to count.*

From the elderly to children, the rolling hill became blanketed with people—families and weary travelers alike converging on the fateful afternoon.

Simon took a deep breath. Even the air felt warm with hope. *A few Pharisee spies must be mixed in*, Simon figured, scanning the crowd and trying to locate them. It had become a sort of game for him. Although they posed no immediate threat, he knew, *They're definitely going to try to cause Jesus trouble in the long run. It seems like it's their number-one mission.*

Jesus finally stood, with his disciples gathering closely around him. Simon and Judas were the only ones who remained standing. After exhaling deeply, Jesus addressed the multitude. "Blessed are the poor in spirit, for theirs is the kingdom of heaven," the divine rabbi began. "Blessed are they that mourn, for they shall be comforted. Blessed are the meek, for they shall inherit the earth. Blessed are they that hunger and thirst after righteousness, for they shall be filled. Blessed are the merciful, for they shall obtain mercy. Blessed are the pure in heart, for they shall see God. Blessed are the peacemakers, for they shall be called sons of God.

Blessed are they that have been persecuted for righteousness' sake, for theirs is the kingdom of heaven."

It suddenly dawned on Simon, *This is what Jesus has been working on with Matthew!*

He looked to John, who mouthed the words *"revealed in good time."*

Revealed in good time, Simon repeated in his head. *Indeed.* But he kept his head on a swivel. *So many people crammed so close to Jesus,* he thought. *This entire scene is a recipe for trouble.*

"Blessed are you when men shall revile you and persecute you," Jesus continued, "and say all manner of evil against you falsely, for my sake."

Simon noted that Jesus's speech seemed different; it was measured, slow, forceful. It somehow felt more deliberate than previous sermons, and Simon sensed that every word was important. *Jesus is at his best today,* he decided, *laying out the attitudes and actions that he wants his followers to live by.*

There was a sudden movement in the crowd, two hooded men pushing their way to the front of the bulging audience. While Jesus's voice faded to Simon, drifting further and further away from his focus, Simon targeted the two men, tracking their every move. With his hackles raised, his senses were so keen that he could feel the weight of the air on his skin. *Not on my watch,* he thought. *Not here. Not today.*

As quickly as the threat had materialized, it disappeared. The two men settled in at the front of the crowd, where the taller one took down his hood. From his eyes, he was mesmerized by Jesus's sermon.

This man is no threat, Simon decided. *Neither one of them is.*

Jesus's voice returned clearly again in Simon's ears. "You have heard that thou shalt not kill and whosoever shall kill, shall be in danger of the judgment. But I say unto you, that everyone who is angry with his brother shall be in danger of the judgment." He took a breath. "You have heard it said, 'Thou shalt not commit adultery.' But I say unto you that everyone who looks at a woman to lust after her has committed adultery with her already in his heart. If the right eye causes you to stumble, pluck it out and cast it away. For it is better to lose an eye than for your whole body to be cast into hell. If your right hand causes you to stumble, cut it off and cast it away, as it would be better to lose a hand than your entire body to hell."

Wha ... what? Simon stuttered in his own head. As was normal, he struggled to understand. He slowly made his way over to Andrew. "Are you getting any of this?" he asked.

Andrew looked up at him. "I am," he whispered, clearly annoyed, "but I've also been listening." He studied his younger brother. "Why are you so distracted?"

Simon scanned the multitude. "There are so many people here, most of them strangers. What are the chances that one or more of them wants to hurt the rabbi?"

Andrew shook his head. "If that were the case, I'm sure Jesus would know about it long before it happened."

Simon pondered this.

"Be quiet," John called out in a forced whisper. "I'm trying to write all of this down."

"You have heard an eye for an eye," Jesus said, "and a tooth for a tooth. But I say unto you, whoever strikes your right cheek, offer the left cheek to him as well."

Huh? Simon screamed in his head. *Turn the other cheek? Did I just hear that right?* The very idea went directly against his nature.

Jesus was on a roll. "You have heard that you shall love your neighbor and hate your enemy," he preached. "But I tell you, love your enemies and pray for them that persecute you, that you may be sons of your Father who is in heaven, for He makes the sun rise on the evil and the good, and sends rain on the just as well as the unjust. For if you love them that love you, what reward have you? Do not even the publicans do the same?"

Simon looked toward Matthew; he could feel his own face burn red from embarrassment.

"If you're only kind to your brethren, how are you any different from any others?" Jesus asked the giant flock. "Don't even the Gentiles do the same? You should be perfect, as your heavenly Father is perfect. Take heed; do not your righteousness before men, to be seen of them, else you have no reward with your Father who is in heaven. So, when you do alms, do not sound a trumpet, as the hypocrites do in the synagogues and in the streets, that they may have glory of men."

Simon scanned the crowd. *Oh, the Pharisees won't care for that one.*

"I say to you," Jesus explained, "they have already received their reward. But when you do good works, do not let your left hand know what your right hand is doing. Do your good in secret, and my Father who sees it in secret shall recompense you." He nodded. "Place your treasures in heaven, where..."

From his peripheral view, Simon detected another sudden movement. He turned on his heels to investigate, when he felt the leather strap on his right sandal snap clean in half. Before he bothered to look down, he studied the area of the commotion. *It's only a mother disciplining her child,* he realized, shaking his throbbing head.

As Simon reached down to retrieve the broken sandal, Jesus's words became fuzzy again. A quick inspection revealed all Simon needed to know. *The leather's so worn and cracked that it's beyond repair.* He shook his head. Whenever he entered his house, his sandals were left at the door—*giving us both a rest from each other. But not out here,* he thought. *These sandals only come off when I sleep.* Fortunately, he had a new pair in his sack: wooden soles, fastened by new, rigid straps of leather. Considering all the walking they did, he sighed heavily. *I can't even imagine the size of the blisters I'm about to suffer.*

Jesus continued with a deliberate, careful pace. "Everyone who hears these words of mine and does them shall be likened to a wise man, who built his house upon the rock..."

Simon's ears perked at the familiar reference. *Built upon the rock.* He smiled.

When Jesus had concluded his sermon, the multitudes were left speechless—and so was Simon, at least for the passages he did catch. *Unlike the scribes, Jesus teaches with true authority,* he thought. The silence of the thousands was deafening.

∝•∞

When Jesus and the rest descended the hill, the astonished horde followed them.

As Simon limped behind Jesus, he turned to John and Andrew. "That was quite the speech," he said.

"You think?" Andrew quipped, still in awe.

"I'm surprised you caught any of it at all," John teased Simon.

Simon shrugged. "I couldn't help it. The crowd was so big that I was distracted a few times and—"

"Well, that's a shame," John interrupted, "because every single word was pure gold!"

Andrew nodded.

"Then I need you to fill me in on what I missed," Simon told them.

Continuing to tease him, both men remained silent—exchanging grins.

Stepping up beside the three men, Matthew slapped his tablet. "Let's eat first, Simon, and then I'll read you everything I have."

Simon was taken aback. "Thanks, Matthew," he muttered, "I appreciate that." Although Simon often struggled to understand Jesus's teachings, he certainly longed to. *And I have to believe that today's sermon is an important one in the rabbi's ministry.*

That night, after receiving some patient tutoring from Matthew and John, who compared notes, Simon asked Jesus even more questions than usual. He concluded with, "How often should my brother wrong me and I still forgive him? As many as seven times?"

"Seventy times seven," replied Jesus, "and from the heart."

Simon took his leave from the campfire to find a rock where he could sit and ponder his master's profound teachings.

Reclining beneath the stars, he struggled to put the puzzle together. Replaying all he had heard on the crowded hill that afternoon, coupled with the details that Matthew had helped to fill in, he decided, *I should be able to see the whole picture by now. But I don't think I do.* It was as blurry as any mental picture he'd ever attempted. Over and over, Simon went through the lessons until they made his head hurt. *Am I really that dense?* he wondered, questioning his own intelligence.

He then began to question his decision to follow Jesus. *Not because of Jesus, but because of me,* he thought. *What if I never get it? What if I'm just not able to?* His inadequacies weighed heavily.

Having been down this rough stretch before, Simon halted the harsh line of questioning. Refocusing his thoughts, he pictured Capernaum. Although the mental pictures made him feel homesick, he decided, *It's better than feeling stupid.*

It was later that evening when Simon recalled one of Jesus's teachings from earlier.

"When you pray, do so in private," Jesus explained during his Sermon on the Mount. "Your Father already knows what you need before you ask Him." Christ then taught them how to pray. "Our Father, who art in heaven, hallowed be Thy name. Thy kingdom come. Thy will be done, as in heaven, so on earth. Give us this day our daily bread. And forgive us our debts, as we also have forgiven our debtors. And bring us not into temptation but deliver us from evil." The master nodded. "For if you forgive men their trespasses, your heavenly Father will also forgive you. But if you do forgive men their trespasses, neither will your Father forgive your trespasses."

Simon repeated this new prayer over and over in his head until sleep arrived to claim him.

Tossing and turning that night, Simon's dreams proved chaotic. Jesus's newest teachings were in such direct opposition to his long-held beliefs that even his subconscious was struggling to reconcile it all.

In what felt like minutes, Simon awoke feeling as confused as ever. No matter how hard he tried to accept Jesus's messaging, he knew that much of it went against his own nature. Feeling desperate, he sought out his closest confidants.

"I just don't understand," he confessed to John and James. "The Romans have lashed Jews for the smallest transgressions. They've forced the elderly to carry their gear on the road, and even tossed them from their own homes so they could sleep in their beds. And these poor people should be expected to turn the other cheek?"

John and James listened but said nothing.

"What if one of those Roman dogs struck you, and then you turned the other cheek and he struck you harder?" Simon asked. "How long would you allow it to go on before ..." He shook his frustrated head.

The brothers, the sons of Zebedee, remained silent.

"And what if someone struck Jesus and he turned the other cheek?" Simon asked, never allowing them to answer. "I'll you tell what I'd do..." He was working himself up into an angry lather. "I'd split his head wide open, just to check how empty it is!" he barked, the devil raging inside him. "'Love thy enemies?' How?"

John and James stood motionless, clearly hoping that Simon's one-sided conversation had come to an end.

Nain, Galilee

The second summer of their ministry had arrived in its full glory, the August heat basting Simon in his own sweat. For reasons unknown, Jesus had picked one of the main roads to travel. *Very unusual*, Simon thought. *He normally likes to remain out of sight whenever possible.*

As they marched forward, Simon noticed that John and James were walking alongside Jesus—like singing birds perched on each of *the rabbi's shoulders.* He snickered. *It's the same when we eat or camp for the night*, Simon thought, *always one brother on his right and the other brother on his left.* Surprising himself, he felt a pang of envy pass through him. *Jesus does love them both, and probably because they're smart enough to hold their tongues most of the time.*

Just then, James told a joke at the head of the line. "John's so cheap that he's given me the same birthday present for years."

"And what's that?" Jesus asked.

"Nothing."

Both John and Jesus laughed.

Maybe it's best to keep it light? Simon thought, wondering whether he should adopt the same approach. He chuckled to himself. *No, that's not me.*

After studying the joking trio for a moment, he had to smile. *The Sons of Thunder are hardly a threat to my position with Jesus.* He glanced up at the relentless sun. *I think maybe it's just the heat that's gotten to me.*

As the weary band rounded a bend in the dusty road, Simon spotted the walls that encompassed the city of Nain. For a moment, Jesus seemed to slow his gait, causing the rest of them to do the same. Simon looked toward the sun. *It must be around two o'clock,* he decided. From the mouth of the city's gate, a parade of veiled women emerged—wailing in grief while instruments lamented above the breeze. *It's a funeral procession,* Simon realized, expecting to skirt past it. But Jesus came to a stop, as though he'd been anticipating their arrival.

By now, a scattered string of mourners began to line the road, sharing their sympathies.

What a sad sight, Simon thought.

As the pitiful procession approached, Jesus stepped up to one of the grieving women. In that instant, both the instruments and sorrowful wails turned to an eerie silence.

Simon glanced at the corpse carried upon the bier; it was a young man, his basalt-white skin gleaming from being recently anointed. *Poor boy.*

"Weep not," Jesus told the boy's mother before touching the stretcher. "Young man," he commanded, his voice deepening, "I say to you, arise."

The dead boy stirred—first his hands and then his legs—until opening both eyes. A moment later, he sat up and looked at his mother.

Moans of pain were replaced by cries of joy.

What just happened? Simon wondered, looking to Andrew and John. They were also slack-jawed in shock. *Was the boy not truly dead?* Simon questioned.

Everyone was shocked. Suddenly, the contemplative moment was broken by the onlookers shrieking their praises—the mourners converted to celebrants. While many ran and fell at the feet of Jesus, the boy's tearful mother met the Messiah's gaze. He simply smiled at her.

Amid the chaos, Simon studied the resurrected boy, realizing that he had indeed been deceased just moments before. He looked at Jesus, thinking, *Like prophets before him, he has raised dead persons to life.* Simon took a few deep breaths to calm his mind and steady his legs. *So, this is what it means to be the Messiah?*

As waves of astonishment, confusion, excitement, and fear washed over Simon, he felt drunk. *If Jesus can raise the dead, then there is nothing he can't do,* he realized, trying not to hyperventilate. *We can accomplish anything. Maybe even resurrect an entire Jewish army?* He felt giddy. *The Romans don't stand a chance!*

That night, although Simon expected some extra-lively banter by the campfire, each disciple remained relatively silent, lost to his own thoughts.

"That was impossible," Simon finally whispered to his brother.

"Exactly," Andrew whispered back.

John smiled. "It's Jesus," he said. "With him, it seems all things are possible."

Simon agreed. *Nothing is impossible,* he repeated in his contemplative state.

When he finally turned in, his fingers interlocked behind his head, Simon stared off into oblivion, completely dumbfounded. *First, that sermon on the mount ... and now this?*

CHAPTER 11

LOAVES AND FISHES

On the road, Galilee

Simon awoke with the same questions—and lack of answers—swirling in his mind. *That remarkable speech and then raising a boy from the dead?* He felt like he was being suspended in a state of awe. The resurrection was unprecedented. *Of course, I believe my eyes and ears; they've never failed me before. But ...* He had no idea how to process all he'd recently witnessed.

Over a breakfast of flatbread, dates, olives, and cheese, he asked Andrew, "What do you think?"

The faithful man could only shrug. "Anything is possible with Jesus, brother," he said, echoing John's assessment from the previous night.

Simon then turned to John, pulling him aside.

John offered a similar shrug. "I'm still trying to make sense of it all myself." He paused in deep thought. "But..."

"But?" Simon asked.

"But I'm thinking I shouldn't be wasting my time trying to make sense of anything." He grinned. "Maybe all we need to do is believe and—"

"And follow," James said, finishing his brother's sentence.

Maybe, Simon thought, nodding his spinning head. *Wait until the wife hears about this one!* He took a final bite of creamy goat cheese before packing up his gear.

They were on the road—with Simon dragging along at the rear—when two messengers approached. Andrew quickly made his way to the back of the cortege to inform Simon. "Those men are John the Baptizer's disciples; they're here to pass along a message from the imprisoned Baptizer. It sounds like John has asked that Jesus confirm his identity as the Messiah."

"What did Jesus say about that?"

"He promised he would, adding high praise of John." Andrew sighed heavily. "There must be more Jesus can do for him."

"What can he do?" Simon asked, feeling defensive. "Besides, Herod would have some real problems if he harmed a single wild hair on John's head. With all his followers..." Simon stopped. He felt bad, knowing that his brother had been a devout follower of John before joining Jesus. *Andrew's in pain*, he realized, squeezing his brother's shoulder. "Let me tell you the same thing you would tell me."

One of Andrew's eyebrows rose in anticipation.

"Stop worrying."

Andrew shook his head. "John baptized us in the Messiah's name, brother. He led us to Jesus, and he prepared the way for everything that Jesus is doing now." His swollen eyes began to leak. "I just hope John's not going to be forgotten."

"Never!" Simon barked. "You need to remember the prophecy that John foretold. 'I must decrease, and he must increase.' You know he was talking about Jesus!"

"I know that," Andrew said, "but after all the years of fasting and living in the wilderness ..." He shook his worried head. "John has sacrificed so much."

Simon stared at him. "I understand how you feel, Andrew, but please don't repeat that statement the next time you're in the company of my wife. She may unload on you on the pains of sacrifice."

As they continued on, Simon was left to wonder about his own place in history. *What is all of this for: the blisters, the haters and the zealots, their threats? The uncertainty. Missing my family. No longer fishing and being out on the water I love.* He looked around at his ragtag band of fellow travelers before his eyes reached Jesus at the head of the pack. *Will any of this make a difference? Will we be remembered?* Simon feared what all men fear—being forgotten. *Only time will tell, I guess.*

John's arrest had caused great distress. He had been thrown into jail for protesting Herod's request to be married illegally. In turn, Jesus had done nothing to secure his cousin's release, and some people were upset over this. Some of John's devout followers were even comparing John's ministry and his meager way of life to Jesus and his disciples "dining at great feasts and being honored at lavish wedding suppers."

Beneath a cluster of shade trees, Jesus finally addressed their resentment. "Can the son of the bridechamber fast while the bridegroom is with them?" he asked. "As long as they have the bridegroom with them, they cannot fast. But the days will come when the bridegroom shall be taken away from them, and then they will fast."

Pondering this, Simon tugged at his short beard. He looked to John, then Andrew and James. They appeared to be as lost as he felt. Jesus often spoke in parables so that the undeserving would not profit by his wisdom. It often felt frustrating to Simon.

Jesus added, "Neither would anyone put new wine into old wineskins, or else the wine would burst the old skins and the wine would be lost. But men put the new wine into fresh, unused wineskins so they can both grow old together. And, when anyone has drunk of the aged wine, he will never desire the new because he says, 'The old wine is good.'"

Listening hard, Simon labored to understand. *Is Jesus explaining that his and John's ministries should not be compared?* He wasn't sure. What he did know was that John's disciples were hurting—*and so is my brother.* He shuffled closer to Andrew and threw his arm around the sad man's shoulders. When Andrew tried to move away, Simon tightened his fisherman's grip.

As John's disciples grabbed their packs, readying themselves to leave, Jesus told them, "John is so much more than just a prophet, because he is the one of whom it is written, 'Behold, I send my messenger before thy face who shall prepare your way before you.'" He nodded. "Truly, I am telling you, among those born of women, there has not arisen a greater man than John the Baptist."

Confusion and then fear struck Simon's heart. *How is this even possible?* he wondered. *Jesus just saved a boy from death, a stranger. Surely, he will save his own cousin? There is no greater man than John. He must be protected.* Simon looked at his brother's face, which was twisted up in pain. *Andrew must sense it too.*

Bethsaida, Galilee

As they approached Bethsaida, they had come upon a crowd that immediately began pushing in on Jesus, maneuvering just to get a better look or to yell their requests for healing.

Here we go again, Simon thought, hurrying to Jesus's side. Ignoring his raw and blistered foot, he deflected people away from the calm rabbi.

Before Simon could prevent it, a woman emerged from the mob and collapsed at Jesus's feet—where she began to wash them. Simon bent to grab her arm when he felt a hand on his back. His head snapped up. It was John.

"Don't," John told him. "She is a friend of Jesus's."

"*A friend?*" Simon mouthed back above the raucousness.

John nodded. "She is Mary of Magdala," John explained, speaking directly into Simon's ear. "He once healed her of seven demons."

Simon looked down as Mary began drying Jesus's feet with her long raven-black hair.

Although she was physically attractive, it was her deep devotion that moved Simon's heart. *Now I have her to protect, too,* he thought, blocking out frantic pilgrims who were seconds away from trampling her underfoot.

They moved on from that crowd to the next and then the next. Jesus healed and he preached in Chorazin, Nain, Cana, Tiberius, Bethsaida, and many other villages and townships on both sides of the sea. He often spoke in mysterious parables: the sower, the cockle, the mustard seed, the treasure trove.

For Simon, each lesson seemed to bring more questions than answers. Jesus was normally patient with Simon and his never-ending line of questions, because of the love they shared. Still,

Simon often kept his questions to himself. *I know I can be dumb at times,* he thought. *I don't need him knowing it.*

No sooner had the thought left his mind when Jesus turned to him and smiled. "You will understand when the time is right, Simon Peter."

Knowing his master could read his mind, Simon returned the smile, briefly considering whether he should ask Jesus to heal his raw, blistered foot. Breaking in the new sandals had proven far worse than he'd expected. *I've limped behind the group for many days,* he thought, *while blisters the size of shekels have grown new blisters.* He quickly put the ridiculous thought out his mind. Given all that he'd seen, this was a very small price to pay. Enduring the pain was starting to feel like a badge of honor.

Jesus turned to him once more and nodded.

Shuffling along, Simon nodded back—his aching feet forgotten.

Limping back home to Capernaum, Simon was both relieved and excited to spend some time with his wife. They kissed like it was their first time.

She finally broke away. "You must be starving," she said. "I've made all of your favorites, even the roasted fish and leeks."

"I am hungry, but that can wait," he said, kissing her again.

When they finally came up for air, Simon asked, "Wait…where is your eema?"

"She's at the marketplace."

He smiled. "How is she?"

"Never better. I don't know what Jesus did to her, but she still spends half her days singing and dancing."

"Dancing?"

She laughed. "It's not pretty, believe me."

Simon joined her in the laughter.

"Enough about Eema," she said. "Tell me everything!"

Simon escorted her over to the table. "You'll want to sit for this. You can't imagine the miracles I've witnessed."

"Are you sure you don't want to eat first and then..."

"The food can wait," he repeated.

"Then start talking," she said, sliding to the edge of her short stool.

Without further hesitation, Simon began to unpack all that he'd experienced since last seeing his beloved. "After we left Capernaum," he explained, still standing, "we traveled back to Jerusalem where Jesus preached to the masses, making the Pharisees angrier than ever."

Sharing the details of the trip, Simon couldn't talk fast enough. At one point, he caught himself and stopped. "I'm sorry, my love," he said, grabbing her callused hand, "I should have asked how you've been faring since I..."

"Don't you dare stop!" she told him, squeezing his hand. "Nothing has changed here, except for me waiting to hear all about your stories from the road."

Simon shared Jesus's sermon on the mount, as well as the boy being raised from the dead at Nain.

"Oh, Simon," she said, her eyes filling with tears. "You have been blessed beyond blessed to follow Messiah."

"I know," he said, nodding. "But I'd be lying if I said it's been easy on me, or any of us, living on the road the way we do. Within every crowd of believers, there are those who want to end Jesus's mission. I can feel the danger wherever we go."

"At least you, Andrew, John, and James have one another," she said.

This innocent comment made Simon think—and smile. *She's right. When life gets dangerous, we have one another's backs. It goes without saying.* The camaraderie they shared made the hardships they endured much more tolerable. *I can't imagine what it would be like to have to experience it alone.*

He kissed her cheek. "You're as wise as anyone I've met out there in the world."

She laughed it off.

"I mean it," he told her.

She stood to dish out some food, gently leading Simon to his place at their table. "Tell me more."

Simon and his wife talked deep into the night, long after he'd filled his groaning belly and the new candles flickered out. *I didn't realize how much I needed to share all of this,* he thought, holding her close to him through the night.

He yawned. *I didn't realize how exhausted I am either.* The world suddenly turned to a tiny pinpoint of light before it disappeared, stolen away by sleep. Simon's energy level was depleted. It was time to recharge.

∝•✕⊃

The next few months were a whirlwind. No sooner had Simon come up for air and leveled his spinning head when Jesus performed another impossible act—a feat that far surpassed reason.

One afternoon, Simon and the others were all in their boat as it pitched to and fro. Jesus had asked that they cross the Sea of Galilee to the east side.

As their master slept below deck, the waves picked up, sending spray over the bow.

While the wind began to howl, tossing the boat around, the apostles became terrified. Lowering the sail, the experienced fishermen threw out the anchor. The waves were gigantic now, creating whitecaps on the violent water. *I hate to wake the rabbi,* Simon thought, *but I have no choice.* His eyes stinging from the sea spray, he could barely make out his brothers trembling on deck. "Master, save us!" he yelled out. "Save us, or we're all going to drown!"

Jesus awoke and ascended the short deck ladder. Assessing the ferocious storm, he looked to Simon. "Why are you so filled with fear, you of little faith?" he asked. Then, holding out his hands, he said to the waves and the wind, "Shalom. Peace, be still."

At that very moment, the winds calmed and the sea went still. As the boat stopped rocking, Matthew vomited off the starboard side.

With the fear of drowning gone, Simon's mind struggled to grasp what he had just seen.

What kind of man is this? Jesus commanded the winds to be still, and they obeyed.

"Why are you so fearful? Jesus asked again, peering straight into Simon's eyes. "Have you not yet learned to have faith? Where is your faith?"

Feeling like a scolded child, Simon could only apologize before offering his thanks to the master for rescuing them all.

What kind of man can command the sea? Simon continued to wonder, his eyes and mind at war over an impossibility. *And yet, I have seen it with my own eyes.*

Several weeks had passed when Simon tied up the boat and the troop took the road back to Capernaum.

Upon arrival, they found a small group gathering outside Simon's home. Jairus, one of the main leaders of the local synagogue, approached Jesus. Overcome with grief, he threw himself down at the rabbi's feet. "Please come and heal my daughter," he pleaded. "She's near death, if not passed already. I beg you, come and lay your hands on her so that she may be made whole again and live."

Jesus told Jairus, "I will heal the girl." They all headed to the man's home.

As they made their way through a jostling crowd, Simon thought he saw an arm reach out and touch Jesus.

Messiah stopped. "Who is it that just touched me?" he asked.

Simon shook his head. "Lord, the entire crowd is pushing to be near you. Many are shoving and—"

"Somebody touched me," Jesus said, interrupting him, "because I felt power go out of me."

A quivering woman stepped forward, telling Jesus, "I've been sick for years. I knew that if I could just touch you, I would be healed." She began to weep. "And I have been. I am healed!" She bowed in reverence. "I meant you no harm, Rabbi. I did not wish to bother you, but I was desperate."

Jesus looked at her as though they were alone. "Be of good cheer, daughter of Israel," he said. "Your faith has made you whole. Go in peace."

Simon shook his head, trying to clear away the cobwebs. A *woman was healed just by touching the tassels hanging from Jesus's cloak!*

As they continued on, one of Jairus's servants ran toward them. "It is too late," he reported, panting. "My master's daughter has passed away."

Jesus shook his head. "No," he said, "she is only sleeping."

When they arrived at the house, only Simon, James, and John were allowed to accompany their teacher. The four men found Jairus in mourning.

"Do not worry," Jesus told him, "I'm sure your daughter is only sleeping."

"She is dead!" one of the physicians yelled out, "I am certain of it."

After clearing the room, Jesus looked up to heaven and prayed. Then, taking the girl's limp hand, he said to her, *"Talitha, cumi."*

Miss, arise, Simon translated in his head.

And she did. Opening her eyes, she sat up—suddenly healthy—calling out for her family. Simon looked to his brethren. *She was dead. The doctor confirmed it.*

Jesus looked straight at the four astonished men and asked that they keep the miracle quiet. "You should feed your daughter," he further told Jairus, "as she will be hungry."

It was the second resurrection Simon had witnessed with his own eyes. Still, he could not fathom or reconcile it. *The dead rise and the sea bows down,* he thought, feeling overwhelmed once again.

This miracle was immediately followed by Jesus healing a blind man—which seemed like a footnote on their journey.

Simon emerged from the intense recollection. *Miracles, indeed,* he thought. *But how? How?*

His head placed in his large hands, Simon was grappling with the barrage of miracles when Jesus told his entourage, "The harvest is plentiful, but the laborers are few. Pray, therefore, the master of the harvest to send out laborers into his harvest."

Although he nodded that he understood, Simon realized he'd just been hit with another lesson that would require hours of dissection and analysis. Sometimes, it was so mentally exhausting.

$$\infty \cdot \infty$$

Days later, Simon had just finished cleaning his teeth with bone and a patch of wool when Jesus announced that he intended to send his twelve apostles on their first solo mission. "Two by two," he said.

How's this going to work, Simon wondered, *with no money to survive on or swords for protection?*

Of all people, Matthew stepped up beside him. "This should be interesting," he whispered.

Studying his slight frame, Simon grinned. "You think Jesus is making a mistake?" he asked, baiting the ex-publican, while also hoping they wouldn't be paired up.

Matthew shook his head. "Mistake? It's not for me to say. I've vowed to do whatever Jesus bids me."

Me, too, Simon thought, surprisingly impressed with Matthew's reply.

"No Gentile or Samaritan cities," Jesus instructed. "Go to the lost sheep of the house of Israel."

Nodding, Simon thought, *I hope I won't be assigned to Judas, Philip, Thomas, or Nathanael either.*

"Heal the sick, cleanse lepers, and cast out demons in my name," Jesus instructed. "I am sending you like gentle sheep in the midst of wolves. I want you to be as wise as serpents but as harmless as doves." He nodded. "Be very careful."

Simon could feel his apprehension rise.

"Beware," Jesus repeated, "you will be delivered up to the courts. You will be whipped in the churches and synagogues."

Simon glanced at the others. Andrew's eyes were on the ground, while John was looking at a nearby hill. The others were all wide-eyed.

"Do not be afraid of them who are able to kill your physical body but not able to kill the soul itself," Jesus concluded. "Rather, fear him who is able to destroy both life and soul in the Gehenna fire."

Simon looked around. *We're all going out, but are we all coming back?* he wondered, swallowing hard. *Will some of us actually be killed? Beaten? Jailed?*

With their packs shouldered, wooden staffs at the ready, and their coin purses empty, Jesus announced the six pairs. "Simon will go with Bartholomew."

Simon exhaled. *I'd rather be with Andrew, John, or James, but I could have done worse.*

"Judas will team up with Simon the Zealot. James with Andrew. John with James the Lesser. Thomas will go with Philip, and Matthew with Thaddeus." Smiling gently, the master then offered instructions on when they should reconvene at their current location.

Without complaint, the six teams started out for all four corners of the wind—determined to heal the sick and spread the gospel.

The trip lasted several weeks.

When the apostles returned from the road covered in dust, hugs were exchanged all around. Jesus smiled from ear to ear while the weary men debriefed, reporting all they had said and done in Jesus's name.

"I'm still amazed at all we were able to accomplish through the powers we've been given," Matthew called out, getting them started.

"We preached to thousands, telling everyone that the kingdom of heaven is at hand," Simon quickly reported, trying not to sound too prideful. "Even the pain in my foot has passed. I've been toughened up enough to take on anything now." He was hardly referring to his blisters.

Chuckling, Bartholomew nodded in agreement. "Thousands of believers," he echoed.

"Although James and I had no money," John said, "we still ate well and were offered shelter whenever we needed it."

"That's the truth," James the Lesser added. "We lived on whatever alms were given us." He nodded. "We were met with kindness whenever it was needed."

Just as Jesus told us, Simon thought, *to be like the birds of the air and the lilies of the field.* He realized that this solo mission had given all of them a chance to put the rabbi's teachings into practice. *This ministry is a way of life,* he realized. *We may be poor, but we're happy and will always be well taken care of.*

Jesus maintained his infectious smile.

"It was also exhausting," Thomas reported, being honest.

Philip agreed. "And although we were rejected and chased at times, we were still able to heal many of the sick."

"Even healing diseases and casting out demons in your name, Jesus," Thomas added, jumping back in.

As they broke bread together, they sat for hours, sharing stories and much laughter. The camaraderie was thick, and their sense of accomplishment was palpable. Jesus remained quiet, listening to grown men who sounded like excited children, sometimes cutting one another off to add a detail they'd just remembered.

Simon looked at Jesus, thinking, *This must be part of Jesus's master plan—sending us out into the world to gather more followers.* He nodded to himself. *On our own, even when he is not there.*

It was late before Simon found himself alone. Laying prone, he looked up into the clear night sky, marveling at the countless stars that twinkled and shimmered above. They brought him back to his boat on the Sea of Galilee. *I miss Capernaum,* he thought, picturing his sturdy boat tied to the dock. He envisioned taking his catch to market, then returning home to his wife. *Oh, my beautiful wife.* He really missed her but knew, *This is where I belong.* Given their recent travels and the lessons learned, he was more convinced of that than ever.

As his mind continued to drift off into the firmament above, he considered heaven. *I wonder what it will be like?* He immediately pictured Jesus's face and smiled. *Heaven is on earth now.*

The group hadn't been reunited for long when John the Baptist's disciples caught up to them again.

"John the Baptist has been killed," they announced. "Herod has had him decapitated, his head delivered on a platter, as his new wife requested."

Monsters! Simon thought, feeling sick to his stomach.

"We claimed his body and buried him," they told Jesus, a hint of resentment in their tone. The dreadful news took the air out of everyone's chest, especially Andrew's.

Simon immediately went to his brother. "Remember," he told Andrew, "Jesus said that there was no greater man."

"I know, Simon. But it still bothers me that we didn't do anything," Andrew whimpered, "that Jesus didn't do anything."

I don't understand that either, Simon thought but kept it to himself. Instead, he took the opportunity to repeat his wise brother's own words. "Jesus knows what he's doing, Andrew. Have some faith."

With a single nod, Andrew walked off to mourn alone.

Simon was also shaken. *I can't believe this. John opened my eyes to the truth and baptized me. Because of him, we met Jesus. How can he just be gone like this?*

Simon looked at Jesus, his concern shifting to his master. For the first time that Simon could recall, Jesus looked disheartened, making him feel his teacher's pain. If there were ever any doubts about Jesus being human, then the news of John's beheading dispelled that. *Jesus is certainly divine, but he's also a man,* Simon thought. *A man who hurts deeply.*

Jesus's sorrow was palpable. And yet, Simon could not understand. *He has saved so many others. Why not his own beloved cousin?*

John's unjust death seemed to focus on a new and urgent phase, with Jesus and the apostles escaping from the large crowds of Capernaum. John's execution had offered them all a frightening glimpse into the real dangers of their mission.

Casting off from the dock, they sailed all day until arriving in the wilderness on the eastern shore.

It'll be good to be away from the crowds for a while, Simon thought as they erected their camp for the night.

Eastern shores, Sea of Galilee, Galilee

The next morning, a small congregation of believers turned into hundreds. Even women had begun to appear, including Mary Magdalene. Followers contributed to Judas Iscariot's bag of coins, carried in his girdle to feed the poor.

The crowd has found us again, Simon thought, hoping that Jesus would dismiss them so they could move on. "Lord, can you send them away now?" he prodded Jesus.

But Jesus pitied the poor. He had compassion on them because they were like sheep without a shepherd. He began to preach and heal the sick.

This went on for hours, with Jesus sending no one away.

The day was growing late when Simon again suggested that Jesus dismiss them. "They have been here for hours, and this is a remote area with no food. They should be thinking about shelter and something to eat while there is still time to find both."

"There is no need for them to go away," Jesus said. "Give them something to eat yourselves."

"We don't have anywhere near enough to feed this crowd," Simon advised, thinking, *There must be five thousand men here, plus women and children!*

"How many loaves of bread do you have?" Jesus asked.

"We have only five loaves of bread and two fish, not nearly enough for a crowd this size."

Jesus smiled. "Tell the people to take a seat in the grass."

Taking the half-empty basket of loaves and the two wrapped fish, Jesus looked up to heaven and asked for God's blessing in prayer. He then broke the loaves of bread, handing them to his disciples.

As the disciples began passing out the bread, they realized it kept coming—one new loaf after the next. Simon marveled that they could not pass out the bread and fish fast enough. An excited murmur traveled through the crowd. It was as though many of them had not eaten for days. People pushed and shoved to claim their share. Greedy hands, large and small, reached out toward Simon and the others. As joyful as the scene appeared, it was equally frightening. *This crowd has become a mob, reduced to fulfilling their basic human needs*, Simon thought. Mothers were more aggressive than men twice their size, resolute in feeding their hungry children.

The line stretched long, with fish and bread being handed out in rapid succession.

Throughout it all, the baskets remained full.

At one point, Simon looked at Jesus. His master smiled; this was not a proud smile but one of pure contentment.

This is how a real shepherd feeds his sheep, Simon thought. In many ways, he still did not understand. It was the truth of Jesus's words—not bread and fish—that would sustain his people for all time.

It took more than two hours to feed the enormous crowd. When they had all eaten and were satisfied, the inspired crowd praised Jesus, giving him thanks. "Hallelujah!" they chanted. "Crown him king! Crown him king!"

In complete agreement, Simon thoroughly enjoyed the crowd's deafening call to power. He looked out onto the swaying thousands and thought, *We have an army big enough to face the Romans.* The fantasy thrilled him even more than the miracle he'd just participated in.

The crowd's chants grew louder, angrier. Simon could see that their enthusiasm was starting to boil over, threatening to become chaotic, even violent. Many were working themselves up into a froth, demanding that they, "March on Jerusalem!"

Jesus stopped the escalating collusion with his commanding voice. "No!" he told them before dispelling the idea that he would not forcibly take his place on any throne.

But why not? Simon wondered. He not only felt disappointed, he felt discouraged.

Escaping the unruly crowd and heading for the shore, Jesus told his apostles, "Sail on without me."

Simon was taken aback, his trepidation speeding up his breathing. "But, Rabbi..."

"Go back, all of you, across the sea, and leave me here," Jesus commanded.

By now, most of the crowd had dispersed but not all. Simon looked at Jesus, then at the crowd, and then back to Jesus. "But, Master, some of these people are..." He paused. "We do not know who is among them."

"Oh, Simon..."

"Jesus," he interrupted, "I'm sorry, but we cannot leave you here alone."

Jesus gestured toward the iron-colored sky. "I am never alone, Simon, not ever."

Simon wanted his words to be true. He had no doubt that angels protected them—especially Jesus. But he still felt uneasy, a feeling that was becoming all too familiar. *Maybe he wants to be alone to pray?* Simon reasoned. *He certainly loves his time alone.*

"Go, at once," Jesus insisted, "while there is still enough light to shove off."

Simon, Andrew, James, John, and the others lingered near the shore until it was nearly dark, still hoping Jesus would reconsider.

He didn't.

Reluctantly, they pushed away from the beach, hoping to catch a late breeze for Capernaum. From the first oar stroke, questions of how Jesus would get back flew around the boat's congested deck.

Simon looked toward the dark sky. *Please, Yahweh,* he prayed, *shroud Jesus in Your angels and keep our master safe.*

CHAPTER 12

WHO DO MEN SAY I AM?

Sea of Galilee, Galilee

As they reached open water, Simon and the others shared their apprehensions. "How do you think Jesus will get back?" John asked, concerned.

James shrugged. "Well, he had a free ride ..." he muttered. No one laughed.

"Truth be told, I'm done worrying about Jesus," Andrew commented, surprising them all. "What's the use? He's so much more capable than any of us, and he has more protection than we could ever provide."

Taking offense, Simon huffed—even though he knew his brother spoke the truth.

Andrew's head gestured toward the starboard side of the boat. A dark, angry bank of clouds was quickly rolling in. "It's us that I'm more worried about right now," he said.

The ashen sky was turning ominous. Studying the horizon, Simon shook his head. "Looks like we might be in for a good storm," he agreed.

"Doesn't look like there will be anything good about it," John said.

Andrew addressed the apostles who were not fishermen. "Hold on tight, men. We may be in for a wild ride."

Under a heavy gale, the sail was taken down. The men took up three sets of oars, fighting to keep the bow windward in the stinging rain. Early night had set in over the water. With Simon at the tiller, the wind began to shriek, kicking up waves that swelled to perilous heights.

While cold water splashed onto the deck, John leaned against the boat's center mast.

Surveying the oncoming storm, he shook his worried head. For a moment, he and Simon exchanged a look—both knowing that this dangerous scene was reminiscent of the time Jesus had calmed the sea.

Only he's not with us this time, Simon realized, feeling a different wave roll over him—fear. His breathing became shallow and labored, while his heart began to thump in his chest—all of it concealed from the men who counted on him to captain the boat.

As the rough waters threw the boat about like a fishing bobber, James tossed out their anchor into a sea as black as the sky.

Simon, Andrew, John, and James had lived and worked on the open water since they could walk. Each man knew this was a treacherous situation.

Racked with doubt and fear, Simon's life flashed before his eyes. *My poor wife is too young to become a widow,* he thought. Yet something deep inside him promised that he had more roads to travel and much more to do.

"The sea is a bit scorned this evening," James called out. "She must have missed us." He finally received some nervous laughter.

"It will die down soon enough," Simon told them, determined to remain their leader, even in the most frightening times. *Especially then,* he thought. *And if I can convince them, then maybe I can believe it myself.*

"A spirit!" John screamed out. "There's a spirit walking on the water!"

Simon looked in the direction of his friend's pointing finger. An apparition—the distinct silhouette of a man—was levitating just above the waves, gliding toward them.

Gasping for the air that had been snatched from his lungs, Simon's knees buckled, nearly yanking him to the soaked deck. Even as terror struck his heart, he somehow managed to remain upright.

As the approaching ghost became larger and more visible, Simon fought off the symptoms that threatened to paralyze him—shortness of breath, a palpitating heart. As if it were a distant dream, he could hear the others yelling, the frantic hum of their voices sounding like terrified children.

Having grown up on the water, Simon had learned to hoist a sail before he could read a single word in Hebrew. *I thought I'd seen everything.* But this vision, this apparition, caused him to rub his eyes until they stung.

The ghost turned toward them. "Be of good cheer," it said. "Take courage. It's me."

I know that voice, Simon thought, recognizing his master's parental tone. "It's Jesus!" he shouted to his brothers, thrilled to see his master safe—even if Jesus was doing the impossible by wandering upon the waves. As if a switch were thrown, all of Simon's fear was replaced by love and a longing he'd never known. "Lord, if it is really you," he yelled above the whistling wind, "then bid me to walk out on the water to you!"

"Come," Jesus called back to him, holding out his hands.

Without thinking, Peter climbed over the side of the boat, stepping out onto the waves. He took one step, and then two. Looking down at his feet, he realized, *I'm walking on water.* But as his faith relapsed to fear, he began to sink. "Lord, save me," he wailed, filled with panic. "Save me!"

Jesus grabbed him by the robe, hoisting him above the waves. "Oh, you of little faith. Simon, why did you doubt?" he asked, a hint of disappointment in his voice. Holding Simon by the arm, the strapping carpenter helped him back onto the boat.

Simon felt like a young boy again, being corrected by his father. But instead of his usual impulsive reaction, he was frozen in a state of reverence and humility.

All at once, the winds complained no more and the waves subsided, the tumultuous water becoming flat and lifeless.

The other apostles bowed their heads. "Truly," they told Jesus, "you are the Son of God."

Simon Peter sat in the bow, catching his breath. *I just walked on water,* he realized. *It was only a couple seconds, a few steps, but I walked on water!* He also realized that he performed this miraculous feat without thinking. *It's when I took my eyes off Jesus and started to think about it—that's when I was at risk of drowning.* He looked at Jesus. *Maybe that's been my problem all along? Maybe I just need to believe without having to understand how or why?*

Feeling the eyes of the other apostles upon him, Simon looked up. Although no one uttered a single word, their gazes spoke volumes. Andrew was emotional, his eyes filled with tears. He had witnessed something a brother never expects to see. In awe, John and James also gawked at Simon, their brown eyes betraying love and a deep respect for his newly elevated position within the group.

Without ego playing any role, Simon could understand how they felt. He had gone to a place where none of them had—*at least not yet.* Jesus had just separated "the rock" from the rest of the pack.

Through unbroken eye contact, both reverence and loving support were offered to Simon by the other apostles as well.

I'm the last person they ever expected to be exalted, Simon thought, dumbfounded. *I'm the last person I ever expected.*

Composing himself, Simon's thoughts flashed to his wife, his hometown, and friends, as he realized he would never be able to do this day justice in the retelling. *Fortunately, that won't be a problem.* His brother and best friends were right there with him, seeing and hearing the very same miracles and wonders. *What a blessing,* he thought, also realizing that this was not by chance. He looked down at his soaked sandals. *Wait until my love hears about this!*

Capernaum, Galilee

Upon their return, a pomegranate sun rose over beautiful Capernaum. Simon shared a few days with his wife, spending every second he could with her. *The fishing can wait.*

He was so happy—and relieved—to unpack all that had happened. "We were caught in a terrible storm until Jesus commanded the wind and the water to be still," he explained. "He then healed a man who was possessed by many demons, casting the evil spirits into a herd of swine that stampeded off a cliff to their death."

"What?"

He nodded, also telling her about the woman who was healed by touching Jesus's cloak, the daughter of Jairus who was raised from the dead, and the miracle of the multiplying loaves and fishes.

"Wow," she said, "that's a lot."

You should have been there, he thought, nodding again. "Oh, and I walked on water with Jesus. It was only a few steps, but..."

"Wait... what?"

After filling her in on the details, as well as how the experience had made him feel, Simon turned quiet.

"Maybe we should invite Andrew, John, and James over for dinner?" she suggested.

"Not yet. Tomorrow is better," he said. "I need time alone with you." He shook his head. "Besides, I spend more than enough time with those oxen."

In the days that followed, word of the loaves and fishes spread, and people sought out Jesus, pursuing more free food. "Rabbi, when did you come here?" they demanded to know.

"You are only looking for me because you are hungry again," Jesus told the crowd. "Don't seek the bread that fails. You're not here because you saw signs and wonders, but because you think I'll feed you. Don't work so hard for the bread that will perish. Instead, seek the food that endures to eternal life, which the Son of Man will give you. For God the Father has put His seal of approval on him."

This was as confusing to the apostles as it was to the horde.

What is this everlasting food that he's going to give them? Simon wondered, taken aback.

They came all this way, and he speaks to them in such a harsh tone? He could empathize, understanding the sting that Jesus's admonishments could bring.

One particular day, Jesus was preaching in Capernaum's large white synagogue to a crowd that was becoming unsettled.

Eager to catch the rabbi in something, anything, Pharisees from Jerusalem were planted throughout the congregation. "What must we do in order to perform the works of God?" they asked.

"This is the work of God," replied Jesus, "that you believe in him whom He sent."

The Pharisees bristled.

Watching from a distance, Simon enjoyed the show. *This one's between Jesus and the Pharisees.* Although he didn't like the religious leaders, he knew, *It's not my fight.*

The rabbi continued. "Indeed, indeed, I say to you, it was not Moses who gave you the bread from heaven, but it is my Father who gives you the true bread from heaven. For the bread of God is that which comes down from heaven and gives life to the world." To the Pharisees, he said, "I am the bread of life."

"Isn't this Jesus from Nazareth?" one of them called out. "Don't we know his mother and father?"

This began to turn the people against Jesus, and the Pharisees were loving it.

"How can he now say, 'I came down from heaven'?" the Pharisees argued, happy to stir the pot.

"No one can come to me, unless the Father who sent me draws him; and I will raise them up on the last day. I am the bread of life," he repeated. "If anyone eats of this bread, he shall live forever... the bread which I will give as my flesh for the life of the world."

Simon hardly expected this strange talk about eternal bread. *Eating flesh?* He tried to dismiss the idea. *I'm confused enough,* he thought, counting more than a few religious authorities amid the crowd, gossiping and looking for any opportunity to turn the people against Jesus. *And Jesus is making it easy for them,* he thought, watching as the crowd grew more dismayed.

"I'm telling you this," Jesus added, "unless you eat of the flesh of the Son of Man and drink his blood, you have no life in yourselves. He who eats my flesh and drinks my blood possesses life everlasting, and I will raise him up at the last day. For my flesh is real food, and my blood is real drink."

This was beyond difficult to understand, with Simon cringing at the words. *What is Jesus doing?* Simon thought. *How can he give us his flesh to eat and blood to drink?*

Many in the crowd were beside themselves. *Eating flesh?* Simon repeated. *Drinking blood?*

The Pharisees were delighted.

Disgusted with this barbaric, cannibalistic talk, some of Jesus's followers stormed out of the synagogue.

Simon looked to his brothers. They appeared to be equally bewildered. Considering all that they'd sacrificed to be here, Simon's heart sank. *This is not good,* he thought.

Even more of the crowd began to disperse. "This is hard to listen to," they complained, many of them intent on following Jesus no more.

Jesus quickly gave his discouraged group of apostles the same opportunity. He looked straight at Simon, asking, "Are you going to leave me too?"

The simple question triggered a visceral reaction in Simon's body that he did not expect. *How could he even ask me this? After all we've been through.* Simon quickly recalled everything they'd experienced together—from being run out of Nazareth to the constant danger, even leaving his wife and the sea he loved. *Never!* he thought. *I will be with you until the end of time.* Knowing nothing would ever change that, he looked directly into Jesus's eyes. "Lord, where shall we go?" he asked. "You have the words of truth about living forever, and we have believed, and we know that you are the holy one of God."

Jesus's gaze rested on him for a never-ending moment.

Simon was surprised that he'd found the right words, words that came from his heart and not his head. *Maybe I really do think too much?* he pondered. *When I don't overthink it, I usually get it right.*

Jesus finally nodded, turning his eyes one by one to each of the apostles, until looking directly at Judas Iscariot. "There are some of you, however, who do not believe," he admonished. "I have told you that no one can come to me unless it is granted him by the Father." He took a deep breath, exhaling. "Did I not choose you, the twelve? Yet one of you is a devil."

Feeling Jesus's angst, Simon scanned the group before stopping at Judas. *Oh, Yahweh be with you.*

For her husband's last homecooked meal for a while, Simon's wife prepared goat stew with salted root vegetables.

"You're the best," he told her, as the delicious gravy dripped into his beard. Simon also filled his belly with leftover roasted fish, expertly seasoned and deboned—all of it washed down with more than a few sips of their best wine.

"This isn't the lavish banquet I've grown accustomed to," he joked, "but it will do." Laughing, she dished out more.

Although Simon would never worry her with such details, there were nights when hope and camaraderie were the group's only sustenance. *And no one ever complains,* he thought.

Later, as they said their goodbyes at the door, he whispered into her ear, "I'll be back when I can."

She kissed his cheek. "I know. Don't worry. We are well," she whispered back. "Just be safe."

Passing through the threshold, he tapped the mezuzah and then kissed the fingers that touched it. "I will," he called back to her.

Jesus and his disciples headed straight for the sea, en route to the Syrian–Phoenician region northeast of Galilee. They traveled the trails off the main roads by day, camping out at night.

One morning, a woman began questioning Simon about Jesus. "I have heard many stories about Jesus of Nazareth and his miracles," she said.

Smiling politely, Simon ignored her and moved on.

Returning the next day, she asked, "Where is Jesus of Nazareth? My daughter is possessed by a demon, and I wish to ask that he come and heal her."

Simon and the others tried to shoo her away. They were still shaken by the last angry crowd in Capernaum, along with the loss of so many followers. *We don't need another miracle right now and all the attention it attracts,* Simon thought.

Finally, Simon informed Jesus about the relentless woman. "You have told us not to go into Gentile areas and to only minister to the lost sheep of the House of Israel. So we have sent her away, but she has been quite persistent."

Jesus nodded but said nothing.

Eventually finding them, the woman hurried over. As she approached Jesus, she fell to her knees and grabbed him by the ankles. "Help me, Jesus," she sobbed. "Please help me. My daughter is possessed by a demon."

Stooping to help remove her, Simon was halted by Jesus's gentle hand.

Messiah looked at the woman. "It is not fit to take the children's meat and cast it to the dogs. The children must first be filled."

"Yes, Lord, that is true," she agreed, "but still the dogs eat of the crumbs that fall from the children's table."

Both of Jesus's eyebrows rose in surprise. "Woman, you have great faith. It will be done unto you exactly as you wish." He then told her, "Go home; your daughter will be healed."

As the apostles huddled together, Judas commented, "A woman?"

This time, it was John who did the rebuking. "Well, Judas, it looks like in the eyes of Jesus, we're all equal."

"Imagine that?" Andrew said, poking fun at their smug treasurer.

Following this discussion, Simon expected that they would break camp and leave.

Instead, Jesus lingered, as though he were waiting for the perseverant woman's return.

And she did return, bringing a crowd with her. As the good news spread, the crowd swelled, many looking for their own loved ones to also be healed.

For three days, Jesus did just that, noticing that most of them had not eaten for the entire time. Taking seven loaves of bread and several small fish, he then repeated the miracle of multiplication—this time, for a crowd of four thousand.

As fast as Simon and his brothers could dig the smoked fish and bread out of the baskets, hungry hands were waiting to snatch up the divine gifts. And as quickly as the fish and loaves of bread were handed out, the baskets were replenished—never emptying.

Even though Simon had seen this same miracle before, he was still amazed. *I like this type of work much better than inciting a crowd to anger,* he thought. *When Jesus is healing and feeding our people, we live a different life ... a safer life.*

Once again, the Pharisees complained as Jesus's followers had eaten with unwashed hands.

"You hypocrites!" Jesus roared, reprimanding them.

That's a compliment for them, Simon thought, gagging on the same hypocrisy that Jesus detested.

To Simon's relief, they finally left the area the next day and headed out into the great unknown again.

For four long days, Simon spent the travel time in deep thought, much of it focused on the days of glory that were sure to come.

As the self-appointed bodyguard and protector of Messiah, he continually questioned his own fighting abilities. No one could ever deny that he was a tough guy. He had made a hard living on the water as a heavy-handed fisherman. He'd been in more than his share of fistfights. *But I'm no trained centurion who has taken lives,* Simon thought. *There's a difference between being tough and being trained,* he realized. *When the time comes, I'll just have to rely on my passion and wits to protect the rabbi,* he told himself. *There's no way those will ever fail me.*

As they walked up the Jordan Valley heading north for the fifth day, Simon daydreamed about being one of Jesus's field generals, helping his leader crush the Romans. Simon imagined the skies opening, the vivid fantasy causing goose bumps to cover his body. *Bolts of lightning and thunder raining down on stampeding stallions and crashing chariots.* He could hear combat-hardened soldiers screaming for their lives. The well-deserved wails made him smile. *After all the pain and suffering the Roman dogs have caused us, I can't wait to hear each one of their pathetic cries.* He imagined legions of angels descending from the clouds, brandishing swords. They slashed their terrified enemies down—one confused column after the next. *Victory,* Simon thought. "Sweet victory," he muttered aloud.

"A shekel for your thoughts," Jesus told him, appearing beside him. Simon shrugged. "Nothing," he said.

Shaking his head, Jesus laughed. "Most thoughts are best when they remain just thoughts."

Simon opened his mouth to counter but thought better of it. *Point taken.* Jesus smiled, before gesturing toward their campsite for the night.

Caesarea Philippi, Syro-Phoenicia

Rising before the sun, they marched up the valley on half-empty bellies, marveling at the beautiful landscapes. As the troop traveled north, rolling meadows, broken up by the occasional hilltop, glistened in the breaking light. Mount Hermon appeared purple in the distance, the grazing white sheep in the foreground matching the mountain's snowy peak.

Eyes wide, Simon attempted to describe the majestic panorama in one word: *Serene.*

At one point, they reached a nook where water from the Jordan River flowed across the tangerine-colored rocks.

As a few of the disciples gathered fallen olives and almonds, Simon was gawking at the mighty oaks when a partridge sang out, welcoming them.

Arriving at a steep hillside on the southern slope of Mount Hermon, Simon decided there was no better view of the Jordan Valley in the Galilean hills. *Just incredible*, he thought, inhaling the warm, sweet air.

"We have reached Caesarea Philippi," Jesus announced, pointing at the city that had been rebuilt by Herod in honor of Emperor Augustus.

At Caesarea Philippi, they passed by the Palace of Agrippa, moving on to the Banias Springs—the headwater of the Jordan River itself.

Simon and the rest had only heard of this distant legendary place. Nearly to Lebanon in the north, he could only wonder why Jesus would bring them so far.

Jesus instructed them to camp and bathe in the crystal-clear spring waters of the Jordan.

The next morning, Jesus gathered the group in front of the Temple of Pan. Simon knew these pagan temples were for the Romans and, before them, the Greeks. *Why would Jesus bring us to this place?* he wondered. *Some sort of important announcement, I guess.*

Jesus asked his apostles, "Who do men say I, the Son of Man, really am?"

"Some claim you're Jeremiah, Isaiah, Elijah, or one of the other prophets," they answered.

"And who do you say that I am?"

The apostles looked at one another, reluctant to answer.

Without hesitation, Simon stepped forward. "You are the Christ, the Son of the living God."

Jesus smiled wide. "Blessed are you, Simon bar Jonas, for flesh and blood have not revealed this to you but my Father, who is in heaven. And I also tell you that you are a rock, and upon this rock I will build my *ekklesia* [church], and the gates of hell shall not overpower it. And I will give to you the keys of the kingdom of heaven, and whatever you shall bind on earth shall be bound in heaven, as whatever you shall unbind on earth shall be unbound in heaven."

Simon nodded his humble gratitude, feeling his face flush.

After more than two years, Jesus had finally explained the meaning of the name Peter [Cephas].

When alone, Simon and his trusted confidants processed the experience in whispers. "Did you hear that?" he asked.

"Every word," Andrew replied.

"Upon this rock, I will build my *ekklesia*?" Simon repeated, his tone inferring more question than statement.

"*Ekklesia*—his religious congregation," John explained. "His flock."

Simon looked at him, still grasping for meaning. His mind suddenly flashed back more than two years, recalling when Jesus had said to him, "You are Simon. You will be called Peter."

"His church, Simon," Andrew said, breaking his trance, "the entire body of Jesus's believers."

"That's why Jesus calls you the rock!" John interjected joyfully. "You finally know."

Simon Peter felt happy and flattered, but it was still all a bit hazy to him. *Obviously, I should feel honored, but what does it really mean? What am I expected to do as ... the rock?*

CHAPTER 13

NEVER ALONE

On the road, Syro-Phoenicia

On their way back to Galilee, they stopped for some much-needed rest and a few gulps of water. "It's good that you know who I am, that I am the Christ," Jesus told the apostles, seated in the shade, "but keep it to yourselves. Do not try to convince anyone I am the Christ. My time has not yet come."

Simon could not fathom why. *If the time is not now, then when?* he wondered. *In Jerusalem for the Passover?*

"I am going to have to suffer many terrible things," Jesus explained, "indignities and tortures. The ones behind it will be the chief priests and the Pharisees. I will be delivered into their hands to be killed. But after the third day, I will rise from the dead."

Simon didn't even remember getting to his feet. All he knew was that he had grabbed Jesus by both shoulders. "Never, Lord!" he barked. "I would never let them take you. Don't say such things!" He was filled with a fearful rage. "Nothing like that will ever happen to you!" he promised, thinking, *Not while I'm around.*

Jesus's loving eyes narrowed, while his mouth twisted to a terrible scowl. "Get behind me, Satan," he rebuked his chief apostle. "You are a stumbling block to me. The things you say are not the things of God but the things of men." This time, Jesus's tone was not merely disappointed; he sounded disgusted or angry—or both.

Losing the air in his lungs, Simon felt like a child on the brink of tears. He struggled to compose himself in front of the others.

Calming himself with a few cleansing breaths, Jesus said, "Listen," gesturing that all his apostles gather closer to him. "If anyone desires to come after me, let him deny himself and take up his cross daily and follow me. For whoever wishes to save his life shall lose it. But whoever loses his life for my sake, he shall save it."

What? Simon thought, still shaking off the terrible sting of being reprimanded so harshly in front of his peers.

Jesus then chose his words carefully. "For whoever is ashamed of me and my words, of him the Son of Man will be ashamed, when he comes in his glory and the glory of the Father and of the holy angels." Slowly, he met each set of eyes. "What benefit is it for a man to rule over the entire world and yet forfeit his eternal life?" He nodded. "There are some of you here who will not taste of death until they actually see the kingdom of God with power, and the Son of Man coming in the full regalia of his kingdom."

Simon looked to John, and then to Andrew—all eyes wide. But Simon no longer wished to ask the questions they were all wondering. He had been humbled, even embarrassed, into silence—and that really took something for the brash fisherman.

When time and opportunity permitted, Simon slunk off into the shadows to lick his wounds in private.

Scolded by Jesus again, he thought, feeling sick over it. Ordinarily, if he misspoke, he was corrected by his master with patience and gentleness. *But not this time.* Not only was he humiliated in front of the others, but he'd also been left confused and frustrated. *I must have needed a sharper lesson this time.*

Pacing like an expectant father, Simon replayed the scene over and over in his mind. *I shouldn't have grabbed him by the shoulders,* he thought. *I realize that. And I shouldn't have yelled at him the way I did. But 'Get behind me, Satan'? How do I go from high praise—being the rock of his church—to this? Satan? Me, the devil?*

He felt someone standing behind him and turned. It was Andrew.

"Don't be overthinking what just happened, Simon," he said, offering his usual solace.

"How can I not, brother?" Simon asked. "'Get behind me, Satan.' What is that?"

"Jesus still looks to you, Simon. Remember that," Andrew said reassuringly. "Maybe because he's giving you more, he expects more from you?" Andrew slapped his beefy arm.

Simon remained quiet, taking it in.

"There are many who'd do anything to be in your position, brother," Andrew reminded him.

As his compassionate brother walked away, Simon remained in solitude awhile longer, trying to hack away at the bitter root of negative thinking. Focusing on Jesus's message made it less painful.

Take up his cross daily? he thought. *Another mystery that's beyond me.* He shook his head. *I'm willing to fight and to sacrifice, but I have no idea what Jesus is talking about.*

That night, the confusion settled in even deeper. Unsure of how to deal with it, Simon decided, *I need to pray.* Remembering the Lord's Prayer that Jesus had taught on that crowded hill, he went to his knees. "Our Father who art in heaven, hallowed be Thy name. Thy kingdom come, Thy will be done, as in heaven, so on earth. Give us this day our daily bread, and forgive us our debts, as we also have forgiven our debtors. And bring us not into temptation but deliver us from the evil one."

Simon recited the Lord's Prayer again and again, until it became his mantra. It brought a great sense of peace. He had no idea what time he finally fell asleep.

Mount Tabor, Galilee

Nearly one week later on their journey south, they arrived at Mount Tabor. *The master looks miserable,* Simon noted.

Jesus looked up the mountain before turning to address the many followers who had heard of his return. "You will remain here and wait for me." He then pointed at Simon, John, and James. "You three will be with me."

Given his recent scolding, Simon felt excited and even a little proud, until he caught Andrew's disappointed face.

"I'll tell you all about it when we get back," Simon whispered to him.

Andrew smiled. "You'd better."

Then Jesus took Simon, James, and John up the narrow trails to the heights of Tabor.

Simon was winded but happy when they reached the summit. He looked out onto the Galilean world from the summit. *Breathtaking,* he thought, branding the view into his memory.

Exhausted, Jesus allowed the men to nap. Simon had just nodded off when he thought he heard muffled voices—*three men.* Sitting up, he looked around. Clouds of light shrouded the mountain, and the view of Galilee below became obstructed. A bright light was shining around the mysterious conversation. Getting to his feet and moving closer, Simon could make out that Jesus was talking to two other men—whom Jesus referred to as Moses and Elijah.

Could it really be? Simon wondered, listening harder than he'd ever listened to anything in his life. *They're discussing Jesus's death and all that will take place leading up to it in Jerusalem,* he gathered, his heart sinking. *Is this a bad dream?*

But he wasn't dreaming. Jesus, Moses, and Elijah were standing together, deep in discussion.

Simon exchanged shocked looks with John and James. "Are you seeing this?" James whispered.

"We are," John managed, his eyes wide and mouth agape.

Simon addressed Jesus. "Lord, it is good for us to be here," he stammered nervously. "If you wish, I will erect three tents: one for you, one for Moses, and one for Elijah," he suggested, wanting to be helpful.

Suddenly, another cloud overshadowed them from above. Jesus, Moses, and Elijah went silent.

"This is My beloved Son, in whom I am well pleased," a voice from the cloud boomed. "My chosen one; listen to him."

Yahweh! Simon thought, immediately going to his knees and covering his face with his trembling hands. Like a young, frightened child, his entire body shook with fear. Through his clenched fingers, he could see a brighter light begin to pulsate. It took all the courage he could muster to steal a peek. *Oh my...* He gasped.

In a state of divine glory, Jesus was now bathed in brilliant light. He wore a robe of bright white that shimmered and twinkled like a million tiny stars. Moses and Elijah, standing to Jesus's left and right, were also glowing. The supernatural vision was overwhelming to the human senses.

Simon shut his eyes tight, afraid to see or hear anything more. *I am not worthy. I am not...* He then felt his master's loving hand on his shoulder.

"Come on and get up," Jesus said, "and do not be afraid anymore."

Simon did as he was told, only to see that Moses and Elijah had vanished, and that John and James were also emerging from their own cocoons. *Moses and Elijah are gone,* Simon realized, surprised by this.

Getting to his unsteady feet, Simon felt as though he had been dreaming and was just awakened. *I may not know much,* he thought, *but I do know that I've just witnessed a vision of the divine Jesus—a glimpse of him in glory I have never seen or imagined.*

Jesus sat alone for a while, allowing the men to gather their wits.

As they descended the mountain, Jesus instructed the three shaken fishermen, "Be sure you don't tell anyone about this vision until after I have risen from the dead."

Risen from the dead? Simon thought, looking sideways at John and James. *What is going on?*

The experience was so consuming that Simon had completely forgotten about the bitterness he'd carried since being called "Satan." More importantly, his faith had been reconfirmed and fortified, strengthening his resolve for whatever the future might hold.

I didn't know what to expect when we were asked to join Jesus on the mountain, he thought, *but it definitely wasn't this.* Although he couldn't put it into words, he knew that he had witnessed the two sides of Jesus—the divine and the human.

He looked to John and James, unable to read their faces. Both looked catatonic. *We just came closer to seeing heaven than anyone ever has,* he realized, *and I'll never forget it.* He looked at John again. *I hope he writes every detail about this one.*

When they rejoined the other disciples, a crowd had gathered. Several of them asked Simon, John, and James, "What did you witness? Tell us what you experienced up there."

All three men were tight-lipped, sworn to secrecy for the time being.

Andrew glared at Simon.

Simon shrugged. "I can't," he whispered. "I promised the master." Andrew shook his disgusted head.

This will be the hardest secret I'll ever keep, Simon thought, *until Jesus is risen from the dead.* He shook his own head, feeling as lost as ever. *When is he going to rise from the dead? How long will that be?* He scratched at his beard. *He's no older than me, so I'll have to keep his secret for decades.*

Amid the crowd at the foot of the mountain, scribes and Pharisees from Jerusalem were also awaiting them. As Jesus approached them, a man threw himself at the rabbi's feet. "Master, I brought you my son, who has a dumb spirit. He suffers terribly. Whenever the demons grab him, he froths at the mouth and grinds his teeth. I told all of this to your disciples, begging them to cast out the demon from him, but they were not able to."

Jesus looked at his apostles and frowned. "Oh, you faithless generation, how long will I be with you? How long shall I bear with you?" His face softened. "Bring him to me. How long has it been since this has befallen him?"

"From childhood," the boy's father reported, placing his son before Messiah.

"All things are possible to him who believes," Jesus advised.

"Help my unbelief," the man begged, his eyes swollen with hopeful tears.

"You dumb and deaf spirit," Jesus said, placing his hands on the young man, "I command you to come out of him and never enter him again."

The boy's face transformed. Muscles relaxed, jaw loosened, and a smile—meek at first, then beaming—took over his joyous face. Jesus had done it again.

The now-joyful crowd swooned in awe, but Simon couldn't help but feel melancholy. *After seeing what we just saw on that mountaintop...*

Several disciples asked Jesus, "Why couldn't we cast out the demon ourselves?"

"Because of your little faith," Jesus told them. Their eyes dropped to the ground.

"If you have faith like a grain of mustard seed," Jesus said, "you will be able to move a mountain."

Although Simon took this all in, his heart and mind were still on the mountain—witnessing Jesus, Moses, and Elijah congregating together, *and hearing Yahweh's voice thundering down from a cloud.*

Simon had expected to discuss the experience with John and James, but instead he found himself alone in prayer. The sudden outpouring of emotion surprised him as he began to cry. It had been building for many tense weeks. He was not used to feeling this vulnerable. So, he sat alone, allowing himself to weep.

Without hearing anyone approach, Simon turned to his left to find Jesus sitting beside him; tears also glistened in the master's eyes.

Jesus placed his hand on Simon's shoulder. Neither man spoke; neither had to. Simon knew that Jesus could feel his strife. *I'm never alone,* Simon realized, *not ever.*

The apostles finally broke away from the crowd, taking an alternate route east of the Sea of Galilee. On their way, Jesus reminded them again that he would soon go to Jerusalem to meet his own death. "The Son of Man shall be delivered into the hands of men," he explained, "and they will put him to death; and having been put to death, he shall rise again after three days." After all the months of miracles and countless roads traveled together, he was clearly preparing his chosen twelve for darker days.

Although every cell inside Simon wanted to rage out, vowing that he would never let this happen, he kept his mouth shut. *I've learned better,* he thought.

Rise again after three days? Simon questioned again and again as he tromped along, unsure of what the prediction meant. *It doesn't make sense. How could God allow His chosen people to hurt or kill His own Son? I can't see it.* Simon was in terrible conflict. On the mountaintop, he had witnessed Jesus be transformed and had heard God, but he also understood that Jesus was human as well. *If only the high priests and Pharisees could have glimpsed Jesus's transfiguration on the mountain, with Moses and Elijah honoring the Christ.* It didn't make sense. *Messiah can do anything he wishes. Why would he allow his own suffering and death?* He shook his head. *Surely, nothing will happen anytime soon, so we have time.*

Although he felt stymied, Simon remained reluctant toward opening his big mouth. *Only to be reprimanded again? I don't think so.*

Unfortunately, there was a price to pay for his silence as well; it was a balled-up fist sitting in the pit of his aching stomach.

It took many hours, but Simon's galloping mind finally surrendered to sheer physical exhaustion. He fell asleep, his subconscious thoughts taking over.

Jesus led Simon and the others down a rocky road on the outskirts of Samaria.

This is foreign territory, Simon thought, having no idea where the unfamiliar road would lead. *I've never been this way before.* As he walked, he considered the thought and laughed aloud. *I've been walking on faith since the very first step I took with Jesus.* He nodded. *Although I'm in the caravan, I'm definitely not driving it.*

Jesus maintained his fast pace, marching toward the unknown.

They were coming upon the edge of a cliff when Simon recognized the place. *We've been here before,* he realized. *It's where the herd of demon-possessed swine plunged to their deaths.* He looked around, confused. *But this isn't right. This cliff is nowhere near Samaria.*

Jesus kept walking forward, straight to the edge of the cliff.

"No!" Simon screamed out, knowing he had a decision to make—*either stop and save myself, or risk my own life by trying to save my master.* His legs froze, refusing to move another inch. *Go ... hurry!* He commanded himself, but to no avail.

As Jesus disappeared off the cliff ...

Awakening, Simon jumped up, panting like a dog. His heart drummed in his chest. Startled from a sound sleep, he didn't know what was wrong. He couldn't breathe. He couldn't think. *There's something wrong,* he thought, *I ... I need help.* He searched frantically for an enemy. There was none.

Suddenly, he felt a sense of doom overtake him; it was so intense that it felt unbearable. He thought his heart might explode, or worse ... *like I might lose my mind.* He was lightheaded, drunk on fear, making him feel like a man who'd lost all control.

The adrenaline rush was more intense than he'd ever known. But when he searched out the reason for it, there was nothing there; no threat or danger for him to defend himself or run from, which made things even more confusing. *What is happening?*

When his legs no longer felt tethered by invisible chains, Simon leapt out of his bedroll and stumbled out of the shelter. Trying to catch his bearings, he stumbled through the small desolate campsite. Each one of his senses were heightened—the smell of burnt hardwood filled his nostrils, while the sounds of animals rustling in the underbrush pounded in his ears. The sky was clear, the air crisp and heavy on his sweaty skin.

Matthew stepped out of his tent. "Is anything wrong, Simon?" he asked, genuinely concerned.

Simon took a deep breath. "Never better," he fibbed, forcing a smile. *It was only a nightmare,* he told himself.

Unconvinced, Matthew slowly returned to his tent.

I need to find peace, Simon thought, heading back to his own makeshift shelter. *I need to pray.*

As Jesus and his apostles traveled back to the Sea of Galilee, Simon couldn't walk fast enough. *I don't know how I'm going to explain everything to my wife, but I need to try.* He gave it some thought. *She'll say I only had a nightmare, but it's what led up to that nightmare that ...* He stopped, sighing. *Maybe I just need rest?* he thought. *Hopefully, she can help me make sense of it all.*

CHAPTER 14

OPEN YOUR EYES

Capernaum, Galilee

Upon their return to Capernaum, Jesus and his weary entourage received a cool reception. The crowd had begun to turn sour on Jesus. Simon couldn't believe it. *This is worse than I could have imagined.*

"Eat his flesh, indeed!" one of them called out. "Beelzebub!" another yelled at Jesus. "Samaritan!" a man yelled out in their direction.

The scribes and Pharisees have done their work well, Simon thought, his blood pressure rising north. But if he were being honest with himself, he didn't understand the flesh and blood lesson either. *I'm certainly not the most educated or cultured man, but I've never considered myself a simpleton either. But this one's way over my head.* He felt ignorant—childlike. *I should be able to understand my teacher by now. I've been following him for long enough ... almost blindly.*

Regardless, Simon also knew he was not going to stop following Jesus. *I'm fully committed.* Even when Simon's mind could not understand, his heart provided certainty.

Staring at the hometown crowd, Simon Peter gagged on equal doses of shock and rage. *They bore witness when the Roman centurion's son was healed by Jesus,* he thought. *All the signs and wonders, the countless miracles—overflowing our nets with fish, healing Eema, even healing a paralytic in my own home—and they've already forgotten?*

Simon Peter was beside himself. Every ounce of pride he'd felt when his people had embraced Jesus was now replaced by uneasiness. *I don't know why, but I feel shaken,* he realized. *I know what Jesus has done. Who he is,* he thought, *and these people changing their minds is unacceptable!* Simon wasn't just offended by this; he felt betrayed. *And I don't see myself turning the other cheek so they'll be able to hurt me even more.*

Simon returned home to his wife, where a long kiss and a hearty soup of barley and lentils awaited him. A basket of leavened bread for dipping also sat on the table.

There's no greater blessing than a good woman, he thought, knowing this was really saying something, given everything he had witnessed.

As he devoured his meal, Simon told his wife, "I realize that talk of eating flesh and drinking blood is not sitting well with many." He chewed a few times. "But since we've been gone, it looks like nearly everyone has turned against Jesus. How?"

"The high priests have been busy," she explained.

He nodded. *I figured.*

"Enough about them," she said. "Tell me everything that's happened to you since we were last together."

What should I share? he wondered, stalling. *I need to feel normal right now, even if only for a few hours.*

"What is it?" she asked.

Skipping past the miraculous vision on Mount Tabor, he said, "Jesus was explaining how he would suffer and die in Jerusalem, so when I grabbed him by the shoulders and—"

"You grabbed him, Simon?" she asked, surprised.

He nodded. "Not my finest moment, but I needed him to know that I'd never stand by and watch anything bad happen to him."

She went quiet. "And how did he respond?"

He swallowed another bite. "He called me ... Satan."

"He what?" she blurted, her brow collapsing into a low, defensive posture. "Why would he ever call you the devil? After all you've ..." She stopped. "What are you going to do, Simon?" she asked. "You plan to stay with him, right?"

"Of course, I do!" he said, his tone louder than he had intended. "I still don't understand what he meant by that," he said, shrugging, "but I think we've gotten past it."

She studied him for a moment, the same way his mother would when he was a rambunctious boy prone to telling half-truths. "If you say so," she said, ladling more soup into his favorite clay bowl.

After dinner, Simon lay down to rest his eyes. He was nearly asleep when he heard his wife clearing her throat.

Really?

Opening one eye, he saw her sitting on the edge of their bed.

"I'm sorry to wake you, husband, but there are three tax collectors at the door. And they've asked to speak to you."

Simon went out to greet them, his chest already feeling as tight as a drum. *Too bad Matthew isn't here to negotiate,* he thought.

"Does your master pay the temple tax?" one of them asked.

A few people had begun to gather outside of his door to listen to the exchange.

"Ya ... yes," Simon babbled, "of course he does."

No sooner had the words left his chapped lips than he knew he should have kept them sealed. *Stupid*, he scolded himself. *They set a trap, and I stepped right into it. Stupid!*

Jesus had awakened and stepped up from behind Simon. "The kings of the world," he bellowed, helping his apostle. "What is your opinion, Simon? From whom do earthly kings take tolls or taxes? From their own sons or from other people?"

Simon said, "From other people."

"Therefore, the sons must be free," Jesus added, surveying the publicans. He turned to Simon. "But unless we want to give them a reason to go against us, Simon Peter, go down to the lake and cast the hook. Look into the mouth of the first fish you catch, and you will find a shekel. Take the coin to these men to cover the temple's tax tribute from both of us."

"A fish?" Simon asked. "With a shekel in its mouth?"

"Do as I say," Jesus insisted.

Later, as Simon made his way to the dock, he continued to shake his head. *Am I missing something again? Is there a hidden meaning behind this ridiculous task? Jesus can't really mean for me to catch a fish and find a coin in its mouth?*

Doubts aside, he did exactly as he was told—using a reed pole and a baited hook.

Within minutes, his pole bent nearly in half, hooking a giant tilapia, as big as any fish found in the Sea of Galilee. *Whoa!* After muscling it in, he hauled it up by its lower jaw and peered into its wide mouth. Sure enough, there was a coin—a shekel—shining brightly. He nearly dropped the flopping fish.

On his way to pay the taxes, Simon's neck grew tired from shaking his head. With the stout fish in one hand and the tax tribute in the other, he thought, *Why should this even surprise me? I've seen hundreds of miracles by now.* He smiled. *This time, it only took one fish to solve our problem.* He looked at the swollen redbelly tilapia. *One with a new shekel in its gaping mouth.*

Stepping up to the publican's barred window, Simon slid the shekel over to him.

"Was it in the fish's mouth?" asked the man hopefully.

"You wouldn't believe me if I told you."

Nodding, the man leaned in closer to Simon. "But I would," he whispered. "I believe Jesus is the Christ."

Smiling, Simon lifted the large fish to show the man. "Just as he said."

The man's eyes widened with approval. "Then it is true!" he said, drawing the Roman sentry's attention. This time, he wasn't whispering.

As Simon walked out and headed for home, he passed two Pharisees who sneered at him. He returned the disapproving look. *The publicans and sinners believe in Jesus,* he thought, *but those who should, do not.* He shook his head. *Another mystery to me.*

Feeling his belly grumble in complaint, he picked up the pace, thinking, *I can't wait to taste what my wife will do with this goliath fish.*

∝•✕

As dinner guests at Simon's home, Jesus and the debt-free apostles gathered in the open courtyard.

Simon's wife and her eema prepared the perfect poor man's feast. They started with flatbread, oil, olives, and cheese. Vegetable stew was served next. The roasted redbelly tilapia was seasoned and cooked to perfection, the flesh falling away from the bones. The delicious entrée was accompanied by cooked greens, the salt cutting through the natural bitterness. A choice of goat milk, water, or wine helped to wash it all down. They had even prepared a sweet dessert of fig and date pies.

"Wonderful meal," Jesus told the women. Everyone agreed, offering their gratitude.

Wonderful, indeed, Simon thought, rubbing his swollen midsection.

At that, Jesus excused himself for a moment.

With the master out of the room, several of the apostles began to discuss their standing in the group.

"Once Jesus's kingdom is established, what positions do you think we'll each hold?" Matthew asked, inciting some lively discussion.

"I hate to break it to everyone," James replied, "but after Simon, John and I are next in command."

"Next in command of what?" Thomas asked.

"Yeah," Philip said, "I can't wait to hear the details."

James was silenced, making them laugh.

"I actually think it should be me," Bartholomew said, keeping a straight face.

"I don't think so," Thomas commented, shaking his head. "I wouldn't follow you to the fish market."

Everyone laughed, Matthew the loudest.

When the ex-publican had composed himself, Andrew cleared his throat for everyone's attention. "Simon has been given the keys to the kingdom, and the power to bind and loose," he said. "What do you think?" He stopped, seeing that Jesus had just returned to the table.

"What were you discussing?" their master asked.

Everyone went silent, sitting upright like children who had just been caught misbehaving. "Um ..." James the Lesser began, with no words to follow.

There was no need to answer, anyway. Jesus already knew. The rabbi slowly surveyed the room, silently making direct eye contact with all twelve of them before he spoke. "If anyone wishes to be first," Jesus said, "he shall be last of all and servant of all." He was skilled at shining a light on human weakness, especially man's temptation toward self-worship.

At that moment, Jesus walked to a window and directed their attention to a small child playing in the courtyard, hiding in the shadows to ambush his playmate.

"Indeed, I tell you," Christ said, smiling as he watched the children play, "unless you turn back and become like little children, you shall by no means enter the kingdom of heaven. Whoever humbles himself like this little child, he is the greatest of the kingdom in heaven." He turned his gaze to meet each of their eyes. "And whoever receives one little child in my name receives me." His face turned ominous. "But whoever causes one of these little ones who believe in me to stumble, it would be better that a great millstone be hung around his neck, and he would drown in the depths of the sea. See that you despise not one of these little ones, for I tell you that these angels always behold the face of my Father, who is in heaven."

Simon studied the small boy, thinking about how Jesus always turned the simple into the profound. *The faith of a child is so modest and calm,* he thought. *They usually don't understand much, but they also don't worry about it. They only need to know that they are loved and taken care of. They'll understand in time ... when they need to.*

As Jesus found Simon's eyes, he smiled proudly at him.

Simon realized that he and the others needed to hear this timely lesson. *We don't always need to understand. We just need to believe.* He looked at his clever teacher and smiled slightly. *I get it. No more needless worrying.* A weight lifted from him, leaving behind a sense of calm that he had not known for weeks. *Just believe,* he repeated to himself.

Jesus received a visit from some of his own relatives asking him to accompany them to the Feast of Tabernacles in Jerusalem. "Manifest yourself to the world," they urged. "Why don't you leave Galilee, Jesus, and go up to Jerusalem, where thousands of your followers are waiting for you? They want to see your miracles and good works. Why instead do you do these things in secret?"

"My time is not yet come," Jesus told them, "but your time is always ready. The world cannot hate you, but it hates me because I give evidence that its doings are evil." He then informed them, "I plan to go to the feast privately."

Later, as the group departed his home again, Simon worried, *Will Jesus ever set foot in my house again or return to Capernaum and its nonbelievers?* The thought of it broke his big heart.

Jesus looked back. "Woe to you," he said, confirming Simon's fears. Simon cringed, feeling a deep sorrow for his own ignorant people.

Rather than travel to Jerusalem with his family, Jesus dispatched seventy of his disciples to be scattered south across the Samaritan countryside. They were to travel ahead of Jesus with the same instructions as his apostles had the year before: spread the gospel, heal the sick, and cast out demons.

They have no idea what's in store for them, Simon thought.

In the higher hills, the oaks had begun to change to fall colors of oranges and reds. Summer had given way to fall, the world seeming a bit slower, calmer. The air felt cooler, cleaner, and the nights filled with more twinkling stars. Although the landscape had lost its lushness, it was still painted green. With the summer sun behind them, many of the crops had been harvested or were in the final process of it.

The towering date palms are dropping their sweet fruit, the olives are being pressed for oil. Grapes are being harvested to make wine. Simon pondered the season. *The wheat is being threshed, laying the fields bare. The people are storing away for the winter months.*

As the veteran travelers forged ahead, leaving behind the bounty of Galilee and Judea, the first leg of the journey seemed more problematic than usual. The desert before them provided fewer resources; food and especially water were limited.

Traveling through Samaria to stay off the main roads, the objective was to arrive in the Holy City unannounced.

At one point, Jesus dispatched several of them to arrange lodging, only to find that the Samaritans were quick to refuse them shelter. "We are sorry, Rabbi," two of his returning disciples reported, "but they turned us away because we are Jews."

What? Simon grumbled in his head. *Didn't Jesus just send seventy disciples to heal their sick, cast out demons, and preach the gospel to these unworthy vermin?* An uncontrollable rage swelled inside him. "Lord, do you want us to bid fire to come down from heaven and consume those miserable Samaritans?"

Stopping in his tracks, Jesus stared at the loose-tongued brute. "You don't know what you're saying! The Son of Man did not come to destroy men's lives but to save men's lives. We will simply keep going. There are more villages ahead where we can find a place to stay."

When am I ever going to learn? Simon wondered, feeling like an errant child once again.

With each step, Simon tried to bury the negative feelings with the hope that they were heading to Jerusalem to finally—and publicly—proclaim Jesus of Nazareth the rightful king and ruler of Israel.

Sukkot, or the Feast of Tabernacles, was always an enjoyable time. Unlike the solemn Passover, people rejoiced during the fall festival, sleeping in small tents or tabernacles. Some even camped out on rooftops. The weeklong festival commemorated the forty-year journey of the Israelites wandering in the wilderness, as well as the completion of the harvest. Along with Passover and the Festival of Weeks, Sukkot was one of three great pilgrimage feasts when Jewish males were required to appear before the Lord in Jerusalem's mighty temple.

I've always loved this festival the best, Simon daydreamed. *Jews building and living in temporary shelters, just like our ancestors did when they wandered the desert all those years ago.* The celebration was a reminder of God's faithful protection and deliverance. *My favorite!*

After four days of difficult travel to avoid the crowded trails, the group camped near the ancient groves close to the Mount of Olives, just as they had in the past. Hiking down in the morning to the bubbling springs of Kidron, they washed and dried their clothes; some even bathed.

"On behalf of everyone, thank you for finally taking a bath," Simon teased James.

The fisherman smiled. "Don't get used to it," he joked. "I don't plan on making it a habit."

Bethany, Judea
After filling water jugs and skins, Jesus redirected the group to Bethany, a small village located just over two miles from the

Holy City. "I wish to introduce you all to some dear friends," Jesus announced. "Lazarus and his sisters, Mary and Martha." He was clearly excited to be there.

Once the brief introductions were made, Jesus took the time to hug each of his friends. Simon watched as Jesus and Lazarus embraced for a long while, both men smiling joyously. *Jesus clearly loves this man,* Simon thought, noticing that his fellow travelers were discerning the same.

"Come inside and rest," Lazarus told the group, welcoming them with a wave of his calloused hand. "You must all be hungry."

As they broke bread together that afternoon, Jesus invited Mary and Martha to follow him as disciples. They eagerly agreed.

They have made an excellent decision, Simon thought, preparing to stay the night. *Jesus treats the women the same way he treats his male disciples. Maybe that's one of the reasons the elders and Pharisees despise him.* He shrugged, giving it more thought. *Treating everyone fairly, equally—now there's a new idea.* He nodded his head in approval, surprising himself. *It's an idea that even I'm still getting used to.*

Jerusalem, Judea

At sunrise, Jesus and his followers took leave of Lazarus's comfortable home.

Beneath a scarlet sky, the group entered the Holy City through the Gates of Damascus, trying to remain unnoticed. It was a futile attempt. The crowd soon noticed Jesus and began to celebrate. "He is here!" they chanted. "Jesus of Nazareth is here!"

Jesus took his place on the temple's main porch and, with the morning sun illuminating his face, he began to preach.

To Simon, it felt like King Herod had built the great temple for moments such as this.

Droves of devout Jewish pilgrims hurried over to listen, while whispers traveled through the crowd that Jesus was "a good man." The people were afraid to speak too loudly, though, as they also knew he was despised by the authorities.

With each word, the people were captivated by the rabbi, inspired to hear more. Simon could only marvel, as he did each time the master preached.

One of Jesus's challengers spoke up. "How can this man have knowledge of letters since he has never learned?" the keeper of the scrolls yelled out. "Illiterate!"

"My teaching is not mine," Jesus fired back. "It's not my own invention but of Him who sent me. If any man is willing to accomplish His will, he will know about this teaching whether it is from God or not, or whether I am just saying it out of my own conjecture." He leaned into the light. "Didn't Moses give you the law, and yet some of you are not really obeying the law? Why are you seeking to kill me?"

"You must have a demon," another Pharisee yelled out from the crowd, demanding that Jesus tell him if he was "possessed."

It was amazing to Simon how quickly Jesus replied.

"You not only know me, but you know my origin. I have not come of myself, but He who sent me is true, whom you know not," the master vowed.

This silenced the crowd. "This is certainly the prophet," some called out. "This is the Christ!"

Oh, this might be it, Simon hoped. *Jesus may be crowned King of Jews right here in the temple!* He surveyed the crowd, catching the nervous eyes of John. Mathew scribbled in his parchment scroll.

The Pharisees and scribes were incensed, some of them scurrying away to report to their leader, the temple's chief priest, Caiaphas.

Seeing this, Simon feared for his master's safety—and possible arrest. *It's only the first day of the feast*, he thought, *and even a blind man can see that the hate Jesus stirs in those of authority is dangerous.*

But Jesus wasn't done. "I am only going to be with you for a little while, and then I will go to Him who sent me. You will look for me, and you will not find me; and where I go, you cannot come."

There was cynical laughter, some in the crowd swinging back like a mindless pendulum. "Where can he go that we cannot find him?"

When Jesus took a break from preaching, Simon was relieved. "Let's tour the city," he suggested looking straight at Andrew, "and explore the different *sukkahs.*"

Andrew happily accepted the invitation.

In every corner, alley, and rooftop of the city, sukkahs had been erected, inspiring a warmth of nostalgia for both brothers. These shelters consisted of at least three walls that were framed with wood and canvas. The roof or covering was made from cut branches and leaves, placed loosely atop, leaving open space for the stars to be viewed and rain to enter. Many of them were decorated with flowers, leaves, and fruits.

"Don't you think that Jesus's tone is more defiant than usual?" Simon asked his brother as they strolled along. "The temple priests are angrier than I've ever seen them."

Andrew snickered.

"What?" Simon asked.

"Which do you want, Simon ... war or peace?" Andrew asked. Before receiving his answer, he added, "You're always dreaming about going to war for the new kingdom, but..."

"With the Romans," Simon harshly reminded him, "not our own people."

"Now the priests and Pharisees are *our own people?*"

"You know what I mean."

Andrew opened his mouth but decided against continuing the argument. A few tense moments passed.

"Do you remember the first time our father brought us here to experience this festival?" Simon asked, wisely changing the subject.

Although Andrew clearly tried to fight it off, a smile sneaked out from the corners of his mouth. "I do," he said, allowing himself to chuckle. "You thought you could stay in any shelter you wanted, and no one would complain—like the entire world owed you lodging."

Simon laughed. "This festival is the best place in the world to play hide-and-seek," he joked.

Laughing along with him, Andrew punched Simon's thick arm. It was a good shot that stung.

I'm not sure how good-humored that punch was meant to be, Simon thought, nodding.

He may get that one for free, but it's his last.

As custom dictated, that night the Hebrew people carried torches, illuminating candelabra along the walls of the temple to demonstrate that the Messiah would be a light to the world.

Simon watched, thinking, *Open your eyes, people. He's here.*

CHAPTER 15

HIS TIME, NOT OURS

Jerusalem, Judea

On the second day of the festival, Jesus was in the temple preparing to preach. Amid the large crowd, several of the conspiring Pharisees were in attendance.

But they're unusually quiet, Simon noticed. *Something's not right.* A strong sense of danger was making his extremities tingle. *Something doesn't feel right.*

Suddenly, several Pharisees pushed their way through the congregation, dragging a woman behind them. Her eyes remained on the ground.

It's shame, Simon predicted.

The self-righteous Pharisees stopped before the rabbi, pleased to report, "This woman has been caught in active adultery. The Law of Moses commands us to stone her to death, but what do you say we should do about it?"

It's a trap, Jesus! Simon screamed in his head. *It's a setup!* He looked at his teacher, whose chestnut eyes revealed that he was well aware of the situation.

Simon pushed his way closer, prepared to defend his master. *Talk about a rock and a hard place,* he thought, missing the irony. *The law clearly calls for her death, and it will be demanded by these hypocrites, who've probably committed the same sin many times over.* Simon knew

Jesus would never condone her death sentence. He'll *show mercy and forgiveness.* The chief apostle held his breath, waiting to see how the predicament would play out.

Jesus remained silent for a long while, making them await his answer. Finally, he took a step forward, addressing the woman's smirking accusers. "Let him who is without sin cast the first stone," he commanded.

Their faces bleached white, and the Pharisees went silent before stepping back to consider their next move.

Turning toward the frightened woman, Jesus asked, "Woman, where are your accusers? Is there anyone here to condemn you?"

"No, Lord, there isn't anyone here. They have left."

"Well, then, neither do I accuse you. Go along now; and from now on, don't sin anymore."

Sobbing, the blushing woman shielded her face, before running away.

My teacher is clever, outwitting his adversaries once again, Simon thought, feeling proud.

More of Jesus's enemies arose to challenge the Lord's words.

"I am the light of the world," he told them, referring directly back to their Sukkot custom. "He who follows me will never walk in darkness but shall have the light of life. You judge according to the flesh. You need to know me to know my Father."

The Pharisees stepped forward. "Who are you?"

"Even the same I said to you from the beginning. When you have lifted up the Son of Man, then you shall know that I am."

These Pharisees were also reduced to silence, before leaving the temple. Jesus's followers, however, were delighted to see him best his foes.

Given the current Jewish public opinion, I can't see how the masses won't accept Jesus as their king, Simon figured. Although he felt a bit triumphant, he made himself show restraint.

That afternoon, leaving the Temple Mount, Jesus led his followers down the steep road to the pool at Siloam. The great *mikvah* (ritual bath), known as the Pool of Siloam, was the largest and most prominent in Jerusalem. Located just inside the walls of the ancient city, this pool had been built in the time of Solomon, receiving its constantly flowing waters from the diversion of the Spring of Gihon at the Kidron Valley. Tunneled through rock, the channel sent the clear, cold waters into the city behind the great walls, giving the Hebrew people the ability to withstand the siege of any enemy for more than seven hundred years. Immensely popular with pilgrims who entered the great city, this pool had stood at the heart of Judaism, protecting the city and its people since the Moabites had built it.

A blind beggar who was well-known in Jerusalem lay near the edge of the pool, waiting for a miracle—or at least a handout. Jesus approached the vagabond.

"Who sinned for this man to be blind?" Simon asked Jesus. "He or his parents?" Like most people, he believed that disability or illness was a direct consequence of having angered God.

"Neither this man nor his parents sinned," Jesus explained. "He was born blind so that the works of God should be made manifest through him." The master looked Simon in the eye. "We must do the works of Him who sent me while it is day, for the night is coming, when no man can work. While I am in this world, I am the light of the world."

Simon nodded that he understood, hoping he did.

Jesus spat in the dust, using his finger to make a paste from the clay. Then, using his thumb and forefinger, he rubbed the anointed clay onto the blind man's stark-white eyes. "Go now," he told the beggar. "Wash your eyes in the pool."

As instructed, the man washed his face in the Pool of Siloam. There was a pause, scores of people watching and waiting.

"I can see!" the man proclaimed, starting to cry. "I was blind but now I see!"

Simon noticed that color had returned to the man's lily-white orbs.

This miracle, which had been witnessed by many, ignited the crowd. They were ecstatic for the poor soul, turning back to see what else they might observe from Jesus.

The Pharisees, however, were enraged. This was a very provocative and controversial act, given that it was performed on the Sabbath.

"Surely, this man cannot be from God, because he does not keep the Sabbath," one of them yelled out. "It isn't proper."

"It's against the law!" another barked.

Simon shook his head. *When will they see past their own ignorance?* he wondered. One of the crowd members yelled back, "Can a man who is not of God, who is a sinner, perform such miracles?"

Exactly, Simon thought, smiling.

Jesus told them, "I came into this world for judgment, that those who do not see may see, and that those who see may become blind."

Even Simon knew that Jesus was referring to the prophecy of Christ. He then watched as Malchus, one of the spies for the high priest Caiaphas, dragged the beggar away.

Simon grabbed John. "What do you think the high priest wants with the healed blind man?"

"To interrogate him, I'm guessing."

Simon shook his head. "I don't know about you, but I'm starting to feel some real danger."

For the first time, John was in agreement on the subject. "Jesus is dangerous to them, Simon. He can no longer be ignored. I see that now."

Simon's chest tightened.

"Our teacher creates disorder, which Caiaphas will want to silence. Jesus's followers are growing and—"

"And the master continues to go into the temple—into their territory—and question their authority," Simon interrupted.

Both men went quiet, pondering some inevitable retribution.

"Why doesn't he just announce his kingdom and use his powers to guarantee his throne?" Simon suggested, sighing heavily.

John stared at him.

"If not during the feast, then when?" Simon asked, feeling his usual impatience and frustration. "This is really coming to a point of conflict," he added.

"Jesus has his own plan," John reminded him. "Everything in his time, Simon, not ours."

As the sun set, torchlit Jerusalem was a city on the brink of eruption. The multitude was split. "Jesus is either a demon or the Christ," they debated.

"If you continue steadfast in my word," Jesus concluded for the day, "you will really be my disciples and shall know the truth, and the truth shall make you free."

The truth shall make you free, Simon repeated for himself. *The truth shall make you free.*

Simon awoke with a yawn, taking a moment to identify where he was. Remembering the tense day before, his neck tightened. Rising from his bedroll, he joined the others, who had already started in on a humble meal of figs, plums, and bread.

Claiming his seat within the circle, Simon studied his fellow apostles as they chatted about the meal and their families back home. Not one of them appeared anxious. *That's odd*, he thought, *given all we've seen and heard.*

The chief apostle opened his mouth but stopped—suppressing his usual tendency to share his thoughts. Keeping his growing concerns to himself, he couldn't help but replay the events of the previous day and all that led up to it.

Lost in thought, Simon looked up to see that Jesus had approached the group. Wearing a smile, and without a word spoken, the master gestured that the group rise and follow him out onto the road. After a final bite of bread, Simon got to his feet.

Here we go again, he thought, taking his rightful place beside Jesus.

On this third day, the Pharisees questioned Jesus in the open, meeting him in the courtyard in front of the temple. "If you are the Messiah, just say it," the wicked men demanded. They then asked for a sign from him, challenging him to prove who he was.

"Works that I do in my Father's name show who I am. My sheep know me. I hear them, and they follow me," Jesus said, gesturing to Simon and the rest. "I give them eternal life, and they will never perish." It was the first time he indicated that he and the Father were one.

Whoa … Simon thought, his anxiety building.

Jesus's identity was now out in the open, triggering great anger. The debate between Jesus and the priests was escalating beyond control.

"Blasphemy!" one of the priests screamed, inspiring the crowd to lift rocks, threatening to stone Jesus. "Demon!"

"In calling God Satan," Jesus said, "they have made the definitive choice."

Simon felt lightheaded, knowing that the punishment for blasphemy was stoning. *We're in real trouble,* he thought. *Many will agree with the Pharisees, calling for Jesus's death.*

As expected, the crowd moved aggressively toward the rabbi.

"He who is not with me is against me," Jesus warned them, "and he who does not gather with me scatters. You brood of vipers."

More rocks were hoisted into the air.

"I have shown you many good works for my Father," Jesus told them. "For which of these are you going to stone me?"

"It is not for your good work that you will be stoned, but for blasphemy," one of the priests replied.

Simon stepped up to protect his master, just as several rocks were hurled in their direction.

Jesus and the apostles fled, with Malchus and several of the high priest's guards taking chase.

As they ran, Simon's mind also raced. *A riot at the temple, the holiest place in Judea,* he thought. *They'll want our heads for this!*

That night, as Simon lay his head on a makeshift pillow, he didn't bother to close his eyes. *There's no way I'm going to fall asleep for a long time.*

Giving his subconscious a break, he analyzed their current situation. *On our last visit, Jesus had become bolder, building his reputation as a healer. But this trip…* He shook his head. *He's pushing it, putting us right smack in the middle of the danger zone.*

Simon understood that those in authority, those who claimed the highest moral ground, feared the loss of their greatest possession—power. *This makes them blind and corrupt, loving wealth and prominence more than God.* Under the premise of enforcing "the law," they committed the most heinous acts while remaining guilt-free. *Power is everything to them.*

He pictured Malchus running off to report to Caiaphas that they had escaped. *That's not good,* he thought. As the highest-ranking Jewish official, Caiaphas's job was to keep peace and law in Judea.

Simon considered his conversation with Andrew. *Jesus picking a fight isn't what bothers me. I like that,* he thought. *It's that he's picking a fight with people who we'll need against the Romans. Why divide us?*

He yawned. *I just hope this isn't the beginning of the end.* He shook off the idea as foolish. *Thank Yahweh there's only one more day of the feast.*

After breakfast, Jesus led them to a small courtyard where a small gathering had assembled to hear what the rabbi had to say.

It was the last and greatest day of the feast and, while the torches still burned in the temple, Jesus announced, "I am the light of the world. Whoever follows me will never walk in darkness but will have the light of life."

Hoshana Raba, or the Water Pouring ceremony, was the final, climactic event of Sukkot.

Caiaphas, the temple's chief priest, officiated the beloved cere-mony. After drawing water from the Pool of Siloam, he carried it to the temple, where he poured it into a silver basin beside the altar, spilling much of it onto the altar.

"Lord," Caiaphas publicly prayed, "provide us with Your heav-enly water in the form of rain."

Thousands of devout pilgrims bowed in prayer.

To Simon's dismay, Jesus took the opportunity to step onto the porch and disrupt the festival.

"But anyone who is thirsty, come to me and drink," the rabbi told the crowd, re-interpreting the scripture with great authority. "Whoever believes in me," he added, "out of his heart shall flow living water." He looked at Caiaphas, letting him know that the rituals were less important than the Savior's presence.

Some in the crowd gasped at this display of defiance.

Simon watched as Caiaphas's face turned blood-red. *Oh no...*

While Malchus, the high priest's henchman, took chase, the crowd erupted in a mix of cheers and jeers.

We need to get out of here, Simon realized, *and fast.*

Jesus, along with his apostles, immediately fled. This time, they went into hiding.

As the guardian of the Jewish people, Caiaphas was the chief defender of their faith. He had no choice but to quell any threats of violent rebellion. It was now obvious: Jesus was a problem that needed to be solved. Jews rebelling against power would never be tolerated, especially at the holiest of holies.

Temple officers were dispatched to arrest Jesus and his followers.

That night, gossip spread throughout the city, many of the people calling Jesus and his followers "rabble" and "illiterates."

The mob is fickle, Simon realized, before skulking back into the shadows. *This is not the game of hide-and-seek I remember.*

While in hiding, Simon unpacked the last few weeks. He enjoyed the power and attention but not the conflict caused by Jesus's growing confrontations and provocations. *I don't get it,* he thought. *Jesus doesn't seem willing to use his power to fight against the Romans, but he has no problem ruffling the feathers of the Jewish authorities.*

Simon wanted to go for a walk but couldn't. Huddled in the shadows, he pictured Caiaphas's crimson-colored face, realizing, *The high priest sees Jesus as a serious threat. Being in collaboration with Rome, Caiaphas is nothing more than the religious leader of an occupied territory who needs to kneel before that butcher Pontius Pilate.* He shuddered at the thought of crossing paths with the violent Roman governor. *And that makes Caiaphas a serious threat.*

He pictured all the big adoring crowds. *Why not return to the way things were when miracles were performed and the people celebrated?* He shook his head. *But now, all Jesus does is poke the mountain lion. Maybe I should talk to him?*

Bethany, Judea

Under the cover of darkness, the group escaped the city, heading straight to the village of Bethany. Like Simon's home in Capernaum, the home of Lazarus, Mary, and Martha sheltered Jesus when he came to Jerusalem. This was Jesus's home base, a safe zone where he could rest or even lie low if there was trouble in Jerusalem.

And we're definitely in trouble, Simon thought.

"Stay with us," Mary and Martha told Jesus. "You will be safe here."

Lazarus nodded in agreement. "Please."

Jesus shook his head. "I will not put you in danger," he whispered.

Simon was hardly surprised by his rabbi's decision. *The Pharisees are angry enough to chase us to the ends of the earth. And if they can't catch us over the next few days, they'll dispatch their spies.*

"Why do they hate you so?" Martha asked Jesus.

"Because they cannot serve both money and God," Jesus explained, speaking to the power struggle that was taking place.

After resting two days and gathering all the supplies they could carry, Jesus and his hooded followers slipped away.

Heading into the wilderness, they traveled east all the way to the Jordan River and turned north until finally arriving at an isolated area close to the desert, between Galilee and the Dead Sea. It was near to the place where Jesus had spent time with John the Baptist. "We will camp here," Jesus announced.

"For how long?" James asked.

Jesus looked at him. "For as long as we need to." They all understood.

If Jesus steps foot anywhere near Jerusalem, he'll be arrested, Simon surmised. *We all will.*

They set up camp but not as the usual temporary site.

We may be here for quite a while, Simon thought, hoping they were not following in their ancestors' wandering footsteps.

Jesus spent much of the next few weeks foretelling their future, giving Simon many nights of restless sleep. Even the suggestion of returning to Jerusalem was unpleasant to him and the others.

As days turned into weeks, both the air and vegetation were beginning to change.

When the wide-eyed fear of Caiaphas had dissolved into a nonchalant shrug, a messenger from Bethany arrived. The man was out of breath, his tunic stained from several days' worth of sweat.

"What is it?" Jesus asked him, gesturing that Judas bring the man a drink of water.

"Lord, he whom you love is very sick," he panted.

Lazarus is ill, Simon thought. *We'll be breaking camp by nightfall.*

The messenger struggled to catch his breath. "Lazarus is dying," he reported. "You must come at once in order for the man to live."

To Simon's surprise, Jesus said nothing. He walked off into the distance before looking skyward.

The master loves Lazarus. He loves Mary and Martha, too, Simon thought. *If Lazarus dies, then his sisters will be left to live alone, which is not an ideal situation for them.*

"Please," the messenger pleaded loudly, "Mary and Martha are desperate. You need to come and heal their brother!"

Jesus has a tough decision to make, Simon thought. *Remain in hiding, or go to his friend and save him.* He shook his head at the dilemma. *If we go back, Jesus might be arrested. But if we stay in hiding, then Lazarus dies.*

Finishing his prayers, Jesus returned to the group. "Lazarus's sickness will not end in death," he said, "but we will not return just yet."

What? Simon thought, shocked. He looked to John, Andrew, James. Each man shook his head, sharing Simon's confusion and surprise.

The messenger opened his mouth to speak.

"Lazarus's sickness will not end in death," Jesus repeated, leaving it at that.

In the shadows of the night's campfire, Simon wrapped himself against the cold. "You saw how close Jesus and Lazarus are, right?" he whispered to John. "Why wouldn't he cure—"

"If Jesus says everything will be fine, then everything will be fine," John said, interrupting him.

"From the sound of that messenger's voice, Lazarus won't last long."

"Stop worrying, Simon," John said. "It's not your job."

Simon approached several others—Nathanael, Thomas, and James—asking the same question.

Each one of them shrugged.

Jesus is in charge.

The morning came, and another one after that, before Jesus announced, "Lazarus is two-days dead. But I am going there to wake him up."

Why would Jesus wait until his friend's situation was hopeless? Simon wondered, believing that the spirit stayed with the body for three days before it finally left. *If Lazarus has been dead for four days, then there's no chance of him coming back.*

"I am returning to Judea," Jesus said.

Why now? Simon wondered. *It won't help Lazarus.*

"Let us go too," Thomas commented, "that we may die with him." Filled with mixed emotions, the apostles set out for Jericho Road.

CHAPTER 16

RAISING LAZARUS

Bethany, Judea

As they traveled back to Bethany, steering clear of the main roads, Simon thought, *Lazarus is four-days dead. He's been wrapped in a winding sheet, treated with myrrh, and placed in a tomb, where he'll stay for a year until his skeleton is pulled apart and placed in a bone box.*

Managing to stay undetected, they were just outside of the small village when Martha of Bethany came out to greet Jesus on the road. "If you had been here," she wept, "my brother would not have died."

She was stricken with such grief that Simon adopted some of it. *She's right,* he couldn't help but think. *The man's passing could have been avoided.*

Reaching for Martha's shoulders, Jesus told her, "Your brother will rise again."

"I know he will rise again in the resurrection of the last day," she said, misunderstanding the rabbi's meaning.

Jesus cupped her face and pulled her close, before speaking with authority. "I am the resurrection and the life. The one who believes in me will live, even though they die. Do you believe this?"

"I believe you are the Messiah, the Son of God," Martha vowed through her tears.

"Where is Mary?" Jesus asked.

Without a word, the woman turned and gestured toward the village, leading him to their home.

They weren't all the way to the house when Mary hurried out to them. "Lord, if you had been here, my brother would not have died," she cried, repeating her sister's very words.

This time, feeling her sorrow deep in his heart, Jesus went to his knees and began to weep.

The master is feeling what she's feeling, Simon realized, witnessing his teacher's immense empathy and compassion. *He suffers the same pains we bear.*

Jesus was clearly shattered at the death of his friend and was sharing in both sisters' agony. From his knees, he grabbed Mary's hands. "Where have you laid him?" he asked.

"Come and see, my Lord," Mary said, taking him to the tomb.

Simon's heart fluttered, leaving him unsure whether it was the result of excitement or fear.

Upon arrival, Jesus commanded, "Take away the stone." Everyone stood frozen.

He's been gone for days, Simon thought. *The smell will be awful.*

"Did I not tell you that if you believe, you will see the glory of God?" Jesus said, gesturing again that they roll the stone back from the tomb's opening.

Jesus then turned to his disciples to look each of them in the eye. When he reached Simon, he paused, ensuring that he had the fisherman's full attention for this next lesson.

Amid the silence, time felt suspended. Only the wind dared to speak.

Lifting his palms to the sky, Jesus prayed. Then, peering into the dark cavern, he raised his hands toward the opening. "Lazarus," he said, "come out."

A long moment of silence passed.

Then Lazarus, wrapped in white linen, stumbled out of the cave and into the light. Everyone gasped, paralyzed from awe.

Simon lost his breath, stupefied beyond words or thought.

"Unbind him and let him go," Jesus said matter-of-factly.

Breaking through their shock, Mary and Martha rushed to their brother, where the three became locked in a long embrace.

His wits returning to him, Simon Peter stared at Jesus. *He has raised a man four-days dead. How? And yet he, too, is a man made of flesh and blood.* Death could only be ordained by God, so when Jesus resurrected Lazarus, he proved beyond any doubt that he wielded the same power and authority. *What more proof is needed that he is the Son of God? Who can possibly reject Jesus now?*

Simon was beginning to believe that faith in Jesus meant that death would be vanquished. *The master has raised the dead before,* he thought, *but this one's different.* He stared at Lazarus. *This man was too far gone. Everyone will hear about this one.* The impossible miracle was sure to shake the Jewish world.

Simon glanced up to notice two temple spies looking on. His excitement began to mix with fear. Grabbing Andrew, he whispered, "Caiaphas's men were watching and saw everything."

Andrew nodded. "And they'll be heading straight back to their boss to report it," he said, his voice raised above a whisper.

This isn't good, Simon thought, *not good at all.* He sensed they would now do everything in their power to put a stop to Jesus's ministry. He could feel it. *Jesus has authority over death. This will threaten anyone in authority at the temple.*

Andrew was talking to him for a few moments before Simon even realized it. "... it'll happen, Simon, you mark my words," he whispered. "How much do you want to wager that by nightfall, the conspiring Pharisees will call for an emergency meeting of the great council?"

The Elders of Zion, Simon thought, nodding in agreement. "I'm not taking that bet."

"They won't allow any risk to their own kingdom for the sake of one man, whether they believe him to be a prophet or not," Andrew added, sighing. "However they decide to proceed, I'm guessing it'll be swift."

Simon took a deep breath. *I agree,* he thought. *I wish I didn't, but Andrew's right.*

Since the Feast of Tabernacles in October, two tense months had passed. Although Jesus had never officially announced his plan, Simon knew they were laying low for the time being.

No complaints from me, he thought, wondering, *Maybe to avoid conflict, we can ask Caiaphas to join us and share the power?*

The fields had changed from green to brown; much of the vegetation had been plucked clean, laying the land bare. Any remaining stalks were matted and faded. Even the orchard's fruit trees were destitute, the bright hues of reds and purples now a dull gold and copper. With their stores in place, the villagers hoped their heavy labor would sustain them through the frugal months.

Through most of December, Jesus and his followers holed up in Bethany, mostly staying indoors during the daylight hours. October through April was the rainy season. *It's not so much cold as it is wet,* Simon thought, *always wet.*

The apostles grew out their hair and beards to protect them from the chillier days. Their tunics, both inner and outer garments, were thicker and made from wool. Sleeved cloaks were also worn.

The female disciples, and there were many among the devout followers, were housed in separate quarters. Their outer garments were longer, with enough border fringe to cover their feet. Many also donned work aprons to protect their outer garments.

Being indoors most of the time, Simon was able to keep his feet clean and his sandals in tip-top shape. *Again, no complaints.*

Even during winter hibernation, the apostles retained their normal body weight, each one knowing how they would suffer the few extra pounds on the long spring marches. Averaging two meals per day, light breakfasts were eaten at midmorning. Dinners were more considerable, often consisting of vegetable stew seasoned with onion, garlics, or leeks. *I prefer the fava beans when they're prepared right,* Simon thought. Barley bread, their main staple, was available at every supper table, along with some type of fish or egg dish.

It might be nice to have some red meat once in a while, Simon thought, knowing it was reserved only for special occasions.

Dried figs, raisins, and apples were plentiful enough, as were pistachios, almonds, and walnuts. Although other fruits were preserved in olive oil, the occasional sip of wine served as the perfect dessert.

To pass all the downtime, the disciples either played board games, a form of checkers, or stared at the rose-gold sunsets. There was plenty of time to think. In Simon's case, there was too much time to think. Day after day, the smell of frankincense, a household incense, lingered in the air. *I prefer the smell of bait,* Simon decided.

Whenever he could risk it, he stepped outdoors to breathe.

On one such morning, Simon was eating a breakfast of flat-bread slathered in goat cheese. He marveled at the first frost of the season that had painted the hills a soft white. The world seemed still, as if it were taking a deep breath before having to prepare for another round of bedlam.

It was a pale, chilly morning. With the harvest complete, nothing much remained to block out the whistling winds. Tightening down on his cloak, Simon looked skyward. *Where do we go from here, Yahweh?*

There was no answer.

Closing his eyes, he prayed, *Please shroud us in Your angels, especially Jesus. I don't know what tomorrow will bring, but I sense it will be challenging.*

When he opened his eyes, he noticed that the pewter sky had turned even darker, menacing. A drizzle turned to rain before the clouds opened up, dumping a deluge of cold water onto the world. Lifting his hood, Simon sprinted for Lazarus's house. *I hope this isn't a sign from above!*

Even when the Festival of Lights was upon them, there was never any discussion about attending the celebration in Jerusalem.

Simon was surprised to have mixed feelings. On the one hand, not enough time had passed to risk a visit to the Holy City. On the other hand, he loved the winter festival, which celebrated the Maccabees's victory over Greek oppression and the rededication of the temple in Jerusalem. It was a proud celebration, as the eternal flame burned for eight days on one day's worth of oil.

What the Jewish people should be celebrating is the coming of the Messiah, he thought. *I wonder if there will ever be a festival dedicated to Jesus?*

Ephraim, Judea

Weeks passed, and the weather turned warm when Jesus took his departure from Bethany. While the birds sang and the trees blossomed, he led his apostles to the little town of Ephraim to rally with a significant number of his disciples.

We're going to Jerusalem for the coming Passover, Simon hoped, and Jesus is bringing an army! He felt sure of it. *It's finally happening! After the resurrection of Lazarus, there's no way anyone will stand in Messiah's way now.*

In another part of his head, a healthy trepidation continued to hum. *God freeing His people from slavery once again, Simon thought, and this time it's the Romans who will pay.*

Understanding the cruelty of his oppressors, he realized it would be a very dangerous atmosphere, nonetheless.

In the distance, Simon spotted a single flower dancing in a fresh field of planted wheat.

He thought of his wife. *I'm still with you, my love.*

On the road, several new lessons were imparted, offering Simon and the others a few small glimpses into heaven.

Two disciples chose to prevent several children from approaching Jesus.

"Have you forgotten what I have taught you?" Jesus scolded them. "Whoever receives one little child in my name, receives me." He then welcomed the little ones with hugs, smiling and laughing as Simon had not seen since the wedding at Cana.

The traveling party also happened upon a wealthy and virtuous convert. Although Simon did not hear the man's conversation with Jesus, he later asked his master, "Why did the man go away looking so sad?"

Jesus said, "I explained to him that it is very difficult for a rich man to enter the kingdom of God, as men find it extremely hard to relinquish their possessions."

"Then who can be saved?" Simon asked for all of them.

"Things that are impossible with man are possible with God," Jesus explained.

"We have left everything and followed you," Simon said, continuing on as the group's spokesperson. "What will we be given?"

"Forsake all in my name, and when the Son of Man sits on the throne of his glory, you shall also sit upon twelve thrones, judging the twelve tribes of Israel. You shall receive a hundredfold and inherit life everlasting. Many that are first shall be last," he added, "and the last, first."

Although Simon was pleased to hear this, he struggled to understand the mysterious pecking order that Jesus often referred to.

Following along the Jordan River, Jesus maintained the lead.

To everyone's surprise, James and John's mother, Salome, made her way from the rear of the entourage to the very front of the column to walk beside the rabbi.

She's going to talk to Jesus, Simon realized, quickening his pace to listen in.

After praising the Lord, she said, "May I ask something of you, Rabbi?"

Never breaking stride, Jesus smiled at her. "What would you have me do?"

Salome looked at her sons, John and James, the deep, maternal love apparent in her eyes. "I ask that my sons are always seated to your left and to your right."

Oh, here we go again, Simon thought, only this time there was no pang of envy. He glanced at the other apostles, who were also eavesdropping. *From the looks on their faces, they like the idea less than I do.*

John and James continued marching, their eyes straight ahead—*like they have no idea what's going on.*

Simon nearly laughed. *James the Lesser might be expected to take the seat at the master's left.* He thought about it. *Then again, Andrew was the first to follow the rabbi, and Thomas had been willing to risk his life for Jesus.* Confident in his own position, Simon was happy to steer clear of the discussion.

Jesus looked at the assertive woman with understanding. "You don't realize what you ask," he said. "To sit on my right hand and on my left hand is not mine to give. It has been prepared by my Father."

Salome nodded her gratitude, dropping back to her place at the rear of the pack with the other women.

Watching this, Simon thought, *Even though Salome was advocating for her children and not herself, that still took hutzpah.* There was a time not so long ago when Simon would have been enraged by the woman's attempt—even insulted. Instead, he realized, *A mother will do anything for her children.*

The other ten apostles were hardly impressed with this scheme to elevate John and James.

Sensing the murmur that grew among them, Jesus stopped to address them all. "Whoever desires to become great among you shall be your servant," he explained, "and whoever wishes to be first among you shall be a slave. Just as the Son of Man came not to be served but to serve and to give his life a ransom for many."

At Jesus's will, they began marching again.

Simon felt a pang of disappointment after this "first is last" statement. *Hasn't Jesus put me first?* he questioned, feeling confused.

Simon was elated that spring was arriving. It was nice to see the flowers in bloom again; bright green fields of grain were growing from the freshly planted fields and silvery groves of olives and emerald vineyards of grapes blanketed the lush countryside. He inhaled deeply, thinking, *I've seen this same view many times, but it always feels like the first.*

There was a lively, festive atmosphere on Jericho Road, with thousands of excited pilgrims converging from all four corners of the Jewish world. Simon couldn't remember being filled with so much hope. His heart overflowed. Although he worried that real danger lurked ahead of them, he had to believe that Jesus wouldn't allow any harm to come to himself or his followers. *He has the power to put a stop to anything he wishes. And after raising Lazarus, the authorities should know better than to go after him.* Feeling recharged, Simon expected to finally reach the long-awaited outcome for which he had prayed—*for more than three years!*

"You're in a good mood. What are you smiling about?" Andrew asked, stepping up beside him.

"We're going to Jerusalem," Simon answered.

"We don't know that yet. Jesus hasn't actually..."

"Where else would we be going?" Simon countered, unwilling to let his pragmatic brother darken his mood.

Once they reached the village of Bethany, Simon felt even more exhilarated.

Jesus and the apostles were invited to dine with Simon the Leper, one of Jesus's friends.

The rabbi accepted his friend's generous invitation.

Happy to give his worn sandals a much-needed rest, Simon was looking forward to breaking bread in the torchlit courtyard.

"Do you think they'll serve that smoked fish I like? Maybe even lamb!" Simon whispered to John, grinning.

John nodded. "Of course," he whispered, joining in the daydream, "and leeks, olives, dried fruit, and fresh berries."

Simon felt his parched mouth begin to salivate. "Some sweet cakes wouldn't be terrible either."

They both chuckled. On the road, even when their bellies growled and groaned, no one complained.

No matter what we're served tonight, Simon thought, *it promises to be a feast.* "And wine," he added, "plenty of wine, I hope."

"Of course," John repeated, trying not to laugh aloud, "jars full of sweet red wine, like Cana."

The sumptuous banquet of bread, lamb, cheese, and fruits was not quite in full swing when Mary Magdalene shocked the apostles by approaching Jesus at the head table. It was unusual for a woman to take such liberties, so Simon watched her closely.

Producing a vial of perfume and oil, she broke off the neck—pouring some of the oil onto the master's head and the rest onto his feet.

Each of the apostles searched the eyes of others in the room.

Going to her knees, Mary then wiped Jesus's feet with her beautiful, raven-black hair.

She's anointing him, as if for burial, Simon realized, the hairs on the back of his tanned neck snapping to attention. *She has taken Jesus's talk of his own death as genuine.*

Some of the disciples were uncomfortable with the peculiar display.

Although Simon didn't care for the gesture, he remembered that Jesus considered Mary a friend. *He healed her of seven demons,* he recalled, deciding to hold his tongue.

The group's treasurer, however, was incensed. "Why did you not sell this perfume and give the money to feed the poor?" Judas demanded of Mary, considering her actions wasteful. "Leave her alone," Jesus rebuked Judas, lightning-quick to defend the devout woman. "Why do you trouble her? She has performed good service for me."

"I was only thinking of the poor," Judas countered, his face burning red from being humiliated in front of his peers.

Jesus paused, taking a deep breath. "You will always have the poor," he told him. "You can show them kindness whenever you wish. You will not always have me."

There was another awkward pause, as Judas glared at his master.

Jesus turned his attention to Mary. "She had to keep this scent for the day of my burial." He nodded. "She will be memorialized for this."

Simon was surprised by the raw emotion in Jesus's tone. He looked to Judas, who was wounded and furious about it. *I understand how it feels to be criticized like that,* Simon thought, empathizing with Judas. *We all make mistakes,* he thought, wondering if he might have misjudged the man.

Feeling shamed, Judas stormed out of the courtyard and into the dark night.

As Simon watched the back of the treasurer's tunic disappear, he smiled to himself. *Who am I kidding?* he thought. *Judas cares less about the poor than keeping as many coins as possible in his purse.*

In the morning, as the sun cracked the horizon and began to infiltrate the darkness, Jesus officially announced, "We will return to Jerusalem for Passover."

The apostles immediately questioned this. "But we were chased out of the city the last time and not long ago," one of them mumbled.

"It is not safe for you there. There are conspiracies," another called out, referring to the rumors they were hearing from other pilgrims on the road.

Simon searched for the voice but could not identify the man.

Andrew sidled up beside him. "What do you think?" he whispered.

"I've felt torn, but I've made peace with it," Simon admitted.

Andrew's jaw flapped open.

Remembering John's recent wisdom, Simon shrugged. "Jesus needs to continue his ministry. It's why he's here," he explained. "And if not in the Holy City during Passover, then what's the point?"

Remaining speechless, Andrew turned his head away; he was not happy but still unwilling to argue.

Simon offered one last shrug, doing all he could to push one simple truth out of his thick head: *We are now on a collision path with both the Jewish authorities and the Romans.*

As they neared the Mount of Olives, Jesus stopped and faced the group. Moving down the line, he looked into each of their eyes—Andrew, James, Philip, Thomas, Matthew, Thaddeus, James the Lesser, Simon the Zealot, Nathanael, and Judas—before reaching John and Peter. "Go to the village over there," he commanded, singling out the two men. "Untie the donkey and bring him to me."

"What if we are questioned by the owner?" John asked.

"Tell him that the Lord is in need," Jesus explained. "He will allow it."

Peter and John exchanged a quick glance. Without another word, they obeyed.

The preparations are underway, Simon thought, the signs as clear as day. *Jesus plans to ride into Jerusalem on the back of the donkey, fulfilling the prophecy of Zachariah and reenacting the crowning of the ancient kings of Israel.*

Along the rocky road, John slapped Simon's arm. "That was very expensive ointment that Mary used on Jesus," he said, "pure nard."

Simon nodded. "I know she loves the rabbi and was tending to him, but the whole thing made me..." He stopped.

"Feel uneasy?" John said.

"Exactly!" Simon shook his head. "I thought it was strange for her to prepare him for burial." He shook off the shiver that threatened to travel the length of his spine.

"Judas didn't care for it, that's for sure!" John said, smirking.

"And I think he liked being reprimanded by the master even less," Simon said. "I know the feeling. Believe me, I've been in his sandals and it's not—"

"Please don't compare yourself to Judas, Simon," John interrupted. "You're very different men."

Simon thought about it. "But Jesus didn't mind. He defended Mary."

John nodded in agreement.

Shaking his head, Simon returned his thoughts to their mission. "Jesus is about to ride into Jerusalem as the King of the Jews," he declared, feeling his eyes moisten.

John nodded again but said nothing.

Simon barely noticed. He was too busy fantasizing about the glorious days ahead.

Just as Jesus foretold, Simon and John found the ass and the colt exactly where the rabbi said they would.

The owner willingly gave them the animals, stating matter-of-factly, "I know of your master's request." There was no further explanation.

With a shrug, Simon untied the braying ass. Before moving an inch, the stubborn animal peeled back its lips, showing off two rows of large, yellow teeth.

"It's smiling at you, Simon," John teased, handling the cooperative colt.

"That's good," Simon said, laughing. "I'll take it as a positive sign."

A few heavy tugs later, the donkey agreed to go along for the ride.

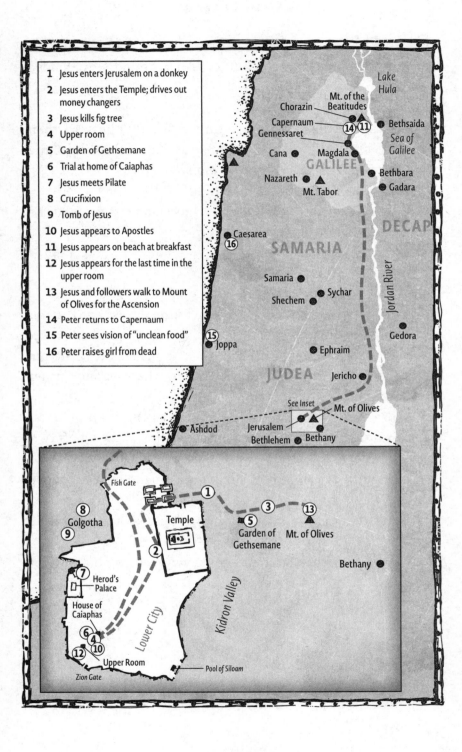

1 Jesus enters Jerusalem on a donkey
2 Jesus enters the Temple; drives out money changers
3 Jesus kills fig tree
4 Upper room
5 Garden of Gethsemane
6 Trial at home of Caiaphas
7 Jesus meets Pilate
8 Crucifixion
9 Tomb of Jesus
10 Jesus appears to Apostles
11 Jesus appears on beach at breakfast
12 Jesus appears for the last time in the upper room
13 Jesus and followers walk to Mount of Olives for the Ascension
14 Peter returns to Capernaum
15 Peter sees vision of "unclean food"
16 Peter raises girl from dead

Lake Hula

Mt. of the Beatitudes
Chorazin
Capernaum
Gennessaret
Bethsaida
Sea of Galilee
Cana
Magdala
GALILEE
Bethbara
Nazareth
Mt. Tabor
Gadara

DECAP

Caesarea
SAMARIA
Jordan River

Samaria
Shechem
Sychar

Joppa
Gedora

Ephraim

JUDEA
Jericho

See Inset
Mt. of Olives
Jerusalem
Bethlehem
Bethany
Ashdod

Fish Gate

Golgotha

Temple

Garden of Gethsemane
Mt. of Olives

Herod's Palace

House of Caiaphas

Bethany

Lower City

Kidron Valley

Upper Room
Zion Gate
Pool of Siloam

PART 3

FAILURE AND REDEMPTION

YEAR 3:
SIMON FALLS,
PETER RISES

CHAPTER 17

PALM LEAVES AND
THE CHILDREN

Jerusalem, Judea

S imon and John returned with the ass and the colt, placing their own outer garments upon them. As Jesus prepared to mount the donkey, Simon noticed that Judas had rejoined the group, returning the apostles back to twelve. *He's more quiet than usual … probably still stewing,* Simon figured. *I get it.*

As they approached the city, still over two miles out, onlookers began to shed their outer garments and spread them before Jesus. Even more pilgrims cut palm branches from the trees, laying them down to create a splendid carpet. Dozens became hundreds, until there were too many palms to count.

With Simon's hair standing on end and his forearms turning to gooseflesh, he held the donkey's reins, feeling honored that he was triumphantly leading Christ to his glorious fate. *This is everything we've been waiting for,* he thought, *everything we've worked so hard for.* They were finally face-to-face with the fulfillment of their divine destiny, the very start of Jesus's magnificent new kingdom.

Amid the majestic chaos, Simon turned to find his master weeping. *Tears of joy,* he guessed—he hoped.

Disciples walked in front of the mounted Christ, as well as behind, shouting, "Hosanna to the son of David! Blessed is he who comes in the name of the Lord; Hosanna in the highest!"

The grand procession passed by thousands, both sides of the palm-lined road teeming with zealous believers who screamed their adoration. Although the love was being directed at Jesus, Simon couldn't help but absorb the amazing energy, accepting some of the abundant love for himself.

This is so much more amazing than I pictured, he thought, feeling his skin tingling, *with nothing but great things ahead of us!*

The crowd pressed in on Jesus, seeking to touch his tunic. "Blessed is he who comes as king in the name of the Lord!"

This time, the mob's excitement did not trouble Simon. The ignorance in him gushed with joy. "Hosanna!" he cheered, completely swept up in the moment. "Hosanna in the highest, and peace to his people on earth!" He was overjoyed, anticipating the climax of Jesus's ministry unfolding right before his eyes.

"Blessed is the coming kingdom of our ancestor, David!" Judas yelled, also caught up in the crowd's palpable energy.

By riding into the Holy City on a donkey, Jesus was announcing—with certainty—his coronation as the King of Israel.

The shouts were deafening, with Simon Peter recognizing fragments of the prophecies and psalms. "Hosanna to the son of David! Blessed is he who comes in the name of the Lord! Hosanna in the heights of heaven!"

After nearly an hour, they reached the Gates of Damascus. Simon instinctively moved in closer to Jesus, using his large hands to deflect the people away from his master. As the teacher's self-appointed bodyguard, it was his duty to maintain order. At this precarious bottleneck, he took his job more seriously than ever.

As Simon felt his shoulder touch the donkey's front quarter, he decided, *Not everyone in this crowd is a believer.* The people's eagerness was bordering on being unsafe. Finally returning to his senses, he told himself, *There are those in this crowd who might be hostile.* He shoved two men away. *Not on my watch!*

Trying to shake off the excitement of overthrowing Roman rule and reestablishing the Jewish kingdom, Simon refocused on the threats. With his head on a swivel, he could already see the temple authorities calling for reinforcements. *Just as I expected.*

Loud enough to wake the dead—or make those same authorities chafe—a chorus of praises for the Messiah continued to ring from the mouth of the city. Many claimed to hear a voice come from above, glorifying Jesus in a thundering roar. Swept up in the divinity of the moment, even some of the temple priests bowed their confused heads in reverence.

Taken aback by this, Simon looked to Jesus for his reaction.

The rabbi shook it off. "They love the approval of men more than the approval of God," he shouted above the din.

Are we in danger? Simon wondered, quick to shake off the first sign of panic. *We must be safe,* he tried convincing himself. *There's no way Caiaphas would risk this massive crowd's wrath.* Then again, he understood that his teacher was the greatest enemy of the High Pharisees—*and maybe even the Romans.*

Simon's thoughts continued to pendulum between excitement and dread.

When Jesus passed through the gates and entered Jerusalem, the entire city had been stirred up into a near frenzy. A half-million people had converged on the Holy City for Passover, and many were greeting Jesus and his followers.

"Who is this?" one pilgrim shouted.

"This is the prophet Jesus, from Nazareth of Galilee," another yelled back. The people were celebrating as though their liberators had just arrived.

Simon scanned the area. *The Romans must be on high alert for possible unrest.*

Well inside the city walls, Jesus dismounted the ass before looking toward the temple, the center of the Jewish world where some people believed God Himself resided.

The rabbi glared at the money-changers' tables located just outside of the building. Before purchasing their animal sacrifices to be laid at the altar, pilgrims were required to exchange their Roman currency for Jewish. *That's not the issue,* Simon thought. *It's where they conduct their business that's the problem.*

Jesus's body tensed.

Oh no … Simon thought, enjoying a brief respite from the sun in the long shadow of the temple. He watched as his master's face contorted. *I've seen that look before. He's angry.*

The rabbi did not wind cords into a whip like the last time. Instead, he simply marched straight toward the money-changer tables and began overturning them—one after the next. Even the vendors' seats were tossed into the warm air. "My house is a house of prayer for all nations, but you have made it a den of robbers. Get out!" Jesus screamed. "Out!"

My house? Simon repeated in his head.

As before, several of the money changers were paralyzed in fear. Others fled, moving as quickly as the gossip that rippled through the marketplace—and beyond.

Although Simon felt an intense rush of adrenaline course through his veins, he thought, *We've been down this road before. It's time to start flipping over Romans.*

Simon was having difficulty reconciling Jesus, who was clearly physically tough. *He has a strong, muscular build,* Simon assessed. *Even his long strides force the rest of us to struggle keeping up.* But usually, his master's voice, his demeanor, were gentle and meek. *Everything is about love, peace, and forgiveness.* He scratched his beard. *And mercy, even for those who deserve none.*

But at this moment, Jesus's blazing eyes and intense tone told a different version of who he was, perhaps his human side. *How can the rabbi's authority ever be questioned?* Simon wondered. *How can anyone doubt a word he speaks?*

Drawn by the uproar, some of the Pharisees surveyed the scene, hurrying off to report the disturbance to their boss.

Simon pointed them out to Andrew. "Look at the mice, scurrying off to their nest."

"I see them," Andrew said, shaking his head. "We're the ones who should be setting traps."

The marketplace commotion, instigated by the radical rabbi, was spreading through the streets like wildfire.

Here we go again! Simon thought, feeling unsettled. *Making a scene at the temple is not going to help our cause with the Jewish authorities. Why does he have to be so confrontational with them?* He turned to John. "Jesus is going to get us all killed!"

John said nothing, remaining frozen in thought.

Simon grabbed at the front of his own throat, feeling as though the noose was beginning to tighten.

"By now, Caiaphas has already been informed that the master drove the merchants from the marketplace," John commented.

This time, Simon did the listening.

"And he'll want the troublemaker immediately stopped," John added, shaking his head. Nodding, Simon looked to the others, noticing that Judas was the only apostle absent.

Where did our treasurer go now? Judas had been making himself scarce, creating some distance between himself and the rabbi. *I wonder what that coin-lover is up to?*

Later, once the tumultuous day's sun had set, they returned to Bethany to rest in relative comfort and safety for the night.

The apostles were relieved to be away from the city—even if only for a few hours.

There's nothing harder than trying to sleep with one eye open, Simon thought.

In the morning, en route back to the Holy City, Jesus approached a fig tree by the side of the road. Announcing he was hungry, he approached the tree, only to find nothing but leaves.

Shaking his head, he commanded, "Let this tree never bear fruit again."

Immediately, the tree withered and died.

Whoa! Simon thought. *What's that all about?*

As the apostles walked behind Jesus, some nervous looks were exchanged. A few of the disciples groaned among themselves. "How did the fig tree immediately wither away?"

"Verily, I say unto you," Jesus explained, "if you have faith, without any doubts, you shall not only do what was done to the fig tree, but you can say to this mountain, 'Get up and move into the sea,' and it will happen. For all things, whatever you ask in prayer, believe you will receive it."

Although Simon listened, he still couldn't get past the cursed tree that they had left in their wake. *That type of cruelty is not who Jesus is,* he thought. *Why would he do that ... kill an innocent life?* Having the power to perform miracles was one thing, but this felt like the opposite—and it shook him.

Jesus was not finished teaching. "But when you pray," the master added, "you must forgive your enemies as you hope to be forgiven."

Simon looked back at the dead tree. *Huh?*

Andrew slapped his arm. "I didn't see that coming, did you?" he whispered.

Simon shook his head, happy that he wasn't losing his mind. "What do you think that was all about? I realize Jesus is hungry, but he's never—"

"I think it goes much deeper than that," Andrew said, interrupting his brother. "Knowing Jesus, there's definitely a lesson in it ... some type of symbolism."

"Like what?"

Andrew gave it some thought. "The tree was fruitless when Jesus approached it, kind of like the temple priests and the people who have refused to believe he is the Christ." He shrugged.

Could that be it? Simon wondered. *Could it be a sign of what's yet to come?*

Every single step that Simon took toward the Gates of Damascus was spent trying to unravel the tangled lesson. *Was that curse actually meant for the Jewish authorities at the temple?*

They weren't two cubits beyond the city's gates when Simon Peter rubbed his neck, feeling the tension start to build off the previous day. Still mesmerized by the dead fig tree, he wondered, *Wielding such power at his fingertips, why doesn't he use it against the Romans?*

Jesus looked toward the money changers but made no sudden moves toward them.

A small victory, Simon decided.

"It's Jesus!" a Jewish believer bellowed, drawing everyone's attention. "He's here!"

Simon inhaled deeply, preparing for the swarming crowd.

It hit like a wave.

They moved slowly toward the temple as the throng grew with each step. Ascending the stairs seemed to happen in slow motion, with Simon struggling to clear the way for his master.

From the moment they entered the temple, Jesus healed many who could not see or walk.

Witnessing the many miracles, even a few of the temple priests appeared to believe in him, but they could not commit.

Other priests and scribes, hearing children hailing Jesus as "Messiah" and chanting, "Hosanna to the son of David" were terribly offended.

"Do you hear what they are saying?" they asked Jesus.

The rabbi replied, "Have you never read, 'Out of the mouths of babes and sucklings, you have brought forth perfect praise'?"

The chief priests and the elders turned ferocious. "By what authority do you do these things?" they barked. "Who gave you the authority?"

Jesus replied, "I will ask you one question, which if you answer, I will tell you by what authority I do these things." He paused. "The baptism of John, did it come from heaven or from men?"

Huddled together, they conferred in whispers. "If we say, 'From heaven,' then you will tell us, 'Why then do you not believe him?' But if we say, 'From men,' then we fear the multitude, as they believe John is a prophet." They shook their heads. "So, we cannot say."

"Then neither can I tell you by what authority I do these things," Jesus told them, shaking his head. "John came to you in the way of righteousness, and you did not believe him. The publicans and the harlots believed him, but not you. You saw and did not repent, allowing yourself to believe."

Simon recalled his recent epiphany when paying off their taxes. *The publicans and sinners believe, but those who should, do not.* He couldn't help but smile proudly. *Maybe I am starting to get some of this?*

Shifting his focus and monitoring everything before him, Simon knew quite well that the Pharisees planned to lay traps for the master or disgrace him to any pilgrim who would listen.

After offering parables of the wicked to them, Jesus asked the Pharisees, "What do you think about the Christ? Whose son is he?"

"David's," one of the finely dressed men answered.

"How is it then that David and the spirit call him Lord, saying, 'The Lord said to my Lord, *Sit you at my right hand until I put your enemies under my feet.*' If David calls him 'Lord,' how can he be his son?" David had prophesied the incarnation of God in one of his descendants, who was now speaking directly to them.

But the temple leaders rejected this final chance to believe.

"Do not be called masters," Jesus told them, "for only one is your master, the Christ. The greatest among you shall be a servant. And whoever exalts himself shall be humbled. And whoever humbles himself shall be exalted."

Sounds familiar, Simon thought, recognizing the importance of this redundant message.

He and the other apostles had heard many of the rabbi's lessons so often that they took his words for granted—their lack of understanding leaving them blindly ignorant.

Jesus was not nearly done laying down the law. "Woe to you, scribes and Pharisees, you hypocrites..."

Woe to you! Simon repeated in his head. While his teacher gave the self-righteous elite two stinging earfuls, Simon spent the time scanning the large crowd for potential dangers.

"Woe to you, scribes and Pharisees, you hypocrites," Jesus continued to repeat, lambasting them with a passion Simon had rarely heard.

At one point, the rabbi explained how the Pharisees had misled their flock and why they would never enter the kingdom of heaven.

The priests and elders were being pushed to a state of madness.

While the shaken multitude gossiped among themselves, Simon would not have been surprised if they had been arrested on the spot. *It shouldn't be long now,* he thought.

As Jesus predicted the crimes the Jewish leaders would commit, the mob remained relatively silent—horrified.

Without warning, Jesus's tone suddenly changed from fervent to sorrowful, commanding Simon's complete attention. The master offered his farewell to the Holy City. "Jerusalem, you who killed the prophets and stone those who are sent to you, how often would I have gathered your children together, as a hen gathers her chicks under her wings. But you would not. Behold, your house shall be left to you desolate."

Is Jesus predicting the destruction of the temple?

"For I tell you that from this time," the master added, "you should not see me until you say, 'Blessed is he who comes in the name of the Lord.'"

Simon felt ice water surge through his veins, knowing there would be no shaking this one off. After listening to Jesus all these months—these years—he could hear the finality in his teacher's words.

How can the master be saying goodbye? Simon wondered, his level of understanding infantile.

Later in the afternoon, Jesus continued to prepare his twelve apostles, explaining Daniel's prophecy of the Christ being slain.

It was an appalling vision and one that Simon quickly pushed away from his mind's eye.

"You will need to carry my teaching to every part of the earth, spreading the gospel among hate," he told his apostles, foretelling the future. "You shall be hated by all nations for my namesake."

Offering more prophesies of the future—of false Christs and deceitful prophets—the rabbi also spoke of the Apocalypse and End of Days.

Simon wanted to cover his ears. *This is too much to hear.*

Jesus then discussed his—Christ's—second coming.

The entire talk made Simon feel like his head was going to crack open. Worse than the terrifying details was wondering, *Is Jesus preparing us, as if he's going away and will no longer be around?*

Simon's face became twisted from the stress. As he considered the possibility, he had never felt so afraid. *How could we survive, ministering to the people without him?*

CHAPTER 18

SETTING THE TABLE

Jerusalem, Judea

On the first day of Unleavened Bread, Simon Peter asked his brother, "Where are we staying tonight?"

"James asked where we should prepare to eat the Passover," Andrew said, "and Jesus told him, 'Go into the city to see a man, and tell him that the teacher's time is at hand.'"

The teacher's time is at hand? Simon repeated in his mind.

"Jesus said that he wished to keep the Passover at the man's house with his disciples."

"What man?"

"A friend of Jesus's," Andrew replied, shrugging. "A man of wealth, from what I gather."

Simon looked at him, awaiting more details.

"I went with James and overheard our host command one of his servants to have the dinner prepared for thirteen in the upper room."

Upper room, Simon repeated in his head. "Thirteen, huh?"

Andrew nodded. "Jesus and the twelve of us."

Hmm... "That's unusual."

Andrew shrugged again. "Maybe he has instructions for us?"

Simon nodded. "So, what do you think will be on the menu? Roasted lamb? Salted fish? Maybe even beef, if the master of the feast is generous," he suggested excitedly. "You said he is rich, right?"

Andrew shook his head. "That's the part you're not going to like."

"What do you mean?"

"It looks like we're in for a simple meal, Simon."

"And what's that?"

"Bread and wine."

"And?"

"Just bread and wine," Andrew repeated.

"I thought you said our host has means."

"He does, but Jesus requested only bread and wine."

Sighing heavily, Simon thought, It *doesn't get much simpler than bread and wine*. The thought stuck in his head. But *why?* he wondered. *Why just bread and wine?*

It was Thursday, just before the setting of the sun. After touring the city all afternoon, Peter and John arrived at their host's lavish home, located on Mount Zion in the upper part of Jerusalem.

Jesus and the other ten apostles were already gathered outside.

The other disciples weren't invited, Peter recalled, but didn't consider that the homeowner wouldn't be in attendance either. The evening was already thick with mystery.

Peter noted that everyone was smiling—*except Judas*. He studied the treasurer's beady eyes. It wasn't easy. Judas refused to hold anyone's gaze for more than a moment. *It looks like something's tormenting him*. Peter thought about it. *If it's because he was scolded by Jesus in Bethany, then he needs to get over it*. He snickered. *He's not the only one in this group to be reprimanded*.

Stepping through the courtyard, Peter wondered why they weren't dining outdoors. *With the sun setting, it would be comfortable enough.*

Instead, they were escorted up a set of stone stairs to the home's upper chamber, where privacy abounded. *Maybe Andrew's right. Maybe Jesus has special instructions that he doesn't want any outsiders to hear.*

As they passed through the room's threshold, each man tapped the mezuzah before kissing the fingers that touched it.

I'm almost as tired as I am hungry, Simon thought. *I hope they've stockpiled plenty of bread.*

As they entered, the room was already dark with the windows closed, brass oil lanterns illuminating the dining chamber. Water basins and clay jugs were available for foot washing. Peter noted that all the preparations for the Passover feast had been made. Looking at the table, he thought, *Andrew was right, as usual ... a simple meal of bread and wine.*

The vast majority of the room consisted of a low triclinium table in the shape of a U. Large couch cushions had been placed on all three sides, leaving the middle open for the servers to work.

As the father of the feast, Jesus did not sit in the middle. Instead, he was seated second to the left, with his beloved friend John on his immediate right.

The apostles often jockeyed for their place nearest Jesus. *This meal is no different,* Peter thought, accepting the last position opposite Jesus.

To everyone's dismay, Judas brazenly claimed the post of honor at the Lord's left. Jesus never objected. Peter took a breath, rolled his eyes, and turned away.

The seating assignments then continued around the table, with the most important guests seated on the left, then descending in hierarchy with the least important of them—the servant—sitting on the far right. *Which just happens to be my seat for this meal,* the chief apostle realized.

Occupying this last position closest to the door, Peter was expected to help serve the others—*whether it's washing feet or serving food.* He was scratching his head over the setup when Jesus offered the meal's opening remarks.

"He who is greatest among you, let him be the least. And he who is chief, he shall be the servant. For which is greater," Jesus asked, "he who sits for the meal, or he who serves it?" Unconcerned with receiving an answer, Jesus continued looking directly at Peter. "It is not he who sits for the meal."

So last should be first and first last, Peter thought, looking at Judas, who was already enjoying his imaginary position of honor. *I get it now.*

"I am among you as he who serves," Jesus said, hammering the lesson home.

From the start, there was so much love in the room, a sense of true fellowship surrounding the table.

Jesus turned to Judas Iscariot on his left. "You are very quiet, friend," he said.

"Am I?"

Simon Peter had been monitoring Judas's strange behavior for some time now. *But Jesus loves Judas and wants him to know that, or else he wouldn't have been allowed in the seat of honor at Jesus's left,* he decided.

Jesus addressed the table. "I've eagerly desired to eat this Passover meal with you before I suffer."

Suffer? Peter repeated.

"I will not eat again until the fulfillment of the kingdom of God," the rabbi told his disciples.

Peter looked around the room to see the same confusion he was feeling.

Rising from the table, Jesus lay his garments aside before girding himself with a towel. Pouring water into the basin, he began to wash his disciples' feet, wiping them with the towel he wore.

Peter looked on in awe as his master washed Judas's feet. *Jesus, our host and greatest of us all, is acting like a servant,* Peter thought.

His teacher approached.

"Lord, are you going to wash my feet?" Peter asked, beginning to rise. "No, you will never wash my feet!" He was taken aback. *This is our leader, and foot washing is a slave's task.*

"If I do not wash you," Jesus told him, "you shall have no part in me."

No part in me rang in Peter's head. Imagination turned to emotion while he considered the prospect of having no part of Messiah. He couldn't help himself. Overcome, he began to plead. "Lord, not only my feet, but also my hands and my head."

After Jesus had finished washing Peter, he dressed and sat down. "Do you know what I have done to you?" he asked, without awaiting an answer. "You call me 'teacher' and 'Lord,' and you are right, because that's what I am. So if I, Lord and teacher, have washed your feet, you should also wash one another's feet. I have given you an example, so that you should also do what I have done for you." He met each of their eyes. "No servant is greater than his master," he explained, letting them know that although he had come as a king, he was sacrificing as a servant. "And no master is greater than the one who sent him."

His example has left no doubt, Peter thought, pondering this important lesson of servant leadership.

Jesus looked around the table. "You are clean," he said, before his eyes fell upon Judas.

"But not all." He took a deep breath, exhaling as though he was expelling a deadly toxin. "I know whom I have chosen, so that the scripture may be fulfilled."

Each man lay on his left side—leaving his right hand free to eat—while leaning on the bosom of the person to his left. Each man's feet were pointed to the outside, away from the food.

Much of the exuberance was lost as the meal unfolded. Peter could feel it. *Waiting for this revolution to begin is exhausting.* He studied his master, thinking, *Even Jesus appears troubled in spirit.*

As if on cue, the rabbi announced, "I tell you that one of you shall betray me. And when it comes to pass, you will believe that I am he."

Peter signaled to John, who was seated directly across from him. It took a few moments before he grabbed his best friend's attention. "John, ask Jesus who..."

"*What?*" John mouthed.

Shocked by this announcement, the other disciples were already turning to one another, wondering whom Jesus was referring to. "Is it I, Lord?" they asked, one after the next.

Trying to contain his frustration, Peter finished his question. "John, ask the master... who will betray him."

Nodding, John leaned on Christ's bosom, asking, "Lord, who is it?"

Peter listened intently, but it was hard to hear from his cushion at the end of the table. Jesus said something to Judas before reaching into the bowl, grabbing a piece of bread, and dipping it into a plate of herbs—according to the old ritual. He then handed the sop to Judas.

Peter watched the exchange, thinking it odd that the master would feed their treasurer.

Suddenly, Judas—looking sick—stood and departed from the meal, slithering away into the starless night.

I wonder what task Jesus has given Judas? Peter wondered. *Maybe he's going out to purchase something we still need for the feast.* He shook his frustrated head. *John will have to fill me in on what I've missed.*

"Woe to the man by whom the Son of Man is betrayed!" Jesus said, loud enough for all to hear. "It would have been better for him had he not been born."

His mouth still empty, Peter swallowed hard. *I don't know who he's talking about, but I wouldn't want to be that poor soul!*

As soon as Judas was gone, the mood in the room changed. It was palpable. Light seemed to fill the upper room's darkened chamber.

"Now is the Son of Man glorified," Jesus said, "and God is glorified in him. And God shall glorify him in Himself, and straightway shall He glorify him."

What is going on? Peter wondered, feeling more lost than ever.

"Little children, yet a little while I am with you," Jesus explained, "I give you a new commandment, that you love one another as I have loved you. By this, all men will know that you are my disciples, if you have loved one another." He nodded. "Peace I leave with you, my peace I give to you. Not as the world gives it, but as I give it to you. Do not let your heart be troubled, neither let it be afraid. I came forth from the Father and come into the world. Again, I leave the world and go to the Father." Jesus looked around the table. "All of you shall be offended in me this night, for it is written that I will smite the shepherd, and the sheep of the flock shall be scattered abroad. But after I am raised up, I will go before you..."

"Lord, where will you go?" Simon Peter blurted.

"Where I go, you cannot follow now," Jesus replied, continuing to show his first apostle patience, "but you shall follow afterward."

"Lord, why can't I follow you now?" Peter asked.

"I have prayed for you," Jesus told Peter, "that your faith may not fail you."

"Lord, I am ready to go with you to prison and death," Peter replied. "I will lay down my life for you."

All the disciples agreed, nodding and vowing the same.

Jesus looked directly at Peter, where his gaze remained. The room went silent. "You will lay down your life for me?" Jesus repeated, shaking his head. "I tell you this, on this very night before the rooster crows, you will deny me three times."

What? Peter thought. *I would never deny you! I would defend you to the death, with word or sword.* "Lord, I would never..."

"Before the rooster crows, you will deny me three times," Jesus repeated.

The group murmured, each one of the disciples feeling disturbed and mystified.

Jesus's attention turned from Peter to the entire group. "Let not your heart be troubled. Believe in God, and believe also in me. In my Father's house, there are many mansions. If it were not so, I would have told you. I go to prepare a place for you. And if I go and prepare a place for you, I will come again and will receive you to myself. Where I am, you shall also be. And when I go, you will know the way."

"Lord, we do not know where you are going," Thomas said, speaking up for all of them. "How can we know the way?"

Jesus took pause. "I am the way, the truth, and the life," he explained. "No one comes to the Father but by me." Jesus asked, "You still don't know me?" There was an awkward silence.

"Lord, show us the Father, and it will suffice," Philip said.

"I have been with you all this time and you still don't know me, Philip?"

Philip turned tight-lipped.

"He who has seen me has seen the Father, so how can you ask me to show you my Father?" Jesus asked, slowly and with great emphasis. "Do you not believe that I am in the Father, and the Father is in me? My words are not from myself, but from my Father, who lives in me." Nodding, he softened his tone. "Believe me, I am in the Father, and the Father is in me."

He is in the Father, and the Father is in him, Peter repeated in his head, thinking this might be the answer to some of his lingering questions. *Jesus has the power of Jehovah, is that it? He raised the dead, power only Yahweh could have. And I'm going to deny him?* He shook his head. *There's no way!* Peter's mind continued to race. *And why is Jesus talking about going to prepare a place for us?*

Simon Peter was still wading through this fleeting epiphany when Jesus took a piece of unleavened bread. Giving thanks, he broke it, passed it to his disciples, and said, "Take this bread and eat it. This is my body, which is given for you. Do this in remembrance of me."

Confused by their master's words, the eleven remaining apostles accepted the bread and ate it.

This is the same talk that angered everyone in Capernaum, Peter remembered.

Jesus then took his cup, and giving thanks, filled it with wine. "This is the blood of my covenant," he said, "which is poured out for many for the forgiveness of sins." He took a drink before passing the cup.

They each took a sip.

How is that possible? Peter wondered. *And what kind of revolution is this?* He still didn't get it. *I've witnessed the power of Jesus,* he thought, *and now the man speaks of his own death!* It was difficult for Peter and the others to hear their rabbi speak like this. *To eat and drink in remembrance of him?* It brought chills.

"Unless you eat of the flesh of the Son of Man and drink his blood, you have no life in yourselves," Jesus explained.

What? Although Peter did not understand, he knew this was important—and drank heartily.

The mood in the upper chamber changed again, becoming more somber.

"If you ask anything in my name, it will be done," Jesus promised, "and if you love me, you will keep my commandments. I will pray to the Father, and He shall send you another Comforter that will be with you forever, the Spirit of truth, whom the world cannot receive, because it does not know him. But you know him, and he shall be in you."

Send a Comforter? Peter questioned. *A Spirit of truth?*

Jesus scanned the room. "If you love me, you will rejoice, because I go to the Father, and the Father is greater than I."

Go? Peter wondered. *When?*

Jesus took a deep breath. "But I tell you, I shall not drink the fruit of the vine again, until I drink it with you in my Father's kingdom."

This comment was followed by a barrage of questions from the confused apostles.

Jesus explained, "He who receives whomsoever I send receives me. And he who receives me, receives Him who sent me."

Peter concentrated on his teacher's words, laboring to understand.

"If a man loves me, he will keep my word," Jesus added, "and my Father will love him, and we will come into him and make our home with him. Peace I leave with you, my peace I give you. Let not your heart be troubled, nor let it be afraid."

Questions flew around the table, while Peter's head was caught in a full spin.

Jesus continued to teach some important lessons. Among them was a lesson of servant leadership, examples of true love and devotion toward even the greatest of sinners.

"Are you not believing?" Jesus asked the group. "Behold, the hour has come when you will all be scattered and leave me alone."

Impossible! Peter thought, knowing better than to voice his disagreement.

"And yet, I am not alone, because the Father is with me." After confirming that he and the Father were one, Jesus searched their eyes. "These things I have shared with you, so that you might have peace."

And we're right here with you, too, Peter thought, somewhat defiantly. *You are not alone, Lord.*

"In the world, you will have tribulation," Jesus warned them, "but be of good cheer. I have overcome the world."

Although the sconces continued to flicker with light, the room seemed to darken.

As the supper ended, Jesus rose from the table, announcing that he wished to go to the Garden of Gethsemane to pray.

Grabbing a sword that hung on the wall, Peter fastened the sharp, flat blade to his girdle. *With all this talk of suffering and Jesus being given up to his enemies,* he thought, *I'm not taking any chances.*

The group exited the upper chamber, with some of the apostles talking and laughing. To Peter, this was madness. *What is there to celebrate after what we've just been told?*

Descending the steep stairs, Jesus led his disciples in the singing of a hymn, the last portion of the Hallel. His tone was not the usual joyous tenor. Instead, each note was filled with melancholy. While some of the others sang with fervor, Peter merely mouthed the words.

"Yah, be mindful of us.
Bless us.
Bless the house of Israel.
Bless the house of Aaron.
Bless those awed by You. Both the little with the big.
Keep us and our children growing in blessing.
And we, with the grace of the God."

Peter considered how many times he had sung this anthem throughout his life. *But this feels very different.* As the others sang, his brain surrendered to its subconscious, his entire body pulsating from a blend of fear and uncertainty.

When they finished singing the hymn, they started toward the Mount of Olives. "The stone that the builders rejected has now become the cornerstone," one of the apostles called out from the rear of the pack. "This is the Lord's doing, and it is wonderful to see."

Remaining silent, Peter stayed close to Jesus.

CHAPTER 19

WOLVES AND SHEEP

Jerusalem, Judea

After that momentous meal, Jesus took his disciples beyond the secure walls of Jerusalem, proceeding across the valley to the Garden of Gethsemane. "I need to pray," he announced.

Peter followed, worried for his master. *Jesus is restless, and his words have become dark.*

He remained vigilant. *What if someone alerts the authorities of our whereabouts?*

"I need to pray," Jesus insisted.

As they walked toward the garden, Peter was still trying to process all that had been spoken and shared. It was not lost on him that this meal felt different from the hundreds of other meals they had shared in their three years together. *The mood in the room. The tone of Jesus's voice,* Peter considered. *There even seemed to be a finality to it … a farewell. He even said I would betray him. Never!* The hairs on the back of his thick neck awoke.

Trying to shift his thinking, Peter wondered, *Where did Judas go? What did the master tell him that made him leave so quickly?*

He stepped up beside John. "Don't you think it's strange that Judas never returned to the supper?" he whispered.

His best friend looked at him with consternation. "Simon, did you not see what happened?"

"I saw everything that happened," Peter said. "I just couldn't hear anything from where I was sitting."

"Well, when I asked the master who would betray him, Jesus said, 'It is the one to whom I give this piece of bread when I have dipped it in the dish.'"

"And he handed Judas the sop!" Peter blurted. *But Judas was seated in the place of honor.*

John continued, "That's when Judas asked, 'Can it be I, Lord? Surely, you don't mean me?' And Jesus told him, 'Do what you have to do, but do it quickly.'"

I missed all of that, Peter thought, before picturing Judas's smug face and becoming angry. "That scrawny little ..." He stopped.

As they shortened the distance to the garden, Peter moved closer to Jesus—his sword half-concealed on the right side of his tunic. Although he was with the group physically, his mind was still back in the upper room. *The master compacted so many lessons into one sitting. It felt strangely frightening. It's as if Jesus needed to get it all out and make sure that we heard him.*

Peter replayed those lessons, one line after the next.

Jesus explained that he was the true vine and that his people were the branches. "Every branch that does not bear fruit, God takes away. But every branch that bears fruit, God cleans it so that it may bear more fruit."

As usual, Peter continued to nod, struggling to keep up. *Being seated all the way over here isn't helping; I know that, for sure.*

Jesus's scanning head stopped at Peter. "There is no greater love than for a man to lay down his life for his friends," he said.

This time, Peter had heard every word. He nodded fervently, proudly.

"My soul is exceedingly sorrowful, even unto death," Jesus confessed to the three of them, obviously battling his own emotions. "Stay here and watch."

"Yes, of course, Master," Peter said, yawning. His eyelids felt heavy.

Moving a stone's throw away, Jesus fell face down on the ground. On his knees in the dark night—beneath the shelter of olive trees—Jesus cried out to Yahweh. "My Father, if it be possible, let this cup pass away from me."

Jesus's childlike pleas were frightening to Peter. *What can the master be afraid of?* he wondered. *He is Messiah, the Christ.* But his teacher was clearly traumatized, and Peter could feel the man's suffering.

Weeping, Jesus looked skyward. "Nevertheless, Your will be done, not mine," he said in surrender.

Jesus's despair was so profound that the sweat on his brow glistened.

However bad this is, Peter thought, yawning again, *we can avoid it and just escape. We have in the past.* He looked to Jesus, deciding, *The rabbi doesn't look like he wants to run and hide from anything tonight.*

Jesus continued to weep.

Peter looked away. His master's anguish was too difficult to watch. *Jesus is in real distress,* he thought. *How could God let His Son suffer so?*

Yawning once more, Peter was unable to keep his promise of keeping watch. Instead of heeding his master's request, he nodded off.

∝•⋈

"Simon, are you sleeping?" Jesus asked, waking Peter. "Could you not watch for one hour?" He shook his troubled head. "Watch and pray that you may not enter into temptation. The spirit is willing, but the flesh is weak."

He's disappointed and angry, Peter realized, accepting the scolding. *I deserve it.* He turned to notice that John and James had also fallen asleep. "I'm sorry, Lord. I'm so sorry," Peter said, having failed the simple test.

Again, Jesus went away to pray. "My Father," he called out, "if this cannot pass away except that I drink it, Thy will be done."

Peter struggled to stay awake, failing once more.

"The hour has come," Jesus announced, startling Peter and the others from their slumber, "and the Son of Man is betrayed into the hands of sinners. Arise, let us go. The one who betrays me is here." Standing over them, the master's brow was beaded with drops of blood, running down his beard and dripping onto the ground.

Peter studied Jesus's face. *I've never seen the master like this*, he thought, feeling frightened and confused. *What does he mean by…*

Peter looked past Christ to see a small mob of officers, chief priests, and Pharisees, accompanied by a detachment of Roman soldiers, coming up the hill. They were carrying lanterns and torches, swords and staves. Peter squinted to make out the silhouette at the head of the column. *It's Judas*, he realized, *that snake!*

Judas Iscariot appeared with the angry group, seeking out Jesus of Nazareth.

Judas knew where we would be, Peter realized, starting to put the puzzle together. *Our treasurer is a traitor of the lowest order.*

Judas walked straight to Jesus. "Hail, Rabbi," he said, kissing Jesus on the cheek.

Jesus embraced him. "Judas, you are betraying the Son of Man with a kiss? Do what you came for, friend."

Judas's face flushed.

Judas clearly gave them a sign, Peter thought. *He must have told them, "Grab the one I kiss; that's Jesus."*

Jesus stepped forward, asking them, "Whom do you seek?"

"Jesus of Nazareth," they answered.

"I am he."

Several of them backpedaled, falling to the ground.

Peter glared at Judas, who now stood beside their enemies. "You treacherous devil," he muttered aloud.

Again, Jesus asked the throng, "Whom do you seek?"

"Jesus of Nazareth," they repeated.

"I told you that I am he," he repeated, before gesturing toward his disciples. "You have found me, so let these other men be on their way."

The apostles inched forward, preparing to defend Christ.

Filled with rage, Peter rushed toward Malchus, drawing the sword from his thigh. Lifting the blade high into the air, he slashed down hard, slicing off a piece of Malchus's ear. The blood flowed freely.

Seeing the damage, Peter thought, *Judas is next!*

Jesus's head snapped sideways at Peter. "Sheath your sword, Simon," he scolded. "Those who live by the sword shall die by it." He glared at him. "Don't you think I could reach out to my Father, and He would send me more than twelve legions of angels? But then how would the scriptures be fulfilled?" He shook his head. "The cup which the Father has given me, should I not drink it?"

Peter didn't dare reply.

Without another word, Jesus grabbed Malchus by the head and healed him, restoring the man's ear to whole. The blood was completely gone.

Jesus has healed the man who is here to arrest him, Peter thought, his breathing near hyperventilation. *How could he heal his enemy?* he wondered in disbelief. *It makes no sense.*

After continuing to teach his disciples on how to be nonviolent, Jesus addressed the hunting party. "You seek me as though I'm a thief, carrying swords and staves to seize me? I sat every day in the temple teaching, and you did not take me there." He looked skyward. "All this will come to pass, that the scriptures of the prophets will be fulfilled."

Everything was happening so fast, making Peter's mind sputter. He did not know anything except, *I will never deny Jesus, and our lives are in danger.* Coaxed by adrenaline, he blurted, "This is your hour, Lord. Put up the sword!"

Jesus paid him no mind.

Peter's eyes darted from one of his friends to the other, and then on to his brother. They had all fallen silent, most of them looking away. He suddenly felt sick and helpless, like he was about to pass out. *Jesus is going to allow them to do whatever they want to him,* he realized.

The chief captain and Jewish officers seized Jesus, binding him and officially taking him into custody.

Jesus looked at Judas with compassion, who shriveled at the look.

"Take them all!" one of the high priests called out.

Peter suddenly came to his senses. The wild rage, the courage—they had abandoned him.

Nothing else mattered but self-preservation. Fear was now completely in charge.

As the apostles fled for their lives, abandoning Jesus, Peter ran the fastest. With each thud of his foot hitting the ground, an overwhelming sense of dread triggered a wave of panic that nearly swept him off his feet.

A safe distance away, Peter stopped. Bent at the waist, he gasped to catch his breath. As his mind spun out of control, he realized that the garden was a place that Jesus and his disciples had customarily visited—*allowing Judas to find us easily enough, and then turn the master over to the authorities.* He wanted to scream but didn't dare. *I'll give away my location.*

Hearing someone moving behind him, he took off again at a sprint. *I'll never forget the Garden of Gethsemane,* he thought, *a place of great betrayal.* He struggled to take in oxygen. *Curse this night!*

When the area seemed clear, Peter stopped again to fill his lungs. He needed to slow his mind enough to string more than two thoughts together.

While he panted, he could still picture Judas's face, leading the Romans to their master—*and betraying Jesus with a kiss.* A murderous rage welled inside him. After recalling the words exchanged between the two, his mind hurried back to the last supper: *The dipping of the bread, Jesus's prediction, Judas suddenly leaving in a huff.* Angry tears welled in his eyes. *Judas sold Jesus out,* he realized. *And for what? To fill his coin purse?* His rage bubbled just beneath the surface. *I'll kill him if I ever see him again, I swear I will!*

Without warning, the rage allowed sorrow to seep in. *Does Judas have any idea what he's done?* Peter's terrible sense of dread returned, a feeling of irrevocable permanence. *All hope is gone,* he thought.

He started to move again, hoping to catch up to Jesus and his captors. *The wolves have the lamb and are taking him to slaughter.*

Hearing a noise, he looked left to see John moving beside him—half-crouched, his face twisted from terror.

Peter nodded at his best friend, who returned the gesture. *How can this be happening?*

Catching up to Judas and his henchmen, Peter and John followed a safe distance behind, staying in the shadows where they could still see their bound master.

All the work and travels together for three years, Peter thought, *forging ahead, and it's all going to come crashing down because of Judas!* His homicidal rage threatened to boil him alive. *I knew the rabbi should have never chosen that serpent!*

Peter pictured the supper table in the upper room, where his mind's eye fell upon Judas's seat of honor. *The world will remember the name Judas Iscariot forever,* he decided, *and that traitor's name will be symbolic of betrayal.* He shook his head. *And yet, Judas was always astonished by Jesus and his many miracles. So, why did he do it? After all the time we spent together, from the south in Judea to ...* He grabbed his beard and pulled at it until pain messages reached his brain, asking him to stop. *Judas was always different.*

He couldn't reconcile it. Judas was assigned as our treasurer, so Jesus had to trust him, right? He was one of Christ's apostles, and Jesus was good to him. It didn't make sense. Why? Why? Was he trying to force the master's hand and see what he would do against the Romans?

Peter marched on, surmising, *Judas must have been overcome by the dark one.* He was breathing heavily now. *Still, Judas willingly decided to betray our master. It was his choice!* A sense of wrath reared its ugly head once more. *And he made the wrong one, the weak-minded, treacherous coward.*

In his mind, Peter took one last look around the table where Jesus and his twelve had broken bread for the last time; he pictured Jesus handing Judas the sop. "Satan!" he hissed under his breath.

As Peter's heart raced and his breathing quickened, sweat beaded on his forehead, pooling at the back of his neck, before racing down his back. *Everything is changing, and not for the better,* he thought, with no idea of how to stop any of it.

He felt sick to his stomach.

Hidden from sight but still advancing, Peter, John, and Andrew followed the guards and their captive toward the dark palace of the high priest.

Eyes wide, Peter willed his legs to move, all the while reminding himself to breathe.

CHAPTER 20

THEY KNOW NOT WHAT THEY DO

Jerusalem, Judea

I t was early morning, around three o'clock, when Jesus's captors led him straight to the home of Caiaphas, the high priest.

Peter followed John, hoping to witness what was going to happen to their master.

Known by Caiaphas, John was allowed to enter the court of the high priest with Jesus, while Peter remained outside, lingering by the door. An eternal moment later, John went out and spoke to the woman by the door to allow Peter admission.

Entering the dimly lit courtyard—the lion's den—at the risk of his own peril, Peter felt paralyzed with fear. *If I'm recognized, I'll also be taken into custody.* He conducted a quick scan, noting that only every other wall torch was being used—creating a poorly lit atmosphere. For a courtyard designed to boast of the owner's wealth and power, it appeared dungeonlike. *Maybe that's a good thing,* he thought. *No one will spot me.* One thought later, he cringed. *They made sure to arrest Jesus in private, not in public. This trial is guaranteed to be the next phase in their filthy scheme.*

An hour passed slowly.

With his hood pulled down level to his eyebrows, Peter saw that the Sanhedrin—scribes and elders—was being convened in the middle of night, where several false witnesses waited to testify against Jesus. *Things look grave.*

The maid stationed at the door studied Peter. "You were also with Jesus the Galilean," she called out.

"I am not," he said, denying Jesus before them all. "I don't know what you're talking about." His heart rate picked up even more. Although Peter had always been fiercely loyal to Jesus, he was learning the depths that mortal men will go to protect themselves, that self-preservation was an involuntary reaction.

Swallowing hard, the chief apostle wondered, Will *the maid let it go, or will she yell out again until someone believes her, sending me to my own death?*

Although the skeptical woman continued to gawk, she remained silent.

Backpedaling into a wedge of blackness, Peter avoided further eye contact, while doing all he could to appear normal. It was an impossible balance, making him twitch even more.

One moment, he struggled not to run off and escape. The next moment, he wanted to hurry to Jesus and do anything he could to help free his master. *You need to do something!* he pleaded with himself, but his legs wouldn't budge; sheer fear had anchored his sandals to the worn stones. His eyes filled with stinging tears, but he fought those off as well. *Any sign of emotion will give me away.* It was as though Peter's morality was being subdued by a greater force, with each horrible moment of inaction creating more distance between himself and his beloved teacher.

Some great defender I am, he thought, hunkered down in the shadows like a hunted rat.

My brothers have been right about me all along. My protection has been a joke.

His heart pounded hard in his ears. *I hope no one else can hear it.* Feeling drunk on fear, he unconsciously held his breath, gasping for air when his body begged to live. Even though there was a stiff chill in the air, his brow beaded with sweat. *Breathe,* he told himself, pulling the hood closer to his eyeline. *Just breathe.*

Servants and court officers stood off in one corner, stoking coals in the fire. As they huddled together warming themselves, Peter nonchalantly joined them to mirror their movements and appear to fit in.

A different maid spotted him. "This man was with Jesus of Nazareth!" she announced to all who would hear her.

Instinctively, Peter rejected the claim, swearing, "I do not know the man!"

No sooner had the disavowal spilled from his lips than the trial was underway. Peter pushed himself deeper into the shadows and tried to listen above the heartbeat thumping in his ears.

∝•⋊

With Caiaphas serving in the role of prosecutor, the high priest began questioning Jesus about his disciples and his teaching.

"I have spoken openly to the world," Jesus told him. "I taught in synagogues and in the temple, where all the Jews come together. I spoke nothing in secret. Why do you ask? Ask those who have heard me speak. They know."

An officer standing nearby struck Jesus. "Watch how you answer the high priest," he warned.

Peter's body instinctively convulsed. He quickly calmed himself.

"If I have spoken evil, bear witness of the evil," Jesus told the officer. "But why strike me if I have not?"

While the Sanhedrin jury looked on, Caiaphas called for any witnesses who could offer testimony.

Two false witnesses stepped forward.

The first man pointed to Jesus. "This man said he could destroy the temple of God and rebuild it in three days," he testified.

Standing from his throne, Caiaphas addressed the accused. "Do you have nothing to say in defense of what this witness has said against you?" Jesus held his peace, refusing to answer.

This trial is a farce, Peter thought, feeling sick to his stomach. *There will be no justice here.*

One of the Pharisees stepped forward, presenting his double-edged question. "Are you the Christ, the Son of the blessed one?"

"You said so," Jesus answered cleverly.

In response, Caiaphas roared, "I order you by the living God that you tell us whether you are the Christ, the Son of God!"

If Jesus answers yes, he will be accused as a blasphemer, Peter realized. *If he answers no, he'll be an imposter.* He quickly searched for John to see his friend staring at him—his dark eyes glistening with tears.

Jesus took a moment before answering. "If I told you, you would not believe me. And if I were to ask you, you would not answer me."

"Are you the Christ, the Son of the blessed one?" the high priest demanded.

"I am," Jesus admitted, claiming divine authority, "and I'll tell you more. You shall see the Son of Man seated at the right hand of power and coming on the clouds of heaven."

Jesus will not be judged. He will judge, Peter thought proudly. Even so, he also understood that this blasphemous claim was worthy of death.

Although it was subtle, Caiaphas smirked.

This is the answer this monster's been looking for, Peter knew. *The high priest can either see Jesus as Messiah, worshipping him as the Son of God, or deem that the man should be sentenced to death for blasphemy according to the Law of Moses.* He shook his head. *It's an easy decision for him.*

Silence blanketed the courtyard, making Peter feel like he might suffer a massive heart attack.

In an impressive display of high theatrics, Caiaphas began to tear at his own garments. "He has spoken blasphemy! What further need do we have of witnesses?" Turning to the council of elders, he yelled, "You have heard the blasphemy, so what do you say?"

The Sanhedrin quickly found Jesus guilty. "He is worthy of death," they called out, announcing his sentence. "Let him die."

This whole trial is a mockery, a gross tragedy, Peter decided. *The Pharisee hypocrites have ignored their own laws so they can condemn an innocent man to death. I'm sure it was their plan all along.* He wanted to scream. *I always sensed we were in danger, but I never saw this coming. How could I have been so blind ... so dumb?*

Caiaphas nodded. "It is beneficial that one man should die for the people." ... *Offering up the lamb of God for us all,* Peter thought, finishing the man's unjust rationale.

Peter struggled not to vomit.

Spitting in Jesus's face, some of the Jews smacked him with open palms. "Tell us, Christ, who is it that struck you?"

Witnessing this abuse, Peter could feel the throb in his bone marrow. He had never felt such a visceral reaction to anything in his life. And yet, he understood, *This is just the start of it.*

Horrified by the great injustice, Peter and John continued to watch from a safe distance as Jesus was handed over to his executioners.

"Dear God, what has Judas done?" John muttered.

How could it all end like this? Peter thought, trying to drum up the courage to help. *This cannot be happening.* Panic coursed through every vein and capillary.

Doing all he could to remain upright and on his feet, Peter looked up to find a man standing beside him and staring at him. It was one of the high priest's servants, a cousin to Malchus. "Didn't I see you in the garden with him?" he questioned. "Certainly, this man is with Jesus. He is a Galilean. Just listen to the way he speaks."

Cursing and swearing loudly, Peter finally vowed, "I don't know what you're talking about. I do not know this man!"

At that very moment, with the first light of morning growing in the east, the cock crowed. Peter's sudden realization of what he had done crushed him. He felt ill as he recalled his master's words, *"Before the cock crows today, you will deny me three times."* He had done the very thing he had promised Christ he never would. *I've denied knowing my master,* he thought, as if realizing this for the first time. *I deserted Jesus when he needed me most.* He started for the courtyard door. *What kind of man does that?* he wondered, weeping bitterly. *Worse than a coward. Now, I'm a traitor.*

As they began to lead Jesus away, his eyes locked with Peter's—peering directly into his fearful apostle's soul.

Forgive me, Master, Peter pleaded in his mind, *please forgive me.*

Despite being manhandled, Jesus maintained his gaze.

There's no hint of judgment in my teacher's eyes, Peter thought, taking him aback even further. *And he isn't looking at my face but into my soul.* Even if it wanted to, there was no way Peter's soul could look away.

Bound and blindfolded, Jesus was led from Caiaphas's mock trial to the Praetorium to be handed over to the brutal prefect, Pontius Pilate.

This might be the last moment I'll ever see Jesus alive again, Peter realized, before the breath left his lungs. His knees threatened to buckle and take him down. *How can this be happening?* The question had become his mantra. *After all we've been through and all the ...*

Peter's mind went blank; anything that had once resembled goodness within him was being drained away.

Stumbling, Peter somehow managed to run out into the dark night. *I could not ask Jesus for his forgiveness,* Peter thought, panicked. *There just wasn't enough time.*

Peter then recalled having denied Christ three times.

I'm a coward and even less than that. He sobbed. *How could I deny my Lord, the man who has taught me and loved me?*

The night seemed even darker.

Everything I've ever known about myself is wrong, Peter thought, weeping hard and experiencing the darkest moments of his life. *Because I was too scared to stand up for him, that's why.*

Searching for a moment of peace, just a sliver of relief, he finally remembered one of Jesus's many lessons.

"Ask and it will be given you. Search and you shall find," the master had said.

Collapsing to his knees, Peter began to pray. *Forgive me, Yahweh, for I have sinned,* he begged. *Forgive me, Jesus!* Tears raced down both cheeks, puddling onto the ground. He knew his treachery was too great. *I can never forgive myself,* he realized, *so how can I expect anyone else to?*

As the morning opened, the chief priests and the elders took further counsel against Jesus to put him to death, while Peter hugged the shadows, remaining on the outer perimeter of the group. When they reached the Praetorium, the Jewish contingent did not enter lest they be defiled and not able to eat the Passover.

Instead, Pilate went out to them.

Peter shuddered when he saw the heartless butcher. *I always believed Jesus would expel the Romans,* he thought, recognizing the painful irony.

Pilate was the Roman military governor of Judea, stationed in Jerusalem, a distant, backwater place far from his home across the Great Sea. Responsible for raising taxes and keeping the peace, Pilate was loyal to the emperor, as well as his own ambitions.

Peter knew that Pilate had a reputation for having a terrible, violent temper. *If provoked, he can be vicious,* he understood, *and he's completely in charge of Caiaphas.*

The Jews were a subjugated people, making Passover a nightmare for the Romans. *A half-million Jews celebrating liberation, when we're anything but free.*

Everyone knew that as long as there were no problems, Pilate allowed Jews to live undisturbed. *But the city's on a razor's edge,* Peter thought, *and Jesus may be considered a threat to Roman stability.* He was starting to understand his growing sense of dread. *Anyone claiming to be a king automatically threatens Caesar.*

Pilate ordered that the prisoner be marched out.

Once the blindfold was removed, Peter could see that his master's face had been marked. *They've beaten him.*

"Behold," Pilate yelled out, "I bring him out to you, so that you may see that I find him guilty of no crime!"

A pang of hope flickered in Peter's chest. He held his breath to hear more.

"Crucify him, crucify him!" several of the chief priests and officers cried out in response. Caiaphas echoed their request.

The hope in Peter's chest faded.

"What accusation do you bring against this man?" Pilate asked the Pharisees.

"If this man was not an evildoer, why would we deliver him to you?" Caiaphas replied.

"Take him yourselves, and judge him by your own laws," Pilate barked, establishing his supreme authority. Clearly, the battle-hardened Roman did not want to get involved, preferring that the Jewish leaders take responsibility for the nuisance.

"We have a law," the high priest explained. "Jesus claims to be the Son of God. According to our law, he must die, and it is not lawful for us to condemn any Jew to death."

"Are you the King of the Jews?" Pilate asked Jesus at the door of the Praetorium.

"Did I call myself this, or did others say it of me?"

"Am I a Jew?" Pilate countered. "Your own people and chief priests have handed you over to me," he explained, trying to decide whether the man was guilty or innocent. "What have you done?"

Nothing! Peter screamed in his head. *Tell him, Jesus. You have done nothing wrong!*

"My kingdom is not of this world," Jesus said. "If it were, my servants would fight to prevent me from being handed over to your leaders. My kingdom is from another place."

"Your kingdom?" Pilate said. "Then you are a king?"

"You say I am a king. For this, I was born. For this, I came into the world. To testify to the truth. Everyone on the side of truth listens to me."

"What is truth?" Pilate asked, snickering. "Take him away. I find him guilty of no crime."

Thank Yahweh!

But the mob was having none of it.

Jesus of Nazareth is popular among the people, Pilate thought, *which is why jealous Caiaphas doesn't want to be seen as his executioner.* He recalled the high priest's impassioned claim. *"Jesus has been perverting our nation, calling himself Messiah—a king!"* Pilate shook his head. *I need to put an end to this travesty,* he thought, interrogating Jesus once more.

Still, Jesus refused to defend himself.

"Have you not heard the many accusations these people have levied against you?" the Roman governor asked.

Again, Jesus gave no answer, not even one word.

Pilate was taken aback. *This man has inner fortitude, I'll give him that.* Although he understood that this harmless-looking rabbi had stirred up the Judean people with his teachings, he decided, *He's hardly a threat of rebellion.*

Jesus continued to breathe easily, his eyes calm and peaceful.

I'm not seeing the panic I usually see in those facing their own death, Pilate realized. "Do you not understand that I have the power to free you or to crucify you?" he asked.

Jesus finally met his gaze. "You would have no power over me, if it were not given to you from above," he told his condemner.

Maybe it's not so much inner fortitude as insanity, Pilate thought, surprisingly amused.

Over an hour had passed when Caiaphas inquired, "Why do you delay, Prefect?"

"I have found no grounds," he reported defiantly. "I obey Rome."

"Any man who claims to be a king opposes Caesar!" the High Pharisee claimed.

That might be the final nail for Jesus of Nazareth, Pilate pondered, before asking, "You would have me crucify your king? He has done nothing to deserve death."

"We have no king but Caesar," Caiaphas said, offering the perfect, politically correct response. "Crucify him!"

Pilate sighed heavily. "Then I will kill your king for you," he finally proclaimed.

Concealed among the masses, Peter watched as Pontius Pilate addressed the mob once more. "There is a custom for me to release one prisoner at the time of the feast," he said, before turning to one of his soldiers. "Fetch me Barabbas."

Barabbas is a violent revolutionary in custody, Peter thought, feeling another spark of hope. *This one felt cruel.*

When the crowd finally quieted, Pilate gave them a choice. "Whom shall I release to you: Barabbas or Jesus, who is called Christ?"

Peter watched as the chief priests and elders stirred up the mob, demanding that they ask for Barabbas's release and that Jesus should be destroyed. To make matters worse, all of Jesus's disciples were in hiding, scattered from overwhelming fear. *There is no one here with an ounce of courage to advocate for our innocent teacher,* Peter thought, remaining cloaked and hooded.

"Which of the two will you have me release?" Pilate barked at the crowd.

"Barabbas!" they screamed out.

"What should I do then with Jesus, who is called Christ?" Pilate asked them.

"Let him be crucified!" they yelled back.

Cold shivers traveled the length of Peter's bent spine. *Please, Yahweh, no.*

"Why? What evil has he done?" Pilate further asked the people.

As though they could not hear the Roman executioner, they continued to cry out, "Let him be crucified!"

This mob will never be swayed just because Jesus is an innocent man, Peter realized, *and Pilate has no choice. He needs to avoid an uprising.*

In a slow and symbolic display of cleansing himself, Pilate physically washed his hands in front of the crowd. "I am innocent of the blood of this righteous man," he announced, before drying himself.

"His blood will be on us and on our children!" the people called back.

The Jews are to blame, Peter thought, *and the Romans have been exonerated.* He couldn't believe it. *How can it end like this?*

A man of his cruel word, Pilate released Barabbas, before having Jesus of Nazareth delivered up to be crucified.

304

Pilate's soldiers immediately took Jesus into the Praetorium, where they gathered around him. Peter moved into a position in the crowd where he could see the nightmare unfold.

The soldiers spat on Jesus and struck him, smearing him with his own blood. They then stripped him, wrapping him in a scarlet robe like a fool. Placing a crown of thorns upon his head and a reed in his right hand, they kneeled down before him. "Hail, King of the Jews!" they mocked, spitting on him some more.

Dry-heaving, Peter realized that this was not the crowning of a king he had envisioned.

Please, Yahweh, he prayed. *Please stop these demons.*

One of the soldiers ripped the reed from Jesus's hand and smacked him on the head with it.

"Father, forgive them," Jesus said, "for they know not what they do."

Like banshees wailing, words of hate and ridicule spewed from the jeering crowd. "Hail, King of the Jews," they screamed. "Hail, Messiah! Hail, Majesty!"

After Jesus had been thoroughly ridiculed, they removed his robe and put his garments back on.

Please, Yahweh, Peter pleaded, as the Romans led Christ away to be crucified. Stirring up the crowd, Caiaphas chanted, "Crucify him! Crucify him!"

Peter was beyond disheartened. He was in despair.

Found guilty, Jesus was sentenced to death by crucifixion. The charge—trying to lead a rebellion against the Romans.

Crucifixion was the most common form of execution for public criminals, slaves, and political revolutionaries. *And when* the leader of a rebellion is sentenced, Peter knew, it's customary that the Romans hunt down anyone affiliated with the condemned man.

With his hood drawn over his brow, Peter slumped back to the rear of the crowd to consider his options, to consider his failure to act and continue his own inner torture. Giant waves of guilt and shame crashed into him, threatening to drown him. I should've been more vigilant, he chided himself. I should've protected him.

While John and the women followed Jesus, Peter did the same but from a safe distance. The rest of the apostles, petrified for their lives, returned to the safe house where they went into hiding.

CHAPTER 21

NO GREATER LOVE

Jerusalem, Judea

Peter couldn't get over it. The scoffing crowd had swung on Jesus like a massive human pendulum suffering amnesia.

Each time the Roman guards insulted their captor, cheers erupted. When one of the soldiers slapped Christ across the mouth, onlookers were sent into a state of bloodthirsty hysteria. Every insult, each strike, inspired a sinister celebration that echoed throughout the Holy City.

The mob has turned feral, Peter thought.

Helplessly observing from a safe distance, he recalled the prophecy: *Foul mouths spat in the face of the Son of God.* This mayhem was beginning to make sense.

Depraved animals, he decided, intentionally focusing on the people's wicked actions rather than his own lack of action.

Peter felt like he was breathing through a bamboo reed as he watched his Messiah being flogged. Christ's wails reverberated straight to the bone. A cat-o'-nine-tails, a heavy leather strap with metal hooks fastened at the ends, ripped chunks of flesh clean from Jesus's back. Each grotesque lash was unspeakably brutal, causing screams of pain and torment.

Dear Yahweh, please stop this, Peter prayed, understanding that torture was a component of the execution. *No more, please!*

With each devastating blow, the Lamb's innocent blood gushed from his torn flesh. As the barbarism continued, several Roman guards mocked and laughed at Christ.

The theater of crucifixion was designed to make an example for the mob to witness, the perfect deterrent for future radicals. *I've seen inhumanity before, but nothing like this,* Peter thought. Although he forced himself to watch, he never lifted a finger or uttered a word in defense of his tortured friend.

Adorned in his halo of glistening thorns, Jesus was whipped and bloodied beyond recognition, his forehead turned to a strip of raw meat.

No more, Peter begged God, *please, Yahweh.*

Once the terrible lashing had ceased, Jesus turned to the woman who had stayed with him through his torture—Mary Magdalene.

"We are with you," she told him above the cheering crowd.

Jesus labored for breath. "Daughters of Jerusalem," he managed, "don't weep for me. Weep for yourselves." He was implying that there would be other things for them to lament over in the future.

∝•∝

The late-morning sun bore down on the evil spectacle as Jesus, weakened and delirious from his pain, was forced to take up the heavy weight of the cross.

Peter estimated that the cross was nearly twelve feet long and six feet across, weighing approximately 165 pounds. He desperately wanted to emerge from the swollen crowd and help his master but again, his legs wouldn't budge. *If I interfere, I'll be carrying my own cross beside him,* he decided. Willing himself to watch, the chief apostle fought within himself over his crushing cowardice. Matching each of Jesus's steps, Peter traveled the slow, painful procession through the narrow stone streets.

While the crowd cheered, armed centurions whipped Christ whenever he slowed. *Jesus could stop this,* Peter thought. *Why won't he?*

Through his tears, the disguised apostle noted that the women—Jesus's mother, Mary Magdalene, and several others—were walking right behind Christ so they could bear witness. John also moved out in the open to join the women. Peter, the more defiant and recognizable apostle, clung safely to the shadows.

Although Peter remained physically unharmed, his entire being—body and soul—was filled with a toxic fear and murderous rage. Panic swelled inside him, causing heart palpitations and dizzying breaths. He fought to march on.

For one brief and surreal moment, the terrified apostle took in everything around him. Children were playing in the street. Vendors were still hawking their wares, while their buyers haggled for better prices. Animals bleated and complained. *There's even laughter.* In the distance, a woman sang joyously. Peter could not make out the words but considered every syllable a blasphemy. *How can the world be going on as normal when it's about to come to an end?* he wondered.

The master's death walk to Golgotha was heartbreaking, watching him struggle with the heavy wooden cross. Jesus stumbled several times. When he finally fell to the ground—face first— Peter again wanted to hurry to him and take up his heavy load. But he didn't. I *can't*, he thought. *If I do, I'll* ... He stopped, cutting off the litany of excuses that was sure to follow.

Jesus managed to get to his feet, clearly blinded by his own blood. As Christ trudged forward, faltering beneath the weight of his mortal burden, the crowd pressed in on him. Some spat. Others threw refuse. All were taunting lustfully.

As Jesus limped past, several Jewish pilgrims called out to him. "Save yourself!" they chided, laughing when he did not.

"Oh, Rabbi ..." Peter said, his pathetic words drowned out by the hooting of the rejoicing crowd. It was like the most horrific dream that he could not escape. *It'll take more than a pinch to wake up from this nightmare*, Peter thought. *It'll take a miracle.* His eyes leaked bitter tears. *And the only one who can perform that miracle looks resigned to his horrible fate.*

∝•✖

They had just reached the rise, starting the ascent to Golgotha located outside of the city walls.

Upon a prisoner's arrival, death by crucifixion is only a few hours away, Peter thought, when he saw his master collapse again.

Agitated by the delay, one of the soldiers summoned a bystander, a man from Cyrene named Simon. "Help him carry the cross," the legionnaire ordered.

With a single grunt, the dark-skinned pilgrim took up Jesus's cross, muscling it through the final street and up the cursed hillside.

That should be my job, Peter thought, quietly sobbing. *I'm the one who should be carrying my Lord's burden.*

The closer they got to their foul destination, the louder the crowd grew. Bloodlust and savagery swept through the shrieking multitude, the cheers growing more harsh and hateful.

Peter couldn't believe it. *Many of these hissing sinners were worshipping Christ just a few hours ago.*

Peter had to coax his legs to climb. It felt as though he were carrying the cross himself, inspiring even more guilt and shame. Reaching the crest, he discovered that two sympathetic members of the Sanhedrin—Nicodemus and Joseph of Arimathea—were waiting for the unjust execution to take place.

Exhausted, Jesus was carried by a centurion the last few yards.

Please, Yahweh, not like this, Peter prayed, hoping against hope for divine intervention. None came.

Without wasting a moment, two soldiers laid the cross flat on the ground. They placed Jesus on top of it, while another fetched a hammer and nails.

I can't bear to witness the rest, Peter realized, starting to dry-heave. *I don't have it in me.*

He quickly searched out John. "I can't..." he whispered to his best friend. "I'm sorry, but I..."

Offering the kindest nod, John whispered, "I know, Simon. It's OK."

Peter turned and hurried away, trying to create as much distance as he could without being recognized. Unfortunately, he could not move fast enough to avoid hearing Jesus's wretched scream. *The first nail driven into Christ's hand,* Peter surmised, imagining Jesus's nerves being severed, shooting bolts of unspeakable pain to Christ's brain. *The pain must be excruciating.* Peter fell to his knees, where he vomited.

Jesus wailed out in agony again.

The second nail, Peter realized, hacking up more bile.

Filled with sorrow, John watched as his best friend and chief apostle scurried down the hill, tripping and nearly falling. *I understand,* he thought, harboring no judgment toward his lifelong friend. John had always been quieter, more nonthreatening than Simon Peter. He was the one who could hide out in the open—*whether in Caiaphas's courtyard or at this damned place.*

I understand, John repeated to himself, watching as Peter's silhouette grew smaller, *but I need to be here for Jesus.* He looked at Mary, thinking, *and his poor mother.*

He turned just in time to see the Roman soldier drive a nail into Christ's left palm. His master's bloodcurdling scream sent a surge of ice water coursing through his throbbing veins.

Please, Yahweh, John prayed, *either save Your Son, or quickly end his suffering.*

At the second nail, Jesus wailed out again.

Have mercy, Lord God.

While Jesus's mother, Mary Magdalene, John, and others kept their front-row seats at Golgotha, Peter decided, *I'm far enough away to be safe.* Stopping, he turned to see the silhouettes of three crosses on the hill—*Golgotha, the place of the skull.* Although he couldn't make out the message, a sign had been placed above Jesus's head. He squinted hard to read it. *I can't tell what it says.*

From his distance, Peter could only presume how his master's demise was unfolding. He pictured the pitiful state of Jesus's pain-wracked body. Being intimately aware of Jesus's boundless empathy, he thought, *I can't imagine the master's trauma, having to* witness his own mother's hysteria while she and the others helplessly watch him die.

Hyperventilating, Peter wondered, *Are the pictures in my mind worse than what's actually happening up there?*

A war cry shrieked down from Calvary, condemning the city and its unbelievers.

No, he realized, receiving his answer loud and clear.

Studying the silhouettes, Peter recalled the cursed fig tree that had withered and died. *If Jesus has the power to take life, then why not use that power now to save himself?*

No answer came this time.

From his safe perch, Peter continued to watch as Christ suffered and died on the hill. He thought about John and the women. *Where have they found their strength?* he wondered. *And why can't I find mine?* He felt like rolling into the fetal position and awaiting his own miserable death.

Hours passed. The weather turned ominous, the sky looking as though it had descended closer to the earth. It was crypt-like—hellish. Peter daydreamed of warrior angels riding in golden chariots to emerge from the black clouds and intervene, their sharp swords at the ready. *If only...*

His mind flashed back to the transfiguration on the mountaintop with Moses and Elijah.

Where is the miracle today? he wondered.

Instead, a cloud of dust blackened the sky into premature night, while several bolts of lightning ripped through the darkness, illuminating Jesus's silhouette on the hill.

I'm sure that legions of angels are here, he thought, *but Christ would never permit their help. If that were the case, he would never have allowed it* to come to this. *Jesus has the power over life and death. He's proven it many times. But it looks like this is one death he's willing to accept. If he wanted to save himself, he would simply command it and it would be so.*

A chorus of screams from the hill reached a crescendo, echoing through the deepest recesses of Peter's mind.

And what did you do to stop this, Simon? he asked himself. *Absolutely nothing!*

Peter felt like he was suffocating on his own shame. Guilt was devouring him from the inside out. He was heartbroken, sick with grief. *All hope is lost,* he thought, *being murdered on the hill of skulls.*

From his knees, Peter recalled Jesus crying out to his Father in the garden the night before. "My Father, if it be possible, let this cup pass away from me," he echoed in a whimper.

It was like he was begging his Father not to turn His face away from him, the apostle reasoned, *as though any disconnection from Yahweh is the only thing that Jesus cannot bear.*

Another hour or so passed; Peter couldn't tell. Time seemed to be frozen in pain.

The sky blackened even more, with several more lightning bolts illuminating Golgotha. The horrid sounds of tearing and ripping echoed across the city, while the earth trembled underfoot. Peter watched as scribes and Pharisees fled for their lives. For the first time in hours, he held his ground.

Jesus has passed, he realized. *He's gone.* He sobbed so hard that he thought he might join his master. *And what a blessing that is.*

The sky lightened a bit, just enough to see the cross in the middle and its lifeless body being lowered to the ground.

Peter could picture Jesus's battered body being placed into the arms of his weeping mother. Worse, he could picture Mary's tears washing away the blood from her son's scarred face. A *mother's love ...*

At that moment, Peter lost access to all his senses—taste, touch, smell. The world suddenly went silent, while his eyes were blind to anything more than shadows and movement.

In his tortured mind, he could hear Jesus's voice as clearly as the moment the rabbi spoke each word ...

"You are Simon. You will be Peter."

"I will make you a fisher of men."

"You are the rock upon which I build my church."

"No!" Peter shrieked; it was not the manliest sound he'd ever yielded, but his intense pain was unbearable. The misery felt so permanent that he would have done anything to open his chest and tear it loose from his broken heart—*anything.*

One by one, Peter's senses returned to him. He could feel a slight breeze on his skin, making his flesh shiver. The distinct smell of earth followed, a sign of new life growing all around him. Unexpectedly, he heard the distant hum of great pain. *Women in chest-pounding grief,* he recognized.

When he could finally see clearly, he wished he'd been stricken completely blind like the man lying beside the Pool of Siloam. *Only I wouldn't want to be healed,* he decided, weeping. *I don't deserve such mercy or grace.*

Taking one last look at Golgotha, where the Lamb had been brought to die, Peter turned and began to stumble into a future of blinding grief and uncertainty. With each step, he openly sobbed, weeping like a child for his master's demise, as well as the death of his own character. *All those moons ago, I had thought the Samaritan woman was unworthy to be in Christ's presence. Yet it was me who was unworthy the whole time.* He shuddered at his own despicable hypocrisy. *And I've always considered Matthew a coward.* He shook his head. *But I'm the real coward.*

Feeling powerless for the first time in his life, a great fear continued to build inside him; this was not so much worry about the future or his own safety. Rather, Peter wondered how he would ever be able to live with himself again. *Everything I've ever believed, all that I thought I was...* "I don't know anything anymore," he groaned.

Faith and belief mean nothing if you don't have the courage to defend them.

Peter never returned to the group or their safe house on that Friday night. He wandered the streets and alleys in misery, without relief from his intense pain. The entire night was a blur, his mind reeling in sheer agony with no way for him to fix what he had broken. *And what I've broken meant everything in the world to me!*

Wave upon wave of panic smashed into him as he began to understand that there was no way for him to right his wrong. *I must be damned,* he decided. Hearing that word in his head, he pictured Judas. *He betrayed our teacher. But was I any better?*

Stumbling through his endless nightmare, pain and grief sawed the chief apostle in half. *This is my punishment,* he decided, *suffering hell on earth.* He wished he had been nailed to his own cross.

He wandered aimlessly. *I had no idea that Jesus was marching toward his death all along.* Dissecting and analyzing each experience, each situation they had encountered over the past three years, he felt like he was being smacked in the face with a boat paddle. *We were whistling past the tombs the whole time*, he surmised, feeling the aching bite of ignorance.

Did Jesus know everything that was going to happen? he wondered. The answer didn't take long. *Of course he did.*

Raising his eyes, his surroundings only confirmed that he was completely lost and alone. He couldn't reconcile it. *I'm the one who abandoned Jesus, so how is it that I feel abandoned by him?*

Within the black abyss, he could hear Jesus's words ring like a ghost bell in his ears. "There is no greater love than for a man to lay down his life for his friends."

As the last ounce of hope drained away, Peter collapsed to his knees where he began to sob, rocking back and forth on his haunches. He no longer knew anything about himself or the world around him. *It was all a failure*, he thought. *The ministry, the mission, and most of all . . .* He paused. *. . . me.* He cried until there was nothing left but a few pathetic whimpers and a lifetime of regret.

Peter wondered and hoped whether the searing ache in his heart might generate enough damage to end his self-hatred, his inexplicable suffering. As he waited for his own end, he closed his burning eyes and prayed hard for forgiveness.

Five minutes passed—or maybe they were hours—when Peter heard his name being carried on the wind.

"Simon," a man called out in a strained whisper. "Simon . . ."

Slowly raising his head, he saw John standing there, his hand extended. The sight of his best friend made him gasp.

"Come," John whispered, "and be quick about it. We have found refuge at John Mark's home."

"We?" Peter managed, reaching for his friend's hand.

"Jesus's mother, Mary Magdalene, Mary of Cleophas, and myself," John explained, hoisting the broken man to his feet.

"And the others?" Peter muttered, his words choked with emotion.

"Back at the safe house," he whispered. "At least we hope."

We hope? Peter thought, not happy about the group being separated. His legs froze—again.

"Let's go, Simon," John whispered, pulling him forward, "we need to move!"

CHAPTER 22

WHERE WERE YOU?

Jerusalem, Judea

No sooner had the two apostles stepped into John Mark's dimly lit home than John turned to Peter.

"Christ is dead," he confirmed in his normal voice. "Jesus is gone."

Female wails of grief filled the room.

Peter struggled to greet Jesus's mother, when Mary Magdalene collapsed into his arms.

She could hardly breathe, never mind speak.

Comforting her, the chief apostle looked up to see that Jesus's mother was looking at him. Although he tried, he could not bring himself to meet her gaze. His crippling shame and debilitating sense of cowardice would not allow it.

Forgive me, he kept repeating in his head. *Please forgive me.*

When he finally drummed up the nerve to look Mary's way, her gentle face told a very different story. Although Peter had never seen such sorrow, there was not one hint of judgment or condemnation directed toward him. There was only great sadness and the understanding that Simon Peter could not have been with her son in his last moments on Earth because the apostle would have surely suffered the same fate.

Peter could see this as clear as day. *I'm being shown mercy and grace when I deserve neither,* he realized. It broke whatever heart remained in his heaving chest, and his body began to shudder. There were few actual tears. Most had already been used up.

When Peter finally composed himself, he studied the fragmented and frightened band. *Who are we without Jesus?* he wondered. *Who am I?*

Breaking his train of thought, Mary Magdalene cleared her throat. "I understand why you could not be there, Peter," she said gently. "We all do."

Mary of Cleophas nodded.

"Even Jesus," John added.

Peter choked on a gasp. When he caught his breath, he turned to Mary Magdalene. "Tell me what our master suffered," he said, the anguish thick in his voice.

She shook her head, reluctant to speak.

"Please, Mary," he insisted, "tell me."

She looked to John, who gently nodded that she honor Peter's wishes.

As she returned the nod, Peter sucked in a deep breath, steeling himself to hear what he could not bring himself to watch.

Although Mary Magdalene agreed to explain what she had witnessed, she decided, *I'll leave out the worst details as they'll do nothing but torment this poor man even more.*

Unfortunately, she still needed to relive the nightmare in her own mind...

"From the moment Jesus was sentenced to death by crucifixion for the charge of being King of the Jews," Mary explained, "I insisted that we needed to follow and stay with him. John tried to warn me, saying, 'It's too dangerous,' but I told him that it's not the same for us women. To the Pharisees, only men are considered Jesus's disciples. As women, I knew we wouldn't be suspicious or draw any attention."

Peter nodded that he understood, and even agreed.

"Jesus Christ of Nazareth had set me free," Mary Magdalene claimed, "and from that moment on, I have followed Christ and never stopped." Her eyes filled with what seemed like an endless supply of tears. "And I'll follow him to the end."

Mary went on to offer the details she wished she could forget, and Simon wished were not true.

"As Jesus was beaten," Mary recalled, "I wondered how we could not have seen this coming. Jesus had been telling us all along." She shook her cloaked head. "If we believed everything else the master said, then why not this? Still, I knew at that point there was nothing anyone could do to stop it."

Mary continued, "Jesus was then forced to carry his cross through the streets to Golgotha. I remember thinking, *Now we will mourn, watching Christ suffer and perish at the hands of our enemies.*

"John, Jesus's mother, Mary, Martha, and a few of the other female disciples joined me on the horrible trip. I knew right away that we would mourn terribly."

Peter nodded sorrowfully.

"We saw you leave before the first nail was driven into Christ's hand," Mary told the chief apostle. "I realized it was too much for you to bear, so I forced myself not to look away when Jesus was laid on the cross, his arms tied to the thick cross beam." Offering some understanding, she said, "We all knew if you were spotted, you'd be hanging alongside Jesus."

Peter could no longer look her in the eye.

Mary glanced over at John, as she continued to tell the passion story. "John was also able to stay since he's never been considered a threat to Jewish authority or the Romans. So he was safe enough."

Mary told how Christ's followers wept as nails were driven into their master's hands. "Jesus screamed out," she said, "his eyes wild with unrelenting pain. 'No!' Jesus's mother wailed, before she fell into my arms where we sobbed together."

Peter would not look up.

"Situated between two bandits," Mary explained, "one named Gestas on his left and the other, Dismas, on his right, Jesus was hoisted upright by rope. His feet were supported by a shallow wooden ledge. Otherwise, he would have immediately suffocated."

The Romans had designed this punishment to last as long as possible.

"Above Christ's head, a sign read 'Jesus of Nazareth, King of the Jews,' and it was written in Greek, Latin, and Hebrew. The Romans were more than happy to mock Jesus in three languages."

Having seen the sign from afar, Peter nodded.

Mary pressed on. "At the base of the cross, Roman soldiers took Jesus's garments and divided them into four parts—one item per man. As the soldiers watched Jesus suffer, one of them suggested, 'Let's not split them but gamble for them to see who wins it all.'"

While Peter stared at her feet, a shiver traveled through Mary's body. "I remember recalling the scripture that was being fulfilled right before my eyes: 'They parted my garments among them, and upon my vesture did they cast lots.'

"Then Jesus prayed aloud, 'Father, forgive them for they know not what they do,' forgiving the very people who were murdering him.

"As pain slowly squeezed the life out of our master, I wanted to scream for mercy! I hurried over to the guards, begging for some wine to give my dying Lord a drink. The guards could not have cared less, so they allowed it.

"Jesus tasted it before refusing the drink. The wine contained myrrh, which would have obviously helped ease his pain. But I realized he was rejecting the comfort, letting us know he accepted his suffering."

Mary took a few calming breaths before continuing to recall the horrible events for Peter. "Throughout it all, some in the crowd wagged their forked tongues at him. 'You, who say you can destroy the temple and build it back up in three days, save yourself!' one jeered. Another called out, 'If you are the Son of God, then come down from the cross.' The chief priests, scribes, and elders also mocked him, delighting in the cruelty. 'He saved others, but he cannot save himself!'

"I wondered how these people could be so heartless... after all the miracles and wonders Jesus performed in their presence.

"'If he is the King of Israel, let him come down from the cross and we will believe in him,' one roared. 'He trusts in Yahweh,' another barked. 'Let him deliver him now, if he wants to.'

"As they laughed at Jesus, some of the crowd took joy in shaming him. Even Gestas, one of the men being crucified alongside Jesus, joined in the ridicule.

"'Are you not the Messiah? Save yourself and us,' he managed through his own pain.

"Dismas quickly rebuked the man, though. 'Have you no fear of God?' he asked. 'Are you not subject to the same condemnation?'

"I think it was around midday, in the sixth hour, when the sun went down, blanketing the entire earth in darkness. I remember looking up at Jesus and realizing that the Son of Man was perishing on a Roman cross, and the darkness was clearly a divine sign of Yahweh's judgment against his murderers.

"Now repentant for his sins, Dismas turned to Christ. 'Jesus, remember me when you come into your kingdom,' he moaned.

"'Today, you shall be with me in paradise,' Jesus told him."

Peter quietly wept.

"Another two hours passed," Mary continued, "with Jesus's breathing becoming slight and shallow. John, Jesus's mother, the other women, and I waited for the merciful end to our master's suffering.

"I turned to look at John, his face glistening in tears. We all expected a Messiah who was going to overthrow our enemies, a King to rule over everyone. No one expected this."

Peter nodded firmly in agreement.

"Right then," Mary said, "Jesus peered down from the cross and looked at his mother standing beside John. 'Woman, behold your son,' he told Mary. Then, looking at John, he said, 'Behold, your mother.'

"It was about the ninth hour when Jesus cried out in a loud voice. 'Eli, Eli, lema sabachthani?'"

"My God, my God, why have You forsaken me?" Peter translated in a whisper.

Mary nodded. "One of the onlookers yelled out, 'This man calls out for Elijah.' That's when I knew it was nearly over, that the Scriptures had been fulfilled.

"Jesus called out, 'I thirst,' but one of the elders responded, 'Let him alone. Let's see whether Elijah comes to save him.'

"Another onlooker immediately ran for the vessel filled with vinegar. Taking a sponge, he dunked it. Placing the saturated sponge on the end of a reed, the man offered it up for Jesus to drink.

"Upon receiving the vinegar, Jesus cried out, 'It is finished.' Then, bowing his head, he yielded up his spirit."

Peter continued to weep—louder.

"At that very moment," Mary said, "the howling winds and swirling dust increased, striking terror in all who witnessed the awful spectacle. At the same time, a strange ripping sound cut through the air. We now know that sound was the veil of the temple being torn in two, from top to bottom! The earth quaked and rocks were split in two. Even the tombs were opened."

She shook her head. "I was thinking that all hope was lost when I shrieked with grief. Even one of the Roman centurions believed and was struck down with immense fear. 'Surely, this was the Son of God,' he claimed. Many people fell to their knees, as they now understood and believed.

But it's too late, I thought. Jesus is gone. As I fell to my knees next to his brokenhearted mother, I realized that I was not surprised by what had just transpired. Jesus had foretold his fate many times. What I couldn't understand was why he didn't stop it. We've witnessed all his miracles, even raising the dead. He could have easily put an end to this at any time. But he didn't." She wiped tears from her face. "From the moment we met, I always had great faith in him. I never needed to understand the reasons for why Jesus said what he said or did what he did. Just knowing he had his reasons was enough for me."

Again, Peter nodded in agreement.

"The Roman legionnaries prepared to break the legs of the three crucified men to speed up the execution," Mary explained, knowing that without the use of his legs to support his body, a prisoner's body weight will dislocate the arms and shoulders, causing the condemned man to suffocate to death. "The soldiers walked beneath the cross and broke the legs of the first crucified thief and then the other. Jesus was already dead, though." She paused to compose herself enough to go on. "So I knew there was no need to break his legs. Sure enough, when the soldier approached Jesus and discovered that he had already expired, he thrust his sharp lance into the master's right side instead—straight into Christ's heart—to confirm he was no longer alive. Blood and water poured out.

"I realized another scripture had been fulfilled," Mary added, reciting, "'They shall look on him whom they pierced.'"

Feeling sick to her stomach, she looked at Peter. The grief was inexplicable.

"Since Jesus died nearly two hours before the sun had set," Mary recounted, "the Pharisees immediately requested that his body be taken down before the Sabbath. They obviously didn't want a martyr decomposing in the sun while his followers became infuriated. They wanted Jesus off the cross, wrapped up, and carried to the tomb before sundown."

By law, no one could work on the Sabbath, so Peter knew time was of the essence.

"After the Romans lowered the cross, I saw Mary take her dead son into her trembling embrace. Seated at the base of the cross, she cradled his head, rocking him like a baby in her arms as I'm sure she did many years ago in Bethlehem. While her tears pelted Christ's bloodied face, she spoke to him. I couldn't hear what she was saying, but I didn't need to know. No one did.

"Then I saw one of Jesus's secret disciples, that wealthy merchant Joseph from Arimathea, hurry up to Pilate, requesting to claim Jesus's body. He seemed intent on properly burying the rabbi with honor, offering his own tomb within the nearby hillside. Surprisingly, Pilate granted the request. I figured the cruel prefect probably didn't want any grave robbers, which might allow the people to think that Jesus did not actually die."

Mary's eyes stared off into the distance. "I watched as Joseph took Jesus's body to his family's recently hewn tomb, where no man has ever been put to rest. It's in a garden just outside of the city's walls. Joseph also offered the linen for Jesus's shroud. Nicodemus came, too, bringing nearly a hundred pounds of myrrh and aloes. We were grateful for the kindness of both men.

"Once inside the tomb, all of us women who had followed Jesus from Galilee began ministering to him. After cleaning his body, Jesus was wrapped in a winding sheet—clean linen cloths treated with spices—in preparation for entombment. As we worked, we wept quietly. When we finished the burial custom, we laid Jesus in the sepulcher and said our tearful goodbyes.

"His mother lingered the longest, of course, before Joseph and two other men rolled a massive stone across the door, closing the tomb.

"Everyone left, except me. We stayed a little while longer. That's when we learned from a messenger that Pilate had given strict orders not to let anyone approach the tomb or its huge stone blocking the entrance. He explained that the chief priests and Pharisees went to Pilate and asked him to order the sepulcher secured for three days, so that no disciples could steal him away and tell the people that he had risen from the dead."

Peter's head snapped up.

Mary nodded. "When I saw a Roman soldier approaching, preparing to guard the tomb, I remembered Jesus said that after three days he would rise again . I knew it was time for us to leave, so we quickly left and found shelter here at John Mark's home."

She exhaled deeply. Even omitting some of the most heinous details, Mary had replayed the entire trauma in her head while she recited the events for Peter to hear. She was now completely exhausted.

Hearing every word that Mary Magdalene had spoken, Peter felt even more devastated. Until now, he thought he'd hit bottom, but he realized that he was still free-falling. More tears flowed.

"Jesus named you the rock," Mary managed softly, "and that will never change. We believe in you, Simon Peter."

"Jesus chose you for a reason," John confirmed, offering a consoling word. "We might not know what happens from here, but we have faith in your leadership."

Mary embraced the chief apostle. "Jesus may not be here physically," she whispered, "but he's still right here with us. You know that, right?" She pulled away to gaze into his eyes.

Peter mustered the strength for a single nod, but he couldn't move past his own self-loathing.

"We're all in this together," John said. "You're not alone. Remember that."

Simon couldn't believe it. *Why the sympathy?* he wondered. *The understanding?* He continued to weep. *I'm being treated better than I deserve.* Although his guilt was not assuaged, he appreciated their loyalty and friendship.

As each of them dispersed to grieve, Peter realized that Mary Magdalene—a person whom he had judged harshly—was at Jesus's side until the very end. *She had the spine to bear witness to the master's crucifixion.* He could not reconcile the depth of the woman's courage against what he lacked. He admired her. *Mary had the strength and fortitude to stay the course and witness what I could not,* he thought, considering himself less than a worthless weakling. *I let myself down in the most irreversible way. Worse yet, I let down my master and friend.* He wept, thinking, *I'm exactly what I've always despised. I'm a coward.*

Kneeling in a corner of the room, Mary wept terribly.

Watching her, Peter wondered, *Who is Mary Magdalene really?* From the small town of Magdala, she was an unmarried woman of some means. She had followed Jesus and the apostles, helping to fund their ministry by contributing her own resources.

It's unusual for a preacher to have female disciples, but Mary has always been one of Jesus's favorites, Peter considered. *And now I can see why.* He nodded to himself. *I can see exactly why Jesus chose her.*

A new wave of grief struck him, causing his wide shoulders to rock with each muffled sob. *But why on earth did Christ choose me?*

Peter looked up to see Jesus's mother suffering in her devastating grief, the sight of her deep sorrow breaking him even more.

He didn't expect it, but his mind pictured the first time he had met the angelic woman. *It was at the Cana wedding,* Peter remembered. *I'll never forget their hug and the deep love they shared.* As his mind wandered back to that beautiful scene, he could picture every detail.

Peter could almost smell the roasting lamb as he pictured Jesus and Mary embracing each other.

Mary is so beautiful, he thought, *inside and out.*

Breaking from the hug, Jesus and Mary exchanged a long look that revealed more about their sacred bond than any words ever could. Jesus then turned to face his disciples. "Mother," he said, "this is Simon Peter."

Rock? Peter thought, swallowing hard. "Simon," Jesus said, "this is my mother, Mary."

As she smiled at him, Peter could feel the air leave his lungs. He struggled to speak.

"I hope my son is taking good care of you," Mary said, breaking the silence.

"He is," Peter managed.

As though she were offering her blessing, she nodded.

Returning to the abysmal present, although he didn't want to, Peter pictured Mary with her dead son cradled in her trembling arms. He envisioned her looking upon her disfigured child, the long, sharp lance pierced into his side, leaving no doubt that he was deceased. *A mother's wound, deep and eternal*, he thought. *And while Jesus's pain is over, hers has only just begun.*

Inconsolable, Peter wept. As his shoulders rocked, he felt two small hands rest upon them. Opening his eyes, he discovered that Jesus's mother was holding him. Within her painful tears, he immediately found consolation—even an undeserved forgiveness. *How is this possible?* he wondered. *In her unimaginable grief, she is comforting me.*

Somewhere deep in his tormented mind, Peter could hear his rabbi's wise voice: "Woman, behold your son. Son, behold your mother."

He hugged Mary of Nazareth tightly, and although he continued to cry, his sobs felt different.

A mother's love is a mother's love.

While the women retired to separate quarters for the night, a barrage of harsh truths taunted Peter in his faithless hours, playing over and over, until only madness remained:

I was faithful and selfless when we walked side by side all those months together; but when the Romans came to take Jesus, I became soulless and self-serving, a spineless jellyfish.

I denied Christ three times but, through my silence and inaction, I betrayed him many more times than that.

Jesus loved me. He trusted me; and to repay that trust, I failed him.

No matter how hard Peter tried to halt this satanic trifecta, it would not stop playing in his throbbing head until exhaustion finally claimed him, and he passed out.

Peter stared at Jesus, who was nailed to the cross. Christ's eyes were shut, his face painted red from his own dried blood.

Christ is gone, the apostle thought, feeling his organs throb with pain.

Jesus's eyes flew open. "Where were you, Simon?" he asked. "I needed you, and you weren't there for me." The disappointment was thick in his voice.

"I told you ... I was afraid, Lord," he tried to explain. "I couldn't ..."

"You were ready to go with me to prison or death?" Jesus said, adding a snicker. "Lay down your life for me?"

"B-but ... but I ..." Peter stuttered. Even now, he couldn't find the nerve to apologize for denying his master three times.

Jesus opened his mouth to speak again. Instead, he shook his disgusted head, closed his eyes, and died.

No!!! Peter tried to scream. But his voice failed him, again.

Peter sprang up from his dream grabbing for his thumping chest. As he struggled to catch his breath, he rolled out of bed and stumbled for the door. *Am I having a heart attack?* he wondered, unsure whether it might not be the best solution.

Sitting alone in the dark, Peter struggled to compose his wits. There were so many unanswered questions. What he did know was that the terrifying dream was simply a stark reminder of his unforgiven sins.

And I deserve every minute of it, he decided.

CHAPTER 23

GO AND TELL PETER

Jerusalem, Judea

As Saturday crept in, the women returned to John Mark's. The day was a long, ominous one. No one could go to Jesus's tomb to pay their final respects because it was the Sabbath, which meant it was against the law. There was nothing they could do but wait. So while the entire world was free to go about its business and celebrate the Sabbath, Peter and the others were imprisoned by unspeakable fear and mourning.

Our master is dead, Peter thought, and we're stuck in hiding. Jesus warned us that his fate was to suffer and die, but he gave no real direction on how to move forward.

Every moment was filled with sorrow, confusion, and intense anxiety.

What will happen next without Jesus? Peter worried.

Throughout the day, the small group learned that the other nine apostles had indeed gathered back together, returning to the upper room.

At least they're safe for now, Peter thought, feeling some relief.

They also received word that Judas Iscariot had hanged himself.

Peter felt confused by this news. *Well, it saves me from committing murder.* He considered it further. *Without repentance and forgiveness, Judas's soul was damned.*

Seconds from this harsh judgment, Peter realized, *I also betrayed Jesus in my own way, and I have not received forgiveness.*

"From what I hear," the messenger disciple reported, breaking his train of thought, "Judas brought thirty pieces of silver back to the chief priests and elders, claiming that he'd betrayed innocence and didn't want the blood money."

"Thirty pieces of silver," Simon Peter repeated, shaking his head. "To hell with Judas."

"I would think so," John commented.

Thirty pieces of silver to betray Christ, Peter thought, *to hand Jesus over to the devil's disciples.* He pictured the traitor swinging from a tree branch. *Maybe he had more courage than me?* For a moment, he considered the same fate for himself but immediately shook off the idea. *That's not courage,* he decided. *If I killed myself, I'd create even more distance between me and Jesus. And I need the opposite of that.*

"And?" John said, prodding the messenger for more details.

The man nodded. "The elders asked Judas, 'What is that to us?' before dismissing him.

"So, throwing the pieces of silver onto the sanctuary floor, Iscariot went away and hanged himself."

Free will, Peter thought, still picturing their treasurer's hanging corpse. *Judas had a choice and lost the battle between good and evil.*

In hope of a single moment's peace, the chief apostle closed his eyes. He immediately saw Jesus's face. "There is no greater love than for a man to lay down his life for his friends," the rabbi said, looking directly at him.

Peter's eyes flew open. "Forgive me," he whispered, feeling another round of tears building.

While they all wept, Peter stayed to himself. *I feel so alone, and I deserve nothing more.*

In the afternoon, John approached Peter. "Simon," he said, "We know you're sick with grief, but…"

Peter's head snapped sideways, halting the spiel.

"We need to compose ourselves," John whispered. "Jesus would expect nothing else." He shook his head. "I can't believe that Jesus's ministry was all for nothing. I just can't."

Peter remained silent.

"After all the signs and miracles…"

Peter shook his head. "But with all of his power, how could he have allowed this—to die the way he did?"

"We need to compose ourselves," John repeated. "We're the master's voice now. Matthew and I have written his words. Now it will be our job to preserve and spread his teaching."

Peter said nothing.

"Simon, have you lost faith in Christ?" John finally asked.

Peter's eyes bore through his friend. "Never!" he blurted, drawing looks from everyone else in the upper room. "It's me that I've lost faith in."

John reached for his best friend's shoulder, but Peter recoiled, heading for a darkened corner to create as much distance as he could.

"Let him be for now," Jesus's mother whispered to John.

"OK," John agreed, "but not for long. Jesus made Simon Peter our leader." Hearing this, Peter could feel a tremor travel the length of his spine.

The Marys left for the night when, after an endless day of punishment and self-loathing, exhaustion finally caused Peter's eyelids to roll. One minute, the world rotated off its axis; the next, it went completely black.

Peter stared at Jesus, who was nailed to the cross. Through a veil of ominous fog, the recurring nightmare of the crucifixion played out—Jesus's screams of pain, the condemnation of the fearful apostle abandoning his master.

At one point, Christ's eyes slammed shut, his face painted red from his own dried blood.

He's gone ... forever, the chief apostle thought, feeling empty, lost, and alone.

Suddenly, Jesus's eyes opened. "Where were you when I needed you most, Simon?" he asked, his voice sounding distant and muffled.

Jesus only calls me Simon when I mess up, Peter recalled, knowing that his recent behavior reached well beyond that. "I was afraid, Master," he tried to explain. "I tried to ..."

"You said you would never forsake me, Simon," Christ said, his pain-laden face uninterested in excuses. "You swore it."

"I'm ... I'm ..." Peter stammered. He tried to apologize, but the words would not come out—stuck in his throat for all eternity.

Jesus mustered the strength to shake his head. "You promised, Simon," he gasped. "You promised." His voice faded to stillness, as he passed away.

No!!! Peter tried to scream. He couldn't. His voice had been silenced.

Jolted again from his hellish dreams, Peter awoke, panting. The horrific dream paled in comparison to the symptoms the tortured apostle suffered upon awakening.

Struggling for oxygen, he sat up straight. As if in danger, his body froze, while his mind sensed the instinctive need to flee. But two invisible chains—the same mental shackles he had been dragging around since the betrayal of Christ in the garden—had tethered his legs once again.

The symptoms came on fast and furious: heavy sweating, hyperventilation, spiraling thoughts of impending doom, nausea, twitching of the body—even a thumping heart that felt like it randomly skipped.

What is happening?

Leaping to his feet, he grabbed his chest, while his breathing came to a sudden halt. His extremities tingling, he stood frozen in place. A moment later, he stumbled from being dizzy and grabbed the wall to brace himself.

He searched the darkness to see his best friend John sleeping. Peter pictured Jesus on the cross, talking to him. It *was only a nightmare,* he told himself, before the truth hit him. *But the nightmare is real. Jesus has been crucified. He's gone.*

Hunch-shouldered and quietly whimpering in his own dark corner, Peter felt like something was squeezing his heart—a *coward's heart,* he thought. *When the time came, I didn't stand up like I swore I would.* He tried to muffle his sobs. *I let everyone down—Jesus, his ministry, myself.*

Wallowing in despair, he never imagined feeling such unrelenting anguish. He began to retch. *Oh no... He* hurried for the door.

In the dusky courtyard, Peter heaved more, his organs feeling like they were being turned inside out. Even still, his emotional and physical pain paled in comparison to what his spirit was suffering.

Where do I go from here? he wondered, looking into an abyss that knew no bottom. *How can I possibly go on?*

The future looked beyond bleak. It *doesn't exist without Jesus—not after what I've done... or not done.*

Peter spent the second night sitting alone in the darkness.

Sunday morning finally arrived. Jesus's mother, Mary Magdalene, and Mary of Cleophas rose and left their lodging before dawn, planning to anoint the Lord's body, a service of cleansing the body and putting oils on it. It was a final act of love.

I'm not sure how we'll get that heavy stone moved, Mary Magdalene thought, heading out. *The Roman guards looked strong enough.*

It was dawn when the women arrived at the garden. Mary Magdalene discovered that the stone had been taken away and the tomb was open. *Where is the Roman sentry?* She looked around. *Nowhere to be found.* She hurried inside the dark tomb.

It's empty, she thought, confirming that Jesus was nowhere to be found. Christ's burial shroud was folded neatly. *Who took him?* she wondered, feeling panicked. *Grave robbers?* It was not an uncommon practice.

Mary ran back to John Mark's house. She woke Peter and John, before excitedly reporting, "The stone has been taken away, and they've removed the Lord from the tomb. We do not know where they've laid him."

This was clearly difficult for the two apostles to believe. "Jesus is not in the tomb where we left him," she reiterated.

With haste, John and Peter began to race to the tomb to confirm that Jesus's body was gone.

Although the sun had risen, it was a cool morning. They sprinted for a few minutes, leaving them breathless. John outran Peter, arriving first to the tomb. Taking a moment to catch his breath, he stooped to look in but did not enter. "Jesus is not here," he called out, panting, "only the winding sheet!"

Without stopping and still gasping for air, Simon Peter burst into the tomb, with Mary Magdalene peeking in from behind him.

Not only the linen cloths, Mary noted, *but also the napkin that had been placed upon Christ's head.* This had been rolled up and placed off to the side by itself.

Both apostles were confused but also afraid.

"Come with us, Mary," Peter told her. "It's not safe here."

Consumed in grief, she said, "Leave me."

Donning their hoods, Peter and John returned to John Mark's, not yet sure what to think.

Mary stayed behind. Standing at the opening of the sepulcher, she wept openly. *And they had to steal away his body too?* she thought.

As she sobbed, she heard someone call from behind her. "Woman, why do you weep?"

Peering into the tomb, she saw two angels dressed in snow-white garments standing at the ends of the stone slab where the body of Jesus had been lain. One stood at the head and the other at the foot of the flat stone.

Sobbing, she answered, "Because they have taken away my Lord, and I do not know where they have laid him." After saying this, she turned to see a man standing behind her.

"Woman, why do you weep?" the stranger asked. "Who are you looking for?"

She did not recognize the voice, mistaking him for a gardener. "If you have taken away my Lord," she said, "please tell me where you have put him."

"Mary," he said.

"Rabboni!" she squealed in Hebrew, reaching out to him. She recognized that it was Jesus. *He is risen!* Her heart instantly lightened.

"Do not hold on to me, because I have not yet ascended to my Father," he told her. She went to her knees. *Jesus has returned in the flesh,* she thought. *The Lord is risen—just as he said he would.*

Jesus told her, "Go to Peter and my brothers and say to them that I am ascending to my Father and your Father, to my God and your God."

Jesus appeared to me first! she realized.

"Go and tell," he told her.

The trusted female messenger hurried back to the safe house to share the news of the resurrection with the apostles. *Just wait until they hear! We have been saved!*

Running back to find the apostles, Mary Magdalene told them, "I have seen the Lord! He is risen from the dead! When I—"

"*Seen* the Lord?" John interrupted, standing.

The rest of them leapt to their feet, gathering closer to listen in.

Mary nodded. "Yes, Jesus appeared to me," she vowed, "and he told me to tell Peter and his brothers that he is ascending to his Father and our Father, to his God and our God."

Peter's face contorted. "You're just upset, Mary. Sit down and—"

"I know what I saw!" she snapped back, refusing to sit. "I did not recognize Jesus at first, but then I saw his face. And I spoke to him. He specifically told me to come to you, Peter, and to tell you."

Remaining silent, Peter looked away to consider what she had just said.

For the first time, Mary held her ground with the chief apostle. "I have seen the Lord and I believe in him," she repeated, raising her voice this time. "I was once lost, and Jesus found me." She nodded confidently. "Today, I am the Lord's witness!"

Peter looked at her quietly. *The tomb is empty.* He suddenly remembered his master's prediction, *"Three days and I will rebuild this temple."* He inhaled deeply. *I need to think,* he decided, hurrying out of the house. *I need to walk.*

As the Sunday morning sun climbed in the sky, Peter walked, pondering Mary's report. *If she's telling the truth, what now? I denied even knowing Jesus three times, just as he had predicted.* His shame was bottomless, affecting his judgment.

Feeling more disoriented than he'd ever felt, Peter arrived at an olive grove. *I don't know what to believe. Can it be true?* he wondered, knowing that women were rarely considered reliable witnesses. *And why would Jesus appear to Mary?* This time, he felt a hint of jealousy. *Why not me?*

He knew exactly why. As much as Peter wished it was him, he feared having to look Jesus in the eye. *I failed him,* he thought, *me ... the one he called rock.* He shook his shameful head. *Some rock.*

Peter was returning to John Mark's when he decided to embrace hope. *I believe Mary Magdalene. Jesus loved her and chose her too.* He nodded. *I believe she has been blessed again, having seen the risen Christ.*

As he reached the front door, he began to ponder the meaning of Christ's resurrection.

I'm not sure what happens now, but ... He smiled. *Jesus is risen! He is alive!*

Stepping through the threshold, Peter announced, "We must return to the upper room and reunite with the others."

Without a single word, they donned their hoods.

After some heartfelt embraces in the safe house, Andrew nearly fell into Peter's arms. "Were you there, brother?" he whispered.

"There?" Peter asked.

"When Jesus suffered?"

"For some," Peter said, shaking his head, "but not enough."

Andrew placed his hand upon Peter's shoulder. "At least you were there for some," he said, gesturing to himself and the other apostles. "We've been in hiding since he was taken."

Peter did not reply. *But you weren't his protector,* he thought, *I was.*

The excitement in the room created a beehive's buzz, as the apostles discussed the amazing report that Jesus was alive.

"He is risen," Andrew howled. "Jesus is risen!"

"Thank Yahweh!" Peter said, hugging his older brother in celebration.

Above the chatter, Peter heard a man's voice say, "Peace be with you."

Startled, Peter scanned the room. *That was not one of the apostles,* he decided, *and the door is locked.* He turned to find Jesus standing before him. Most of the air left his lungs.

"Why are you troubled?" Jesus asked. "Why do doubts rise in your minds?" He showed the disciples his scarred hands and pierced side. "Look at my hands and my feet. It is I, myself."

Except for Thomas, who was not present, the apostles were ecstatic when they saw Christ. Peter was also in awe, overjoyed by the sight of his fallen friend. The rest hurried to their master, each of them touching him.

Jesus isn't a ghost, Peter realized from a distance, *not a hallucination.* He stared at his master's transformed, glorified body. *This is Jesus, and he lives!* Peter's body rushed with adrenaline.

"Sit with me now," Jesus instructed.

Overwhelmed with emotion, they did as they were told—with Peter sitting farthest from his master. *Jesus has defeated death,* he realized.

After they had spoken for some time, Jesus departed the same way he arrived—with the front door remaining locked.

Quietly celebrating, the apostles were thrilled to have seen Christ.

Jesus is risen, Peter thought, feeling the enormity of that truth before a hint of shame returned. *But I have lost my place with him. I can't imagine Yahweh welcoming me into His house.* He inhaled deeply. *Still,* he thought, his eyes filling, *all that matters is that Jesus is alive!*

Later, when Thomas returned to the safe house, the other disciples told him, "We have seen the Lord."

Thomas shook his skeptical head. "Unless I see the nail marks in his hands and put my hand into his side, I won't believe."

The others snickered at him.

"Ye of little faith," John commented, echoing Jesus's own words.

After eight days, with the apostles still locked in the safe house, Jesus appeared again.

Peter looked at the door. *It's still secured*, he confirmed.

"Peace be with you," Christ said to them all, before specifically turning to Thomas. "Put your finger here into my hands. And put your hand into my side."

Thomas felt the nail holes in his master's hands, as well as the wound in Christ's side—before falling to his knees.

Watching the skeptical apostle receive the physical proof he had requested, Peter also thought, *Ye of little faith.*

"Do not be faithless, but believing," Jesus told Thomas.

"My Lord and my God!" Doubting Thomas cried.

"Because you have seen me, you have believed," Jesus told him. "Blessed are they that have not seen and yet believe."

Although he nodded in agreement, Peter continued to fear seeing the disappointment in his master's eyes.

At last, all of them believed that this was Jesus Christ, the Son of God.

After a brief time spent in fellowship, Jesus left them again without opening any doors or windows.

Peter kicked himself the moment Jesus left the room. *I missed my chance to ask for his forgiveness. So stupid*, he thought, sitting paralyzed. *I was too ashamed to ask, and I may never have the chance again.*

Three days later, Peter decided, *Enough time has passed. It's time to leave the Holy City and travel home to Galilee.*

From the moment they hit the road, the eleven apostles realized that the truth was spreading: "The Lord has risen and has appeared to the apostles and many others."

Before long, a winded messenger approached. "Who's in charge?" he asked, breathing heavily.

Everyone pointed to Peter.

"Word has reached the chief priests that Jesus is risen," the emissary reported to the head apostle. "After investigating the rumors, they assembled the elders and decided to bribe the soldiers, instructing them to tell the people that Jesus's disciples came by night and stole him away while everyone slept."

Oh, is that what we did? Peter thought sarcastically.

Without any feedback, the envoy added, "It's said that the soldiers took the money and are doing exactly as they were instructed."

Peter couldn't help but grin. "Well, they're obviously scared, and that's not a bad thing." He thought about it. "Let them tell their lies. We know the truth and it's our job to spread that truth far and wide." He looked to the other apostles.

Each one of them nodded with conviction.

Picking up the pace, Peter thought, *Even the elders believe Christ has been resurrected.*

His grin threatened to turn into a full-blown smile.

CHAPTER 24

SWEET REDEMPTION

Jerusalem, Judea

Uncertain of what else to do, Peter decided the group would return to Capernaum and he, perhaps, to his life as a fisherman.

As Peter walked, he felt numb, thinking about his wife. *I can't wait to tell her that Jesus has risen, but I also have no choice but to share the shameful details that led up to his crucifixion,* he realized, feeling a brew of mixed emotions. *My love may never look at me the same way again,* he worried, picturing the disappointment in her beautiful eyes.

En route back to Galilee, the apostles and their entourage passed the Kidron Valley. Circumnavigating the village of Bethany, as well as all their friends who lived there, they never stopped. Instead, they headed down the steep hills past Jericho and the Dead Sea before making their way north along the Jordan once again.

Spring in Galilee was magical, a tapestry of fragrant flowers covered the countryside in a quilt of vibrant colors. The dank smells of the earth, waking from its hibernation to create new life, filled the warm air. While birds offered their joyful song, emerging crops with an uneven line of shoots and stalks competed for the sun's attention.

Whether the sun shined down or the clouds dumped buckets of water on them, the group marched on, heads down and feet aching.

Someone laughed, the innocent cackle reminding Peter that the group was ecstatic over their master's resurrection. *Does anyone else feel guilt or shame?* he wondered.

With each mile, the chief apostle did all he could to project positivity. *I'm supposed to be their leader,* he thought, feeling the heavy yoke around his neck. *Jesus specifically chose me for the role.* Although the thought seemed clouded at the time, he was doing all he could to walk forward in faith. *I need to believe that Jesus knew what he was doing when he picked me.*

Some of the apostles exchanged worried whispers among themselves.

Peter never bothered to eavesdrop. *Our only priority is to stay alive, so we can do Jesus's work.*

Andrew and John stepped up beside him.

"How are you holding up, Simon?" Andrew asked, matching each step.

Peter shook his head.

"Jesus is risen!" he shot back, smiling.

"Amen, brother!"

"But..."

"But?" John asked.

"But I wasn't there for him when he needed me most," Peter explained. "I—"

"Jesus is alive," John interrupted, "and that's the only thing that matters."

"I know," Peter said, gratefully. "I know."

Both men dropped back, allowing Peter to take the lead alone.

Capernaum, Galilee

After three short days, the apostles reached their final destination, Capernaum, before breaking off into their own directions.

Peter stepped over the rise to see his wife standing outside their home, waiting for him. *Oh, my love ...* His heart raced and then sank. It was the first time he'd ever felt that way since he had met her.

She waved frantically at him.

He stopped. The emotion he'd kept at bay since the betrayal in the garden—the shame, the guilt, the sorrow—came flooding back, shame mixed with the inexplicable joy of knowing that Jesus was still alive. His eyes swelled with tears.

Before he knew it, Peter could feel his wife's gentle hands on his shoulders.

"Simon," she whispered, "tell me ..."

"They crucified Jesus," he reported.

"We know," she said. "Word reached Capernaum days ago. I've been worried sick about you. Where have you ...?"

"And before Christ died, I denied him," he confessed in a single breath.

"Wha-what?" she stuttered, her face becoming frozen.

Nodding, one lone tear broke free and raced down his tanned cheek. "Three times," he confessed further.

"Husband ..." she gasped, spreading her arms for a hug. But Peter did not go to her. His shame would not permit it.

"Oh, Simon ..." Ignoring the rallying onlookers, she locked her arms around him and refused to let go. "No matter what happened, Jesus knew that you loved him."

Peter remained silent.

"He still does," she added, "I just know it."

Composing himself, he whispered, "That's not all of it, though. Jesus is risen." She stared at him, her mouth agape.

Joy overtook shame, bringing a smile to Peter's weathered face. "He has been resurrected and appeared three times, once to Mary Magdalene and twice to the rest of us."

"What?" She tried to understand.

The grin disappeared. "I can't forget what I did. I denied Jesus. Now I can't even muster the courage to meet his gaze, never mind ask for his forgiveness." He shook his head.

"Let's go inside, where you can explain everything to me," she told him, pulling at his arm.

Peter was mindlessly led. Passing through the home's threshold, he tapped the mezuzah before kissing the fingers that touched it.

For hours, Peter replayed his every action and inaction, until finally turning in for the night. Before dozing off, he couldn't help but smile.

Jesus is risen, he reminded himself. *But do I still have a place in his kingdom?* The grin vanished.

The following morning, Peter opened his eyes to see his wife seated beside him on the edge of their bed.

"I'm right here, Simon," she said, grabbing his hand. "You're not alone."

"I know," he said, pulling her into his arms. "What would I ever do without you?"

"You'll never have to know," she whispered.

A bit later, after a light breakfast of cheese and olives, Peter decided to return to fishing. *It's what I know*, he reasoned. *I need to provide for my family, and doing something normal might clear my mind.*

From the shore on the Sea of Galilee, he scanned the beach. Beyond the drying racks and baskets awaiting the day's catch, small fires were being stoked. Fishermen spliced ropes and mended nets, several of them greeting Peter with a respectful nod of the head.

He returned the gestures.

For the chief apostle, the life he had once lived no longer held the same passion. He had experienced so much more. *I've been to the mountaintop with Christ,* he thought. *There's no coming back from that.* For more than three years, he had thrived in a world of hope and love.

Is that all gone now? he worried.

Looking out onto the water, he knew he was changed. *I'm not the same man who left Capernaum. I'm different, much different.*

On their travels back from Jerusalem, Peter had thought he might be able to go back to where he'd once been—*where everything began.*

He now understood. *I never will.*

That night at his own dinner table, Peter broke a piece of bread, before remembering his last supper with Jesus.

"*This is my body,*" Christ had explained. "*Take it and eat it. Do this in remembrance of me.*"

Taking a bite, Peter began to chew. *Jesus is risen,* he thought, smiling. *But will I see him again?*

Swallowing, he thought about the many lessons Jesus had taught him, his teacher's words still ringing in his ears and his heart.

"*No servant is greater than his master,*" Jesus had said.

Isn't that the truth, Peter thought.

A few hours later, when he could not stay awake a moment longer, Peter went to bed—fully expecting to toss and turn. *If I do see Jesus again, how will I … ?* He stopped, beating back an onslaught of emotions. *How can I ask for his forgiveness?*

Closing his eyes, Peter prayed for mercy, that he might avoid the tormented nightmares of his betrayal and the crucifixion that followed.

The next morning, Peter sat on a rock, looking out on the Sea of Galilee, still feeling lost. *But where else can I go?*

Rays of sunlight struck the body of water, making it shimmer like a thousand morning stars. This sight, which had once stolen his breath away, offered him little comfort. *Have I lost my love for the sea?* The rhythm of the lapping surf, which had always soothed him, made him shiver. Even the beloved smell of drying fish irritated him now.

He surveyed the scene below. *This is where it all started fewer than four years ago,* he realized. *A lifetime ago.*

Peter could still recall life's daily struggles as a hardworking man being double taxed, some for Rome and the rest for the locals. *It was nearly impossible to make ends meet.*

He shifted his weight. *And then I met Jesus, who promised a new world, a better world—even salvation.* He inhaled deeply. *I was one of the first to be called the rabbi's disciple, and it didn't take much convincing.* He'd been more than willing to learn and follow.

Immediately drawn to Christ, Peter was excited to be following such a charismatic teacher. *Jesus was unlike any scribe or Pharisee. He was real—true.*

Peter stared at the sea. *Jesus said I would be a fisher of men, luring others into his following. But what does that mean?* he wondered. *Catching people? It is hard to imagine anyone listening to me.*

Throughout their travels and the many months together, there was so much Peter didn't understand. *The only thing I was ever sure about was that I would remain the master's devout follower.* This truth still existed in his bones.

Unfortunately, Peter had always struggled to understand Christ's teachings. *My head normally swam in confusion.* He nodded. *I was always worried about being two steps behind.* Peter knew he was a problem student, asking too many questions. He had difficulty understanding basic lessons and simple instruction. *But Jesus was patient with me. When he did tease me, it came from a place of love.*

New tears rose in Peter's eyes. *What did Jesus ever see in me?* he wondered, staring at the water for a long while. *He must have seen something I either lost or can no longer see in myself.*

Peter's mind went back to Caesarea Philippi. As if they were still there, he could picture the apostles debating about Jesus's identity.

Jesus turned and asked his disciples, "Who do people say the Son of Man is?"

They looked at one another.

"Who do you say I am?" the master asked.

"You're Messiah," Peter said, professing his faith from his heart. "You're the Son of the living God."

Pausing to emphasize his response, Jesus said, "Blessed are you, Simon bar Jonas. I tell you, you are Peter, the rock, and upon this rock I will build my church."

Returning to the present, Peter pondered, *The rock upon which I build my church?*

Not truly understanding what this meant, Peter had become Jesus's right-hand man—and everyone knew it. *It was surprising, even to me.* He was not well educated, nor was he multilingual. He spoke in Aramaic, which needed to be translated into Greek before being written.

But I had the passion to walk by Christ's side, he realized. *When people laughed and spit at Jesus, I shielded my master. And when the crowd threw punches or stones, I was there to protect him.* His eyes filled again. *Until I wasn't...*

He refocused on the sea he once loved, trying to clear his mind.

Some rock I am, he thought.

That night, Peter did not return home until late.

What's the difference? he thought. *I'll never get any sleep anyway.*

The following afternoon, Thomas, Bartholomew, and the two sons of Zebedee talked on that same hill.

"I am going fishing," Peter announced and meant it. They were nearly two weeks beyond their time in the upper room. "We need to do something normal."

"I've missed scraping and scrubbing the nets for transfer to the drying racks," James joked. "We need to fish!"

Peter smiled.

"We'll go with you," the others told the chief apostle.

Minutes later, for the first time since returning home, Peter stepped into his boat, beneath an azure sky, with a few puffy clouds skulking by.

The rhythm of the sea's ebb and flow, lapping at the shore, made Peter hurry to leave the dock. He hoped that he might look forward to smelling like old fish and new sweat again, to unfurl his boat's sail to the wind. *I don't care.* Usually, Peter would be yearning to go to market with a full day's catch, the larger fish strung on loops of twine, with the smaller sardines taken in baskets or casks. *I couldn't care less,* he thought. *None of this matters anymore.*

Stripped naked, a long night of drift fishing beneath a dusky sky led to empty nets and a bare cargo hold. *Who cares?*

As the sun began to rise, the apostles were not far from land, when they saw the silhouette of a man standing on the beach.

The stranger called out, asking, "Have you eaten?"

"No," the weary fishermen called back.

"Cast the net on the right side of the boat. You'll find fish there."

They looked at one another curiously, before doing as they were told. They quickly discovered that their net was teeming with fish—more than they could haul on board.

"It is the Lord!" John yelled excitedly. He pointed at their teacher.

Hearing this, Peter froze, but only for a moment. Girding himself, he dove into the sea.

Unwilling to wait for the boat to dock, he swam for the shore.

James, Andrew, and John all laughed. "Now there's the Peter we know," one of them commented.

Once on the beach, Peter raced toward his master. *This is the moment I've been praying for.* He was not about to squander it again.

YOU WILL BE PETER

Jesus outstretched his arms toward his first apostle, the warmth requiring no words.

Peter collapsed to his knees in front of Christ. *Jesus has come for me*, he thought, feeling unshackled—free.

When the rest of the apostles beached the overflowing boat and stood on land, they saw a fire already burning, with bread awaiting them.

"Bring some of the fish you have just caught," Jesus told them.

Feeling his strength once again, Peter helped drag the full net onto land. *There must be more than 150 here.*

"Come and break your fast," Jesus told them, before taking the bread and giving it to them. He did the same with the fish.

This is the third time Jesus has manifested himself to us since rising from the dead, Peter realized.

As they ate, the fire popped and crackled, offering warmth as well as a soothing aroma.

During some nervous small talk, Peter kept stealing looks at Jesus, watching as the campfire helped illuminate the goodness in his master's chestnut-colored eyes. He tried to summon the courage to ask for forgiveness, but before Simon Peter could speak, Jesus did.

Jesus stood and turned to face his chief apostle. Looking him straight in the eyes, after what seemed like an eternal pause, the master said calmly, "Simon bar Jonas, do you love me more than these?"

Peter swallowed hard. "Lord, you know that I love you."

"Feed my lambs," Jesus replied. Then, after another long moment of peering into his chief apostle's eyes, Jesus asked, "Do you love me?"

He's allowing me to declare my love, Peter thought, *to say what I couldn't during his arrest.* He could feel shame's iron grip beginning to slip away. "Yes, Lord, I love you," he replied more fervently than the time before.

"Tend my sheep," the Lord said, pausing.

Then, gazing deeply into his eyes, Christ asked, "Simon bar Jonas, *do you love me?*"

Peter felt annoyed. He couldn't help himself. *How can he not believe me? I've already told him twice that I...* His eyes filled with tears. "Lord, you know all things. You know that I love you."

"Feed my sheep," Jesus said, with his eyes locked on Peter's. The long gaze spoke of love, forgiveness—restoration.

Christ's eyes unlocked something in Peter, draining away all the guilt, shame, and self-loathing he'd been drowning in. He looked to his right to see Andrew and John both crying.

"Feed my sheep," Jesus repeated, concluding the merciful reinstatement. Closing his eyes in prayer, he blessed the food.

John was the first to recognize the symbolism, the merciful meaning of the three questions. He turned to Andrew. "Three times he has asked your brother," he whispered. "Do you understand?"

Andrew's tears rolled down his cheek. "I do," he whispered, nodding. "Jesus is relieving my little brother's torment." He choked on the emotion. "Our ... our master is restoring Peter." Tears glistened in John's eyes as well.

Andrew reached out to touch Peter's shoulder, when the meaning hit the anguished apostle. *I denied Jesus three times. Now he's asking that I profess my love three times.*

I will! I will! Peter vowed in his soul, no longer feeling like the gutted fish before him. The Lord had given him an opportunity to atone for his triple denial with three affirmations of love. *I am whole again,* he thought. *Rock solid!*

Andrew and John smiled at him through their tears, making Peter realize that this glorious redemption had not only affected him. *The entire movement has been revived!*

Calm overtook the group as John handed Jesus a piece of broiled fish.

Christ ate it for all to see.

I have been given mercy, forgiveness, and redemption, Peter thought, tears streaming down his cheeks. *I have been redeemed!* Jesus was restoring Peter as the leader of the apostles.

Smiling broadly at Peter, Jesus told the four apostles, "Everything must be fulfilled that was written about me in the Law of Moses, and the prophets, and the Psalms." He nodded. "It has been written that the Christ should suffer and rise again from the dead the third day, and that repentance and remission of sins should be preached in his name to all the nations, beginning from Jerusalem."

Peter understood. *From now on, I will do whatever Jesus commands me to do.* He could breathe easily for the first time since that terrible night in the garden. *I've been given another chance, which I will not waste!*

The four disciples sat in a circle on the beach with Jesus. It was windy, the campfire licking at the murky sky.

Jesus told them, "All the authority on heaven and on earth has been given to me. So make disciples of all nations, baptizing them in the name of the Father and of the Son and of the Holy Spirit."

They vowed they would.

Our mission is to spread the word! Peter confirmed. *Our ministry is all about going out into the world and gathering followers for Jesus.*

Smiling, Jesus placed his hand on Peter's shoulder. "Indeed," he said, adding a single nod.

Fishers of men, Peter thought, smiling. *I finally get it.*

Late into the night, Jesus and his joyful apostles sat together, sharing in their loving fellowship.

Detailing his expectations and their roles going forward, Jesus was clear about having to leave them, as well as putting Peter in charge of his church and its leaders.

"I won't let you down again," Peter vowed to Jesus—and himself.

Christ also offered Peter a foretelling of his future. "When you were young, you dressed yourself and went wherever you wished. But when you are old, you will stretch out your hands and be dressed, and be carried where you do not wish to go."

Stretch out my hands? Peter thought, not understanding. Looking at John for a reaction, he watched as his friend shrugged. *I'm not sure what it means, but time will tell.*

Jesus looked at Peter. "Follow me."

Peter's eyes filled with jubilant tears. *Jesus is my teacher, my friend, the Son of God.* He felt reborn, his life's purpose firmly set before him.

I can't wait to tell my wife and finally sleep again.

CHAPTER 25

I AM WITH YOU ALWAYS

Jerusalem, Judea

Peter was no longer suspended in a catatonic state. He had been awakened in a glorious way. A few days later, he and the Galilean contingency, including Mary Magdalene and Jesus's mother, joyfully returned to Jerusalem, rejoining their fellow apostles to celebrate the Feast of Weeks as Jesus had instructed.

I'm looking forward to all of us being together again, Peter thought.

When they arrived in Jerusalem, they made their way to the upper room located south of the Zion Gate within the walls of the Old City.

Our safe house, Peter thought, stepping in. *The same room that our last supper with the Lord took place.* A quiver traveled the length of Peter's reinforced spine. He could still picture Judas seated beside Jesus while the master fed him the sop.

He scanned the large room. *So many memories here. Some good...*

Peter felt like they were on the mountaintop when they had broken bread together at the last supper. He could still feel the love and fellowship that filled the room.

Many memories were horrific...

Peter vividly recalled returning to this very room to hide from those who had put Christ to death. *This space is the lowest valley I have ever traveled through in my life,* he decided. *The hours of torment, the depressing days and sleepless nights.* He took a deep breath, exhaling slowly. *The room where I learned my final lessons from Jesus, washing feet and being a servant. Now we will wait here until he sends his instructions and until we receive the power he promised.*

As the meeting of the eleven commenced, Peter decided, "Judas Iscariot should be replaced to bring our apostleship back to twelve."

Two men were brought forward: Joseph called Barsabbas from Cyprus, and Matthias from Judea.

United in prayer, the apostles asked the Lord to show them which of the two devout disciples should become the twelfth apostle.

"Lord, you know the hearts of all men," Peter prayed aloud. "Of these two, which would you have us choose?"

Lots were cast, and the lot fell to Matthias. They'd found their new apostle.

"We are whole again," Peter announced with confidence. The group celebrated.

They were just about to eat bread and fish, washed down with the water they had carried, when Jesus again appeared in their midst. The apostles immediately worshipped at his feet.

Philip offered food to Jesus, who blessed it and began to eat, drinking from the passed cup—the holes in his hands still apparent.

After speaking for a time, at four o'clock in the morning they left the upper room with the apostles following their master out of the city, once again, toward Bethany.

As long as we steer clear of the garden, Peter thought, drawing a wry smile from Jesus.

The sun was burning away the last of the morning clouds, when the faithful group assembled on the central height of the Mount of Olives. *Exactly where Jesus appointed us,* Peter thought.

"This is the fortieth day since the resurrection," John reminded the group, pointing out the significance of the day.

Besides the apostles—Peter, John, James, and Andrew; Philip and Thomas; Bartholomew and Matthew; James, the Lesser; Simon, the Zealot; and Thaddeus, who was also known as Judas, the son of James—nearly five hundred men had also gathered, along with many women, awaiting Christ's divine wisdom.

"Lord, will you restore the kingdom of Israel now?" one of the men called out.

Standing atop a massive rock, Jesus cleared his throat. "It is not for you to know the times or periods which the Father has fixed by his own authority. But you shall receive power when the Holy Spirit descends upon you. And you shall be my witnesses, both in Judea and Samaria, and to the remotest part of the Earth."

Looking to Andrew, John, and James, Peter nodded confidently. They were receiving their marching orders.

"All authority has been given to me in heaven and on Earth," Jesus explained. "Go forth, and make disciples of all the nations, baptizing them in the name of the Father and the Son and the Holy Spirit." He nodded. "Go into all the world and preach the gospel to everyone. He who believes and is baptized shall be saved. But he who does not believe shall be condemned."

Saved, Peter repeated in his thick skull.

"Signs shall accompany those who believe," Jesus added. "In my name, they shall cast out demons and speak with new tongues. They shall take up serpents; and if they drink any deadly thing, it will not hurt them. And they shall lay hands on the sick, who will recover."

Fishers of men, Peter recalled, finally able to understand.

"The Father has sent me, as I send you. If you forgive the sins of any, they are forgiven them; if you retain the sins of any, they are retained," Jesus told them, continuing to explain what he wanted and expected. Offering several commands, he concluded with, "You are to remain in the city until you are invested with power from on high. I am with you always, even to the end of the world."

While the crowd discussed this in hushed whispers, Peter watched as Christ and his mother exchanged private words of their own.

Peter could not hear what either of them was saying. *And I don't need to know,* he decided. *No one does.*

In a moment suspended in time, Jesus paused to look at every face one last time—hundreds of them. Without a word, Christ spread his pierced hands and looked up into the sky. Accompanied by two angels, he slowly began to rise off his scarred feet.

Several of his followers gasped.

Jesus, my Lord and Savior, Peter thought, feeling consumed with unconditional love.

Hovering just above them, Christ smiled at his apostles, Mary Magdalene, and his tearful mother, before ascending ever higher until a giant billowy cloud swallowed him whole.

Amid more gasps, some began to weep while more sang out prayers of praise.

Two youths with long flowing hair appeared before the group. Both radiated a white light that was unmistakable.

The Lord's angels, Peter thought.

"Men of Galilee," the messengers said in precise unison, "why do you stand gazing up into heaven? This Jesus, who has been taken away from you into heaven, will come in the way that you have seen him go into heaven."

Before anyone could gasp again, both angels vanished.

Tears raced down Peter's cheeks. *We have been blessed,* he thought. *We've witnessed Jesus die, come back to life, and now ascend into heaven.* Looking skyward again, he smiled through his tears. *Beyond blessed.*

As their master had instructed, the inspired troupe returned to Jerusalem. They gathered in the safe house, the home of John Mark, as well as homes of other friends and believers nearby. They were near the large upper room where they had taken the Last Supper with Jesus, the same room where they had seen the resurrected Jesus just three days after his death. And now they gathered daily to pray, to reassure each other by sharing the tales of their sightings of Jesus, and to wait.

Peter remembered the words of the angels: *Until we are invested with power from on high,* Peter admitting he was unsure what that meant. *I may not understand what is coming,* he thought, *but I will not question the Lord's words again—not ever!*

The wait was not long, only a few days.

It was Sunday, exactly fifty days since Christ's resurrection, when a loud sound came from heaven like the rush of a mighty wind. It filled the entire room, startling everyone to his or her feet.

Peter watched as tongues of fire, licking at the air, descended upon each one of them, consuming all the apostles.

All at once, everyone was filled with the Holy Spirit and began to speak in foreign tongues.

Peter watched as John and Andrew rambled on in gibberish. He then turned to see James and Matthew frozen in a state of rapture. *It's a miracle!*

Hurrying out the front door and bounding down the stairs two at a time, Peter discovered that the other apostles were at his heels. *They must feel the same need to share what has just happened.*

As he reached the courtyard, he discovered a large crowd, hailing from all nations under the sun, had already gathered to investigate the ruckus.

"What was that loud noise?" one of them asked. "Was it an earthquake?" another inquired.

In response, the apostles began to answer their questions in each of their native tongues: dialects from Mesopotamia, Judaea, and Cappadocia. From Pontus and Asia, Phrygia and Pamphylia, Egypt, and the parts of Libya about Cyrene. Even the native Roman tongue was being spoken fluently.

The crowd was confounded, each man listening to the apostle who spoke to him in his own language.

"Don't they all speak Galilean?" one of the onlookers asked, in awe of the spectacle.

Amid the confusion, the apostles continued to preach the mighty works of God in tongues they had never known.

"What does this mean?" a dark-skinned woman asked, completely perplexed.

"They are drunk!" one of the men yelled out.

Standing up for the eleven, Peter spoke loudly. "You, men of Judaea, and all you who dwell in Jerusalem, hear my words: These men are not drunk! It's only nine o'clock in the morning. This is the prophecy of Joel that has come to pass."

To Peter's own surprise, each one of his words were filled with authority and conviction.

I've been given the gift of tongues, he realized, *and now I can go forth and preach the gospel.*

This was Peter's maiden speech, his first sermon, and he knew it. Drawing in a deep breath, Peter belted, "Men of Israel, hear these words: Jesus of Nazareth, approved by God, gave you mighty works and wonders and signs. Him, being delivered to lawless men who crucified him, whom God raised up, having him overcome death." He nodded. "Whoever calls on the name of the Lord shall be saved."

The growing crowd moved in closer.

"Brethren, as prophesized by the patriarch David, Jesus died and was buried, and his tomb is with us today," Peter preached. "David spoke of the resurrection of the Christ, who knew no sin. God raised him up, for which we are all witnesses. Being exalted at the right hand of God and having received of the Father the promise of the Holy Spirit, he has poured forth what you see and hear."

Bolstered by the Holy Spirit, the chief apostle had never felt such courage his entire life.

Even when I was young and foolish and didn't know any better, I didn't feel this invincible.

"Let all the house of Israel know assuredly that God has made this Jesus, whom you crucified, both Lord and Christ."

Hearing this, the crowd was moved—hushed, still. "What can we do?" a Jewish voice called out.

"Repent, every one of you," he told them, "and be baptized in the name of Jesus Christ, so you may receive the gift of the Holy Spirit. This is a promise to your children and even those from afar."

Many went to their knees.

Peter proclaimed, "Jesus is both Lord and Christ," before inviting the people to repent and "Save yourselves from this corrupt generation."

By nightfall, believing Peter's heartfelt words, nearly three thousand souls from many nations were baptized and received into Christ's new church.

Returning to the upper room, John whistled, getting Peter's attention.

"What?" Peter asked, curious about his friend's joyful grin.

"Three thousand netted in one day," John said. "Good for you, fisher of men!"

Peter smiled. "No," he said, "good for them."

Fully comfortable in his role as leader, an emboldened Peter and the apostles returned to the safe house's darkened threshold.

As they gathered for their evening meal, the new leader stood to direct them, as Jesus instructed. Bowing his head, the lead apostle took a piece of unleavened bread. Giving thanks, he broke it, passed it to his fellow apostles, and said, "Take this bread and eat it. This is Christ's body, which is given for you. Do this in remembrance of him."

The eleven other apostles accepted the bread and ate it.

Peter then took his cup and, giving thanks, filled it with wine. "This is the blood of Christ's covenant," he said, "which is poured out for many for the forgiveness of sins." He took a drink before passing the cup.

They each took a sip.

John smiled before repeating their master's words: "Unless you eat of the flesh of the Son of Man and drink his blood, you have no life in yourselves."

"Amen," they said in unison.

CHAPTER 26

NO MORE FEAR

Jerusalem, Judea

Peter thought about all that had happened in the fifty days since Christ was resurrected. *I was broken, unable to breathe, to even think straight. I'd never felt so disheartened and hopeless in my life. And then Jesus appeared to us. And I was filled with joy but was still too ashamed to beg my Lord's forgiveness. And I suffered more, much more.* He nodded to himself. *Until returning home to Galilee and seeing Jesus on that beach.* His eyes filled. *And I was forgiven, offered grace and mercy once again.* He sighed heavily. *Sweet redemption.*

It was Jesus's plan all along, Peter realized. *To teach me. To mold me. To give me the tools I needed to be a leader and preach the gospel throughout the world.* Without true humility, Peter could not understand true love. In his role, he would also need to be forgiving and merciful and just. *I am representing Christ, preaching his words and baptizing in his name.* He smiled wide. *Gathering the flock unto my master.*

Without having been brought to his knees and completely broken, Peter could not have been made whole again—*prepared to do my master's work.*

Late into the night, Peter continued to ponder all that had passed.

He had been schooled on the writings of the prophets, which proclaimed that the Son of God would be sent. *It has come to pass,* he thought, grasping the mystery of Christ more deeply. *Now, it feels like my brain is finally working at full speed.*

Nearly everything Peter had always wished for and expected was completely off. *Jesus didn't destroy the House of Israel*, he realized. *He completed it.*

Days later, it was late morning when Peter and John proceeded into the temple. A man, lame from birth, laying at the temple's massive door, caught their attention.

"Alms," the poor soul begged. "Alms."

Fixing his eyes upon the lame man, Peter told him, "Look at us." The man locked eyes with the stout apostle.

"I have no silver or gold," Peter said, "but what I have, I give to you. In the name of Jesus Christ of Nazareth, walk."

Taking the man by the right hand, Peter raised him up. Immediately, the man's feet and his ankles became strong, and he began to walk. Entering the temple with Peter and John, the beggar praised God with every step taken.

Praising God, others watched as the man walked for the first time in his life. The worshippers realized that it was the lame beggar who sat for alms at the Beautiful Gate.

In curiosity, the mob ran to Solomon's Porch to see what had happened.

Seeing the gathering crowd, Peter instinctively began to preach, "Men of Israel, why marvel at this man? Why fix your eyes upon us, as if it was our power or godliness that made him to walk?" He shook his head. "The God of Abraham, and of Isaac, and of Jacob, the God of our fathers, has glorified His servant Jesus, whom you delivered up and denied before Pilate, even when he was determined to release him. But you denied the Holy and Righteous One, instead asking for a murderer to be released to you."

As the chief apostle delivered his second sermon, the crowd grew larger and larger.

Looking to his left, he saw the High Pharisees and elders standing there, watching and listening.

They look annoyed.

Something in the back of his mind expected that he'd start to feel heart palpitations, shallow breathing, heavy sweating. There was none of that. While his heart rate continued at an even pace and his breathing remained uninterrupted, his fiery words came easily, each one filled with confidence and conviction. *There's no more fear,* he realized. *None.*

"You killed the prince of life," Peter preached, "whom God raised from the dead, for which we are witnesses. By faith in his name has this man been healed, whom you now see."

Many in the audience lowered their eyes, fixing them on the ground.

"I know that you did it in ignorance, as did your rulers," Peter said. "But the things that God foreshadowed through the words of prophets, that his Christ should suffer, have been fulfilled. Now repent!"

As he spoke, Peter saw the crowd pushing closer, their eyes entranced by the words Jesus had put into his mouth. He also saw the High Pharisees' faces change from agitated to legitimately threatened. Again, he felt no symptoms of fear. *I have the Holy Spirit in me now. There is nothing on this earth that can stop me, even though the temple priests are furious with me.*

For all to hear, Peter was proclaiming that Jesus had been resurrected from the dead. Until now, Jewish authority had no reason to feel threatened by a few uneducated Galileans. The apostles had given no proof of Jesus's powers. But *a man, lame from* birth, *has been healed in Jesus's name,* Peter considered, *and things have changed.* Even knowing this, he still felt no fear.

While the crowd praised God, they believed Peter's words.

At the conclusion of his sermon, Peter and the apostles were apprehended and dragged away—but not before they had gathered five thousand new believers to Jesus's growing flock.

Elders, scribes, even Caiaphas convened, asking, "By what power, or in what name, have you healed this lame man?"

Filled with the Holy Spirit, Peter told them, "You, rulers of the people and elders, you question this good deed performed for a lame man, asking how he was made whole. You should know, as should all the people of Israel, we performed this miracle in the name of Jesus Christ of Nazareth—whom you crucified and whom God raised from the dead. In no other name is there salvation."

Having believed the apostles were ignorant fishermen, they were taken aback by this new hutzpah in Peter and John. But given that a lame man—standing before them—had been miraculously healed, they could say nothing against it.

After convening in private, the religious leaders returned to Peter and the apostles, ordering, "From this day forward, you are forbidden to speak of or teach in the name of Jesus!"

Both Peter and John shook their heads. "Is it right in the sight of God to answer to you rather than to God? If so, then judge us. We cannot help but to speak of the things that we have seen and heard."

Finding no grounds for formal punishment, the High Pharisees let them go after offering a few final threats.

Peter stifled a laugh as he exited the courtyard. *They have no choice,* he realized, *because the people would be outraged.* Looking skyward, he gave all glory to God for his newly found courage and the opportunity to further spread Jesus's words.

The lame man was also released, returning into the city to spread the truth far and wide.

Ignoring the temple's warnings, Peter and the apostles continued their fellowship, teaching Christ's followers how to properly pray and break bread in the Lord's name.

Each time they shared the gospel, fear came upon their audience. With the help of multiple signs and wonders, many new believers were converted, selling their possessions and offering them up to those in need.

Day by day, the apostles became increasingly popular with the people, gaining more followers with each sermon.

During Peter's homilies, the words came easily to him. He was well spoken for the first time in his life. His preaching was more than inspired. It was divine. *But I can't take credit for any of it. I'm merely doing the work of my master,* he understood. *These are not my words, unlike those I've fumbled over and searched for my entire life. These are my master's words.* Peter was no longer speaking from his mind but from his heart, where the Holy Spirit now dwelled.

Peter became the good servant he had been taught to be. By merely surrendering to that, his life took on more meaning and purpose than he could have ever imagined. *I always thought I was a fisherman, that I was born to be a fisherman and would die a fisherman.* He smiled. *I wasn't wrong. Except now, my nets are the true words of Christ.* The catch, teeming and overflowing, was being gathered to bring glory and honor to Jesus's name. *By being baptized and believing in*

Christ, they have been saved. I've only been a conduit, a vessel, a sturdy ship used to make the journey possible.

Jesus has finally made me the man that my wife can be proud of, Peter thought. *No more stumbling in the dark. No more searching for answers that I could never find on my own. I know my path now. I know the way.* He nodded confidently. *My direction is set to true north. My ship is seaworthy, sturdy enough to push through any storm. Jesus's words will fill the nets to overflowing.*

Peter excitedly set off to spread the word of the gospel. *This time, I won't let Jesus down,* he vowed, singularly focused on his life's mission. *I almost threw it all away once, but never again!*

EPILOGUE

I AM PETER

Capernaum, Galilee

Eighteen years after Pentecost had passed, Peter and his wife returned to Capernaum to pay respects to her eema, who had recently died.

Standing at the kind woman's tomb, Peter thought, *I wish we could have made it home in time to hold her hand as she passed.* He felt his wife's hand tighten on his. *She feels the same.*

As they said goodbye in prayer, Peter thought, *Eema loved and believed in Jesus Christ as much as any of us. She is saved.*

His mind immediately went to Jesus's time with the woman, making him smile. *I wonder if he would have healed her this time,* he wondered, before shaking his head. *No, we all have to die at some point.*

This simple truth made Simon Peter contemplate his own mortality. *Yes, we must all die.*

Staring at the tomb, he prayed. *Receive Eema into Your embrace, Yahweh ... in Jesus's name. She loved Your Son dearly.*

As they walked away, Peter never let go of his wife's hand.

"I'd like to spend some time in the village, visiting with some old friends," she told him.

"Of course, of course," Peter said. "I'll meet up with you later. I have somewhere I need to go first."

She grinned the same grin that made him fall in love with her all those years ago. "To see your first love?"

"Yes," he said, kissing her weathered cheek. "It's been much too long since I've seen the Sea of Galilee."

In no great rush, Peter headed northeast toward the shores of the Sea of Galilee. He could feel the air change on his olive-toned skin before he ever saw the water. Closing his eyes to allow his other senses to take it all in, he kept moving forward. *After all these years, I can still walk each step blindfolded.*

The sound of children's laughter caused his eyes to fly open. Scanning the area, he thought of his friend Jesus. *The master was a child magnet, always smiling and laughing freely with them,* he remembered. *Children loved him wherever we went.* Although Peter never saw the children, he couldn't help but echo their joyful laughter.

It's sad to think that many will never know the sound of Jesus's voice, the love in his eyes. But the master preached, "My words will never pass away." *Christ's words are eternal, as is his sacrifice on the cross.*

At the top of the last rise, Peter slowed his gait before stopping. As the cool air caressed his neck and arms, the soothing rhythm of the lapping surf made him smile again. *Home,* he thought, detecting the smell of decomposing fish. *Home, sweet home.*

Moving a few steps to his left, he claimed a seat on his familiar rock, just west of the road; it was the same rock where it all began. He loved this perch and the view of the sea below.

Was this seat more comfortable when I was a younger man? he wondered. He adjusted his position, sliding free from a jagged fist of granite that protruded from the center of the massive stone. Looking down at the rock, he shook his head. *You're still a pain in the backside.*

Finally comfortable, Simon Peter bar Jonas looked out onto the water. *The sea is like a sheet of expensive silk today,* he thought, becoming hypnotized by the beloved scene before him. *I've been gone so long.* He nodded to himself. *Many years have passed since I pummeled poor Yussif in the tavern.* He snickered. *I can thank Yahweh; I'm a changed man.*

Earlier in his life, Peter had admired brawn. *If you were strong and gruff, you had my respect.* As he grew and matured, he began to admire wisdom—true knowledge. *This is a lifelong aspiration I may never reach.* When he finally grew up, he admired kindness. *Faith without works is dead, so if believing in Jesus is the way, then good works is proof of that.*

There was such a sense of peace in Peter's soul. *What I've seen and been blessed to do along the way . . .*

He closed his eyes again, allowing his mind to travel back, to reflect on his journey and his evolution from fisherman to chief apostle.

The last two decades have been filled with baptisms, repentance, and new believers saved. Peter and his fellow apostles filled net after net with souls for Jesus. *After being forgiven and redeemed, the only thing that has mattered is helping others find the same.*

Thanks to the Holy Spirit opening Peter's heart and mind, it all made sense now. *It's as clear as the Sea of Galilee after a summer storm,* he thought.

Simon Peter could finally connect all the dots—from John the Baptist and meeting Jesus for the first time, to the three years of following Christ in his ministry, watching and learning. *The last supper, the betrayal, the mock trial, the scourging.* He stopped, vividly remembering how he had feared for his own life. *I could not be there* to protect my master, and I suffered terribly for it. It all made perfect sense now. *Jesus was building muscle in me, making me strong, stripping away all I didn't need and replacing it with everything I did.*

How could I forgive others in the name of Jesus Christ, if I didn't understand forgiveness and the value of it? Peter realized. *How could I refuse to sit in judgment, unless I understood what it feels like to be judged and had once wrongly judged others? How could I heal the sick, if I suffered from my own ailments, carrying burdens that forced me to focus on myself? I could never show mercy, had I never been given mercy.* He nodded. *The same for grace.*

Peter loved being lost in such thought. *Jesus knew that if I was going to help transform the world, then I would have to be transformed, myself, first.* He grinned. *I can't believe how much of my foolishness the master put up with.*

Although he had paid as close attention as he was capable during each one of Jesus's sermons, he only now understood. *The entire three years was the lesson! Children may not always listen, but they do watch. And Jesus taught by example.* The chief apostle felt a gentle peace to finally grasp it. *I must follow Christ's example to the best of my ability, and only through the Holy Spirit is that possible.*

Peter thought about all that had transpired since receiving Christ's powerful spirit in the upper room. *Thousands upon thousands of Jews joined the new church,* Peter recalled, *as long as we kept the Jewish laws and traditions. The Torah was read, and the Hebrew psalms were sung.* Peter and the apostles—no different from the rabbis in the synagogues and high priests in the temple—preached homilies and offered explanations.

Assigned the role of high priest by the Lord Himself, Peter ensured that the prayer for the Last Supper was shared with the growing congregation. He also established at each service that the bread and wine be consecrated in remembrance of Christ.

"Father, look with favor upon these offerings and accept them," the early priests recited.

"And this ceremony shall never change," Peter commanded.

While establishing these new ceremonies and customs, the apostles taught, "Whatever you have, give to the poor, and you shall possess treasure in heaven."

As a result, Christ's followers did not claim wealth or property. Everything they possessed was common to them—*except in the instance of Ananias and Sapphira.*

Peter still shook his head as he revisited the story of a wealthy couple, Ananias and Sapphira, who had joined the church, vowing to follow Christ's teachings. Selling a portion of their property, they intentionally withheld a percentage of the profits—only offering up a partial sum to the apostles and the church.

Sensing their dishonesty, Peter questioned the husband. "Has Satan filled your heart to lie to the Holy Spirit?" he asked. "Why have you kept back part of the price of the land?"

Without hesitation, Ananias lied. "We did not withhold any money from the church!"

"How could you have conceived this thing in your heart?" Peter roared. "You have not lied to men but to God."

Wide-eyed, Ananias slumped to the ground, breathing no more.

After the dishonest man had been wrapped and buried, word spread about his untimely death, causing great fear among the people.

Three hours later, Peter approached his wife, Sapphira, who had yet to hear about her husband's demise. "Tell me whether you sold the land for the amount your husband has claimed."

She nodded. "Yes, my husband tells you the truth."

"So, you have both conspired to lie to the Holy Spirit," Peter said, shaking his head. "The men who buried your husband are waiting at the door, and they shall carry your body away as well."

Sapphira fell at Peter's feet, where she died.

Feeling sorrowful, Peter recalled his master's words. *It is easier for a camel to go through the eye of a needle than for a rich man to enter the kingdom of God.*

The same young men who buried Ananias carted the dead woman out, burying her beside her greedy husband.

After holding Ananias and Sapphira accountable for their sin, Peter went on to heal many in the temple, which inspired many more conflicts with the high priests and elders.

Who would have ever thought that John and I would travel back to Samaria to lay hands on the new believers and teach them about the word of God? Peter considered, chuckling at the irony of it. It had taken years, but he had finally overcome his bigotry toward these life-long enemies. *We also traveled to Lydda and many other places to preach and convert believers in Jesus Christ.*

Peter recalled a man named Aeneas, who had been palsied and bedridden for eight endless years. "Aeneas, Jesus Christ heals you," the apostle told him. "Arise and make your bed."

Standing on his own two feet, Aeneas began to walk.

Lydda reverberated with the news of the miracle and the people believed, many converting to the new faith.

Only days passed, when two men from Joppa approached Peter. "Please come with us. Tabitha, a devout follower of Christ, is very ill. We must hurry."

Peter went with them. Upon arrival in Joppa, he was brought into the upper chamber only to find several widows standing over her corpse, holding the coats and garments Tabitha had made while she was still alive.

Dismissing them all, Peter went to his knees and prayed. Turning to the body, he said, "Tabitha, arise."

She opened her eyes, and when she saw Peter, she sat up.

Offering his hand, Peter pulled her up, before calling in the widows. "Weep no more," he told them. "Tabitha is alive."

Word of the miracle spread throughout all of Joppa and across Israel, adding many new believers to their ranks.

The Spirit then compelled Peter to stay in Joppa for a time. *I'll stay with Simon, the tanner,* he decided. *He has a comfortable little place by the sea. This place is filled with Romans and Gentiles of every race, but the Lord wants me here.*

One afternoon, Peter was up on the roof praying, when he became hungry. While calling down for some food, he suddenly fell into a trance, watching as heaven opened above him. A great sheet appeared, descending as though it was being let down by four corners upon the earth. From his knees, Peter stared in awe; the sheet contained all kinds of four-legged animals and creeping things of the earth, as well as all the birds of the heavens.

"Rise, Peter," a voice from above called out, "kill and eat."

Shaking his head, Peter scrambled to his feet. "No, no, Lord," he stammered, "I have never eaten anything that is common or unclean."

The voice spoke again, louder this time. "God makes nothing that's common or unclean!"

This was repeated three times before the sheet ascended, disappearing into heaven.

Mystified, Peter struggled with what this vision might mean. He hadn't taken two steps when the truth smacked him, nearly knocking him off the roof. *All people are welcome in Christ's church!* he realized. *God does not discriminate when it comes to receiving His word.* His once-bigoted heart was filled with love and joy. *Of course! Everyone's welcome at the Lord's table!*

While Peter thought on the vision, the voice called out one last time. "Behold, Peter, three men are seeking you out. Go, meet with them, and do not question their request. I have sent them."

As Peter made his way down the old wooden ladder, three messengers were already waiting at the tanner's gate. *As promised,* he thought, approaching them. "How can I help you?" he asked.

"We have traveled a full day, dispatched by our master, Cornelius the centurion."

Peter nodded. "Whom do you seek?"

"Simon," they said, "his surname is Peter."

"I am Peter, the man that you seek. Why have you come?"

"Our master is a righteous man who fears God and is a good friend of the Jews," they explained. "He was warned by a holy angel to send for you, so that he may hear your words."

Without questioning anything, Peter invited them into the house, feeding them and putting them up for the night.

In the morning, the four men traveled north from Joppa along the coast of the Great Sea together. As they entered Caesarea—not Philippi where Peter had made his confession of faith, but Caesarea Maritima—Peter couldn't believe his eyes. The city, glowing from buildings of pure white marble, was exquisite. *Another of King Herod's crown jewels,* he thought.

This amazing port was home to the palace of Herod Agrippa. Other than the temple in Jerusalem, Peter had never seen such grand buildings or opulence. Ships larger than any he had ever seen, much less sailed, lined the docks of the deepwater port—sailing across the Great Sea, even to Rome itself.

When his guides brought Peter to the centurion's home, Cornelius fell at the apostle's feet, worshipping him.

Peter grabbed his forearm. "Stand up. I am also just a man." He glanced around. *It looks like the soldier has gathered all his family and friends to welcome me.*

Peter wasted no time in sharing his truth. "You, yourselves, know how it is unlawful for a Jewish man to enter the home of someone who is not Jewish," he explained. "And yet, God has recently showed me that I should not call any man common or unclean. This is why I've come without anything to gain. So, tell me, why am I here?"

Cornelius cleared his throat. "Four days ago, I was in deep prayer when I saw an angel of God appear. 'Cornelius,' he called out, 'your prayers and alms have gone up as a memorial before God. Send men to Joppa and fetch Simon, who is surnamed Peter. He is living in the house of Simon, a tanner.' So I quickly sent for you." His last few words sounded choked from emotion. "I ... I am so grateful that you have come. Now we are here in the sight of God to hear all the things that you have been commanded by the Lord."

Peter took a moment before responding. Contemplating this man, who commanded a vast army and ruled over such a great city, Peter marveled at the power of the Holy Spirit to alter the lives of all men. Having been lifted from such a modest background, Peter felt humbled at the opportunity to lift these people up. "Truthfully, I believe God loves and respects every person, from every nation, who fears Him and does righteous works. He is Lord of all."

Hopeful looks were exchanged throughout the room.

"The word, which he sent to the children of Israel, preached good tidings of peace by Jesus Christ," Peter explained. "After the baptism, which John preached even to Jesus of Nazareth, God anointed him with the Holy Spirit and with power. He went about doing good, healing all that were oppressed of the devil, for God was with him." He slapped his broad chest. "We are witnesses of all things that he did in the country of the Jews as well as Jerusalem where they killed him by hanging him on a tree."

For the first time, Gentiles were hearing about Jesus Christ's ministry—and were awestruck by Peter's words.

"God raised Jesus up on the third day and manifested him, not to all the people but to witnesses that were chosen by God," Peter preached. "Appearing to us, we ate and drank with him after he rose from the dead. He charged us to preach to the people and to testify that this is he who is ordained of God to be the judge of the living and the dead. As the prophets witnessed, everyone who believes in him shall receive forgiveness of their sins."

While Peter spoke, the Holy Spirit was poured upon all of them—even the Gentiles. The Jews were amazed.

At the conclusion of his sermon, Peter commanded that they be baptized in the name of Jesus Christ. "And do not wait."

I caught a lot of griping over that one, Peter recalled. Many believers in Jerusalem were not happy that I had kept company with the Gentiles. Paul was the most upset over it. Looking skyward, he grinned. Fortunately, I only answer to one master.

My, how Christianity has spread quickly, from a small group of followers in rural Palestine to the greatest cities in the world, Peter pondered, as he shifted his weight on the rock. There are those who do not believe, still waiting for the coming of the Messiah, but the number of believers continues to grow.

Ten years after Pentecost, Peter convened the Council of Jerusalem. A conference of the Christian apostles from across the world gathered in Jerusalem to discuss several important topics.

The church was growing, and we needed to get organized, Peter recalled. I can still picture all the apostles in attendance, as well as some of the key disciples—Paul, Luke, John, Mark. He grinned. Lots of strong personalities at that conclave.

Led by Peter and James, the lengthy meeting hosted a great debate over the church's membership—Jews and Gentiles.

"Let's sort it all out," Peter began, clearly in charge. For reasons that still reached beyond his understanding, he had been chosen by Christ. *And I'll never let Jesus down again.*

The others waited for him to speak.

"This is no longer a Jewish-only faith," Peter announced. "It is now a universal religion to include Gentiles. All who believe in Jesus will be saved."

Although it was rare, Paul of Tarsus, who sat in favor of the Gentile Christians, agreed with him.

Paul boldly acknowledged Peter's sole leadership of the church, deferring power and primacy to the chief apostle. After all, Peter had been chosen by Jesus and walked with him.

Hour after hour, they discussed the church's expectations of its body. It was eventually determined that Gentile Christians were not bound by the Levitical ceremonial regulations of the Jews, except for the so-called apostolic decree: "Abstention from what has been sacrificed to idols and from blood, and from what is strangled and from fornication."

At least we were able to compromise on certain issues, Peter thought. *Maintaining peace and unity in the church was just as important as anything else.* He shrugged to himself. *Bottom line, we decreed that Gentile Christians would not have to observe the Mosaic Law of the Jews.*

As they poured the foundation of the early church, some of Christ's followers—now choosing the name "Christians"—insisted that Gentile Christians from Antioch in Syria obey the Mosaic custom of circumcision. A delegation, led by the apostle Paul and his companion Barnabas, was appointed to confer with the elders of the church in Jerusalem.

At the end of the conclave, Peter gave assignments to each of them to preach the gospel. "James will remain in Jerusalem," Peter announced, "while the rest of us will head out into the world to baptize in the name of Christ and preach his word." He then listed where they would each travel.

Renewed, Peter settled in Rome, continuing to move forward with courage and confidence. His greatest task was to claim people for the kingdom of Jesus—*even if I have to travel to the ends of the earth to do so.*

As he continued to reflect across the past eighteen years, Peter's heart sank—remembering as the persecution of the early church began to intensify. *Stephen was stoned to death. And my beloved brother, my childhood friend, James, was beheaded.* His eyes filled. *On King Herod's orders, we lost a loyal and reliable apostle who can never be replaced.* He shook his head. *All because Herod wanted to cause trouble for the church.*

Peter allowed himself a moment of silence to remember his fallen friend.

Those were very dark days, Peter recalled. *When Herod realized what he had done made him popular, he had me arrested and thrown into prison. Thankfully, one of the Lord's angels set me free!*

Staring out at the glorious sea, he inhaled deeply, filling both his lungs and his soul.

With James being martyred in Jerusalem, he thought, *it was the right decision to move the church to Rome.* He nodded confidently. *The light shines in the darkness, and the darkness shall not overcome it.*

Returning from his bumpy trip down memory lane, Peter felt at peace, even though his backside was now asleep.

On the leisurely stroll back to his wife, Peter considered his fellow apostles, men who had been uprooted from their professions—*picked for each of us long before we were ever born.*

Generations of fishermen rearing fishermen, apprentices from long lines of artisans. He smiled.

Fishing families do not produce blacksmiths. We were born into our life's path, and family legacies are not easy to walk away from, especially to follow a man who spoke in mysterious parables. Every minute took faith and some fairly thick skin.

Peter pictured each of the apostles' seasoned faces. Now brothers, one and all, he thought, considering all the love they shared. The courageous camaraderie, the faithful fellowship, and the forgiveness we have given freely to one another. There is nothing we cannot do, he realized. Jesus has trained us. He has prepared us. He empowered us with the Spirit. And we shall continue to go forth and do his work.

At last, Peter understood. The big moments often brush past us without us understanding their weight. He smiled again. The master always knew, even when we didn't.

Now, as an elder, Peter could see the power of each moment he'd been blessed to experience. Thank You, Yahweh!

He drew in a lungful of air, exhaling slowly. I have been blessed, chosen by the Son of God. Although it had not been an easy road, Peter could not have imagined a greater adventure or purpose for his life. I have so much to be grateful for.

Reaching Eema's house, he considered his own mortality. I need to get back to Rome to see John Mark, he decided. I am going to tell him everything, so that he can put it in writing. I believe it is time to write these stories, to be shared for generations to come. He nodded. John and Matthew must do the same.

Passing through the home's threshold, Peter tapped the mezuzah before kissing the fingers that touched it.

Grabbing the water basin, he prepared to wash his face and feet, when he again heard Jesus's words in his ears.

"You are Simon. You will be Peter."

Peering into the basin, he caught his aged reflection. *My beard has grown longer and is starting to turn white.* A grin worked its way into a smile, taking over his tanned and weathered face.

"I know who I am now," he said aloud. "I am Peter."

AFTERWORD

"*I* am Peter, the Rock, and I will go forth and build his church." With humility, childlike faith, and obedience, this brash man evolved from fisherman into saint. Peter's story of redemption is the foundation and cornerstone on which Christianity was established.

Simon Peter...

- was chosen by Jesus Christ as the unquestioned founder and leader of his church
- is responsible for founding and leading the most influential and enduring institution in the history of mankind, the Christian church
- would record his eyewitness story—and in doing so, co-create the first gospel—by dictation to John Mark around the year AD 53
- wrote the two letters named after him in the New Testament (from Rome near the end of his life) to encourage the new believers in the growing churches across the known world
- would live to be about sixty-five years of age; his last thirty-three years were devoted to establishing the church and preaching the gospel as he was directed to do by Jesus Christ
- would be crucified in Rome, as predicted by Jesus in John 21:18–19—at the site of the Clementine Chapel—by Emperor Nero. Since the second century, church tradition

has taught that Peter was crucified upside down, as he did not feel worthy to die upright as had his Lord and Savior

- is buried beneath the altar at Saint Peter's Basilica, Vatican City, where you may see the tomb holding his bones to this day.

For centuries, every June, a life-size statue of Saint Peter has been crowned in Saint Peter's Basilica with a papal tiara, ring of the fisherman, and papal vestments as part of the Feast of Saints Peter and Paul.

One of the most powerful figures in all human history, Peter was a giant, chosen by Jesus.

Simon of Bethsaida was the "Everyman."

The timeless message of hope dictates that each one of us is offered the same chance Jesus gave Simon Peter. We all make mistakes. We all have flaws. But like Peter, we can also receive forgiveness and get back up again.

Like Peter, despite our failures, we all have a chance. A chance to evolve from "Simon" to "Peter." Just as it was for Simon, it is a journey that takes a lifetime.

SELECTED BIBLIOGRAPHY

Walsh, William Thomas. *Saint Peter the Apostle*. New York: Macmillan, 1948.

McArthur, John. *Twelve Ordinary Men: How the Master Shaped His Disciples for Greatness, and What He Wants to Do with You*. Nashville: Thomas Nelson, 2002.

The Abbé Constant Fouard. *Saint Peter and the First Years of Christianity*, translated from the second edition by George F. X. Griffith. London: Longmans, Green, and Co., 1892.

Maier, Paul L. *Josephus: The Essential Works*. Grand Rapids, MI: Krogal Publications, 1988.

Armstrong, Garner Ted. *Peter's Story*. Flint, MI: Garner Ted Armstrong Evangelistic Association, 1981.

Binz, Stephen J. *Saint Peter: Flawed, Forgiven, and Faithful*. Chicago: Loyola Press, 2015.

Lockyer, Herbert. *All the Apostles of the Bible*. Grand Rapids, MI: Zondervan, 1972.

Bruce, F. F., *Peter, Stephen, James & John*. Carlisle, UK: Paternoster Press, 1979.

Lewis, C.S. *Mere Christianity*. New York: Harper Collins, 1952.

Walsh, Michael. *Roots of Christianity*. London: Grafton Books, 1986.

Haag, Michael. *The Quest for Mary Magdalene*. New York: Harper Collins, 2016.

MEET THE AUTHORS

Jerry Lathan is a first-time author who brings a wealth of knowledge in telling the remarkable story of Simon Peter. Combining his lifelong interest of history with a decade of research on the life of Simon Peter, Jerry has unearthed and painted missing details on the evolution of Simon—the brash fisherman who became Peter. Over the past forty years, Jerry's national award-winning construction company has focused on the preservation and restoration of historic structures, national monuments, and historic churches, in particular. His deep interest in the lives and journeys of historic characters are central to his calling in authoring *You Will Be Peter*. From Jerry's time as co-owner of Big Easy Studios in New Orleans, producing more than a dozen major motion pictures, he has come to understand the incredible power of a good story. A culmination of his own life's work, Jerry has focused tremendous effort in producing and sharing the real and relatable story of Simon Peter, the very flawed man who Jesus chose to build His church.

Steven Manchester is the author of the soul-awakening novel *The Menu* as well as the '80s nostalgia-series *Bread Bags & Bullies* and *Lawn Darts & Lemonade*. His other works include #1 bestsellers *Twelve Months*, *The Rockin' Chair*, *Pressed Pennies*, and *Gooseberry Island*; the national bestsellers *Ashes*, *The Changing Season*, and *Three Shoeboxes*; the multi-award-winning novels *Dad* and *Goodnight Brian*; and the heartwarming Christmas movie *The Thursday Night*

Club. His work has appeared on NBC's *TODAY* and CBS's *The Early Show* and in *Billboard* and *People* magazines. Three of Steven's short stories were selected "101 Best" for the Chicken Soup for the Soul series. He is a multi-produced playwright as well as the winner of the 2017 Los Angeles Book Festival, 2018 New York Book Festival, 2020 New England Book Festival, and 2021 Paris Book Festival. When not spending time with his beautiful wife, Paula, or their children, this Massachusetts author is promoting his works or writing.

Visit: www.StevenManchester.com

Amazon: https://www.amazon.com/stores/author/B001K8Y14C/about

Facebook: https://www.facebook.com/AuthorSteven Manchester